D

and the

Sword

Legacy of the Phoenix
Book One

Beverly L. Anderson

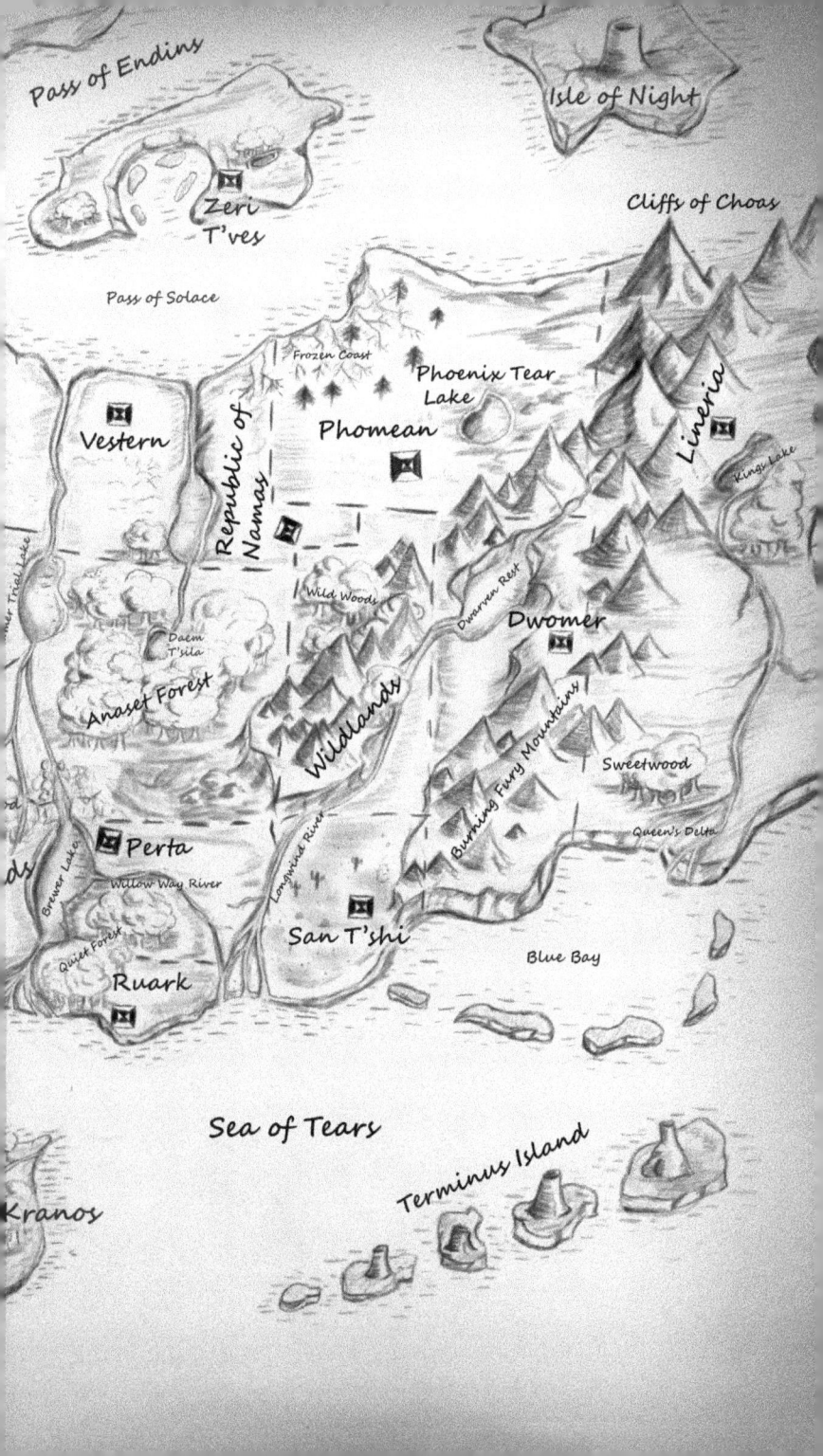

CONTENTS

Legacy of the Phoenix is dedicated to a lot of important people in my life, both current and past. I like the idea that people come into your life for a reason, a season, or a lifetime, and I truly believe all three are important to our lives. I still think of people I've worked with for years at a time, yet haven't seen since I left that job. People I knew in high school changed and we all moved on. This series of books has taken many years and a lot of courage to publish. It's a work of my heart, and I truly fell in love with the concepts and characters. I only hope that those I love can realize how important they have been in my life, even if they were only in it for a short time.

Acknowledgements

I'd like to extend my heartfelt thanks to everyone that helped with this book over the years. All the people that have read and helped me revise this in preparation for this to be released. I have more people than I can name that have been influential in the creation of the fantasy world of Avern.

Special thanks to all the wonderful Kickstarter backers!

Casey King

Andrew McCullough

Meghan Thomas

Paige Ward

I'd like to acknowledge my amazing artist, Leah Blis. She did a fantastic job on the cover as well as the map of Avern! I cannot express how thankful I am to have such an amazing and talented artist doing work for me.

https://creativelea2.wixsite.com/leah

PLAYLIST

Enjoy the music that I feel like fits with the Legacy of the
Phoenix series!

INTRODUCTION

Welcome to the first book of the Legacy of the Phoenix. First, I want to thank you for picking up this book.

The world of Avern awaits within these pages. Avern is a creation born of my love of fantasy and a lot of playing of Dungeons and Dragons. Many years of both these have led me to want to create my own world. World building and character creation have always been things I love and writing a book like this gets to engage both those abilities.

There are so many interesting things awaiting you on your trip through the world of Avern, and I truly hope you enjoy your stay.

I decided to write a fantasy series aimed at adults because many fantasies are aimed at younger readers. Adults can read and enjoy fantasy, and I wanted to create for those that do. In these pages, you'll find many themes that relate to a great many people.

If you're wondering about the genre of the book you picked up, it is fantasy with a queer erotic romance twist. In this first book, there isn't a lot of romance, because things are just getting started! Subsequent books in the series will have more of a focus on the romantic relationships between characters, which will include heterosexual, homosexual, and queer relationships as well as depictions of polyamory. In the world of Avern, there are as many ways to be queer as there are in our world today.

I hope you take this journey with me and stay through all seven of the books for this series. I have a long story to tell, and I want you to come along for the trip with me. The world of Avern awaits, and I will be your guide.

CONTENT LISTS

Please note, this is a list of all possible content for the entire Legacy of the Phoenix series. Each book will have this same page in it. Any of these things may be present in any of the books, and may not be present at all in the book you are reading. Please be aware of these things as you go into these books. Some things may be warnings, while others are simply things that are present that may be something a reader may choose not to read.

Explicit sexual content (both heterosexual and queer)
Rape or other non-consensual acts committed by antagonists
Polyamorous relationships
Various genders and identities
Graphic violence typical of a fantasy setting
Graphic torture of multiple types
Abuse, both past and present
Descriptions and depictions of war
Political discourse
Racism/Speciesism/Misogyny/homophobia/other bigotry by antagonists
Post Traumatic Stress Disorder and other mental health issues

PROLOGUE
The Roll of Ages

The ages roll on endlessly,
Whether we move ourselves or not.
We must move,
Or be rolled over and forgotten.
—Serista, Seer of the Noran t'Kalima

The world of Avern has changed. Nearly a thousand years ago, the world as we knew it came crashing down upon us, changing forever. The Divine left us alone, and the Old Ages all ended. There weren't any reasons we mortals could understand. There were no explanations offered; they were simply gone.

But how could we know such a thing, we've been asked? Perhaps they were still there, and we didn't realize it. Perhaps they had just withheld their powers. They might have gone quiet. This was possible in the beginning. The effects on priests were the first signs. At first, the people thought surely some evil had come to the world, and the healing powers of the holy priests had been staunched. But then the emissaries of the other side came forth angered that we had somehow interfered with their unholy abilities to channel their deity's' influence. After several skirmishes between the two sides, it was revealed neither had the power of the gods on their side. The effect was immediate. Houses of healing were no longer healing the minor maladies of their local populations. What had been easy to remove, small things such as pox or poison, remained. The Houses of Healing changed within a few short years; instead of magical healing, they sought herbs and nature's own remedies to the things they once removed with a wave of the hand.

Some would continue to argue that it was impossible that the gods were gone. Even with the irrefutable evidence of the priests' powers leaving them, they said we were not faithful enough, so they had gone quiet. Then more were left without power. Those who said the gods were withholding their favor rethought things when they heard of the complete disappearance of the Keeper of Stars' chosen children, the Oracles.

In our world, magic was once very simple. Wizards used the three spheres of magic, the darkness, or psychic magic, the light, or spirit magic, and the elemental, or nature magic. Only a few could practice two of these spheres. Elemental and darkness could be combined to use time magic. Elemental and light could be combined to use spatial magic. Finally, and by far the most common of the secondary magic was the combination of light and darkness, yielding the ability to practice cycle magic.

Long ago, there was rumored those who could practice all three spheres which yielded a tertiary magic, but in the last thousand years, these mysterious Oracles have not been seen.

There were many which had no training in magic, sometimes called sorcerers, sometimes called demons and devils. Springing from the psychic abilities of darkness, those with natural abilities arise now and then, which are called prophets. Those who hold in them the innate ability of the Spirit magic of light were called the Seers. Finally, those who naturally held the power of nature were named the druids. These are now gathered and taken to the Forge of Magic as soon as they are born, and a mark is seen on the child.

Prophets are marked with vivid purple eyes. Seers are marked with pale eyes which turn white when their powers are used, and the Druids are marked with hair tinged green in color. Once they are found, they are sent to be trained at the Forge. Strangely, they are never seen from again.

None, however, have been born with the Mark of the Oracle. In fact, it has been lost to time what the Mark of the Oracle was.

The power of the wizards was rising, however. Their abilities were not as great as it once had been, but they still had more magic than the average person. All wizards were to be trained at the Forge, and under direct control of the leaders there. Any misuse or unauthorized use of magic was punishable by magical tortures and death. The people began to fear magic, and with that fear, the governments began to assert their control. None were permitted to use magic without official papers for it. Those who dared to do so could be sent to prison, or worse.

So, why did the Keeper of Magic, Kalimourne, choose to Abandon us? It was obvious she had indeed left now that the chosen Oracles were no more, and magic had diminished. Perhaps the Mother of Elves is the one which pains me the most to think of leaving us alone. She was so gentle and caring for all, not just her children. What would she say today if she knew her children killed any not of their kind on sight without question? The other Keepers, of Life, Nature, and Death, were also gone. But without them, the world moved onward without many problems, at least that we could see. The loss of the Keeper of Magic, or the Keeper of Stars, as she was also known, was keen.

Nay, no more Oracles rose to power. Instead, wizards learned of the Spheres of Magic. Many held the hope they may have had the powers granted by the Path of Stars, or perhaps the sorcerous talents, but they never did. Wizards who were found to have the Talent were trained in their chosen Sphere, and no matter what, their choice could not be altered, and they could not learn more than one. They were found to have the ability of psychic magic, spirit magic, or elemental magic alone. Wizards came to the forefront of the battle for the truth, but their magic could not find it. Seers and Prophets could only see a veil before their vision. For some reason, it was as though a dark thing had descended to block what they normally would see. It seemed the gods wished to be left alone after all. So, the mortals were left to debate without magical aid.

For years, the debate raged. Did the Divine simply leave us because we were unfit? Did they leave because they were bored with us? Why? There were many sides, and the debates turned to fighting, and the fighting to wars.

The Elves said nothing; they simply closed their borders and made it near impossible for travel near their homelands. Long winding roads had to be built to pass them by as the power over time and space had been lost, and portals were no longer possible. The Dwarves retreated to their underground citadels and were rarely seen, and always surly when encountered. The Orcs waged wars across the wildlands with the shifters. The Beast Lords rose to power and combated the Orc forces which threatened to raze entire provinces. The gnomes of the Seran Jungle stayed out of things, remaining insulated in their own small world. Places that had been bastions of hope and commerce became desolate and worthless.

It did not matter. There were no gods left to ask, so the truth would remain untold. Until the dawning of the Ages of Destruction, the arguments continued. For many hundreds of years, the very lands rose against the people, and great destruction followed. Homes were ruined, and the very landscape was altered. But eventually, nearly two hundred years ago, the Ages of Destruction ended.

The Age which followed was something that not many could understand as the same as the previous Age. It brought no destruction, or at least, not the destruction they had seen in the previous Ages. Instead, the Age of Law had come. Lands began to organize and form nations. Rulers came to the forefront of every land. No one was left to their own devices, instead all had someone to answer to. Roads were built, and people trained in many ways. Perhaps, though, we forgot too much. We forgot that Law can be as deadly as any other power. During this Age of Law came the time of the Regulators.

The various kingdoms came together in the great Council of Magic, a place of learning and research, and decided that because magic was precious, it should be controlled. It was decided a representative from each kingdom would be a part of the creation of a force of skilled individuals they dubbed the Regulators. Their job was to discover those with the Talent, those born with the Marks, and bring them to the Citadel of Magic in the mountains north of the great kingdom of Lineria. The Citadel was not in the governance of any one kingdom, but instead governed by all kingdoms. At the beginning, it was a place of learning and solace for those born with magic still in their veins.

Thus, the Regulations were created. Their most powerful wizards began to cast webs throughout the kingdoms, enabling them to detect unauthorized magic use. And eventually, anyone who was not registered within the kingdoms was apprehended and taken to the Forge. No one was allowed in or out of the Forge save those who ran the building. Those taken there by force were never seen again. Nestled as it was in the mountains north of Lineria, there was no way in save magic, and the only ones who knew how to get in were the High Wizards.

As the Wizards have come to power, so have governments using fear and oppression come to power alongside them. Alliances between powerful countries keeps the people in check. The non-humans hide from the humans out of fear and hatred.

Now is the Age of Chaos, when the world is changing rapidly

The Veil stands before us like a black curtain which shrouds the end of times. Prophets have always seen the future, and now they cannot. The answer is quite simple; the shroud is the herald of the End Times. The End Times herald the end of the world. Avern as it is now will be no more. The prophecies are clear about only one thing. When the End Times come, the Eternal One will be reborn for a third time on Avern. The first time brought life. The second brought death. We know not what the third time will bring. And the world will forever be changed, and most likely destroyed. The prophecies simply stop at the End Times. The only other possible explanation is perhaps the End Times is still an area where events are yet to be determined. I would like to believe it.

For the last thousand years, and for five thousand years before, Prophets of Avern have agreed on one thing. There has always been a point in the distant future which they cannot see past. There is a point when everything is simply black. Prophecy upon prophecy has been written, but they simply stop now. For the first time in our long history, events are being written without foreknowledge. How things will happen, none know. Perhaps it will simply be that all the magics pass from this world. Perhaps the world will end after all. No matter.

The End Times have come.

I'm the last of my kind, faithful to my last days to the Truth Speaker, though her gentle touch I've never felt, and will never know. I find no one to take my place, no one who wishes to work in the name of those who Abandoned us. That is sad, but perhaps one day the Divine will return. Perhaps we shall know one day. I am in my seventy-fifth year, however, and it is unlikely I will witness any changes. I would love to chronicle such changes, though, in the name of my goddess.

By the Truth Speaker's pen, I swear to the truth of this book's words.

—Excerpt from the Book of Lost Ages, penned by Vranimina Vertrica, Last Truth Warder, in the Year 4999 of the New Age

CHAPTER ONE

SOLSTICE EVE BLOOD MOON

The moon rimmed in fire red,
Will bring tidings of the dead.
So, watch the skies, child born high,
For they in wait for you lie.
—Avernese children's rhyme

T he world was dark, snow-covered, and quiet. The winter
moon hid behind the clouds now, disguising its nearly
full berth. The snow that covered the mountains both north
and east lay heavy, and the fall had only abated within the last
few hours. The mountains had finally decided to don their
winter cloaks, as the season had come late this year. Tomorrow
was already the first day of Thrakmor, the first month of winter,
and the winter solstice. It was a typical Solstice Eve, though,
with great festivals and celebrations going on all over. Luckily,
the snow had abated soon enough for the people of Lineria to
make it to the streets to celebrate.

A chill carried on the air, though, which Captain Jovan Lis-
tenrissas did not like at the slightest. He stood on the battlements and watched the flickering lights far below. People cele-

brated this year again, but he could hear none of it, for the castle stood on the side of the King's Mount, high above the capital city of Meitan's Rest. Only two months ago, the Winding Down was celebrated in much the same way. He thought that the depressed people of Lineria needed to get their minds off things during the celebrations. The winter had come late but had come hard and icy. The last two days, the snow had fallen over a thick ice that had rained down before it began. It had frozen all commerce in the kingdom.

He dragged a hand along the gray stone, his leather and wool gloves protecting his fingers from the snow and ice coating everything. It rose on the merlons, which almost came to the top of his head and dropped into the depth of the embrasures which were level with his waist. He wore a heavy woolen cloak, deep red and trimmed in gold. These were the colors of Lineria's crest, a gold rampant mountain lion on a red background. His leather armor creaked slightly when he walked, but it was far better than the armor some of his men wore. Granted, it was lined heavily with wool for the winter months, so it was much bulkier than he liked.

Jovan had been many things in his life, a fighter, a ranger, a thief, and now a captain in the palace guard, but he always chose mobility over protection. He couldn't imagine the misery some of his men were in wearing those tin suits, as he mockingly referred to them. He shook his head, his black hair free under the edges of the fitted leather cap he wore and coming down to just over his neckline. It wasn't really regulation, but everyone let him by with it. No one would deny Jovan's abilities when it came to being a captain of the guard. He had an intuitive sense of trouble. Since he'd joined the guard, he'd caught seven infiltrators from neighboring armies, as well as tracked down seven deserters. That didn't even count the multiple times he'd found spies in the kingdom at large before he'd been transferred to the palace guard.

He moved onward, his left hand now on the short sword at his hip, his right using a spear to walk with. He left strange impressions in the fresh snow, almost like some three-legged creature. Jovan smiled to himself. Bartholomew had not been making his rounds in the last hour; there were no tracks added to the ground since he'd last come by. Only a tracker, however, would notice that among the snow dusted tracks already there. And tracking was one thing Jovan did best.

He saw him leaning in the crenel in the wall next to the bastion at the northwestern corner and saw him staring downward. Jovan said nothing but knew his lady had been by to wave up at him as she usually was at this time of night. He paused for a minute and let Bartholomew straighten back up and turn towards him.

"Captain, Sir!" he said with surprise.

Jovan waved it off. "Mina came to wave up at you again, I see."

Bartholomew's jaw dropped, and Jovan hid a smile. "Um... yes... sir... I'm sorry sir, it's just I don't get to see her much and the only time I can is when she comes to wave at me, I mean I'm sorry I haven't been on my round waiting here for her..." he rushed onward.

Jovan shook his head and put a finger to his lips, and Bartholomew finally quieted.

"It is okay, I know what it is to love," he said and went to lean on the wall beside the young man. The cold was cloying, penetrating even the layers of leather and padding on his arms. It froze the stone to its very heart this night.

Jovan could see the relief flood Bartholomew's pale face at his words. The people of Lineria were fair skinned, especially here at the palace in the northlands. Close to the Ice Crown, the people were mostly all of light complexions, and had flaxen to red hair. The cold and wet carried on most of the days, only the deep of summer bringing warm sun to the chilled lands. Jovan smiled, pulling off his glove slowly and stretching his olive-toned skin. He was twice as dark in skin color as most of the Linerians. But of course, he wasn't Linerian. He slipped his glove back on and smiled at Bartholomew. As usual, he looked at Jovan with a mix of awe and confusion, as though he really didn't know what to think of this man who was gentle yet stern at the same time.

Jovan turned away from him and stared out over the water-less moat. There was little need of a filled moat with a castle stronghold built into the side of a mountain. The mountain protected the entire east side, and the wall tapered into a craggy rock moat, a completely natural formation. The wall itself was around thirty feet tall, and the moat reached another twenty before the bottom of the chasm. There was a spot just on the other side that looked like someone had stood there for a while. Most humans wouldn't be able to see such a thing, but Jovan could. Well, honestly, he wasn't human at all. Sometimes, like now, it amused him greatly to masquerade among them, and for the last three hundred years, he'd done just that. Jovan turned to Bartholomew.

"Is she worth it all, my boy?" he asked, and watched as the young man's light brown eyes glowed.

He nodded furiously, making a tinny ringing sound with his helm hitting his neckpiece. "Oh, yes, sir! She's the most beautiful and caring and lovely and beautiful woman I've ever met!"

Jovan didn't laugh, only smiled and nodded. "That's good, Bartholomew, that's good. If you love her that much, take care of her, and she'll return your love, you know."

Bartholomew smiled, revealing reasonably white teeth for his age. Jovan couldn't help but notice a lot of humans didn't take good care of themselves. Maybe it was because they lived less than a hundred years that they didn't often worry about caring for themselves. The boy had a leg up on many of them. He looked up into the sky and saw the moon had finally come out from behind the snow clouds . His eyes widened slightly, and he stood with a sudden stiffness, which was quite uncharacteristic of the ordinarily casual and easy-going Jovan.

"Bartholomew, do you see that?" he said, pointing to the full moon. Around it, a ring of soft red glowed.

The young man stared. "Yeah, strange."

"That's a blood moon. It's an ill omen. Something is going to happen tonight, something evil..." He paused and shook his head. It couldn't be. It was perhaps since he left home that he had felt the tickle in his brain of the old prophecies, before the Prophet's power failed.

Bartholomew chuckled, but it was an uneasy chuckle, and Jovan looked at him with an arched eyebrow. "I don't think so; I think it's just smoke."

Jovan leaned back on the battlement with one elbow against the arrow loop in the merlon behind him, his initial shocked attitude and worry apparently fading from his face as quickly as it had come. "Smoke?"

"Yeah, didn't you hear? There's some sort of forest fire to the northeast, up past the mountains in Phomean," he said, pointing towards the west, where, of course, nothing could be seen.

It was at least fifteen miles to the mountains, and perhaps ten more miles still to cross them, at least a two-day ride on horseback. Jovan caught the slight shake of the man's finger as he pointed. Jovan got the impression Bartholomew was very good at pretending he didn't understand the significance of these large events in the world.

"Forest fires? Why would they let them get out of control?" he asked, thoroughly confused by the idea, standing up and staring, his casual demeanor slipping once again. Even his bright blue eyes could see nothing out of the ordinary.

"Well, that has to be it," Bartholomew continued, narrowing his eyes at his captain. "The scouts have been reporting a thick haze in the area which they dare not cross, and it smells like smoke to them."

Jovan turned to him sharply, blinking his eyes several times. Once again, the mask of ease fading completely from his face this time, replaced by obvious concern and worry. "For how long?" he asked.

Bartholomew turned to him and straightened up. "I think the last week or so..."

"A week! Has anyone reported it to the king?" he exclaimed, dropping the spear to the ground beside him in shock, his usually controlled expression wild-eyed. The king might have been ill, but we should inform him of such things. He, like Jovan, would likely recognize things for what they just might be. He saw the confusion on Bartholomew's face, but he had no time to explain why smoke would put him in such a state. Sometimes, he believed they learned nothing in their lifetimes!

Bartholomew shook his head, and Jovan ran towards the king's chambers across the parapet. A forest fire indeed! As he thought and ran, he let himself go, and only Bartholomew behind him noticed the fact he left no tracks in the snow as he ran. What fire mage in his right mind would let one ravage for a week? It was true they could be beneficial sometimes, but for a week? No, it was no fire. It couldn't be. If it had gotten out of control past the elemental mage's capability, they would have requested Linerian assistance, and he'd gotten no requests. He was willing to bet he knew what it was, and it had nothing to do with fire and a lot to do with magic. It might have been forbidden. Magic of a kind that hadn't been seen in the last thousand years if he didn't miss his guess. As he ran his leather cap rode up higher on his head, revealing to any who cared to look distinctly pointed elven ears.

Jovan was indeed more than he appeared and was, in fact, a renegade Whispara t'Kalima, or as the common people called them, the air-kin elves. He'd left his home in the Anaset Forest because he did not want to live his life only among his kind. He carried the *vanasta*, or the wandering ways, as the old druid told him when he was young. That had been before he and his father had died, and Jovan lost all reason to stay in the Anaset. His sister had watched him go, knowing he could never return, for to leave the forest was punishable by death among his people. Should Jovan somehow survive return from the outside world, of course, which was known to be unfriendly toward the magically inclined elven peoples.

Jovan took a hard turn and leapt gently across the short expanse between the outer wall and the inner wall. There was only one place that was close enough for Jovan, and only Jovan, the jump across, and it was close to where he'd left the dumbfounded Bartholomew. Even then, the leap over the outer courtyard was at least twenty feet, and it was impossible for most to believe anyone could jump it. Jovan forgot he could be seen and made the leap anyway, garnering the attention of a couple sleepy and alcohol weary guards below. Both looked at each other and didn't say anything, believing they'd definitely drank too much at the feast before they came on duty.

Jovan ran quickly across the snowy ice, not slipping one time despite the slick nature of the stone he ran on. His mind was too busy working over the things he had seen, and he honestly wasn't even thinking about the thirty foot drop off the wall if he slipped. But then, Jovan's body had a way of taking care of itself without him having to think about it. He took a run at the stairs leading up to the keep wall that stood even higher than the inner wall and ran across the stone expanse between the four towers. He was on top of the main building and passed a couple guards who briefly stared but didn't bother him. He was the captain on watch tonight. He ran down the steps leading down into the building that spiraled downward for two stories and exited into the grand hall below.

Jovan came to the hand carved doors to the inner sanctum of the castle and kept running. All along the walls, paintings of the king's slain wife Good Queen Anaya appeared, and paintings of his two daughters, Keiara and Sealla. The king's wife had died mysteriously to a poisoning that was never identified soon after Jovan had come to Lineria, and he regretted it greatly because she had been a beautiful soul. Jovan had been this way so many times; he barely noticed them. In fact, he barely paid any attention to anyone here save the King himself, and possibly the other Captains. And even the other Captains had to admit, Jovan had far more knowledge than any of them, almost as though he were older than he looked.

If only they knew how old he was, they would be so surprised. He'd already lived through many of their lifetimes and had many more left to go, unless he got himself killed. He paused before turning the corner and tucked his hair back into place and pulled his cap down once more. He came to the end of the hallway and turned left into the next one to find his way blocked by two of the House guards. Outside on the battlements and in the courtyards, he could control things; in here, he could not.

"Let me through, I must see the king!" he announced.

He could see the light coming toward the doorway and stepped back, assuming the King had heard his voice. Even in his sudden poor state of health, he would speak to Jovan, surely. He trusted Jovan more than anyone, and Jovan has a suspicion he knew more about Jovan than he let on.

Sealla stepped out instead. Jovan's face unconsciously scrunched up at the sight. She was dressed in great finery for such a late hour he thought, noting the fine scarlet satin and black velvet gown she was wearing. A strange outfit for an hour after sunset, when most of the castle was sleeping. Her golden hair was pulled back from her face in a tight bun on top of her head, and as she turned Jovan saw she held the King's crown in her hand. She put it behind her and faced him.

"Captain, I'm afraid father has passed from this world," she said quietly, and Jovan's anger built.

She carried no remorse and no tears at the fact. Her eyes were dark and revealed nothing, and Jovan was certain they were supposed to be gray. Things were beginning to clear in his head. They had been gray, he thought, recalling the paintings along the walls. She was not the same, and he sensed the power inside her, and it was not her own. The power was dark, and he could feel its malevolence. He bit his lip. It was as though an aura of darkness was surrounding and emanating from her.

"What was of such importance?" she asked quietly and there was an edge to her voice which threatened to pierce Jovan and let his lifeblood.

He shook his head. "Just some matters of the guard. It can wait, my lady, until a later time."

He bowed graciously to her and she turned and walked away without a word, and almost without a sound. Jovan's breathing had grown deeper though, and he knew he had to leave now. The pieces were beginning to fit together. She was the cause. If she were indeed the one causing the haze as he now suspected, she would find out about his origin in no time, and an elf among humans was as good as dead. He ran back to where he'd left the bewildered Bartholomew standing, leaping the gap in the walls again, and making sure the two guards below would believe they'd certainly drank too much. Bartholomew still stood there, waiting.

"I must go, Bartholomew, I fear my time here has ended with the King's death. I have to beat that smoke, or my life won't last long," Jovan said nodding to the young man, whose face became even more confused. He knew nothing of the King's death and wondered at why the Captain would be running from it.

He hopped up onto the crenel with the lightest of steps, almost as though some force propelled him and smiled, pulling off his cap and brushing his hair from his face, revealing the elven ears. Bartholomew started to say something, but Jovan leapt from the crenellations and whispered a word to the wind and was lifted into the air. He breathed in the wind as it whispered back to him. It was the most amazing feeling in the world, and after fifteen years as a Captain of the guard in Lineria, he was glad to be riding the winds again. Of course, this had nothing to do with his air-kin elven heritage. Even the old druid could not explain his ability to speak to the wind like this and have it do his bidding. Of course, Jovan knew what was coming after he landed. He could only hope to land somewhere relatively safe, but he was taking a huge risk in the winter of the north. There was a chance he, with no supplies, would freeze before morning when he landed.

Bartholomew watched for a moment. He looked slow. In fact, most considered him clumsy and dull witted. He was slow to anger, slow to laugh, and even slower to act, but he was not what he appeared. He had always known something was different about his captain, and now it explained things. His mother would have known what to make of it, but they had dragged her away to the Forge many moons ago. He blinked slowly and then looked up at the Blood Moon. Yes, it was indeed a Blood Moon, the one his mother had spoken of the day before she was taken away.

Awakening, eyes of night fluttered in the depths of darkness. The call had come. Slowly, slowly, the heart within began to beat and pump dark fire once again. How long had it been? How many years since her breath filled a body? Stirring within the warm confines of a mortal form, the dark began to uncoil and fill the body. How long indeed? Reaching out to touch the children, she recoiled. The mortal form began to weep, also asleep in the world of Avern.

Gone? Where had they gone? Her precious children, so many, and she could touch none of their minds. After a panicked moment, she remembered, yes, they were gone, that is why she had chosen to come. She needed to find them.

The others? Where were the others? Darkness reached out and sought the light, touched its sleeping form and she smiled. Darkness reached out again and felt the sleeping forms of the others, the warmth of the fire, the sturdiness of the earth, the soothing of the water, and the touch of the air. She was the first to awaken to the world. But she was sleeping still within this new mortal form. Something had to release her, something would have to break the barrier between her and the mortal soul and allow the two to become one.

Opening her mind to the cosmos, the connection to the Maker and Unmaker solidified, and all that was known to the Maker and Unmaker was known to her sleeping mind. So much, so long a time had passed on the world. She knew the cosmos were cut off to her children and had been so for many centuries. She knew without the sustenance of the cosmos, the time of their end would be coming soon, too soon. Why had

29

it been so long? Why nearly a thousand years? She did not know the reasons; she only knew there had been no change that the Maker and Unmaker could tell. Of course, that was why she came to the world of Avern. Beyond the reach of the mortal world, the Maker and Unmaker could merely mark the passage of time, but not necessarily the events of the world they watched. She was their connection to the children who kept the balance. But the balance of the world was gone, and if something wasn't done quickly, there was going to be a catastrophe which even she could not phantom for the people of Avern.

She sighed in silence and rested. The storm would be here soon, and she would be the storm-bringer. She took comfort in the fact the presence of the other five were there yet sleeping. She was unsure why she was needed first, perhaps because of the mortal body she had taken up residence in. But time passed slowly as she slept. So warm, she was, but soon it would be cold. Like a newborn babe howling in terror at the sudden light and cold after the comfortable safety of the dark warmth of the mother's womb, she would come screaming into this world.

Ahead of him he saw the haze creeping from the mountain ranges. He sucked in a breath sharply. How did she draw enough power to do this? It was the same dark power he'd sensed in her, like coiling black death. He had been here for fifteen years, and in that time, his senses of her had never indicated she could have that much power to work with. She'd always been a strange child, and he'd watched her grow into her magical ability. He'd also never sensed the power he'd sensed from her tonight in the hallway. Something had changed recently and changed drastically. He sped the wind along at an even more frantic pace, though as he did, he felt his strength waning. He knew now what it was. A binding barrier spell, on the grandest scale he'd ever seen. He had to get out before the spell finished binding the borders...

There was an unusual sound above him as Jovan neared the border, looking for a gap in the barrier that was not quite complete. His power was waning faster than he'd have liked, but he'd managed to turn a day's hard horseback ride into a six-hour wind ride. Unlike moving over the terrain, he didn't have to go up and down the nearly impassable passes, most of which were blocked with rockfalls these days, making a straight line from the capital city to the border with Phomean where the edge of the Windsong Mountains met the Burning Fury Mountains. He still had at least a day's walk ahead of him to get out of the mountains and into the nearest town in Phomean, however. He glanced up, the winds nearly dropping him as his concentration shifted. He blinked several times then lost complete control of the winds and went into a spinning dive toward the ground, managing to cushion himself with the surrounding air somewhat. Luckily, he was only about fifty feet from it, but he hit with a cracking sound as his wrist shattered on impact. He had managed to get through the barrier though and was in Phomean, but as he rolled to his back his eyes locked on another pair of eyes in the tree above him.

She was stark naked, and despite the fact, her nakedness was the last thing he noticed. The first was the striking resemblance to Keiara, except it couldn't be her, Keiara was blonde haired, this woman had jet black hair, and Keiara's eyes were vivid blue, not black like this woman. It could not be the first princess, after the king's death, she would now be queen. He didn't know this woman at all, but still longed to reach out to her. But besides that, what make Jovan's heart stop was pair of great nearly transluscent black wings spreading out from her back, making her look like some sort of dark angel of death. For a moment, Jovan wondered if he was dead, and somehow Keiara all this time had been hiding a secret that she was a reaper of the dead.

Behind her, the grayish barrier finished knitting together, and there was a sound like silent thunder as for a moment the gray shimmered and shined, then it was simply gone. To any who looked, there was nothing beyond the barrier at all, no land, no sea, nothing. Lineria lay behind, but none could get to it now without Sealla's magic opening the way. Jovan swallowed hard and stood up, the exhaustion beginning to flood him. He stumbled to the side, and without thinking tried to brace himself with his right hand. He screamed out and fell to his knees as soon as the pain from the shattered remains flooded him. Then he stared at up her, she still looked at him from her perch, perfectly balanced, perfect in the moonlight with snow falling around her. And Jovan sighed. The threads of ancient prophecy began to tie together in his mind. If he remembered all of it correctly, this was only the beginning. The snow began to fall heavy once more, but Jovan simply slid into darkness, the pain in his wrist a memory just like the sight of the dark princess.

The Forge was cold in the uppermost tower this evening, the eve of the Solstice. Nestled in the very north east of Lineria, close to the Cliffs of Chaos at the edge of the Cragtooth Mountains, the Forge was a huge citadel built at the base of Throgu's Mouth, facing the Sea of Terster. There was no way in or out of the Forge save by magic, the rugged cliffs and impassable sea on one side, and the meeting of the three mountain ranges on the other three sides. If the site was forbidding, there was good reason. For many years, the dealings of the Forge were best kept hidden from the view of the general populace. The intention they stated was to keep people safe. They gathered those with magic in their blood to train them. Of course, what was said and done were two very different things at the Forge of Magic.

Yes, it was Solstice Eve. Here, no one celebrated. No one dared make joyful noise. The door opened in a tower on the farthest north east section of the citadel. From the tallest room, one could clearly see for miles across the icy Sea of Terster, and just in the distance make out a land mass. Some thirty miles off the coast sat the Isle of Night, an even more forbidding landscape than that which surrounded the Forge. The island was volcanic, and very active, and now and then filled the air with ash and forced those who lived in the Forge to close themselves up and wear masks to keep from breathing in the poisonous substance. Right now, a great gout of smoke puffed up in the distance, and they knew another ash storm would be coming.

"Master?" a feeble voice said carefully.

A dark figure was silhouetted in the window. Thin, gangly, with a wild and messy bunch of black hair on top of his head, he appeared much too young to be called "master". He turned his head slowly, his eyes burning red as he locked eyes with the pale old man before him. Despite the frightening aspect of his eyes, the old man did not flinch nor react, merely waited for his master to acknowledge him. The boy nodded.

"He's here," he said slowly. "Do you want him to come up?"

The slim figure nodded, and then turned his red gaze back out the stone window to the snowscape before him. His eyes rested on the red rimmed moon and he smiled, teeth jagged and sharp exposed to the world for a brief moment before the grisly smile faded. The door shut gently, almost without a noise, and soon after it reopened in the same manner.

"Massster!" the surly voice of the newcomer said, hissing in a very subtle way as he spoke.

A man in a garishly red cloak stood in the doorframe and stared around the sparse room. His eyes, black and rimmed in red rested on his master. He waited for his master to speak, and pushed back the red hood of the cloak, revealing a bald head covered with scales. His tongue constantly flicked across his lips, as though tasting the air around him. A closer look would reveal the forked nature of his tongue. The figure at the window sat on the sill still, one leg planted firmly on the floor, the other laying angled along the stone. He turned his red eyes on the cloaked man.

"Your quarry," he said in the voice of a child. "It has been released. The barrier near Phomean. You'll know it. Report back which quarry it is."

The man nodded and bowed deeply. "Your will to my hand, massssster."

"And don't lose it," the boy said, turning his red eyes away and back out to the snow. "Your punishment will be eternal. Play with it all you desire, but bring it living to me, and willing, it must be willing to sacrifice itself to me. The power is useless if it is not given."

The man swallowed hard and left the room. He was always shaken after meeting with the master. Those eyes, red with a black pupil, they were so unnatural, but oh so powerful. He smiled and relished the thought of pleasing the master by bringing him his desires. He walked down the stone stairs which had an eerie quiet to them. All sounds here in the Forge were muffled. He entered the next room where there were four figures trussed up to the wall, their faces twisted in agony. Around their necks were thick collars with glowing blue stones. He walked up to one of them, one he knew very well.

"Are you well, Nilest, my love?" he whispered to the male human.

Tears flowed from his hollowed eyes. "Please, help me, such pain, I loved you," he gasped.

The red cloaked man kissed the man on the cheek. "I'm sssorry, love, but my master requiresss your magic, and Master comesss first."

He turned and glanced at the others, all had their hands chained above their heads, and their feet were chained directly to the wall. The other three were also in pain like Nilest, their faces contorted as the bands on their necks drew off their spiritual energy. They had perhaps a week before they were drained completely. It was a long process, taking perhaps a month or more depending on the power of the wizard, but the benefits to the master were enormous.

He glanced at the slight old looking servant standing beside the door bent with more than age. He wasn't actually old; he had been made old by the process those on the wall were going through. Having his spiritual energy removed had left him a shell of the man he once was. Some did not survive the process, but those who did became obedient servants to the master, their free will obliterated.

He stepped out the door and was greeted by a black-haired young woman. Despite the cold, she wore a pair of short breeches and a leather vest. Her long black hair whipped around her as she perched on the wall. Her eyes were bright and vivid in the night, taking in everything around her.

"Hey, how's it going, Cage?" she asked cheerily.

The red cloaked man turned to her. "Tyla. I sssee you're here, as usual."

She smiled broadly. "You have quarry. You should drop the hissing, you know. I don't think your quarry will just go running off with a guy that hisses when he talks. And the snakey

35

look has to go, you know. You'll get chased out of every town you come to."

"Yeah," he said nodding. "I'm the first. And I will drop 'the hissing' as you sssay when I need to, it is an effort to do so. And I can alter my looksss to sssuit my needsss...just like you. Masssster providessss all our needsss, sssisssster..."

"Yes, he does, but the hissing is annoying as the nineteen hells of Sherba," she said, rolling her eyes with a grin. "I can't wait to prove myself to Master."

Cage nodded. "I have to go, Tyla. Keep the massster happy."

The young woman grinned even wider. "Of course. Happy hunting!"

The red cloaked Cage smiled finally. "Oh, hunting is the bessst part, you know, and then I'll make this quarry mine, body and ssssoul."

As he walked away, his body began to change. The red rimmed eyes began to shift into a much more pleasing gray blue, and his bald, scaled head shifted into a nice shaggy hair of a blonde shade. His pale face darkened to a light tan shade, and a rough beard began to grow. He shook his head and cracked his neck.

"This should do," he said in a mild tenor toned voice, the hissing sound gone, and a smile came to his lips. He hated the cold, but he wore an enchanted set of metal bracers which kept his body temperature up during the cold, one of the reasons he could walk about so easily despite his unique physiology.

He walked a long way before he stared up to the sky and to his luck saw the constellation he needed finally.

"Well, time to summon my new friend," he muttered and cleared a circle on the ground.

After drawing some intricate runes, and throwing some materials in the middle, he recited a verse in a tongue not heard on Avern since the gods had been in the heavens. After a time, there was a loud crashing sound and a great column of smoke and lighting stood in front of him.

"Summoner, why have you summoned me?" a booming voice announced.

"To do my bidding."

"What is your bidding, summoner?"

"You will bind me to another in the Zypher."

"Doing so will destroy both."

Cage grinned. "Yeah, I've heard that before."

"Your bidding is ours to do," came the answer from the smoky pillar. "Summon me when you wish."

The smoke dissipated, and Cage approached the gray barrier. He glanced up to the east and saw the sky lightening. So, the night of the Blood Moon was coming to an end. It had been a good night. The King of Lineria was dead, and the puppets didn't even know they had strings. He smiled a crooked smile and wondered how long it would be before they knew. He touched the barrier, at first it was solid and somewhat spongey feeling. He poked at it a few times then walked through it. He adjusted his pack and headed down the mountains into the country of Phomean and toward his target. He hoped it would yield some fun, at least. He really did not like to be bored.

CHAPTER TWO

A Princess becomes an Outcast

The King is good, the King is kind,
The best king you will ever find.
He loves his family and us all,
Hail to the King, never to fall!
—Linerian Chant

A young girl, just turned eighteen, lay drowsing in her bed when a pair of armored and armed guards came rushing into her room.

"Princess Keiara!" one of them announced, the one with the pretty blond hair, Vermace.

The young blonde jerked her head up. "What?"

"The Queen is on her deathbed!" the guard said motioning to her to come.

She jumped to her feet and ran past them down the hallway into the room where a great ornate canopied bed sat. An intricately carved phoenix sat at the apex of the headboard, its great wings spread, almost embracing those who lay in the bed. The eyes were set with black opals. Keiara had seen the bed many times, but now it was looming and giant in the large open room. Kneeling beside the bed was her father, King Meitan, his dressing gown still on. Behind him stood Keiara's twelve-year-old sister, Sealla. Sealla stood with her back against the wall and staring into space, in shock.

"Mother!" Keiara said, dropping to her knees on the floor beside her father.

The woman in the bed, a once beautiful nymph, lay sweating and shivering. Her face had drained of all color, making her already pale skin ghostlike, her once bright golden hair laying limp and sweat matted around her head. Her bright blue eyes were dull and cloudy, and her lips were tight and drawn in pain. King Meitan, his great blond shaggy hair and beard askew and looking decidedly not kingly wept openly, staring at his beloved wife. Keiara groped for her mother's hand. It was like holding ice.

"What happened?" she gasped.

Her mother had been dancing hours ago at the ball. Laughing and drinking wine, she had sent Keiara to put her protesting sister to bed. Keiara found the function dull, so she had headed to bed afterward, but had listened to the music floating up from the ballroom for three hours at least before she had dosed off.

"Poison," said the physician standing on the other side of the bed. "Of a type I have never seen and I cannot tell how to treat. It is fast, and we don't even know where or when she contacted it."

"Mother, please, you have to fight," Keiara said desperately. "I can't lose you now..."

Queen Anaya smiled weakly. "Shhhh, sweet love. You will be fine."

Her voice was fading quickly, and she motioned to Keiara. She pulled her closer.

"I love you," she rasped, burying her face into her daughter's fine hair. "I love you, but you will...never...be a queen. You...will...be...much greater...than a mere...queen..."

She released her and fell back into the thick golden pillows in death. Keiara stood slowly, her father looking expectantly for his wife's final words.

"Love, she professed her love for us," Keiara said, her eyes strangely dry and her heart beating strangely slowly.

She looked over at her sister who stood staring at her mother's body, neither crying nor moving. The king pulled his dead wife close, swearing to murder the perpetrator with his very hands should he ever find them. Then the world spun into darkness for her as Keiara felt the world slip out from under her. Was it a memory?

The world in the dream now turned hazy. She knew it was a dream now, not a memory. It felt like a dream, and there was the knowledge in the back of her mind. She was staring off a cliff into a dark ocean. Above her the light of the moon reflected off the waves. She turned and faced a group of people. She heard her own voice speak, though there was something different about it. Somehow it was stronger, more forceful. A strange mark graced her face and meant so much even in the dream.

"The world changes. The Veil lifts. We have no time left to prepare. It is now, or the world will die. Now we shall all die, gratefully."

She felt something moving and thought for a second that the ground was moving. She realized though it was someone shaking her to wakefulness.

"Keiara...wake up..." someone whispered urgently.

Keiara's clear blue eyes flickered and then flew open as she felt the guard's hands on her body grow more insistent. Her own guards shouldn't be coming and waking her in the middle of the night, and then pulling her from the bed. However, those feelings changed from bewilderment to fear as just that happened.

"Keiara, I'm sorry," the guard to her left whispered his face hard, and his mouth nearly not moving. Jermal was his name, and his blue eyes carried a sadness that made Keiara's heart burn. He was indeed sorry. The other guard didn't look at her. Vermace was his name. Keiara remembered him for his pretty blonde locks of hair. He'd been there when the queen had died.

The guards roughly pulled her to a standing position and she desperately tried to shake them off her. She couldn't help fighting them, especially if they truly did not wish to be doing what they were doing. They held tight and wouldn't let go. They yanked her roughly into the hallway, nearly carrying her between them when she resisted them. This was wrong. Something was very wrong.

"What is this? Stop this! Jermal! Vermace! Please, what are you doing?" she muttered in a half sleeping fashion, the words thick and slurred. Something wasn't quite right with her. She was awake but not able to move fully.

The remnants of the dream clung to her memory like filaments of sugar candy. She felt daft, her heart still heavy with the memories of her mother. What if something had happened and the guards didn't answer to her father any longer? A flicker of fear blossomed in her heart, and as she was pulled from the room her eyes went to the windows which lined the corridor. Outside, the clouds were gathering as if for another snowstorm, but the full moon rimmed with red was what caught her attention. Her breath caught in her throat. A blood moon, her father had warned her of that omen. It was an omen of death. Could father have died? He had been so sickly these last few weeks.

If father had died, though, why would her guards be doing this to her? She was the heir to the throne so if the king had died then she would be the ruler of Lineria. Keiara was still trying to figure it out when her sister, Sealla, appeared before her with a loud cracking sound. Keiara hated when she did that. She may have been a wizard, but she didn't have to flaunt it. Keiara had never shown any inclination to the arts of magic, in fact, when the Master had come to look at them, he's shook his head at Keiara, telling her father she had no magic at all in her aura.

The guards pushed Keiara to the ground, her nightgown billowing around her like an iridescent silver cloud, and her blonde hair falling to the ground in front of her, pooling there in front of her like a golden puddle. She lifted her head and pushed the strands of hair away from her face as she sat back on her heels. Sealla stared down at her with scornful dark gray eyes and began to laugh at her. Keiara tried to stand once more but the guards pushed her back to her knees.

"Stay down, please," Jermal whispered in her ear as he pressed her to the floor. There was pain in his voice, as if he was fighting against something.

She felt the scratches forming there, and the slight dampness of the blood. She stayed there and stared up at her sister and realized she held the crown in front of her. Sealla was dressed well, as always, in fine red satins and black velvets. Her own blonde hair was pulled away from her face, making her radiant. But her eyes reflected no inner beauty, only coldness.

"Father died a few minutes ago. The old goat never knew when to quit, did he? Never saw a man hang on for so long. That would make you queen, my dear, wouldn't it? You are, after all, the elder of us and of the age to rule. And he did pronounce you his official heir last spring," she said with a coldness which did not belong to a woman who had just lost her father, especially such a doting and caring father.

Keiara felt a lump in her throat and her eyes misted over. She could not keep the tears all the way back, and they began to trickle from the corners of her eyes. She'd loved her father more than anything in her life. He'd been a kind and gentle father, and an even kinder ruler. Suddenly the world became so real and vivid around her, the last vestiges of sleep fell away from her mind and she could see and hear everything around her in utter clarity. The cold, gray stone of the walls closed in on her and the vaulted ceilings of this, the uppermost level of the castle, were so close, trapping her. When she spoke, she couldn't keep the quiver from her voice.

"Yes, it would make me the queen, so why are you doing this, Sealla? Father never wished us to fight over the crown, that's why he chose to let you pursue magic, and train me to lead," Keiara was so confused by all of this. She could not really understand what her sister had done.

She felt like her heart was breaking, too, knowing her beloved father had died without her there for him, after all she had been there for Mother. But her mother's words rang in her mind, that she would never be a queen. Had her mother, on her deathbed, been given a bit of Prophecy? Had she seen what would happen only ten years from her death? Keiara remembered her little sister, silent and still, in shock, or so they all had thought. Sealla had never had any interest in the crown, only in her magic, and even more so after their mother had died. Every year she became stronger in her magic, and more distant from their father and Keiara.

"I've been trained since birth to rule, and it is my right. What is happening?"

Somewhere, in the back of her mind, a voice spoke to her. She couldn't understand the words; she only understood the intent. Something was going to change, and there was nothing that the new queen of Lineria could do about it. Her mind echoed again with the memory of her mother's soft, gentle voice telling her she would never be a queen. The soft voice repeated the words her mother had uttered again and again in Keiara's mind.

"Keiara, you are a little idiot, aren't you? I am going to be queen because I am taking over Lineria. I am usurping your power my dear. And there is nothing you can do about it, and oh, are you weak and unable to fight? Too bad, my poison works well on annoying elder sisters too," she said with a pleasant smile on her face. Her eyes flashed and were so very dark, so black.

"P...poison?" Keiara gasped, recognizing the lethargy that was clinging to every limb and every part of her. She could barely move her arms and legs, and were she to stand, she would only return to the floor. She'd poisoned their father, and then she'd poisoned her.

In her hands Sealla turned the crown of Lineria, as though a toy. It was a fine piece of work, rich golden in color, with each of the three points in the front tipped with a clear diamond. Rubies, sapphires and emeralds decorated the whole way around it. Keiara stared at it, understanding dawning, but still not able to admit it. She couldn't imagine her younger sister, whom she'd taken care of as a child, doing this to her. For twenty-eight turns, Keiara had been groomed to lead, and Sealla groomed to stand by her side as the Palace wizard for twenty-two of those turns.

"But it is mine! I'm the rightful heir and the armies will stand behind me! You can't kill me! I'm your sister! You already killed father..." Keiara couldn't keep the pleading sound out of her voice. Something told her she was wrong. Sealla had already committed regicide and patricide once tonight and being her sister would not save Keiara.

Sealla smiled. "No, I can't kill you, and I can't keep you here, so what oh what should I do?" she said tapping her forehead with the crown, a sardonic look on her face.

You should kill her, a voice whispered to Sealla's mind.

For a moment Sealla's head tipped to the side and her eyes glazed over a frosty blue and then turned greyish black again. She glanced beside her, where an old set of armor that had belonged to her father stood. In the gauntlets sat a rusty sword. It wasn't pretty, or sharp, or anything special, but Sealla smiled. Her father had gone halfway across Avern to acquire the suit and sword, and she'd always thought it the most hideous thing in the castle. Fitting.

"Jermal, come here," she said.

Jermal released Keiara, her arm dropping limply beside her, sending shockwaves of pain through her body as it fell, and went to where Sealla stood. Sealla smiled, reaching out and taking his long knife from his belt. Jermal stood at attention beside his impromptu liege but Keiara saw the fear creeping into his eyes though he was trying to keep his face blank.

"See, Jermal, you've served me well, but now...well now your purpose is far greater than you know." She smiled again, that same cold smile. She then took the long knife and ran Jermal through the chest with his own knife.

Jermal immediately coughed and fell to his knees and looked up at Sealla, who was now wiping blood from her hands onto a handkerchief. She'd slid the crown down her arm and it now rested at the crook of her elbow, the points facing toward the dying man. Jermal's eyes pleaded with her for a reason why. She smiled and dropped the handkerchief on the floor at her feet.

"No, you did nothing wrong, sweet servant. Well, you fought off my magic, so I guess you did do something, didn't you? I can't have strong willed guards now can I and well; I needed a scapegoat for my sister's death," she said softly, then her face changed to show one of horror and shock.

"My! What a horrible night it was! First our dear father dies from a wasting illness, then my dear sister is murdered in her sleep by her most faithful servant. What a terrible day for Lineria," she said, spinning the crown nonchalantly around her left index finger.

There was a dull thump as Jermal slumped over, blood pooling around him, his life already extinguished. Keiara stood transfixed by the sight. It was as though she couldn't believe what she had just seen. She swallowed and looked up, just in time to see Sealla raising the old rusty sword and moving forward, the crown still spinning in perpetual motion around her right finger. The remaining guard had slackened his grip, mostly out of shock, and Keiara jerked away from him and scrambled to her feet as fast as she could. But her body was dull with the poison.

"Still not awake, my sister?" Sealla said, walking slowly after her sister. "Yes, it was in your drink last night, and father's. I've been doing it for weeks now to make sure you and him stay asleep and don't wake to find me in the middle of something. But last night there was something special added to them, something that father's been getting for a few weeks now."

Keiara couldn't believe what she was hearing now. How long had she been hiding this malice? She still scrambled away from her sister, towards the end of the hall where the blood red moon was framed at the top. She stood there, her back to the cold, rough stone, knowing the blood moon was there for her, and her father.

I am here, came a voice in her mind. Do not fear. Two souls will become one soul tonight.

Keiara looked up at the moon one last time, and then turned in time to watch Sealla drive the surprisingly sharp blade through her chest. And at that moment, when the blade pierced her heart, she began to laugh manically. To the disenthroned queen of Lineria it felt like the most excruciating pain and bountiful joy ever. Sealla backed away suddenly, leaving the blade buried halfway in her sister's chest. Laughter?

Sealla watched as Keiara's blood poured out of her mouth, nose and wound, her chest heaving with each gushing flood of blood from her chest. She had pierced her heart. She knew she had. The strike was true, through the bone and through the heart, the incantation she'd uttered beforehand made sure of it. Why was she still standing? Yet there she stood, laughing, her head hanging down, her face completely obscured by her long thick blood-stained blonde hair. She slowly fell to her knees, her hands clutching feebly at the sword in her chest.

"Thank you," she rasped. "Thank you...for...releasing...me..."

Sealla stepped back again, eyes growing lighter as she did so. The voice in her mind was silent. As she watched, the blood that was pooled at her sister's knees began to catch fire. But it was no ordinary fire, it was black, and soon it was leaping up all around her, up to her shoulders, up to her head, and then, nothing of Keiara could be seen; only the strange black flames which had consumed her were visible. There was a clattering of metal on stone within the flames, sounding like a sword falling to the castle floor.

Then just as suddenly, the flames receded. Sealla blinked her eyes blue, if cloudy, once more, the voice, and the power in her mind, gone completely.

"Keiara?" she whispered, not recognizing her sister in any but shape now.

The figure stood slowly from a position on hands and knees on the cold stone floor, gripping the hilt of the sword as she did so. Her face was still obscured by her hair, but her hair was no longer blonde, it was black as night itself. She was completely nude, her clothes burned away by the strange flames, but she stood proudly. She lifted her head and shook back the hair from her face. From her left eye, as though a flood of black paint had spilled from it, a black mark burned in the way that stars burn...only without light. Her eyes themselves had turned black but within them twinkled stars and swam eternity.

With a voice that was both Keiara's and not Keiara's, she spoke.

"Who I was I am still yet am no longer. Who I am, I was always, yet never was. Only with these words do I leave you, Sealla, and your master. Both of you should fear the return of the six into this world. It begins."

With that, she let out a sound like a shriek and a wail, and her body writhed in pain as from her back a pair of black feathered wings burst forth. She rolled her head around for a moment and stretched the wings to their full span, then folded them down and in one graceful move leapt from the window bearing only the naked, rusted blade with her.

Keiara stood in the tree and wondered why Jovan was here. She knew he was injured, as she'd seen his tumble from the sky. She would also have liked to know how he managed to fly as well. She leaped down from the tree, falling lightly on her bare feet beside Jovan's crumpled form. The snow melted where her feet touched the ground. She kneeled and rolled him into her lap. She pushed back his hair and saw his elf ears. Ah, so Jovan had a secret of his own. She gently brushed his cheek. Then a shot ran through her from her fingers to her head. She blinked and vaguely, she realized she would be seeing Jovan again before long. She kissed him gently on the forehead, then set his wrist with a makeshift splint and bandaged it with his shirt, which she ripped into strips. She wrapped him in his cloak, which luckily was one of the good winter cloaks from the guards' tower. His breath was fine; he had collapsed from exhaustion. A flicker of understanding bubbled in the back of her mind as to why this was, but it wasn't complete yet. She still wasn't fully of one mind.

She hefted him easily, and for a second was surprised at the fact. She still didn't understand exactly what was happening to her, but she knew she was still Keiara, but not her at the same time. She found a small cave, placed him inside, and built a small fire at the opening to keep him somewhat warm. She smiled as she left him, knowing the time would come when they would meet again.

Keiara landed in the field sometime later and her form changed to normal, the wings receding. Once more the pain assailed her, and it was like nothing she'd ever felt in her lifetime. It felt like her very bones were coming apart and reknitting. She stood for a second, naked save her hair and breathed deeply, the blade in her hand. She looked around her and saw a nearby house with laundry outside it, strange at this hour, but she guessed they must have forgotten it. She sneaked towards the stone fence and saw none looking. She reached out and grabbed the first two things she could and ran toward the town lights she could see. She stopped behind a boulder and pulled on a pair of pantaloons and a white ruffled shirt. Unfortunately, she hadn't robbed a woman's home. She stared down. What dress for a queen to wear, she thought.

She walked into the village, named Niliern. It was a large one, and she knew she would probably find what she sought here. Though she wasn't really sure what or who she was looking for. She knew she would know when she saw it. She glanced up; night was deep by now. She shook her head. She hadn't flown too long or far; she wasn't far inside Phomean. But still, she'd landed close enough to what she was seeking to make her errand easy.

She headed toward the main inn and tavern in the town, a large three-story building called the Stabled Pony. She pushed the door open and stillness caught her attention. All eyes were on her. She looked to be one of the few females in the bar. She put her head down and stumbled in and seated herself at a table in the shadows. She took a breath. The mark on her face would get her unwanted attention and she knew it, even if the flowing black hair that reached nearly to the back of her knees didn't. It was usually a mark of nobility or royalty to have long hair, and the longer their hair the higher the rank. This was no law, but it was general custom. Still she looked around, seeing smoke rising slowly into the air from pipes. Eyes diverted to her for a moment, and then returned to conversation with friends and companions at each table. She sighed. A bar wench came over, and she ordered a cup of water, for she was parched. She paid with a copper penny she'd picked up on the road; luckily it was enough for this.

Soon enough a drunk man came and sat with her. She looked up from the shadows, her black and silver eyes glittering.

"Ya aren't quite normal, are ya?" he slurred. He was obviously so drunk he couldn't even see straight, so she doubted very much he would remember anything she said to him.

"Leave me be," she muttered. "I don't want to hurt you."

He laughed lightly and turned around to his cohorts. "Ya hear that, the lady doesn't want to hurt me. I guess that's good, huh?" he said and a man at the next table laughed with him. He turned his bleary brown eyes back to meet Keiara's own black ones.

"You sure have a pretty figure under those clothes. Don' see many women beside the working sort who wear those type a clothes, what d'ya say I give ya about seven golden pieces and you make my night?"

Keiara tried as best she could to not show her distaste. It did not work. Here she was a queen, and this man was accusing her of being a common whore? Inside, the subtle voice laughed with her at the situation.

She reached out and grasped his face and turned her head to the side. "Leave me be, you dirty perverted man. Or I will show you what kind of work I do."

She let go of him and he fell back. Keiara realized where she touched him, there was a red hand mark as though he had been burned by her very touch. She didn't care, not in the least. She was a queen. Or at least she was supposed to be a queen. She was quickly coming to realize she wasn't going to ever be a queen as she'd always dreamed.

She leaned back and waved the serving wench over. "Red wine. He's paying," she said gesturing at the man who had just been at her table. The young girl nodded and set off back to the bar.

She brought the wine and sat it down. Keiara stared for a minute. No, she was indeed no queen, or even a princess, any longer, and she had to come to terms with it. She was no more a queen here than the serving wench. She sighed and drank deeply of the wine. Fate was very cruel. She crossed her legs, and realized, no not many women wore pants like she had on now, most were in skirts except those brave or crazy enough to go seek their fortune as mercenaries. Truth be told, Keiara had never before now worn pants. She didn't care for them, though, and wanted to find something else.

She closed her eyes and felt for what she was seeking. It was near. Very near. It was as if it had sensed her coming time and had arranged to make its way to her. Yes, whatever it was, it was sentient, very much so, so did that mean it was a person rather than a thing? She wished she knew what, or who, it was she was waiting for. She would wait. It would come to her. And when it did, she would...what?

Finally, a man came in. He wore a dark cloak, and there was a golden hilted sword across his back. He went to the bar and ordered a drink. That was him, it had to be. She held her breath and waited. She closed her eyes and felt the presence she was seeking. Yes, it was there, in him. So, it was a person, and not a thing. She opened her eyes and watched him carefully.

The man stopped, obviously feeling someone watching him. He turned, and Keiara saw his full figure, a tall striking man with good build, his eyes a piercing blue, and his hair a wild cropping of yellow upon his head. He wore a gritty beard and moustache, as if he had not had the occasion to shave in a while. His eyes met hers and she drew him to her like a fly to the spider.

He sat down. "What do you want?" he asked. "You've watched me since I came in."

He felt like an insane person sitting here. He'd come here for some reason, and now he didn't know what it was. He stared at the woman in front of him, dressed in men's clothes, and not very good ones at that. They didn't even fit her. So obviously she wasn't a mercenary, what then, a harlot?

She arched a brow, the one over the eye that had the black mark flowing down from it. "I don't want anything except someone to help me and I think you are that person."

He pulled a drink from his glass as the bar wench set down a cup for him. "Why should I help you?" he asked slowly, his voice smooth and calming. She wanted his help? There was something intoxicating about her though, and he almost felt his façade slip away. It was so intoxicating he almost felt the urge to grasp her and pull her to him in an embrace.

She smiled. "You have a soft spot for ladies in distress."

"No, I don't," he answered, starting to stand up, he felt if he stayed, he might give in. The longer he looked at her the more enraptured he became with her.

"Wait. I might have what you need, in the end, Myrstand, paladin of Aren."

He sat back down, slowly, feeling his determination give way slightly. He should have left. But how did she know his name? And how did she even know of Aren to speak the name of the Paladin-father? Most hadn't heard or spoke his name outside his order in hundreds of years. And currently, his order consisted of Myrstand himself and a few scattered and crazy old fools.

"How would a woman of the night know what I need? I am a man of morals and means. I do not mingle with the gutter trash of this world."

Keiara paused. "Then why are you here? Certainly looks like the upstanding paladin came into an Inn that caters only to the dregs of society."

That was the key. Why indeed? He looked around the room to see gamblers, mercenaries, harlots and worse. There was no reason for him to be here, yet here he was. It was difficult enough to make a moral way for himself in these days, let alone walking into a den of filth. He was trying to leave, but he just couldn't. Even as he sat here accusing her of being a harlot, he couldn't believe his own words. It was fear of her that drove him to push her from him like this. His heartbeat had quickened in his chest, and his blood sounded like thunder in his ears.

He looked her over. "I do not know, and I wish I did. I was drawn her by some force I cannot explain." He drank again from the glass, and it was then Keiara noted the drink was water, and no spirit. "I thought it may have been Aren's will."

"It is Aren's will, in a way. If it is Aren's will to help the weak. I offer you nothing but a chance to be my defender, my companion, and save this ruined world."

He set his glass down and bit his lip. "Why would I defend you? And what will I defend you from, those who refuse to pay? I've had enough of this; I do not know why I even bothered to come here."

He stood up and turned to leave.

Behind him, she stood up, picking up the sword that leaned against her chair and walked to the doorway. He looked up as he untethered his horse and saw her in the doorway. She stepped outside as the wind kicked up. He noticed that she had no cloak and wore no shoes. He turned away from her to get ready to leave. Why should he care if she as cold or not?

"You insult me, and now you turn your back on me?" she said, her eyes bright despite their blackness. Her hair fluttered gently in the breeze.

He turned to her, a mild look, desperately trying not to reveal his heart's devices. "Oh, and how is that, my lady?" he said the last with such sarcasm that it took all within Keiara not to slap him, but inside another feeling began to well.

"I am no lady of the night. If you do not want to help a good and just woman reclaim her rightful throne than you are no warrior of light and goodness, as I thought you were. My name is Keiara of Lineria. My father died this eve and my sister, the second child, Sealla has taken control of my kingdom."

He laughed. "You are a liar. Keiara of Lineria I have seen. She is fair haired and blue eyed."

He tied the last of the ropes on his mount and swung upward. "You are a wonderful tale spinner, you should ask the keeper if you can earn coin in a proper manner by telling tales in there."

"I was Keiara of Lineria. I am now still Keiara, but I am not. I have claimed my true nature this night. You can choose to believe that the Mother of Gods walks the world of Avern once again in order to free her children from their imprisonment, or you can choose to ignore me and go your own way. I am the Phoenix of the Dark returned. Come to the Ironside Cliff tomorrow night. I will be there until I set off to find those who will aid me in rescuing my children from their torment."

With that she rolled her head and let out a sound that was a mixture of a scream and a shriek and he watched as from her back a set of black, slightly translucent wings emerged. She closed her eyes and ran a hand over the rusted sword in her other hand. "This quest will be long. Do not come if you will not die for me. Do not come if you will not die for Aren. Do not come if you will not die for this world."

With that her great, black wings beat down once, sending snow flying in every direction and setting Myrstand's horse to rearing on his hind legs. And all Myrstand of Darna, the last Paladin of the Light of Aren, could do was watch in amazement as he saw the beginnings of a prophecy come true. Above, the clouds moved to cover the moon rimmed in red as dawn began to color the eastern sky the night of the Blood moon was over, that was only the beginning for the broken world of Avern.

CHAPTER THREE

A PALADIN BECOMES A CHAMPION

Balance is the key to all life.
Without the balance of life,
All would perish.
—Ancient aphorism, unknown origin

M yrstand of Darna sat alone and pondered things. He sat inside an Inn called the Leopard's Paw. He found it greatly ironic since it was likely that no one in the place had ever seen a leopard. Smoke permeated the place, as it was around dinnertime. There was not a table left unseated, and the vast majority of those seated around the room were drunk or on their way to drunkenness. Today had been a special day. It wasn't a good special day, just special day. It had been the Anniversary of the Abandonment, the first winter solstice of the 999th year of the New Age, or as some Seer's claimed, the Age of Chaos, of their world. And it was also the beginning of the last year before the End Times which had been prophesized thousands of years ago, even before the Old Age. The portents were in place, and prophecies began to unfold. But as always, prophecies were like double-edged swords, just because they bespoke one thing did not mean it would happen the way one thought.

He thought of the hauntingly dark woman he'd met last night in Niliern. He knew what she could have been, and if she was the one spoken of in the Prophecies, then it meant for certain the End Times would come. His mind dwelled on her, though. Still, here in Diverson's Port, he wasn't so sure he should have agreed to meet with her. He shook his head; his mind fogged as though he had been drinking the spirits that made those around him so loud. There was a constant din, and the bar maids made their way through treacherous territories of drunkards grasping at them. Myrstand shook his head.

He drank no liquor. He never did. It was undignified to allow oneself to be out of control. But the code he lived by felt like it was slipping away. His allegiance to a lost and forgotten god was fleeting at best, and most thought him horribly out of the times. Aren had Abandoned him, so why should he seek to make the Lord of Paladins happy? The gods were gone, why pay allegiance to them? He'd nearly ordered a drink of spirits upon entering here.

He ran a hand through his blonde hair. He was tired too. If he was to meet her, he should go now. He was drawn to follow her. He did not understand in the least why. It was unfathomable for someone like him to chase the trail of a creature of pure darkness and chaos and not desire to destroy it. So why was he here, thinking of taking off after her up the mountain to the cave she spoke of? His heart beat heavily at the thought though. She'd needed help, and her face was like ivory darkness. He shook his head. No matter what, she haunted him, and the things he'd said to her haunted his memories. His code had gotten in the way of his heart and now he wondered if it was even worth it.

He ordered another glass of water, and waited, though for what he did not know. It was like destiny was speaking to him, though the language was one he did not comprehend. He sighed and kept to himself, like he always did, keeping an ear open though just in case.

"Can ye b'live that man?" a rough, drunkard's voice bellowed from the bar.

"Yer full o' it, Mern. Ye donae know what yer jabberin' about," another equally inebriated voice said.

"Nay, nay, I saws it with me own two eyes!! Distapeared, all of 'er is gone!" the first drunkard, Mern apparently, continued.

Myrstand perked an ear. The gentlemen were at the bar directly behind his table, so he could not see them, but their loud voices penetrated the din around them quite well.

"Nay, cannae be, I tells ya!" the second answered, and Myrstand heard him take a deep draught of the ale he was apparently consuming in mass quantities.

There was rancorous laughter from a near table, just then and Myrstand missed part of Mern's response. " ...then the wholed damn place up and was gone! Wholed kingdum, Jacab, just up n gone from the world!" There was a pause. "I's knows! I's been to Lineria. Recent like too, and she wuz a bo-be... pretty place, she wuz. King wuz good, two daughters I wouldn't 'ave minded spendin' the night with!" there was another burst of laughter from them. Myrstand did not turn to look.

Lineria was gone? Myrstand's mind worked at the thought. That was strange. Very strange. It was true that Lineria was difficult to get too. The convergence of three mountain ranges, the Windsong Mountains, the Burning Fury Mountains, and the Cragtooth Mountains all surrounded the kingdom. The majority of the Burning Fury was occupied by the dwarves and the earth-kin elves, but a large population of dark-kin elves had taken to dwelling in the surface locations in Dwomer and

Phomean, in particular in the small area where the Cragtooth Mountains converged with the Burning Furies. Lineria was also bordered on two sides by the ocean, and the Mourning Islands to the south made it nearly impossible for all but the most skilled boatman to get through, and the ocean to the east was dotted with dangerous reefs and rocks, making the route treacherous. But to disappear? There were passes, artificially made of course, in the mountains, and there were various magical means to get there. Any Wizard with control of the Temporal Sphere could take you there, but if they could not get in it would appear the kingdom was simply gone. Besides that, the Forge, or the magical research facility, was located in the Windsong Mountains just north of Lineria's capital of Meitan's Rest. That place was linked with the capital cities of Phomean, Darna, Vestern and Luxen.

Could it be the black eyed one had been the Lady Keiara? He shivered at the thought. Keiara had been preened from birth to be the queen of the great and powerful kingdom of Lineria, and her younger sister, similar to Keiara in all ways save her eyes were gray as a storm on the night's horizon, and there was a sinister feel about her the good Myrstand did not care for. It was more than possible. But how could it be? There were so many elements he just did not understand right now. He laid his head on the table and tried to stop thinking.

Without knowing the reason, he rose and headed for the door. He could hear nothing but the haunting voice in his mind, and his memories spun in his head and certain ones locked in place, memories he did not know he knew... Memories of time immemorial, and places he'd never been. Things no mortal should know. Was she showing him these things?

Soon, the good paladin was outside, staring into the void of night that surrounded him. His breath was heavy, and plumes of smoke puffed from his mouth, for it was chill here, this close to the northern frost wastes where great ice lands floated. It was not snowing yet. He pulled his woolen cloak tight and was thankful he'd worn his winter boots. He walked now, his horse whinnying to see him go without him. He turned and then mounted the horse. It was time to go.

"Let's go, Tarm," he told the animal, which understood.

He rode onward, coming closer to the mountain pass which looked easy for a horse to navigate. It was a long way up to the cave, but even in the moonless night, he could see some sort of light coming from it. The night was silent and cool, though a flake or two of snow had begun to float down to the piles of snow that lie even on the ground already. The winter solstice was nigh, the eve having come and gone. There was a snow cached quiet that reverberated off the soft white palate around him. He looked up as he guided Tarm through the rough path upward, ever upward. Just what would wait for him up there?

After some time, she awoke on the hard floor of the cave she'd told Myrstand she'd be waiting at. She remembered flying up here after her meeting with Myrstand, but not much afterward. It was the stress of altering her body in that way, on top of the other events, had sent her into a deep and quite dreamless sleep. She shivered. It was cold up here. She hadn't noticed it when she fell asleep the night before. She stood slowly. She stumbled toward the opening of the cave. There was a long, sloping path leading up to the opening, easy enough by horseback, and she figured it would take a person on horseback maybe an hour to make it up to this spot. She glanced, and the sword lay tossed to the side.

She leaned down, bending her knees and reached out for it. She touched the handle, and she was shocked by a vision in her mind. She pulled her hand back as though hurt. In a way, it did hurt, though not physically. She was breathing heavy as she licked her lips. What was with this sword, and why had she hung onto such an old and rusted piece of junk? Was it because it was what her sister had plunged into her? She knew... Now, the thoughts slipped away like smoky shadow. She sighed. She stared at the sword and realized a medallion laid beside it. It looked ancient, as though it had been lying in the cavern for a very long time. She picked it up and placed it around her neck. A jolt of pleasurable pain struck through her body. The incomplete tearing of the veil had left her confused, but the touching of the ancient metal had ripped the rest of the barrier between the two souls completely apart. Black flames erupted from around her body.

Nothing could be seen except the raging black fire. The long years of being locked to the task of awakening the dark phoenix were over, and the wounded world's salvation would be born.

Then, Keiara felt weak, so weak, and visions and memories from time unknown came flooding into her from somewhere she could not name. She saw the beginning of time, the empty world filled with life, the second coming of the phoenix and the beginning of the cycle, then she felt the ripping as she, the Eternal Phoenix, was ripped apart into six pieces, and then she came together with the phoenix of life, and the gods of the world were born, then the elves, then much, much more, and then she felt the tears slip from her eyes within the black flames. If only the mortals knew the truth of the Abandonment, they would understand. The Dark Phoenix would do her master's bidding once more.

Keiara had never felt like this. Even when Sealla had killed her and she burned the first time, she had not felt something so intense. It was like touching a candle and liking the pain it caused. Except this was more, there was no pain. The flames felt as though they consumed her, and soon, she screamed, though from release or pain, she did not know. Then it was all quiet and still. For a moment she felt as though she did not exist. She saw nothing, felt nothing, and then she felt herself burst forth once more, as though from the ashes, the fire hot on her fresh skin. Briefly, she was the phoenix, and then she was the woman. She breathed deeply.

The fires had died away and the only thing on Keiara was the amulet. The amulet was pure obsidian with an etching of what looked like a large, black birds on it, surrounded by flames. Keiara stood still.

There was a flash, and the medallion disappeared, melting into her skin.

"I am reborn," she said.

Keiara stood and found herself face to face with Myrstand, though now, she was totally naked, and he was staring open mouthed, his hands slack on the reins of his horse. Keiara for a moment couldn't understand what was wrong, and then she glanced down.

"I suppose I should remedy this," she said glancing up at the gaping paladin, who had also gone pale as a ghost.

She closed her eyes, and for a moment, was encompassed with black fire, and when it was gone, she was clothed once more. She wore no color save black now. Her gloves fit her like second skin. The boots were heavy and good. She wore a shirt with no sleeves, and a long thick tiered skirt. A cloak billowed around her as well, with a dark thick hood. She felt the mark on her cheek burning. She had complete control of the form, and she had become one, she was not Keiara carrying the dark phoenix. She was simply Keiara, the Dark Phoenix.

Myrstand wasn't quite sure what to think as he watched the completely naked woman burn in black fire and reemerge clothed. She smiled gently and approached him, the once rusty sword now in a black sheath at her hip. She stopped in front of him and placed her gloved hands on his shoulders and stared into his face.

Her voice was soft, "You want to know what I am?"

He slowly nodded, unable to take his eyes off her face.

"I am the Dark Phoenix. I have many names. I live many lives. I am one in the same. I am the creature that lives. I am the creature that dies. I am the voice in the night. I am the whisper on the wind. I am the shadow that moves silently. I am the breath that whispers in your ear. I am the muse in the darkness. I am all there is to fear. I am all there is to love. I move and hide in the shadows. I am to be hated and to be loved. I am something that cannot exist. I am also something that is all too real..."

Myrstand blinked finally and realized as he did he was staring at legendary Dark Phoenix. One of the progenitors of the Gods. The Divine had been birthed by the union of the Dark Phoenix and the Light Phoenix, the two which had remained after the Phoenix had been sundered by the Maker and Unmaker after the Phoenix had brought the Flame of Asumbar, the Flame of Life, to the world. This was the creature spoken of in the prophecies that came before the End Times, when all prophecies failed to see any more. The End Times were the point no Prophet could See past.

"You are confused by this," her haunting voice continued. Myrstand simply stared at her black eyes. He swallowed. It was the same voice as the dark woman who had claimed to be Keiara, yet different.

The air was cold against Myrstand's skin, and he shivered, though the warmth from Keiara's body radiated outward toward him. Something about this made sense to the lonely warrior.

"Sealla meant to murder me and grasped the only sword nearby, one she thought worthless, but was the only one that would release my essence in one stroke. For thousands of years, I've waited. Born once more into the realm of life, I waited inside the body of the chosen, a veritable seed ready to bloom forth from her soul. The chosen was the princess Keiara, for reasons which are unimportant now. I am Keiara, still. Sealla's soul was planted with seeds as well, though of a different kind. The one responsible is our greatest enemy, though I will not speak of it in the open. It is because of this enemy I have been sent by the Maker and Unmaker to set things right. This outside force wished Sealla to kill her sister. However, this is something even the great Maker and Unmaker could not understand completely, so these plots are mine to unravel."

She paused and sat down, still exhausted from her reclamation of her memories. Myrstand slowly dropped down beside her, unable to take his eyes off her at all.

"I am a beast of darkness, of entropy and change if you will. I am a beast of chaos. You are my champion of light, and you are my champion of order. All your life you have sought your cause. You have never found it because I did not exist yet. I do now, and you know what I speak is true. It is the Light I seek, because between the Darkness and the Light there casts the Shadow, and though I don't understand it completely, it is the shadow we're seeking. Sometimes light may not illuminate the darkness, it casts too many shadows to be effective and the darkness squelches it. I am one of the Eternal," her voice trailed off and she stood, slowly walking to the opening of the cave. He followed her.

She stood and stared at the sky, and Myrstand did the same. The moon was full. There had been an eclipse earlier in this night, the night of the hidden moon.

He turned and stared at her again. His heart ached at the sight of her, and he longed to lay aside all else and lay with her. He shook the idea away. Why would he think such things? He was a chaste and pure man.

She spoke now aloud. "Will you reconsider your refusal to be my champion?" she asked, her voice unsure for the first time. "There are abilities within you which you do not know how to tap yet, and now that I have recovered my entire mind, I can teach you."

He stared into the infinity in her eyes, the black patch over her left eye swimming with the very bleakness of chaos incarnate yet suffused with stars.

Could he do this? His eyes gravitated to the medallion around her neck, and his hand grasped the one about his neck. The one on Keiara's chest was pure obsidian and etched into it was an engraving of some sort of bird surrounded by flames. Around Myrstand's neck hung a medallion he'd been given by an old man in his order. He said it was something very special. It was made of a metal that was a silvery color and was etched with fire.

"You bear the symbol of the silver fire. You are my Champion. Will you take your place by my side and oppose those who would undo this world before our very eyes?" she asked one last time and stared into his pale blue eyes.

Myrstand breathed deeply her beauty, and whispered, "Yes."

Jovan awoke cold, but not frozen to death, which actually surprised him greatly. He hadn't completely expected to survive the trip. It had been a gamble especially with the freezing temperatures up here. He sat up, wincing as the wrist he'd broken shifted, and realized he was safely covered in a cave with a dying fire outside the opening. He remembered hazily the woman he thought was Keiara but couldn't have been. She must have done this. It was the only answer. Whoever she was, she'd made sure he didn't die during the bitter cold night. He quickly gathered his stuff but doing so one armed was exceedingly difficult.

He stared up and realized it was not the same night. Somehow the fire had survived the night and most of the day, and now the moon was high again. He was starving, and curiously he smelled cooking meat close by. He began trudging through the snow toward the smell and saw a man sitting alone at a campfire. He looked up at Jovan's unceremonious coming.

"Well, there, you look a fright," the man said, grinning up at him from the fireside. "It will be dark soon, and the night is so bitter here this close to the peaksss. Join my fire?"

Jovan glanced about for a second, cradling his arm against him under his cloak. The man looked to be human enough, wearing a garish red jacket over a black shirt. He had a cape attached to the shoulders of the jacket, the cape also black, and wore simple black pants. Aside from the bright red jacket, he looked like any other traveler. Jovan, even in a kingdom where red was one of the royal colors, rarely saw people wear it. His own red and gold cloak was the exception, of course. The captains all had them. His smile was genuine, but there was something, and Jovan wrote it off at the moment to being chilled to the bone with the cold and the numbing pain in his wrist.

He wore a heavy black cap over what looked to be a mop of brown, shaggy hair. He had a couple days of stubble on his face, making him look like he'd traveled several days at least on the trail. His smile lit up his grayish colored eyes in the light of the fire, and Jovan could detect the fine lines of beginning age around those eyes. They were at the same time hard and clear, but there was a guardedness that Jovan could detect, perhaps because of his non-human senses. He wasn't an old man, but he wasn't young either. A fine scar crossed his right cheek, but Jovan could tell it was old. His jaw line wasn't really strong, but it wasn't weak appearing either. Appearances told Jovan he was around thirty and human. Of course, appearances were deceiving often times.

"I s-s-see you're from Lineria, tough luck, that's where I was heading. Damned barrier. Did it catch you?" he asked, taking a bite off a rabbit he'd roasted.

Jovan sighed deeply. "Yeah, can't get back home," he said. He smiled then. "I'd help you if I could, but..." he said, holding up the wrapped arm.

"Come, s-sit, s-sup with me," he said. "Name'sss Cage. I was headed for work as a mercenary, hoping to catch a caravan to Phomean or something, but well, barriers tend to put a stop to trade."

Jovan carefully navigated the slope and sat on a log opposite the human. He pushed his leather cap down again, making sure of his ears being covered. He smiled up as he handed him a spitted rabbit. He noted the lisping sound this fellow had when he spoke, but it could have been the cold as well. He was about to start chattering on his own as it was.

"Thanks, it was going to be a cold, hungry walk to Niliern like this."

Cage smiled again and continued eating. "What happened to your arm, if you don't mind? Looks fresh, there's fresh blood on the bandages."

Jovan chewed thoughtfully for a moment. He couldn't very well tell him the truth, now could he? Saying he was flying and got distracted by a naked, flying woman who may or may not have been the woman who was supposed to be the queen of Lineria right now would get some strange looks and a laugh. And might get him killed depending on who this guy was. He said he was a mercenary, but mercenary was a standard response when you didn't want people to know what you were really up to.

"I was clumsy. Headed down a slope, looked up when the barrier snapped into existence and slipped, caught myself, but messed up my arm in the process..." he said after he's swallowed.

Cage nodded. "Happensss to the best of us, friend. You say you're headed to Niliern?"

Jovan nodded, continuing to eat in silence. The less he said the better right now. He'd feign being tired and pretend to sleep. As an elf he didn't require as much as humans anyway, and he'd had more than enough while he recovered from using his powers.

"Ah, well we can travel together. You look fit enough to take care of yourself, even one handed, since you're a captain of Lineria," he said looking up at the eclipsing moon.

Jovan nearly choked. This guy was pretty good, observant, and knowledgeable of the local kingdoms if he knew the mark of Linerian captain. He cleared his throat. "Yeah," he muttered through a full mouth. "I'm...er I was just a captain of the palace guard."

Cage glanced up. "Aren't you a little far west of the palace?"

Jovan groaned inwardly. That's why he wasn't supposed to talk yet. He didn't have everything planned out in his head. Instead, he snorted. "Yeah, well, that's a story in itself…"

"Well, we've got time, eh, friend?" Cage said, and Jovan couldn't help but note the glint in his eyes as he spoke.

Jovan smiled, "Yes we do!" he commented around a mouthful of rabbit. He had to think quickly about what to say…else he was going to look like a fool in front of this guy and it wasn't for sure yet what his intentions were.

"Well, first, let me know how much of the recent events in Lineria you know of, so I know how far back to start?" Jovan asked, hoping he didn't appear like he was fishing for information, which of course he was.

Cage thought about it for a second. "I heard the old king was dead from a merchant passing this way, but that's about it."

Jovan tilted his head to the side and thought a second. That was of course impossible because no one had known except the palace guards, and he and the woman he had seen were the only two to escape the massive barrier. He smiled, though. "Oh, okay then I don't have to explain that part!" He ripped off another bite and chewed it for a moment.

"Well, they decided there was some sort of foul play with his death, so they decided to send a guard patrol out to check the outlying areas for signs of encroachment. We were the first to find out, so rather than wake and panic everyone else, the palace guards were sent out. I was following a few fresh tracks in the snow. I guess I went a little too far before Lady Sealla's magic created the barrier, so now I'm stuck," Jovan said shaking his head. "I'm going to head to Niliern and see if I can find one of the portals back, but I don't know if that will work, she might have sealed them off."

True or not, Cage bought the story, as he nodded and grinned. "Well, it is quite unfortunate, my good man. Well, we can travel together at least. Our waysss may part at Niliern, no doubt, but at least I'll have company on the way!"

Jovan smiled, his eyes focused on the fire. For some reason, he was starting to trust him implicitly. "I should sleep, now, should I take a watch or something?"

Cage smiled into the fire, and for a second, Jovan caught a glimmer of something in his eyes again. "Nah, my man, you rest easy and recover from your injury. Nothing will bother ussss this night."

Jovan nodded and rolled over and pretended to sleep, something he was used to doing over his years of pretending to be human. He, as an elf, didn't sleep in the same manner as humans and other creatures. The t'Kalima put themselves into a trance, very similar to what humans did when they chose to "meditate". In this state they "dreamed" of many things wonderful and strange. Some believed they saw visions from the lives of ancestors. Others just thought it was dreaming. They also tended to need less rest than most other creatures, and as a good side effect were less susceptible to sleep inducing magics and herbs.

He deepened his breathing and closed his eyes, instead spending the time to focus on healing his injury. Another odd thing about him, besides his ability to get the wind to do what he wanted it, was his ability to heal faster than normal especially when he focused on the injury. This, too, took energy, but not as much as getting the wind to hold him aloft, but since he was supposed to be sleeping, it wouldn't matter. In his mind, he imagined a globe of white healing energy flowing from his head down to the wrist. It didn't work fast, and he'd have to concentrate on it for several hours to do anything more than suppress the pain.

After a long while, Cage stood up. Jovan listened intently, regulating his breathing still. Cage walked away from the fire, out of the range of human hearing, but not out of Jovan's elven hearing range. Jovan peeked through his eyes and watched.

Cage looked up at the sky and smiled. He moved his hand in an intricate design that had there been a paintbrush in his hand would have revealed an intricate seven-pointed star with a spiral in the center. After a rush of air, the area surrounding Cage became nothingness. He closed his eyes and felt for the presence.

"Contact made. Air esssssence. Not yet transformed. Doesss not appear to know hissss true nature. Male human from Lineria. Injured, will travel to Nilern with him. Operation will commensssessss in three dayss. Will meet up with Pin in five dayss... will contact if thingss change."

Jovan nearly lost his breath. Operation? What was this about? He was talking about him. Just then the area of blankness around Cage dissipated and Cage returned to the fireside and laid down. There was a hissing and a loud rustling sound. Jovan swallowed trying not to get noticed as not sleeping.

"Pretty," Cage whispered, a large python curling around his arm. "Where did you come from? Come to ressst with me. No, leave him be, he'sss my prey."

From what Jovan could tell, he was sleeping. He did not even trust his senses now, however.

CHAPTER FOUR

A SERVANT BECOMES A SAVIOR

The Veil falls over the Sight.
The Veil falls over our ways.
The Veil heralds the end of us,
The Veil has numbered our days.
—Seer's Lament, Lucienda Trimas

Keiara looked down into the main area of the cavern that she and Myrstand had found the previous night. They had left the small cave where her powers had awakened to find something closer to the ground, and closer to Niliern, where she was sure things would begin to happen. The cave was large and had several high chambers that only she could get to by her flight. Myrstand was sleeping now, lying in a sleeping bag, curled into the fetal position on the floor. Keiara couldn't help but smile at him. He had not one idea about the truth of his potential and the real reason he was here. But he would understand soon. Someone was going to need him soon, and she would leave him to sleep for now.

She sensed one of her blood growing nearer. The second. And as she closed her eyes, she felt the third, and not far behind, the fourth. The fifth and sixth were further away, but they grew nearer each moment, making their way steadily toward her. She knew the next to join her, it would be the fae born child.

Thinking of her reminded her of her sister. The seeds had been planted long ago in Sealla. She sighed. She hated to admit her sister had become someone else and she'd never noticed. At first, Keiara tried to believe it was a sudden change. But now, viewing the past Sealla's life with the clarity only the dark phoenix could give her, Keiara realized it was something that had not occurred recently. It had been coming for many years. And it made the part of Keiara that was yet human cry for the soul of her sister.

She stepped out on the ledge and saw Myrstand was no longer asleep. He had sat up while she had been thinking of Sealla and was now thumbing through an old book of some sort. Keiara leaped off the ledge and landed beside him with a soft thump. He looked up and a ghost of a smile lit his lips, no longer surprised at the strength and grace she had.

"I have found the one you will be seeking today," she said, laying a hand on his shoulder.

"Oh?" he said and looked up at her.

She sat on the ground beside him. "This will test your faith in me, Myrstand. You must trust me, and you must return with her."

Myrstand looked at her. "What do you mean?"

Keiara smiled. "She is a sweet girl, nearly eighteen turns, who was a servant in my household, but when you find her, she will be in grave danger by the servants of the dark."

"I will do this for you, where is she?" he asked, though, never thinking twice more about it.

The mists curled around the castle in the damp of the early morning. The guards were not as vigilant as they should have been after the long Solstice Eve celebrations the night before. Many of them had become incredibly drunk and then come in at the morning dawn for their duty watch. Some wobbled at their stations. Some slept against their spears as they looked out across the world of white. The dawn captain was in similar state and did not chide his men for being somewhat lax at the hour it was.

Some noted the absence of one of their captains, the third watch captain, Jovan. He had been there during the night, and Bartholomew had been on watch with him. Bartholomew, however, did not know what had happened to him. At least if he did, he wasn't telling anyone about it. He simply left at the dawn and headed to the barracks. Truth be told, Bartholomew did not know what to make of what had happened. After Jovan had taken to the wind, he had simply thought about what he said. Then he thought of the night, beginning with a blood moon, and then this night, when around midnight, there was supposed to be an eclipse, according to the last palace Seer. Perhaps portends that his mother had told him about as a child would indeed come true. Then, before he slept, his thoughts slipped to Mina, the dear sweet girl he wanted to marry, and he remembered what Jovan had said to him the night before.

Bartholomew was well asleep by the time Queen Sealla made her first edicts. He would only hear about them that night before he went on duty, and once more, he would remember Jovan's words of the night before. Bartholomew, unlike many of his fellow young guards, knew more about things than anyone would guess, and no one would ask him. Bartholomew, though he acted surprised at what Jovan had to say, already knew what was to come to pass. His mother had been a powerful prophetess and would slip into nearly comatose states of sight and ramble on for hours, series after series of prophecy and vision. Despite the fact that Bartholomew did not have them written down, he remembered well many of the things she said in her high, lilting sing song voice.

He remembered well one time she spoke of the blood moon. "The queen shall rise from the ashes of the withered tree, rising up like something that no one will ever be able to see, after the blood moon rises full on the horizon, and the night of the hidden moon has come to pass us all. Then there shall come the daughter and son, who will rise up strong and true, never to fall. First though the false shall rise and take hold, and everything will wither grown old."

Like all prophets, it was hard to know what exactly the meaning of the words was. But all seers saw the truth, encrypted or not. The words when he woke brought him no surprise.

At early morning the announcement spread throughout the kingdom that the king had died during the night. He had finally succumbed to the long and now fatal illness he had contracted. A strange thing, since the king had always been a healthy man. Sealla had made the announcement, or rather Queen Sealla the first. Apparently, Keiara had left the castle shortly after her father's death and had not been seen since but was accused of murdering her father and trying to kill Sealla when she was caught in the act. Since Keiara was guilty of regicide, she would have been put to death anyway. And Sealla's job as the next in line to the throne was to take her place, of course.

Many in the castle did not believe it. In fact, most of those in the castle did not believe that. However, it did not matter anymore. She was no longer here. For whatever reason, she was gone, and they were left under Queen Sealla's rule.

The first order, on the first day of winter, was simple. Any with a Mark of Sorcery were to be brought to her at once. No matter how poor their skill, how young or old, any who showed a mark were brought to her. Normally, those with the Mark of Sorcery who had never shown awakening power were allowed to remain with their family, but those who showed awakening power were sent to the Forge with the rest of those with the natural powers. The order was not explained, only given, and all over Lineria, the few remaining people with a Mark of Sorcery were gathered. They were told they would not be harmed if they did not resist them. Strange guards worked for the kingdom now, ruffians and villains all, and they were not always as gentle as the people were used to, so fear spread out among the kingdom. Some ran. Some hid. Those who were caught trying to run were killed by the guards for trying to escape the Queen's edict. Treason was the charge, and a charge which carried a death sentence. Some escaped to find the mountains a wall of dark mists they could not penetrate and found the mountain night too much to survive.

The spell was a rather simple one. It constructed a nearly solid wall of mist and fog that penetrated everything from the sky to the ground, through the leaves and through the bushes; it forced its way through and blocked all travelers. The magical bonds which had once connected Lineria to other lands were severed as well, making special movement impossible. But no spell is perfect.

Among the barriers of fog and solid darkness, a group of tall rocks stood. They had been, at one point, a religious place, but it had been lost to the mists of time to those of Lineria. The ironic thing about the rocks was it had been a place to worship Pherome. Pherome had been the Great Hunter, and closest servant to the Keeper of Nature. None used the stones anymore. There were seven stones, standing in a perfect circle. After thousands of years, though, some had fallen, and two or three of these stones were at the place where the barrier around Lineria had formed. One had fallen on the stone next to it, and formed a small triangular gap underneath it, just big enough for a small person to squeeze through. And that was exactly what the small girl named Lena did. Unfortunately, the Lineria Calvary had a way of tracking those like her, and was right behind her, using a magically crafted rod to open a gap in the barrier that Sealla had created.

The thunder of hooves was loud behind her. She ran as hard as she could, but her speed was nothing compared to the Calvary that chased her. She'd gotten out, and their job was to make sure she was duly punished by death for her treason. She had, after all, run from the Queen's edict because she was sure they would find her powers were awakened now. Her breath came in ragged gasps as she slipped and slid down the falls and drifts on this side of the mountains she'd just come through.

She was neither quiet nor hidden. She simply ran. Her small size allowed her to go places where the mounted war riders couldn't, but they could go around and over, eventually finding her. Her dark gray shift was ripped and torn nearly to shreds from the scrub brushes which populated this side of the mountains. Her hair was matted tight to her head, and her eyes reflected only fear.

Tears ran down her face at a frantic pace, though not out only of fear, but also out of what she knew would come to pass.

She didn't know what to do, she really didn't. She'd never had to make this sort of choice, she either had to run after Keiara's disappearance, or she would die at the hands of the new Queen. She crashed through some grass and nearly ran over a log. She slipped and spun, skidding down an embankment to a stop at the bottom. Her breath was heavy, and she could smell the fear on herself, it was so strong. She was sure the horses would come. But she heard distantly a scream, and then the loud whinnying of a horse.

Lena of Lineria leaned back against the bank and forced herself to catch her breath. She was scared, and pain radiated from her ankle where she'd fallen. She looked down and noted the swelling and knew it was hurt somehow. She was done for if one of them came this way, she could no longer run. She began to crawl away, looking behind her until she impacted with something. She turned and looked down seeing a pair of boots. She sat back, avoiding her ankle and looked up at a tall darkly cloaked man. Her eyes went wide. Had they found her?

For a second before he spoke the world exploded before her eyes, and to the man standing before her they went totally white for a second. To Lena, she saw the future, or at least a piece of it. It was a difficult thing to interpret, for she saw a large black bird rising up and eclipsing the moon, and then something brighter than anything she'd ever seen flashed before her eyes. Then it was gone. The moon will rise full on night, and then the two will take flight. Dark will eclipse the silvery moon, and then light will follow ever so soon. The words echoed in her mind as the world swam back to existence before her eyes. Her visions were like that, both in pictures and words, making her a very rare Seer. Unlike a Prophet, she could only receive visions pertaining to those she was seeking, enchantments, or a specific person. It meant the vision was about this man before her. She turned her eyes, now heavy-lidded back to the figure.

The man paused for a second, recognizing she had the sight by the look. He stared for a second, obviously thinking. She didn't dare move even if she could.

"So, this is the fierce beast those horsemen were after," he said, and Lena found she could not move on her own. She was frozen.

"Come with me," the deep voice commanded, and she did, as though her body was moving of his accord. The moon was bright, but she could not see. She limped on her injured foot which hurt so much she thought she'd scream, but she found she could not scream.

She followed the cloaked figure silently and as she walked, she saw three men laying in a pile, all dead. She could only move her eyes, and she saw blood splattered all over the ground. She was scared despite the fact that whoever this was had rescued her. If he could kill three men so easily, what would he do with her?

The world shifted away again, this time though with less force, and she felt the impact of the world onto her body as though she'd fallen a great distance, and then she stood. She turned and faced herself, and bared thick long fangs, dripping with blood. Her own eyes stared back at her lit with some sort of black fire. The frail and weak shall ascend and become strong, and then shall rise up to right the wrong. The fury of death shall rise in her veins now, and then she will speak the vow. She swallowed hard and the world swam back. She hated visions of herself. Sometimes the sight was fickle and let her see her own future. But nothing had ever disturbed her like this. She continued to walk and suddenly she felt the weight of destiny.

Soon they came to a cottage, and she followed him in. The inside was devoid of light, and she could see nothing, but soon she felt hands on her, undressing her to her waist. She was frightened but still she could not move. She felt him there, by her neck. He moved in front of her, and she saw his face for the first time. He was so handsome. She could not see his eyes, but the cut of his jaw was smooth and square, and his nose was proud. His long black hair hung down past his shoulders.

"Such a beast to need three men to chase her down..." he whispered. He leaned close and breathed deeply of her. Lena didn't know much about vampires, but she knew they fed on the life force of mortal beings. They were undead things and abominations, but they were also powerful. His ability to hold her with his commanding ability was only one of the things that he was capable of.

"What do you have there, Devon?" a female voice spoke from the side where Lena couldn't see.

The man, Devon, raised his face from the hollow of Lena's neck. "Tres, look at this sweet, tiny morsel I have found..."

The woman walked in front of her frozen form. She reached behind her and turned up a lamp and Lena could see her finally. She was eerily beautiful, pale and almost glowing in the dim light. Her eyes were yellow like a cat's, or a demon's, and her face was angular, with an almost sharp chin and nose. Lena swallowed as she leaned in close her and deeply breathed of her like Devon had moments before.

"Oh, Devon, how lovely. She smells...different...she's human?"

"As far as I know, but I haven't taken a sip yet," he said, smiling.

With that Lena gasped as he sunk his fangs into her neck. She wanted to scream but she was frozen in place. Just as suddenly he let go and sighed so deeply.

"Amazing. Faeblood. She's a changling. Oh my, I haven't had such a taste in hundreds of years..." he said.

She felt his hands release her and the woman leaned over from in front of her and sank her teeth in the other side of her neck. A feeling of coldness was creeping over her as she stood there. Then she heard a shout from outside. The female vampire released her and then stared into her blue eyes with her own yellow ones.

"Sit down, don't move," she commanded, and Lena was powerless to disobey.

The door opened, and another woman came in, this one with long blonde hair and vivid, orange-colored eyes. She was smiling, her fangs dripping with blood, and she dragged a male figure in through the doorway. He was tall with blonde hair, shaggy and unkempt. He wore metal armor, and there was a sword at his hip. His hands were bound in front of him, and she was dragging him by a short lead attached to it. His mouth was gagged, and his eyes covered with a silk sash.

"Aiya, what is this? Why is this one tied up?" Devon asked.

The blonde vampire smiled broader. "It is wonderful! He's a paladin, I found him wandering around the woods near here. I can't charm him! I've never met someone I couldn't charm, so I thought I would share such a rare feast. I see you've thought the same."

She tied the lead rope to a ring on the wall and sat beside Lena. "Aw, but you started without me," she whined and lapped at the blood dripping down her naked chest. She shivered.

Tres slid the blindfold off the newly arrived paladin, and he locked eyes with Lena. Lena blushed deeply, though how after they'd drained so much of her blood, she wasn't sure how. He stared at her until she looked away.

The female now, the one with the dark and short hair began nuzzling around his neck. Lena could see that he was obviously struggling against the bonds, but the vampires had used their unnatural strength to make sure they didn't come loose. Devon touched his face and he jerked away.

"Aiya, take a drink, that one is amazing. She's a changling and something else, but it is delectable. Don't drain her, she's mine," he said, petting the paladin's struggling head. "We'll save this sweet morsel for after she's drained. Been a while since I've had my fill of holy blood, they don't have many of them anymore."

Lena watched as they stripped some of the paladin's armor away, revealing the tanned flesh of his neck to them. Around his neck were two symbols, one a disk with fire etched into it, and another with a strange mark that Lena did not recognize. Tres grabbed the unrecognizable one and ripped it from his neck, tossing it aside with a hiss. Then she slipped fingers into the band of his pants, and he jerked away from her again. Lena could see the fear etched into his face and knew they were in trouble if they didn't get away soon.

"Oh, my Devon, so sweet," Aiya said as she stood and traded places with him.

Devon sat down beside Lena and petted her face gently and then roughly bit into her chest just above her heart. Lena gasped, realizing that slowly whatever he had done to her was wearing off. She felt her blood draining from her, and her head became light, but it wasn't really like she was dying. Something was rising in her.

The two female vampires watched Lena and Devon now and stopped playing with the paladin. They exchanged a look with each other, and Lena wondered how long this was going to take.

"Devon, she should be drained by now," Tres said softly.

Devon moved backward and stared as blood flowed out of the wounds they'd each given her still. She shouldn't have had blood yet to bleed. In a second, Devon realized his mistake. Water began to pour out of his nose and mouth at a torrential rate suddenly. Aiya and Tres both went to him and dropped to their knees beside him. Lena was flexing her fingers and her toes as they did so, their attention no longer on her. Lena could feel the wounds closing, and she could feel her strength returning to her. She looked over at the paladin, and she leaped from her seat and bolted across the small room, pausing only to rip the hook from the wall which held his hands bound. Then she thought about it and stopped to grab his armor before she pushed him through the door. She got him outside and then pulled apart the bonds with a hand and Myrstand removed the gag.

"Let's get out of here before they recover," he said in a whisper.

Lena stood still for a while then looked at the blond man. "They won't recover."

The paladin only paused for a second before he set out at a run. Vampires weren't the only thing out this hour. His horse was tethered relatively close to the cottage, and he quickly untied him lifted her onto his horse, who bucked slightly at the strange smell. The paladin soothed him with words of comfort. He settled down soon enough. He led the horse and let Lena ride as he walked beside. He handed her his cloak to cover with for the duration of the ride.

They rode in silence until they reached the cavern. Myrstand led Lena inside. Once inside, Lena sensed something overwhelming.

"Lena of Lineria," a haunting voice said. Lena started. "Or should I say Lena Darkfyre now that Myrstand has brought you to me."

The woman turned and despite the changes Lena knew Keiara. She fell to her knees in front of her, as Lena could still see Keiara there, for one with the sight always saw beyond appearances.

Lena knew Keiara would surely remember the trials she'd gone through because she was gifted with such powerful sight at such a young age. Lena's sight had begun at the age of eight, and she had been hard pressed to understand what many of them meant.

"Stand child. Come to me. You are of my blood, now drink of my own blood and remove the impurities from you that the vampires have given you."

Slowly, she pulled an arm from under her cloak and staring at the young woman showed her wrist. Lena's eyes widened, and the red began to glow in her eyes though she could not see it. Lena felt the temptation rise and knew that she could not resist if offered blood. Keiara slid a sharp nail across her wrist and blackish blood began to flow, dripping to the floor, and burning away in fire the second after.

Lena's eyes burned red for a second and she latched onto her wrist. Lena suckled on the wrist like a babe at its mother's breast. She kneeled and leaned back against Keiara's strong form and drank deeply. She bore no concern for taking too much from her, only the need to drink. Myrstand watched, his face beginning to line with worry at the sight he was seeing. He started to step forward. Keiara raised her other hand, and Lena only continued to drink the sweet nectar that had been offered to her.

"Fear not, Myrstand," Keiara said with a smile. "I purify her with my blood, just as the fires purified me."

Keiara kneeled and wrapped her arms around the Lena. Lena remembered playing with Keiara as a child still, and she knew that the princess must have remembered too. She was now only eighteen turns of age. She though had remained small and childlike, and gentle. She looked no more than fifteen, and her demeanor was also like a child. Lena slowly felt the hunger lessen in her, and outwardly, the red of her eyes turned dark, nearly black.

Keiara spoke softly then. "The creatures who would find each other the most hated will gather to defend our world. The light and dark shall fight side by side to bring back those who've been stolen from us, and to restore the balance."

Lena pulled away from Keiara's wrist and stared up at her. Keiara looked at the Paladin. "You are the light, and she and I are the darkness that falls, and she will kill with no remorse when you cannot kill because of your oath to goodness. And there are others we have yet to gather. The balance must be returned, but there will be time for that discussion later, we've not come to that yet.

"She's more than she appears, so it may have been that the vampire blood wouldn't have taken anyway, but I would prefer to be sure and speed removal of the negative effects. Because of what she is, she will retain the vampire's strength and fury. She won't be a vampire; she will be more than one."

Lena stood slowly and stared at her princess, no, her friend. Keiara smiled and asked, "Do you embrace your fate, my seer in the darkness?" she asked.

It was always a free choice, no matter what, even after all of this. Lena closed her eyes and felt new feelings inside her. She stared into the infinity of blackness around her eye and saw the truth of what would happen if she did not join her.

"Yes," she whispered, answering the one person who she saw eternity in.

CHAPTER FIVE

A Monk Becomes a Student

There will pass into the world
fires of life and death
carried forth by the Eternal Phoenix.
—Litany of the Ages

"Yes!" Sanna yelled as the bald and bearded man went flying. He hit the ground and rolled to a standing position in one smooth motion.

"Very good my student," he said with a grin. "Like the phoenix rises from the ashes, you have risen from your old self."

She smiled and did a couple flips. Things had changed much. She had trained under this man in the months which had passed since she'd touched the essence of fire. Somehow, when she had taken the black gem, she'd appeared in the room of the Monk of the Sacred Flame, Glasdaow. He'd only been a few rooms down in the Inn and had hidden her in his bed with him when they came searching all the rooms. Somehow the woman they saw in the monk's bed was a different one than Sanna. Her only explanation was the Gem clutched desperately in her hand at the time.

Glasdaow smiled and bowed to her. "You are almost ready to be on your own, my young firebird. Time has healed your scars even. You are a sign of hope in our world," the older man said.

He'd taken Sanna on almost as a daughter. Across her back and down her arms were tattoos not unlike his own, of fire and of the mythical phoenix. Tattooed flames covered her right arm up to her neck, and a fire flower was on her belly. There were others covered by her clothes. The markings were very distinct.

He nodded to her and beckoned for her to follow. She was led into the small shrine. Glasdaow picked up a bowl which had always sat there. He looked at her holding up the bowl and whispered some words in an ancient language.

"Touch the bowl," he said.

She reached out and grasped the bowl around each side. In the bowl a fire sprang up. Glasdaow nodded slowly and placed the bowl back on the alter. He dropped some incense into it and whispered some more words.

"The training is complete. Destiny will come to you soon." He nodded to her as the flame burned higher. "Yes, you are a Monk of the Sacred Flame..."

He stared though, seeing more than that. There was something more to Sanna than just being a simple Monk of the Sacred Flame. Her mastery of fire went beyond that of any he had ever met, and she was almost immune to damage, the moment she was cut, flames would encircle the wound and heal it. He watched as Sanna bowed her head in reverence.

He smiled again. "It is time. I feel it."

She looked up at him, frowning. "Time? For what?"

"All young birds must take flight, and you are no different, Sanna. I sense that your future is not here at this old monastery. No, your future is out there. And you must embrace it."

Sanna lifted her arm adorned with the flames. "You said I still need to earn the last flame. The flame of the past," she said softly, a slight tremor to her arm.

"That flame is one I cannot force to happen, and one that will come in time. I sense that you will be best able to serve others in the direction of Lineria. There is a darkness growing there, one that even the coming Veil cannot obscure from me."

Sanna knew that his words were true. She, too, had sensed something dark in the east. She excused herself, going to her room, and finding her things.

It was time.

Sanna waved to Glasdaow as she walked away, wearing the clothes she had crafted for herself. Tall, supple boots which went over her knees nearly halfway to her hips gave her both protection and movement. A red and black dress left some of her tattoos prominent, in particular it didn't cover her shoulders or her right arm at all and left most of her back and right side open, but as tight fitting as possible allowing her to ability to tumble and flip as she needed to. It of course had a pant underneath since it was short to leave her legs free. She wore black leather gloves and a black cloak with deep crimson on the inside. They allowed her freedom to move. She had a walking staff which was more than a staff. In the top was mounted the gem of fire. So, it was that she carried a piece of the essence of fire out of the mountains north of Lineria. Today, she had cut off her hair as a signal that all her old life had been left behind.

Myrstand checked on Lena, as she had fallen asleep among the furs that they'd used to make a bed for the small girl. She was sleeping well as the early morning sun began to make its way into the openings at the top of the cavern. She was exhausted by the night they'd had last night. Myrstand shivered to think of it. It would have been worse than dying for him. He moved from that open area into another open area.

Myrstand looked into the cavern where Keiara was sleeping and let the torchlight fall on her. His breath caught once again in his throat, and his mind began to think thoughts that it should not. Years of training and learning had made him a chaste man, and in fact in his life he'd never lain with a woman. He'd held to the Code of the Paladin, and not broken from it once. He'd been sorely tempted in his time, but the thoughts had never entered his mind like this. It was as if there was some other pull between him and this woman he'd never met before a few days ago.

Now the temptation was mounting like never before. She'd never given him reason to feel this way; she'd never seduced him. She'd used no magic on him, for he would have known. But still, every time he glanced in the room, and the torchlight danced off her ivory heart shaped face his heart stopped in his chest. He looked now and the only thing he could think of was embracing her. He felt such love towards her, as well; it wasn't only lust. He felt like she was the perfect being, and that he had to be with her. He licked his lips and turned his back.

Your thoughts are not evil, Myrstand, the voice he knew too well whispered in his mind. He turned to find Keiara had sat up. She stretched, the covers falling away from her. Her black hair was mussed from tossing in her sleep, but her dark eyes nearly glowed in the room. She yawned; her thin white hands coming to the dark rich lips of hers and Myrstand nearly lost all restraint. He held on though.

"Come in, my Paladin, we must speak."

At her words, it was like a wave of cold water washed over him. The desire melted away, and he was staring at the woman who would change the world.

He entered and stood before her. She nodded toward the pile of bedding, and he sat down and faced her. "Yes, my Lady?" he whispered.

She didn't straighten herself at all, simply began to speak, as though it were a natural thing.

"There are things you must know. Things you do not wish to know. Things that will change the way you think forever." She shook her head, as though shaking away the sleep. Myrstand listened intently.

"The Dark Phoenix, what I have become, is only the beginning. The others will come," she said crossing her long legs under the blankets.

Myrstand made a face. "The phoenix of light?" he asked.

She nodded. "Yes, and the others."

"Who are they?" he asked, growing confused.

She shook her head. "I only know of what I said already of that. Any further of it cannot be Seen. The Veil has blocked all viewing of that." She picked up her waterskin and drank. "I may be the emissary of the Maker and Unmaker, but I am not the One."

Myrstand drew his brow together. He'd never heard mention of "the One."

"Keiara, what do you mean, the One? You are the emissary of the Unmaker, you are the force of chaos, death, destruction, and some say evil? What do you mean of the Maker?"

Keiara's face changed; a look of near remorse crossed it. "Here I will bring an end to your world as you know it, Myrstand, and I'm so sorry."

"What?" he whispered, inching closer to her.

"There is the Maker and Unmaker. Not the Maker and the Unmaker. There are not two, only the One. I am perceived as the Unmaker's hand because I am the darkness. But that is incorrect; I am the emissary of both just as the phoenix of light is as well. The One is both of what you call the Maker and Unmaker. The closest to being a set of two separate entities is the Dark Phoenix and the Light Phoenix. I suppose I could be perceived as the Unmaker, and the phoenix of light as the Maker, but we are both merely the Hands of the One. Don't you see, balance beyond all else must be kept?" Keiara's voice was soft and enthralling.

Myrstand couldn't comprehend what he was hearing. One of the creators of the gods sat before him and was telling him the basis of all belief was wrong. "So, my life's endeavors of seeking to destroy the Unmaker are fallacy? It cannot be done?"

He was rewarded by Keiara's gentle smile. "Would you destroy me now that I am here? No, you cannot. Inside you know the truth, all that live know the truth. You cannot destroy the Unmaker without destroying the Maker. They are one in the same. Without one the other cannot exist. Imagine a world without the Unmaker, if you will, where nothing died, nothing decayed; no room was made for all the life the Maker brings. There is a delicate balance that was begun with the Flame of Asumbar was brought to the world not once but twice."

Twice? Myrstand had learned at his grandfather's knee what the Flame of Asumbar was; the Flame of Life, and the order of Monks of the Sacred Flame worshipped it as the catalyst of life. Or did they? Did they worship it as both? They had no desire to kill, but they did when they had to do so... He looked back at Keiara saying nothing but understanding somehow. Somehow it just fit.

"But the Litany says..." he began.

Keiara smiled again. "The Litany as you know it is wrong." She appeared to measure his reaction, and when he made none she continued. "The Litany is far older than you can imagine. It was penned millennia ago by Samastain herself as a witness to events. It's written in an ancient language that likely those of the blood of the phoenix can read. But the version you know has been changed, altered, and rearranged far more than you realize. It's the fallacy of mortals not the Litany. There is no remaining copy of the original save one, and it is the original and holds more power than any can imagine."

She stood up slowly stretching her long limbs out. Myrstand found his mind slipping to what he wanted more than anything. Every move she made sent shivers up his spine. She wore a black, long shift with no sleeves, and it covered her up entirely, but it didn't matter. It was as though his imagination was creating scenarios.

"The Veil will fall soon. The Veil is what blocks the Prophets and Seers. It is coming to bear very soon. When it does the only thing that can break it is the True Litany, but I cannot know how that will occur. It must be recovered. It's hidden away on the Isle of Night in the northern sea. No mortal soul may read it. I am not sure how it will be retrieved. Without it the balance cannot be righted. We must head out to past the Cliffs of Chaos and across to the seas," she said and then turned to see Myrstand.

She stopped suddenly, staring at him. He watched her intently. Her face softened, and he looked at her. She swallowed, a woman for the moment and not the Mother of Gods. He felt the wave of desire wash outward from her, and it was met with his own desire.

"I don't understand, Keiara. I've been a Paladin for many years, and I've taken a Vow of Chastity and a Vow of Purity, and right now I want to break them both. I've never lain with a woman. I've never had the desire to lay with a woman. I've never been so selfish as to do something for myself alone. And I've never contaminated my body with desires of the flesh. I've been trained to not feel these things, but now they are all I feel. I'm descending into..."

Myrstand did not finish his sentence for Keiara dropped down in front of him, lips hovering inches from his own. She wrapped her arms around him. "You need no vows any longer," she whispered.

He stared into her silver flecked eyes and saw only Keiara the woman. She leaned in, silently asking permission, before he leaned toward her in answer. Their lips met for the first time, and Myrstand felt the world shift around him. He moved his hands to slide up her back, tongue flicking out to request admission to her mouth, and she opened in answer. He found her tongue eagerly entwining his own as he searched her mouth, descending into an ocean of sensation like he had never felt. She pulled back, panting just slightly and smiled at him.

Her hands went to the armor he was wearing, and with deft movements of her fingers, she began removing it. He was in a fugue state, really, not sure what he was doing as he helped her with the removal. When she reached the shirt underneath, he captured her hands and kissed her knuckles gently. She looked at him with those haunting eyes and then reached for the base of his shirt. She slipped it up and over his head and he felt the touch of the chill air on his skin. He was shivering at her touch more than the cold that surrounded them. She trailed her finger down to his belly button and glanced up at him again.

"But I can't...I'm honor bound..." he whispered.

"Honor bound to me, now, I am the Mother of your gods..." she whispered and kissed him full on the mouth once more.

He paused for a moment, pulling back from the kiss and absorbing what she had just said, and then embraced her and allowed the desires and wants he'd never let take over before control his every motion. His hands were furious as they stripped the rest of his armor and her light clothing from her supple body. Her breath on his skin was so familiar, but how could it be? There was a feeling that was soul deep, as though this were nothing new for the two of them, but it was impossible. Then again, the whole situation should have been impossible because he was about to lay with a woman for the first time, and it was the mother of gods...

The clothes piled upon the floor slowly, and the torch lay near the doorway, giving just enough light in the early morning darkness. His hands traced up her sides to her full breasts and he squeezed the flesh there with his hands, sliding his fingers over the nipples that were erect from the cold or the stimulation, or both. She sighed, arching back from him, proffering her bosom to him as his hands glided over the soft skin. He'd never touched a woman in such a way, and his fingers nearly tingled as they moved down to her stomach and hips.

"I don't know what to do," he whispered, almost chuckling at the ridiculousness of that statement right then.

She smiled though, leaning toward him, and capturing his mouth once more, arms encircling him in another tight embrace. He felt her naked body hot against his despite the cold, and he felt his own body spring to life from her closeness. He felt his face heat up more as her hands slipped down between his legs and gripped him tightly, her hand giving him sensations he had only ever given himself before he had taken his vows. It had been several years since then, and his body was more than willing to react to her gentle yet firm grip.

"You've grown in desire," she whispered to him as her hand stroked his slick length. "My desires for you grows as well," she said, taking his hand and sliding it between her legs into her wetness.

He was still unsure of what he was doing, but he pressed fingers forward into the damp warmth she offered him, and found that she reacted to his touches, making small mewling noises in her throat. She grabbed his wrist, sliding his hand upward, guiding his fingers with precision. He felt a nub of flesh and she let out a deeper sound.

"There," she whispered, and he knew it must be a pleasure spot for her. He swallowed and nodded, rubbing gentle circles where his finger pressed and feeling her shiver under the touch. "That's it," she told him, her own hand continuing to stroke him.

"It's so warm," he said, looking up and locking eyes with her. She smiled in return and leaned over to kiss his lips again.

"We can make it warmer," she said and smirked at him, letting go of him and moving his hand from her. "I want to feel you entirely, Myrstand of Darna."

His breath caught and for a second, he panicked and wasn't sure what to do, but he didn't need to do anything. She moved to straddle his lap where he sat, and he felt himself sliding into her core. He gasped, feeling the enveloping sensation and he controlled his own reflex to thrust upward as she settled herself on his lap.

"Let your feelings guide you," she said, writhing slowly on his lap, just enough to tantalize him. "Do what you feel is right."

He nodded; mouth slightly agape for a second as he processed everything he was feeling. He then began sucking on her chest, lips and tongue occupied by the supple flesh there. She moaned a little as she began to move faster on him, causing him to feel his member twitch inside her depths.

"I can't do it so slow," he whispered, and moved to lay her on her back. She went with him, legs clutching around his body as he slid out and back into her. She clutched him around his neck and pulled his mouth down to her own as he began thrusting deeper into her, his body on fire in the cold cavern. Every motion sent more shivers through his body.

She nuzzled her face into his neck, and he felt her mouth on him, biting gently into the flesh there, tongue flicking against the skin. Her breath was hot and panting. "You're filling me, my dear Myrstand. Now, fill me with your essence."

He almost felt his body crest at her words, but he knew she had not reached completion yet. He may have been inexperienced, but he had learned the basics from an older boy when he was young. He knew just as men reached a climax, so did women, though he was not sure exactly how he would know. Then, he remembered the bud of flesh she had shown him. He leaned back, leaving her lying back, and slid his hand between them, finding the spot once more with his fingers. She arched, breasts heaving as he began to thrust and rub at the same time. He wasn't going to last much longer, so he hoped he was doing the right thing.

Then he felt her start to squeeze him, her body spasming as she let out a long, low moan, legs flexing around his hips. He thrust through it, his own body beginning to come to an end. He groaned out loud, feeling the sensation from his toes on up as he felt it coming onto him faster and faster. His motions became almost frantic as he moved within her body. Finally, he thrust deeply into her and felt the sensation of release wash over him with such power it took his breath from his chest. She clutched him as he came, his heart speeding in his chest. He pulled away and lay down beside her, breath still fast.

"That was amazing," he whispered, truly having never experienced anything like it before.

"Of course, it was," Keiara answered, sitting up and putting a hand on his chest. "When it happens at the right time, it cannot be compared to anything else. It is an act of ultimate love."

"Love?" he asked, turning to her, eyes wide.

She smiled at him. "Yes, my paladin. Love. I love you."

"How can you say that? We've only known each other such a short time?" he asked, but he knew he too felt the same emotion of love for her.

"We've known each other before," she said, leaning down and kissing him again.

"I don't understand, but I love you as well," he said with a look of wonder on his face.

"Just know that what you feel, I feel as well. We are meant to be together, and it is all that matters to me," she said, stroking his chest for a moment before she placed her head on him.

"To be in love with the Mother of Gods," he said staring at the ceiling.

She pulled the furs over them and sighed. "Forget what I am, and focus on who I am. And I am Keiara, you lover."

He nodded, threading fingers through her dark hair and thought about it. Was this meant to be? Was this what the Lord God Aren had intended for him? He clutched her tightly, though, knowing that what he felt was genuine. He wondered what the future had in store for them. Mere days ago, he had been sure of his future in all ways, but now, things had all changed. He found Keiara had fallen to sleep in his arms and he smiled because it was perhaps the best feeling he had ever known. He laid there for a few more minutes until sleep finally claimed him.

A pair of blue eyes shined in the darkness at the opening of the cavern and there was a giggle like fairies gathering.

Sanna attracted no attention as she sat in the back of the tavern, a bottle of whiskey and a glass in front of her. She sat by the window, her green eyes staring at some unknown distant place. She swirled the strong drink in the glass and drank it. She'd drained half the bottle already. She sighed. She couldn't even drown her sorrows in drink; she didn't have the capacity to get drunk for some reason. She sometimes wondered if it had always been like that. She licked her lips and stared into the tavern, her eyes shifting between the patrons.

With training, she'd calmed the furies inside. With training, she'd accepted the torture she'd endured. With training, she'd done a lot of things that no one should have been able to do. The training was everything. But now, far away from the mountains she trained in, she felt the fury rising in her chest. Everything triggered the fire within.

Here a man roughly handled one of the bar wenches. Here another man slapped the woman that sat at his side. There another man tried to grab another bar wench's breast. And there a night lady allowed herself to be fondled in public as the coins passed from his hands in her own. Sanna met eyes with her and read the pain within the smiling face.

Sanna gulped down another drink of the whiskey, wishing to hell she could get drunk. She vaguely wondered why she was drinking the stuff when it tasted horrible and had no merit without the ability to make her lose her senses. She didn't notice the man who had come up close behind her and was staring intently down her front. She jumped when he dropped his hand onto her bare shoulder.

She looked up, silently cursing the fact he'd snuck up on her.

"Well, now aren't you an unusual customer in here," he said smiling and sat himself beside her

She narrowed her eyes at him and wondered what he wanted. He was shorter, nearly an inch shorter than she by what she could tell, and his eyes were red and bleary with drink. Their color was a dull brown, and his hair nearly matched. It was raggedy and chopped at odd angles, as though he'd done it himself. His skin was a ruddy brown, so he was obviously from one of the more southern kingdoms, perhaps Ruark or Petra. He was dressed reasonably well, but not outlandishly, so she could tell he wasn't a noble or a man of money. He wore a cloak with a red colored hood attached to it.

"I must say," he said as he drank of a tall glass of amber colored ale. "This place would be more interesting with more like you around." His voice was deep and rumbling, and Sanna could see how he likely took in the affections of women.

She sipped the small whiskey glass. "What do you mean, 'more like me', I might ask?"

He smiled; his teeth were yellow but otherwise healthy. "Well, you're a traveler. Maybe even something more. You've got the marks of the fire monks, so you must have stayed with them for a while."

Sanna leaned back, crossing her legs over one another, the leather of the boots making subtle creaking as they rubbed against each other. "So, you know of the monks. Then I suggest you leave me be, then. I was trained by them."

The man smiled. "Huh, I heard they don't train women. So, I doubt that very much."

Sanna felt the fires raise. "You doubt my word?"

"Of course, I do. You're a woman. You're no different from the bar wenches or the whores in here. You're here seeking something, and I can give it to you, and pay you for it..." he said, sliding his hand to her leg above the top of her boot and under the edge of her skirt.

It was like someone had lit an explosion off in the back of the room. No one in the tavern really saw what had happened, all they knew is that one minute they were enjoying themselves, and the next there was a wave of heat rolling through the room followed by the cracking of the table. The red-haired woman stormed out of the door, leaving the man who had been sitting with her unconscious in the middle of the broken table. No one, not even the man, was sure what had happened.

When Niliern's authorities reached the Resting Pony a few minutes later, the man was identified as a man wanted in Ruark for the rape and murder of the King's daughter two years before. They gladly kept the five thousand gold piece reward for delivering the man to the kingdom of Ruark, but there were whispered words of the strange woman who had really taken down the Scarlet Hood of Ruark.

On the far side of the room, a man with a bandaged arm sat drinking lost in thought when his friend returned. The second man, wearing a red shirt, sat down, and asked what happened.

"The most amazing thing ever, Cage."

Cage looked around at the chaos. "Amazing thing? Looks like someone got their ass kicked over there. Was it a big brawl? Come on, Jovan, I leave for a moment and all the action happens."

Jovan drained his mug to dull the aching in his arm. "It was the red-haired woman with the staff. She did it."

Cage looked at them dragging off the man in bindings. "What? By herself?"

"In less than a minute, I'm not kidding. I didn't even see him do anything, or her either. One minute she was sitting there, and that guy sat down with her. You saw how she'd been putting away whiskey since she got here, I figured I might have to intervene if the bastard started anything with her, but I didn't get a chance. He was up in the air and through the table with such force I felt it through the floorboards. Turns out he's a wanted man, the Scarlet Hood or something like that. But she left, and those knuckleheads are taking the reward."

Cage furrowed his brow, looking thoughtful for a moment. "If I didn't know better I'd say you were smitten by the lass," Cage said, flashing a goofy grin for a second.

"Yeah," Jovan said, resting his half drunken head on one hand and smiling in an equally goofy manner.

Cage nearly snorted. He was smitten with her after all...

The day passed with the two wrapped up in each other. Lena used their stores to cook a meager meal of dried meat and vegetables. As the evening came she went into the room where they slept in each other's arms. She gently touched Keiara's shoulder and she turned and looked at her.

"Mistress," she whispered.

Keiara smiled. "Please, don't call me that..."

"Yes, mistress," Lena answered, gaining a dim smile from Keiara, and continued. "I've made a stew for the meal."

"Alright, it is time for Myrstand to set out for our next addition," she said standing, not even really noticing her nudity. She stretched and replaced the black frock she'd been wearing and then shook Myrstand to wakefulness.

"Is it morning?" he whispered.

Keiara smiled and beckoned as she walked away. Lena stared at him as he stood up and he grinned at her. Then, realizing he was naked he dropped back into the bedding.

"Get out of here!" he shouted, his face burning red. Lena giggled and ran after her mistress.

Slowly he dressed again and then headed outside to relieve himself. He realized it wasn't morning, in fact it was nearly twilight. He rushed back inside to find the two women doling out a stew.

"It's already..." he started.

"Yes, almost dusk. Hurry and eat, you must meet the monk," Keiara said, smiling.

Myrstand cleared his throat and quickly ate. "Monk?" he asked around a mouth of hot food.

Keiara nodded. "She's a monk of the sacred flame, and she's not easy to miss."

Myrstand nodded and finished his food. He grabbed his sword and bag and headed out. Not easy to miss? He wondered what exactly that meant.

Sanna was still full of a fury born of anger and fire as she headed in the direction of the mountains. It was then she looked up and noticed the man dressed in armor who stood in the road ahead of her. She stopped and stared. He had a shock of wild blonde hair on his head and stood beside a large chestnut colored horse. For some reason, it was like Sanna knew who he was at the same time as not knowing. It was as if she knew destiny had come to call on her.

He approached her and nodded to her. "I'm Myrstand of Darna, the emissary of the Dark Phoenix. I've come to bring you to her."

She nodded slowly. "Sanna," she said reaching out her hand.

"Sanna," Myrstand nodded. "She said to seek the monk of the sacred flame," he commented, shaking her hand, firm and with little doubt. She returned the handshake, and Myrstand noted it was stronger than most men's handshakes.

She didn't ask any more questions, simply walked past him where he had come. Myrstand walked beside her, and he noticed she stood nearly as tall as he, and he could not take his eyes off the staff she walked with. He'd never seen a gem like it. They came to the cavern Keiara had come to call home. He walked in and saw no one at first.

"Myr!" she heard.

Myrstand was nearly tackled by a small, frail looking woman child. He hefted her up in his arms easily. She was only about five feet in height and might have weighed a hundred pounds.

He set the young woman down and kissed her forehead. "You're back! I was hoping you wouldn't have trouble on the road," she announced.

He smiled. "Yes, Lena, I am, meet Sanna," he said, motioning to the redhead beside him. Lena looked up and smiled.

Then her smile melted. Sanna stared at her for a moment, having seen the pointed canines which signaled the fact she was not entirely human. She was friendly enough with the Paladin, so she didn't understand.

"What is it?" Myrstand asked Lena softly, noting her change in demeanor.

Lena blinked a couple times. "You are—"

"Welcome, Sanna," a loud female voice boomed suddenly, interrupting Lena's words. From a higher ledge something dark floated down, and then it walked forward and as it got closer, Sanna saw it was a woman with flawless ivory skin, and eyes like the night, and over the left eye and cheek, infinity rested. Sanna didn't speak. She saw all possibilities in the woman before her.

"Perhaps I can even answer your questions of your path, child," Keiara said as she came forward and grasped her by the face and stared into her emerald eyes.

Lena stared for a moment. "But you're—" she started, but then glanced sharply at Keiara. She said no more, as it appeared

Keiara knew what she was going to say. Sanna saw the paladin staring at the girl and she was curious now what the young Lena would have said as well.

Sanna watched as Myrstand turned his attention to Keiara and his face changed. Unlike with the girl Lena, there was a look of utter awe and adoration on his face. He was obviously enraptured by the dark woman, and Sanna understood why. She would be the kind to bring anyone to her side in a moment.

"Do you come to me, willingly following me, Monk of the Sacred Flame?" the dark and beautiful woman said, in Sanna's mind, and out. And Sanna knew, there was always a choice. "Do you come to me willing to let me train you how to quell the fires within you that you cannot yet control? Do you come willing to do what I ask of you?"

"Oh, yes," she said and bowed to her.

CHAPTER SIX

A RANGER BECOMES A DISCIPLE

Into the night, into the end, we walk.
Into the day, into the beginning, we walk.
We were here when it began,
And we shall be here when it ends.
—*Therma Lesteransas, Last Whispara t'Kalima Oracle*

N ow, Jovan drowsed sleepily and quite happily in a bed, but it was a very hard bed. Suddenly he felt a jolt and tried to turn over. That was when he realized he wasn't in a bed but was instead laying on hay in the back of a wagon. He tried to move and realized with dawning horror his hands and feet were both bound and staked into the side of the wagon. The gag in his mouth was soaked in something bitter to the taste, and he guessed it was some sort of sleep-inducing potion. Suddenly the wagon jolted to a stop. He held his breath and listened intently.

"Just a load of hay for the Jebbens farm down the road here, next to Vrastima." It was Cage's voice. Why was he tied up in the back of a wagon with Cage driving it? The last he remembered they'd said goodnight after drinks in the tavern...

There were voices otherwise, then he heard, "If it be hay, ya don't mind if we take a look, do ya?" asked a gravelly voice. Obviously one of the outer guards in the tower at the edge of Niliern.

"Of course not, my good sir, all you'll see is a big load of hay," Cage continued.

The flap at the end was lifted, and light washed over him. He struggled against the bindings and made noise against the gag as best he could. The guard was middle aged, scarred and weathered. He looked around, reached inside the wagon, and looked to be poking at the air. He then took his blade and made as if to stab the hay, and Jovan gasped against the gag as the guard thrust the sword. Right above Jovan's face it hit some sort of barrier and stopped with a "thunk" as though it had hit the bottom of the wagon.

Oh please, thought Jovan. Realize it isn't the bottom of the wagon; realize you hit something a good foot above the bottom of the wagon...

The guard closed the flap and Jovan's hopes were dashed. He wasn't smart enough to notice the dimensions were off, but then, that's why the spell was effective, because most people didn't notice.

"Alright Mister...?" the guard asked.

"Twofell, Tiberias Twofell," Cage answered with ease and Jovan couldn't believe this was the man who had helped him through the wilds and got him to Niliern with such speed. He'd even taken him to the healer and paid for the treatment of his wrist. And then, last night, he kept buying him round after round...and Jovan laid back his head with a thump, realizing how much it was pounding at the moment. The oldest trick in the book. Then he realized his headband was gone. Cage knew he wasn't human. This wasn't good. Was he taking him to get a reward? He had heard of elf hunters in his days back in Anaset, but he'd never seen one in the human world... Then he remembered the strange conversation with no one he had overheard. He had assumed Cage was waiting for someone, and in that he assumed he would have a chance to fight. He didn't think Cage was supposed to deliver him.

With a jerk, the wagon set off again and Jovan wondered just how the hell he was supposed to get out of this.

Keiara rolled over sleepily and found Myrstand once more gone. She sighed. He was a conundrum. If only he knew all the truth, but it was something that he had to find in his own good time, not something she could reveal. Just like the others. She had to hide so many things and she wished she did not, but once they awakened, then she would have to hide nothing.

But once they were awakened the end would come. And she couldn't see that at all.

She stood and headed out into the wider main cavern where Lena and Sanna were cooking some eggs Sanna had retrieved from a nearby tree. It smelled lovely. Keiara smiled and then saw Myrstand cleaning his sword again. It was as if he had to have something to do. They ate in silence and Keiara finally broke it after she'd finished.

"Well, I suppose some explanations are in order for our newer members, though I'll have to do this twice more, I suppose," she began, stretching catlike from her sitting position on the floor.

"Tonight, at sundown, Myrstand and Sanna will go and retrieve one more of our blood," she said.

Sanna interrupted her there. "What do you mean by 'our blood'?" she asked.

Keiara looked at her for a moment. "Well, the whole of it is complicated, but the short version is the eternal phoenix binds us together."

Myrstand and Lena exchanged looks. "It is the reason Lena did not succumb to three vampires, why her blood never ran out, and why they were destroyed after feeding from her. She carries abilities of water, and because of that, her injuries are healed by it, and her blood was not consumed entirely because her body protected itself by feeding them water that they assumed was blood. It is also the reason Sanna has the ability to defer much damage, and why she heals so fast from wounds. A mortal wound on either of you may not have any effect because water protects you, Lena, and fire protects you, Sanna."

Lena and Sanna nodded. Myrstand wondered what protected him if he was of this "blood" like the others.

"Myrstand and I are different, though. I am of course the bearer of the essence of the dark phoenix. Myrstand has other things which protect him, such as his faith and his paladin's honor. Tonight, you retrieve someone I've known a long time and never realized the truth about until now. He will be in danger by the time you find him, and that is why I also send you Sanna."

Keiara took a deep drink of her waterskin. "After tonight, there is one more making his way toward us, then we may set out toward the Isle of Night to retrieve the one true litany. Hopefully, we'll find more clues as to what we're supposed to do along the way."

"Should we make ready with supplies then?" asked Myrstand.

"Yes," Keiara answered and stood slowly. "Enough supplies for a week for six."

With that she walked to the door and looked out as the crisp winter morning dawned. She grabbed the sword beside the opening and smiled back at the others.

"I'll go for a morning walk, I'll be back in a while," she said and walked out, fresh snow crunching underfoot as she went.

Myrstand watched her leave. His heart easily skipped two beats. He'd kept his distance since his moment of weakness, but he couldn't help himself, he was continuing to be drawn to her. She was intoxicating, and it was the only way to describe the sensation he got when he was around her.

"What is she going to do with a rusty sword?" Sanna muttered as she stood and stretched. She began rummaging through the bags.

Lena stood and came and got Myrstand's plate. "You like my cooking, Myr?"

Myrstand smiled and stood slowly. "Of course, dear."

He reached out and ruffled the young woman's hair. She was so small compared to both him and Sanna, being not only young, but small of stature. Sometimes he thought of her as a child, when she was really more than eighteen turns, and a woman. But there was something so childlike about her. But Myrstand yet worried about the vampire attack. No matter what Keiara said, she had been drained by three different vampires, and yet showed no ill effects, and had even gained abilities of one of the foul beasts like strength and speed. He wondered if she had the other capabilities that one of those monsters did, and vaguely hoped he'd never find out.

Sanna approached, a bag in hand. Myrstand smiled at her. Keiara had said she'd endured much, and Myrstand wasn't really sure what that meant.

"Myrstand, I've been going over supplies here, and we don't have near enough to make it very far," she said with a shrug. He noticed she was very formal with him. It made him feel like he was in charge, and he wasn't.

He nodded. "Well, we're close to Vrastima. It's a small village, but the people there are good enough. It will take about an hour to walk there for you, so you best be going. Going back to Niliern would be a mistake for you," he said nodding toward Sanna. "Take this," he said handing Sanna a bag of coin.

"It should be enough to buy what we need. See if you can find a sturdy draft horse and a cart. I'd like to be able to take enough food and water with us, so we don't have to depend on finding it along the road. I'll have Tarm of course, but he's not good at wagons."

Sanna nodded. "You don't wish to come with us?" she asked.

"No, I'll stay here, there are many preparations to make..." he said, staring out the doorway.

Lena smiled broadly, then blurted, "He just wants to be alone with Keiara again."

Sanna frowned at her, and Myrstand felt his cheeks heat up at those words. He turned to her and gasped, "Lena!"

Lena smiled and turned to the much taller Sanna. Myrstand wondered at the way Keiara had stopped her from saying anything when she first saw Sanna. In a way he wished she hadn't. Then again, maybe they were better off not knowing what the Seer had seen. Sanna then took her hand, and they headed off, Lena nearly bouncing beside her with glee at getting to go out into the township.

Myrstand shook his head as they walked away. He hoped they didn't get into trouble. Lena was strong, but a group of mad villagers could bring her to her end easy enough with one fell swoop of an axe across her neck.

"Be back before sundown, that's when we're setting out," Myrstand called after them.

The cart jolted to a stop once again, and Jovan's breath caught as he was slammed up against the side of the wagon roughly this time. He waited for a few moments and the flap of the wagon was thrown open and he found himself looking at Cage, but he looked a lot different than he had the night before. He wore a thick, black hooded cloak and Jovan could barely discern his face within it. His clothes had lost all air of being jovial, and his face had not a trace of mirth in it.

"Imagine my surprise to find out you are an elf," he said in a low and dangerous voice. "Not only are you worth a great deal to my master, but you are also worth a great deal of coin to many others. So, I had to decide whether to gather the coin first, then charm the elf headhunter and take you back, or just hand you over to my master."

Cage leaped easily into the back of the wagon and tapped the invisible barrier over Jovan's head. "I need the money, so we're going to the elf headhunter's house in Vrastima first, where I'll be gaining a few thousand gold coins and then I'll charm him into forgetting it ever happened."

Jovan swallowed hard. So, the elf hunters did exist. He struggled in vain against the bindings.

"Oh, sweet Jovan, don't struggle so, you'll cut your wrist and ankles up. I mean, the pain from your wrist should be returning soon after the medication the healer gave you wears off soon, you don't want to make it worse than it is."

Cage leaned over the clear barrier and for the first time in his life, Jovan felt a stabbing fear of someone because the look in his eyes was like an animal or a demon. "If I only had more time with you. You can't imagine the fun I could have. Of all the flesh I've tasted, elf kind has never been one."

He tapped on the barrier twice and it shattered like invisible glass. He then reached down and pulled Jovan up and out of the hay by his shoulder. He'd already unclasped the bindings from the side of the wagon and Jovan, focused on his own internal horror at his captor, hadn't even noticed. He tied a lead to the rope around his wrists and untied his ankles after he got him sitting on the end of the wagon. Suddenly the pain exploded in Jovan's shattered wrist, and he screamed against the gag. Cage smiled inside the black cloak.

"Shouldn't have struggled so hard, sweet elf. You injured it worse. You didn't think I actually paid to have them repair it, did you? I had them give you a pain medication. I mean, no need to mend it, once master gets you, you'll be dead."

He then yanked hard on the rope, pulling Jovan by the wrists off the back of the wagon to the ground. Jovan was completely immobilized with pain for a moment as he dragged him to his feet. Jovan stumbled as he looked up, the sun bright in his face. It was well past noon, easy late afternoon if he didn't miss his guess. The bitter taste in the rag was getting annoying and he sputtered against it. Cage turned back and smiled.

"I wasn't originally prepared for an elf. It wasn't until the third time I drugged your drink last night that you passed out. That's when I figured something wasn't right, then when I took you upstairs and found out you were an elf, well, wasn't I surprised. The herbs only are effective for humans, so I just tripled the dosage on everything to keep you out as long as I could, but of course, it didn't last as long as I'd hoped anyway. Not much experience with elves."

Jovan gagged, feeling his stomach lurch. Cage rounded on him immediately grabbing his face by the chin. "Puke and I'll kill you, Jo-Van," he said spacing out his name. Jovan nodded slowly, swallowing hard at the bile rising in his throat.

Cage smiled then patted him on the cheek. Then his eyes seared into his face again. It was as though he were thinking something horrible. He then stepped back. "Good boy," he said. "Maybe Master will let me play with you before he kills you, oh I'd love that."

Cage yanked him roughly towards the house in the middle of the cove of tress ahead of them. Jovan's moan was muffled by the haze which crossed his vision. The only thing he could feel was the grinding of the rope against the shattered wrist. Cage knocked on the door slowly.

"What?" came a gravelly voice from inside.

"Present, old man, provided you've got the coin I want," said Cage.

The door opened slowly, and a wizened old man stuck his head out. He smiled at Cage and then waved them in. Cage pulled him painfully up the stairs, and Jovan wished he was still unconscious. The inside of the house made Jovan's stomach lurch even worse. He felt his head go dizzy and he stumbled and fell to his knees. The old man laughed.

Cage grinned down at Jovan who stared horrified at the "trophies" on the walls. "What, Jovan? See anyone you recognize?"

To his horror, Jovan did. The term headhunter wasn't an overstatement as Jovan had always assumed. Preserved elven heads were mounted on bases and stared back at him. There was a large board on which ears were mounted, at least fifty of them, and Jovan could see they belonged to at least five of the six houses of the elves by the color. Some of the trophies were old, he could tell, and some were fresh, like the last of the ears on the board which still were red and raw looking at the edges. He felt his stomach churn as he locked eyes with the preserved face of someone he did indeed know, his own sister, the eldest of his sisters, Jokeiva. Her brilliant green eyes shined back at him, and there was no mistaking the beautiful head of bluish white hair she had inherited from their mother. She had been in the forest when he left, so how did her head end up mounted on this...this freak's wall of horror?

The wizened old man reached out and lifted Jovan's head and stared at him.

"Noble blooded Whispara, if I don't miss my guess," he said, his voice gravel on Jovan's ears.

"Noble?" Cage asked. "Then the price goes up."

The wizened old man might have had eyes of brown at once, but now they were gray with age and nearly blended with his gray, lined face. "Of course, young man. Of course. Nobles don't come cheap. An extra thousand. I'm seeing he is eyeing my princess, me guess a'course is that's his sister."

Cage glanced up at the female elf's head and back to Jovan, who had not shifted his tearful gaze from her beautiful face, his own eyes filled with tears. "Well, I think you're right, old man. Well, won't they make a pretty pair for your wall? Been awful careful, I have, to keep his face pretty for you."

Jovan wasn't sure what to do. His heart was beating so hard in his chest; he didn't feel the deathly stillness of the air around him. He didn't even notice when Cage grabbed his throat and started coughing. The old man looked into the room and called out something, but Jovan didn't see or even hear it. He didn't see the old man drop to his knees gasping for breath. Jovan didn't even feel the pressure on his own lungs as they themselves were being starved for air. Without even realizing it, he'd managed to create a vacuum around him by commanding the air to leave the space. And it wouldn't be long before he collapsed himself. But he couldn't see it, couldn't feel it, only the white-hot fury of his sister's face burned into his mind.

Suddenly, there was a bang at the door and Jovan blinked, on the edge of unconsciousness, and felt the coolness of air rushing back into to him. He took a huge breath and realized Cage was on the floor gasping for breath and so was the old elf hunter. He heard the banging on the door.

"Jubel, I knows you there, now answer, saw th' cart, you got a new un?" came a female voice.

The old man, Jubel he guessed was passed out cold, and Cage was gasping great gulps of air just on the verge of unconsciousness. Jovan stood shakily and took one last glance at the face of his sweet sister and took a running aim at the door. He slammed into it with his shoulder and went tumbling down the short stairs and landed on his back. He found himself staring up at a shocked old woman, probably the old man's wife. She had a look of confusion, but Jovan managed to get to his feet and took off at a run into the small wood. He saw a village ahead, it must have been that Vrastima they were talking about. He couldn't get the gag out of his mouth, though, it was tied too tight, and his hands were bound so only the last two joints of his fingers were free. Tears rolled down his face as he thought of his sister, and he knew she must have come to find him. And for his eldest sister to come, and not his brother Jomel, something was terribly wrong in the forest of Anaset.

He burst out of the trees and onto the main street of the small village and scared a couple of children who were playing with a ball near there. He ran up to the little girl closest to him and held out his hands, hoping she'd understand he needed to be untied. Instead, she screamed and all four of the children ran into a nearby house and he heard the bolt slam shut. He slumped his shoulders.

"Through here, you idiot," he heard Cage's voice, and a shiver ran down his spine like he'd never felt before at his voice.

"Jovan, come out come out," he called. "The things I'll do to you for that little trick are beyond your imagining, elf."

He had to hide, and fast. He saw a stable and headed toward it, hoping the horses would mask him somewhat until they passed him by. He got inside the doorway easily enough and slid underneath into a stall with a huge stallion. The stallion snorted at him menacingly and Jovan nuzzled his head against the beast's neck quickly and hummed under his breath. Just as quickly the stallion nuzzled back, calmed by Jovan's actions and sounds. Basics of being one with nature was learning to calm beasts of nature. The old druid had taught him well. He got behind a bale of hay and crouched down at the stallion's rear hooves, hopefully the most dangerous place for anyone to look to find a fugitive elf.

The general store had everything they needed, including the wagon. Sanna loaded it up out in front as Lena paid the rest of what they owed. Waterskins, rations, rope, sacks, block and tackle, lanterns, oil, chalk, fishing supplies, hunting knives, and now they just needed a good strong draft horse to pull it. Luckily, right next door to Vert's Supply was Vert's Stable. Vert was a busy man.

"Okay, Sanna, he said to ask the stable boy to show us the draft horses. He said there's one we can have for free, too," Lena said coming out. She still limped a little on the foot she'd injured a couple days ago.

"Free?" Sanna asked, looking over to the stable. "Why free?"

Lena shrugged. "Says he's worthless, no one can get him to do anything. I'll stay with the wagon; he might not like my scent right now."

Sanna growled under her breath. She headed over to the stable and saw the boy standing in front of the building. He was short, almost half of Lena's size, and as she got closer, she realized he wasn't a child at all, but a Halfling. She smiled. She hadn't seen those in a while, but she supposed they were here and there.

"Hey, Vert says you can set me up with a draft horse. Said there's one for free if I can handle it."

He nodded, reaching out his hand. "Crumel's the name," he said. "And yeah, if you can handle Maelstrom, he's all yours. No one has been able to yet, and we're tired of him taking up space."

Sanna looked at the other draft horses, and then saw the big stallion. She smiled. The name badge read Maelstrom. She walked up to the stall and saw the horse was strangely calm. Even the other horses, the ones not "wild" like this one bucked and snorted at her approach. For some reason this one didn't do that. Then she heard it. Ragged and heavy breathing coming from behind him. Suddenly the doors burst wide and a man in a black cloak stood there, looking back and forth.

Crumel walked up. "Can I help you?"

The man stared around the room, locking eyes with Sanna for a moment then the Halfling. "You seen anyone come in here in the last few minutes?"

The breathing halted inside the stall when the voice spoke and Sanna understood. Whoever this was, they were running from him.

Crumel shook his head. "No, just my master's customers, if you need a horse go see Vert next door."

The man looked at the ground, as though looking for footprints, and Sanna shifted to her right, moving to disturb the footprints in the dusty area not covered with straw.

"Are you sure? He's about my height, his hands are bound, and he's gagged. Some kids said he ran in here," he continued.

Crumel shrugged. "Look if you want, but there's no one here but us."

The man walked in and started looking into each stall. Then he came closer to Sanna's position and Sanna pulled her cloak tighter around her, covering her tattooed arm, just in case. She heard whoever was hiding behind the horse shift and take a couple quick breaths. The horse began to prance the closer the cloaked man came.

"I wouldn't mess with him," the Halfling yelled.

He looked over at him and frowned, his hand falling on Maelstrom's gate. "Why's that, small master?"

"He's trampled two people who got in his stall. Ain't anyone getting in there with him," Crumel said and lifted his shirt, showing the recent horseshoe shaped bruise on his ribs. "And I wasn't even all the way in the pen when he did this. Other two's dead. Anyone who comes near those hooves dies. Vert's about ready to put him down."

Inside the stall, the large horses began to snort violently and stomp his front hooves at the intruder. The cloaked man looked inside, and the horse reared up and hit the gate with his two front hooves and letting loose a loud whinny. The man stepped back.

"Yeah, I see what you mean, little master," he said and continued down the row to check the other pens.

He eventually was satisfied and left. The Halfling shrugged. "So, I can have him?" Sanna asked, motioning to the stallion.

Crumel snorted. "Sure, get that horse out of here, and he's yours, but I'm heading back to the shop, I'm not standing out here while he tramples you."

Sanna nodded and waited until the little man left. She then gently opened the gate, hearing the quickening of the breathing.

"Be calm, both of you," she said softly, and heard the sharp intake of breath. "He's gone, come on out."

From behind the hay bale in the stall, a dark-haired man poked his head out and locked eyes with Sanna. He slowly stood up, looking around and seeing they were alone, he fell to his knees shaking. Sanna rushed into the stall, and to her surprise, the horse edged over, allowing her to pass. She grabbed the gag and he started to sob uncontrollably and fell against her. She was surprised and held him against her and patted his back as he sobbed into her chest.

He started to stammer out words that were half formed. "My sister, she was there, and if she was there, it meant something was wrong. My brothers! Why wouldn't my brothers have come instead? What happened? Why? What is going on and where are they now?" he nearly moaned in her arms. She didn't say anything and eventually he sat back on his feet and wiped his eyes awkwardly with his bound hands. She only took a knife from the scabbard on her thigh and cut the ropes apart.

"I'm sorry, I'm Jovan," he whispered after he got himself under control. "I just couldn't...his eyes were too much...then the heads...my sister...and he...so many ears..."

Sanna had no idea what he was talking about but then realized among his long black hair were a pair of elven ears. She sucked in a breath and reached into her pack and pulled out a scarf she often used to cover her face. She reached for his head, and he pulled away instinctively. She patted his shoulder, and he was amazed to see she wrapped the scarf carefully around his head, covering his ears carefully.

"You should come with us. You can tame the horse, I take it?" she said softly.

Jovan nodded, looking embarrassed now that he'd broken down in front of her like that. "I'm a ranger of my people, I can handle any animal."

She nodded. "Okay here," she said, taking off her cloak and wrapping around him. She noticed he had no shoes either, and the bottoms of his feet were crusted with blood, but there wasn't much to be done about it right now. "Come on, quickly, before that man comes back. You can explain later. I don't know what's happening, but anyone who can commune with nature is okay in my book, and that man was not anyone I would want someone to be caught by."

Sanna saw Lena look up as they neared. Once more, a look crossed her face as though she wanted to say something. Instead, she smile broadly as they approached.

"Let's go, we've got to hurry back!" Lena announced.

Sanna stammered for a moment but quickly hooked the horse up to the wagon as Lena led the cloaked figure to the wagon seat and as she looked up, she saw her whispering to him. Down the road a way, she saw the dark cloaked man walking toward them. Lena and the elf were in conversation about something, so Sanna hurried with the harness because now she was exposed fully, and she of course did not look anything like the commoners.

"You!" the cloaked man screamed from down the road. "The fire monk, you've got him with you haven't you, you bitch!"

"Hurry!" Lena said, throwing the reigns into the elf's hands.

Sanna nodded to them. "Go, I'll handle him."

Lena looked back. "Are you sure?"

Sanna grinned. "Keiara has been teaching me, but she hasn't quenched the flames by any means."

"Stop!" he yelled as Lena and the elf took off in the cart at a full gallop.

Sanna stood in the center of the road, and he ran to her. He tossed back the hood revealing a mildly handsome face, but a face that triggered an intense feeling in her. The eyes, something about the eyes. He looked a lot like someone she had once known, though she couldn't recall who it was at the moment.

"No, you stop," she said, a dangerous edge to her voice.

He held up both his hands and as she watched a strange swirling blackness began to form. She thought for a second that it was enough of that. She closed her eyes and held out her hands and whispered to the fires within.

A jet of fire shot out from both her hands at the spell he was casting, throwing off his concentration and surprising him. He frowned and pulled a sword on her and ran forward. She read his face.

"You fire slinging bitch; you won't stop me from serving the master's will!"

Well, that wouldn't work much better. In two steps, she sidestepped his thrust and put herself behind him. She spun and planted the heel of her foot on the back of his neck sending him sprawling, unconscious. He should have stopped.

Lena put the wagon beside the cave and took the elf by the hand and led him into the cavern. Myrstand stood ready at the door with his arms crossed. The sun was starting to slowly sink in the west.

"You two are late…" he began and then realized it was not Sanna with Lena but a man. "Who's this? And where's Sanna?"

"I'm here," Sanna said, strolling in easily. "I was just a little behind them."

"It still doesn't answer who this is, and why you're late?"

Keiara came up behind him and placed her hands gently on his shoulders. "Don't worry; you don't have to leave now."

Myrstand furrowed his brow and turned to look at his dark lady. "What, you mean this…?"

The new arrival stood transfixed as he removed Sanna's cloak and stood there numbly. His one wrist was crudely bandaged, and his other was red and raw. He was barefoot, his pants tattered and torn especially at his ankles, which like his wrists were raw and red. His eyes were red and swollen, and as he took off the red scarf from his head, he revealed a set of elven ears.

"Jovan," Keira said, stepping toward him.

"It is you," he croaked, his eyes welling with tears. He stood there silent and confused for a moment.

She smiled and held up his injured hand. "I'm so sorry I surprised you and you fell like you did, I tried to make sure you survived the exhaustion and the cold, but I didn't anticipate an enemy finding you instead. Unfortunately, there are things that I cannot See."

She motioned to Myrstand, and he came to stand beside her.

"Here," she said, handing him Jovan's bandaged wrist.

Myrstand looked at it with confusion. "What am I supposed to do with it?"

Keiara gently unwrapped it to reveal a swollen, red and bruised wrist and hand. The treatment it had gotten being bound to its twin had been worse than Jovan realized. The pain at the wrapping being removed sent him to his knees. Keiara gently held up his hand as he finally was able to succumb to the nausea that had been threatening to overcome him ever since he'd been pulled from the wagon. He supported himself with his other hand and finally sat back up and wiped his mouth, heaving great breaths of air.

"You can heal, Myrstand. Just believe in that," Keiara said, handing Myrstand his hand once more.

Myrstand swallowed and kneeled beside the elf. He closed his hands around Jovan's wrist and closed his eyes. From his hands a brilliant white light encompassed the wrist and Jovan's look of pain began to fade. Myrstand himself didn't understand it. He was only concentrating on the act of healing, and he was finding himself doing what he was thinking about. After a few minutes though, he felt like he had drained every ounce of his power and he released Jovan's hand. He opened his eyes and looked down at the elf's wrist to see it still somewhat swollen and red, but nowhere nearly as bad as it had been.

"By the Lord of Paladins," he whispered and then his eyes rolled up into his head and Keiara quickly moved behind him and caught him.

Lena gasped. "What happened to him?"

"Don't worry, just the exhaustion, just as you were exhausted after your battle with the vampires, he has done the same, using his power to the limit. Now, Jovan," she said, turning to him.

He looked up at her slowly. "Before you can no longer stand, I have a question. Do you come to me, and become my agent of your own will?"

Jovan looked at her, then glanced over to Sanna, who was staring silently at the scene, and all he could think to say was, "Yes..."

He smiled for a second then felt the world fading from existence around him, and quick as a flash, he fell into Sanna's strong arms. She looked up at Keiara who was smiling down at her. She stared into the elf's face, swollen and red from tears, and Sanna's heart ached. Could he understand her pain? Would he want to?

CHAPTER SEVEN

A DWARF BECOMES A BELIEVER

Should you meet me in your travels,
Give me a piece of bread, and I will bless you.
Give me a kick to the shin, and I will curse you.
Give me neither, and I will leave you be.
—*Teberas Hinder, Beggar Prince of Vestern*

"Whatever you do, Moryn, you must protect your sister," the taller and older dwarf said staring down into the young boy's face. "She's special, you know that. You're special too, and I'm sure yer mom is gonna tell yer sister the same thing. One of six pair o'twins born fifty years ago today. Now, go enjoy yer coming of age."

With that, he pushed the young dwarf out into open room which was filled with all the children who had a birthday this day. The six pairs of twins were seated together. Moryn sat down beside his sister. He nodded at her. He already knew they had both been told the same thing. Beyond all else, watching out for each other was at the heart of what the twins did.

He watched as his father, Margreth Stormhearth, leader of the guild of metallurgists. His mother, Alaga, stood beside him.

127

Also present were the parents of the other twins. While a child's birthday was a special occasion, the six twins born fifty years ago in the year of twins were coming of age today. They would all be able to marry and start their families, choose their pathways in life, and decide on what they would use their various talents for.

Moryn's father cleared his throat. "Welcome, and healthy days to all who celebrate their birth today! Today is a very special day for not only are we celebrating the birth of several children tonight, we are celebrating a coming of age for the only six children to be born in the year of twins. Six pairs, twelve children, born in one year is a phenomenon in itself, but twelve children born the same day in that year, as twins, is simply a miracle.

"Since the Abandonment, we've all doubted that the divine still looked down on us, but that year, there was little doubt, someone out there was looking out for us after the skirmish at Raphel Lake where we lost so many to the Noren's magic and steel. To add twelve children in the next year was the start to make up for the loss of sixty strong dwarves that day. May they rest in stone," he whispered. "But we are not here to morn but to celebrate!"

There was a round of raucous applause that rang out through the chamber. Moryn looked around. They had these massive gatherings once a week to celebrate birthdays of the children, but normally this grand hall was a dining hall. They normally all ate dinners with the rest of the dwarves, and very rarely did a dwarf not eat dinner in the main hall. Miira looked at him and smiled. They had plans for later and were looking forward to it.

"Now, bring the feast!" Moryn's father clapped his hands loudly, and the cooks began passing out massive trays of food to each of the large, stone tables.

"I guess this makes it worth it," muttered Tamba Graystone, one of the other twins sitting beside Moryn. He smiled at her.

He'd always liked Tamba's company. Unfortunately for Moryn, Tamba's interests lay with his sister, Miira, and not him. He had hopes to at least father her child one day, even if he couldn't marry her.

Miira nodded at her. "Of course, the food is good, and we didn't have to help!"

The smell was amazing. Roast meats, vegetables, mushrooms, and tubers filled the room. Miira and Moryn both filled their plates, and for the first time, a tray of mead and wine was sat down on the table. Miira took a large goblet of vetrenberry wine and Moryn took a goblet of sweet gloomhoney mead. They ate forever it felt like. Then it was time for the presenting of the coming of age gifts. Each dwarf was given one gift from their parents, and then allowed to have free time as adult dwarves for a few hours before the night gong was rung.

Each parent of the twins came and encircled the table where the twins sat. Each set of twins was comprised of a boy and a girl, and each mother stood behind her daughter, each father behind their son. Each one held a square box which was about the size of a large melon. The young dwarves turned around and each accepted the box. As one, they removed the top to find their present inside.

Moryn found a pair of stone colored gloves. They sparkled with pieces of stone, diamond, emerald and ruby, and he could sense already the earth magic woven into the fibers of the gloves. He looked over at Miira, who held a set of soft black boots. They were made of some sort of animal hides that were tanned and inscribed with magic runes of all sorts. Inside the boxes was also a perfectly clear stone inscribed with a single rune, the rune for home... Sometimes called a homequartz, they were magical stones all dwarves carried that were tuned with their home hearth in the citadel of stone but shattered once they had been used. Making one took a lot of time, and a lot of effort, so it was only given at the coming of age presentation.

Moryn looked over, seeing each of the other ten had various items and their homequartz. There was nothing said, the parents all turned and left, followed by the rest of the groups of dwarves, leaving the twelve newly come of age dwarves. Moryn put on his gloves immediately and felt the strength of stone surge through him. Miira pulled on the boots and Moryn noted that her steps and her sounds were muffled. Tamba, who had received a silver headband with a diamond in the center, hugged Moryn and Moryn sighed, smelling the mint she used on her hair. Then Tamba embraced Miira with a hug followed by kiss which made Moryn turn away after a few moments.

"Son of a stone, girl, breathe," he muttered as he went to talk with the others.

Tamba's brother, Terverath, shook his head. "You would think they'd find a quiet place, or at least go somewhere else," he muttered as Moryn approached.

"Well, now that they're of age, they can be open about their love for each other," another one of the twins, Vertran Breakstone. "I wouldn't mind being either one of them's child father, though..."

Moryn and Terveran both glared at him. "Sorry! I forget that they're related to you two..."

Vaerba, Vertran's sister snickered. "Well, they'll have to choose a child father eventually, but once the child is born, they'll be able to care for them without any interference. Can't help who you fall in love with!"

"I wouldn't mind spending some time with you, Moryn," muttered a female voice behind him. Moryn turned around to be looking at Lavada Masonhammer. He swallowed, staring into her grayish green eyes.

"Lavada, you know I like you and all..." he stammered, stepping back.

She pouted. "Moryn, you know the best you'll do with Tamba is be her child father, you need a mate, not a girl who won't love you except as the father to her child. She's in love with your sister, so get over it and take advantage of my overly emotional state right now on my celebration night when I've had too much wine..."

Moryn fell over a stone bench. "Lakwath! Help! You're sister's after me again!"

A dwarf that other than being male was identical to the female trying to embrace Moryn came over. "Sister, you're embarrassing yourself, you know I've known Moryn a while now, and if you want him to like you, play hard to get, look how much he loves Tamba and he can't have her!"

Lakwath steered his sister away and Moryn sighed. The Crystalhands, Keda and Kambreth, came up and lifted him up from his place on the floor.

"I don't think she's going to ever let you be, Moryn," Brea Silverore said walking up behind him. "She's been after you since we started school at ten years old."

Moryn nodded. "Tell me about it. It isn't that I don't like her, she's nice enough, just not my type."

Brea's twin, Brandeth clapped him on the back. "Of course not, you've got a thing for watching Tamba and your sister kiss."

Moryn frowned at him then skulked away. "Oh, come now, I'm just kidding, Moryn!" he called.

He headed down some of the more unfamiliar corridors. No more was he limited by the color of the corridors. After a while he found himself lost in the mazes of corridors marked with the black, red and yellow flags. Black meant they were dead ends, red were dangerous or set with traps, and yellow were ones that were unexplored completely. Those were the three colors that underage dwarves were not permitted to go down. Now, no one stopped him as he wandered, thoughts on many things at once. Then he realized there were no more flags. And he couldn't remember which way he'd come.

He frowned and sighed. Well, this would be a difficulty. He fingered the homequartz in his pocket but didn't want to use it so frivolously. There might be a time that he really needed to make it back home, and besides, all he had to do was wait for Miira to find him.

Miira realized at once that Moryn was gone. She felt the roiling confusion and sensation of being lost and she knew he'd been lost in the corridors.

"Tamba, Moryn's gone and lost himself, and I've got a feeling of foreboding. We should go look for him before something happen," Miira said to the dwarf who was holding her right hand.

"Brother!" Tamba called, and he looked over. "Moryn's got himself lost."

Terveran stopped his conversation with a few of the other twins and nodded to her. "We'll be back, Miira will find him, no doubt."

Together the three of them took off, Miira leading the way. She had an intuitive sense of where he was, almost like a compass in her mind pointing toward him instead of north. All of the twins had this same ability as well as some sort of low-level telepathic link with each other.

"He's not scared, he's just waiting, he knows we're coming to him. Tamba, keep track of the turns," Miira said.

Tamba had a piece of chalk she was marking the walls with as they went. It was a basic cavern exploring rule to have chalk with you in case you needed to find your way back. Moryn of course had left without his pack, leaving him without any of the tools to ensure he could return the way he came.

It took a while but eventually they found Moryn sitting in an alcove.

"What are you doing, wandering off like that, brother?" asked Miira smirking.

Moryn shook his head. "Got tired of watching you two make it in front o'me."

Tamba and Miira exchanged blushing glances. "Yeah, sorry, the moment kind of took hold."

"Let's just go, Moryn," Terveran said with a smile.

Together the two pair of twins set off back the way they had come until they came to an unmarked intersection.

"You marked them all, Tamba," Miira said, looking around in the darkness.

"I know I did," Tamba said, turning around like her lover. "Someone has cleaned off the chalk marks. The stone is wet on all four walls."

"Look what we have here," a strange voice came from down the corridor ahead of them. "A few little rats in the trap I set."

Miira, Terveran, Tamba, and Moryn immediately stood back to back with each other and began slowly turning so they could all see in each direction.

"Four nice fat ones," another voice said from down a different corridor.

There was a female giggle. "Twins, it looks like, what a gift."

"Noran," Terveran growled.

"Oh, now little dwarf-master, don't be so derogatory when you say our name," the female said in a singsong voice. "After all, we've caught you, and now we'll kill you."

Miira reached back and pulled her great axe from her back. Moryn stood at the ready, needing no weapon. Terveran's hammer was already out, and Tamba's crossbow was aimed into the darkness. They'd never seen a real fight before, but they would give them everything their youth would allow.

"They're going to fight us," one of the male voices called, echoing slightly.

"Seems that way," the other male voice answered.

"All the more fun," the female said, a quiver of excitement to her own voice.

With that, for the dwarves, the entire world exploded. Noran were known for their mastery of explosives and chemicals that the dwarves had not, so the group should have been prepared when the rock face exploded to their right. However, these two sets of twins were not battle hardened, and did not know of the treachery and sneakiness of the Noran's ways. They had heard tales of entire caves collapsing at their behest, but who knew what came from the mouths of the old ones was true and what was exaggerated. Apparently, they didn't exaggerate as much as the young ones had thought.

Miira coughed out lung-fulls of rock dust and felt a hand near her. She gripped it and pulled, and a coughing and sputtering Moryn came up. The entire area was blocked, leaving them with one corridor to go down. On the other side, they heard metal clashing as the other twins fought with someone.

"Tamba! Terveran! Are you alive?" Miira screamed through the rock.

After a while an answer came. "We're here; are you and Moryn both alive?" Tamba asked, her voice faint and distant.

"We are, but we're blocked in, the stone is unstable, we'll have to all move from here before any more collapses. What of our attackers?" Moryn said, his voice thick with the dust.

"Dead, well a male and female, anyway. I don't know where the other one we heard is. He may have been blocked off like you two," Terveran answered, sounding equally distant.

"Look we're going to try and find a way out this way, can you two get home from here?" Miira asked.

Tamba tapped twice on the rock. "We'll get there, you continue down that way, if I'm right it leads to the surface, and you'll be able to come down a different place."

"Right, see you back home!" Miira yelled, touching the rock gently.

There was a rumbling above them. "Come on, sis, this is going to come down on our heads if we don't move, now."

Miira nodded and the two dust coated dwarves scrambled through the rubble into the corridor. They looked back as the rocks gave way and filled even more of the open space in. They slowly moved down the corridor, hoping Tamba was right and there was an exterior cave close by that they could get to the surface by. Of course, there was the problem that neither of them had been to the surface before.

Keiara looked exhausted to the others as she wandered around their little dwelling lost in thought. She turned to the others.

"Gather up, the last of our group will be met at the mountains to the east of here," she said, turning on her heels and disappearing into the darkness of an inner cavern once more.

Myrstand shrugged and set about the work. Jovan, still sleeping, was curled up against the wall. Sanna sighed and shook her head. He was just a man after all, why should she worry about him?

She hitched up Maelstrom and began loading the wagon with Myrstand's help. There was an eerie silence settling around them as they felt something significant coming their way.

Lena sat down beside Jovan and gently shook him to wakefulness, or at least she had thought he was sleeping.

"Yes?" he asked as soon as her hand touched his shoulder.

"Oh!" she said, recoiling a bit. "I thought you were sleeping."

He sat up against the wall, every part of him sore. "I'm an elf silly I don't sleep."

Lena looked confused. "You don't sleep?"

Jovan smiled again, brushing his black hair from his face. "Not like humans sleep, anyway, it's called different things, reverie, trance, meditation, whatever, but we're more aware than humans are when we rest."

Lena nodded. "We're heading out to our final companion," she said with a smile.

Jovan nodded and stood up. His bones creaked, and he felt like his wrists and ankles were trying to come apart. Oh well, he thought as he headed to help with the preparations.

Keiara watched them from above now. She was confused. One more, just one more was missing, so why was she sensing two?

Moryn and Miira surfaced into the bright sunlight. "That's odd," Miira commented. "Why is our night their day?"

"That is odd," Moryn said slowly, looking around. "It was near high moon by our time when we left."

"Nothing odd, dwarf-kind," came a voice from behind them.

Cloaked in black they saw the light-colored eyes of a Noran who had followed them from the caves below. "Now you can die," came the voice from below the heavy black cloak.

"It isn't necessary, we won't attack, we just want to go home, you can too," Miira said holding up her hands in submission.

The Noran held up a crossbow dripping a green viscous fluid. "There's no quarter between us, and you know it."

"Well that's not very sporting, now is it," a voice above them said. Miira and Moryn looked up and saw a pair of legs swaying above them in the large tree. "I mean, no weapons drawn, what harm are they?"

The Noran looked up above them, almost dropping his aim on the dwarves. "I can tell you are an elf. Face me coward."

Miira watched as a tall elf dropped down gently beside her. "Well, yes I'm an elf, as are you, but you're Noran, if I'm not mistaken."

Moryn frowned. "Another elf? But the Norans are elves, but you don't look like them..."

The elf smiled. "Of course not. I'm Whispara, otherwise called Air-kin elves, while the Noran are the dark-kin elves. I know the Noran hate the dwarves, but my short friends, I guarantee they hate us more."

The dark cloaked Noran hissed. "Cowards, all of you. I'll kill you and these dwarves and go home with three heads instead of two."

Moryn looked up. "Whispara? How many kinds o'elves are there anyway?"

"Name's Jovan, by the way, good dwarf. And there are six kinds of elves. None of us really get along with each other, my people have an uneasy peace with the earth-kin elves that live in the northernmost reaches of these mountains," Jovan said, leaning on his staff casually. Both the dwarves had dropped their hands by this point.

"Enough talk!" the Noran screamed.

"Yeah, I'm growing a bit bored, Jovan," came a female voice from behind the Noran.

The Noran spun around, switching his vision from the dwarves and Jovan to the new addition. A red-haired woman with a tight outfit showing a lot of fire themed tattoos was standing directly beside the Noran.

"Want to take care of him, Sanna?" Jovan asked still casually.

The elf was unsure how to handle this situation, but before he could even think about it, he found himself pinned to the ground the unnaturally fast red-haired woman. His weapon was discarded, and he had both arms pinned behind him with her sitting on top of them.

"Now what do we do with him? Keiara would definitely want us to keep him alive," Jovan said walking up.

Moryn yelled out, "Wait, he's going to..."

They all heard the snarling sounds and looked down to realize the elf was foaming at the mouth.

"Poison," Miira said. "They carry it in a capsule inside pouches sewn into their cheeks. They'd rather die than be captured alive. There's no quarter between our people."

"Well damn," Sanna muttered. "Can't be helped I suppose."

She stood up and gestured to the two dwarves. "Come on, you two. You're expected."

Miira and Moryn exchanged a glance, and a thought, "What?"

"Keiara will explain everything, and you two are?" Jovan said, motioning them forward.

They glanced at each other quickly. "Miira and Moryn Stormhearth," Moryn said slowly.

They had camped close to where the dwarf twins had come up, near another cavern which led underground. Keiara stood in the sunshine as though soaking up something she was without inside her. Myrstand walked up behind her and wrapped his arms around her waist tightly. She covered his pale hands with her own and smiled, memories of time immemorial to the mortals flooded her ancient mind, times when his hands had held her before. She closed her eyes for a moment and reveled in a time much simpler when she knew what was happening and knew the future.

"So, your 'one' is really two now?" Sanna's voice came from a few yards away.

"I'm not sure, Sanna," she said, not needing to turn to know there were two dwarves there. "I am not the all-seeing mother of gods in this body, you know. I am simply Keiara sometimes, and this is one of them."

Myrstand released her and turned to see the two disheveled and dirty dwarves standing behind them. Both looked confused and he could understand that.

Jovan clapped the male on the back. "Moryn and Miira," he said with a smile. "So amazing, I've never seen one of them before."

Moryn looked up at him with an arched brow. "Keep it up and you won't be seeing much outn them eyes o' yours when I'm done."

Jovan leaped lightly out of the way and smiled again, even broader. "They're everything I heard and more!"

With that Jovan turned and trotted up a way so he could keep a watch out. Sanna leaned against the rock and crossed her arms waiting for the introductions or whatever she had planned. Lena came running up to stand beside her looking around with those bright eyes of hers.

"So who are you and how did you expect us?" Moryn asked, Keiara's back still turned.

"I remember, you know, when dwarves took their first breath," she said her voice a haunting melody that caught on the wind. Miira and Moryn exchanged glances. Keiara stared into the sky.

"Out of all the people of the world of Avern, you were an amazing creation. The spark of life given to you by the phoenix of earth, grown from the very rock itself. I helped a bit, I suppose. An entire race alone is very difficult. The humans were created between me and the phoenix of light, and then of course, my daughter laid with each of us to create the elves. But you dwarves, you were special, because the phoenix of earth was insistent that you were to be his alone. But I did help, if just a little. Igniting the spark by yourself, it is oh so difficult."

"You're trying to tell us that you are..." Moryn began. "The Dark Phoenix of legend?" Miira continued.

Keiara turned around finally, focusing her black eyes on the twins before her. "I am the mother of gods, though diminished in the mortal form."

There was a shared glance between them and Keiara could pick up the nearly telepathic resonance between them. So, the earth essence had been split between a pair of twins.

"No, I'm not insane, as you believe Moryn," she said smiling gently.

"I didn't..." he started.

She stepped forward. "No, you didn't say anything, it passed between you and Miira. What proof do you require? I've already gained allegiance of Jovan and Sanna who you met, Lena over there by Sanna, and Myrstand here, the last paladin of Aren. So how do I convince the dwarves?"

She came forward and sat on a boulder near them and stared. "For Myrstand, his magical abilities allowed him to sense my truth and power. For Lena, she knew me long before we encountered each other here. For Sanna, she could sense the flame of Asumbar within me. For Jovan, his elven history and knowing me in the past made him my companion. So, what is it that will make the dwarf a believer?"

Miira and Moryn glanced at each other again and then back at the strange dark woman. "If you are who you say you are, show us."

Myrstand frowned. "How do you mean show you?"

Moryn turned to him. "Humans may have lost the stories, but elves and dwarves have not. You are said to have the power over the dark circle of magic, psychic magic, and all magic of the mind and illusion. Show us that which will make us believe."

Keiara smiled. "Oh, the wonderful, pragmatic dwarves. No lovely words, no fancy parlor tricks, no transformations, for you. You strike to the heart of the matter and to the source of my ability. Very well. I will show you what will make you believe."

Myrstand stepped forward. "Wait, if you are master of mind and illusion, how do they know you won't show them something false?"

Keiara smiled. "Therein lies the trick, lovely Myrstand. Unlike other races, dwarves are immune to psychic illusions. Their minds are as strong as the very stones they were brought to life from, and if I attempt to show them anything untrue, they will not see it. Only truth can be shown inside a dwarven mind."

She stood between the twins and gently placed her right hand on Moryn's right temple, and her left hand on Miira's left temple. She lifted her head up and her eyes changed, burning brilliant purple white.

141

"See the truth of the past," she said softly.

Inside Miira and Moryn's mind, the world was like a play upon a stage. They viewed the creation of the dwarves, and while it was not exactly as they had learned in school, they knew much time had passed. They saw a different figure but knew it was the same one who stood before them. They saw the war of the Noran, they saw their own births, and then they saw the events of the day in rapid succession.

Myrstand, Sanna, and Lena all watched as nothing at all transpired, except Keiara standing there. Then she removed her hands, and her eyes returned to their normal black star speckled color. She stepped back and crossed her arms. She stared and waited. Split in twain, the essence of earth was definitely within them both.

"So, will you follow me?" she asked, the eternity around her eye swimming with stars.

Miira and Moryn glanced at each other and nodded in unison. "Yes," they said together. Behind them, the sun began to set.

CHAPTER EIGHT

THE PUPPET QUEENS

Her breath is like the death.
Her death is like the breath of doom.
She is the wind of the end.
—Song to revere the Black Queen

B rian Demia walked with determination down the hallways
of the great castle of Lineria. Great kings and queens had
come and gone who had lived inside this castle. He looked up
at the portraits of the great ones that had come before. He
stopped and stared into the face of the last king, King Meitan.
He had truly been a great man. He was kind, generous and
understanding. He'd married a woman who had given birth to
two daughters, though. And some scorned him for it. Many
thought after the queen's death he should have married once
more and tried for a male heir. He did not. He stayed true to his
wife. As he should, Brian thought.

Brian swallowed hard and walked on. Queen Sealla was not
her father's daughter. She was evil. She was hateful. Keiara
would have made such a wonderful queen. Brian smiled as he
thought of the lovely girl he'd grown up with. She was so sweet

and wonderful. But now, she was not here. And Sealla had used some of the darkest arts on the Avern to remove Lineria from the rest of the world. Brian was no wizard, and he certainly didn't understand what had been done, all he knew was his family could no longer be contacted by any means, and because of it, Brian felt as though the world had ended. Perhaps it had, and Lineria was all that was left.

He walked onward and passed many people he knew. They all averted their eyes as he walked by them. They all knew all too well what it was which would occur soon. He sighed and did not let it affect him in the slightest. It was to be, and he could not help it. He did not indicate he held any fear in his breast, for he did not. His world had ended when Keiara had been killed or cast out, or whatever had happened. He'd vested so many hopes and dreams into her, and they had been squashed by Queen Sealla. But even as unknowledgeable as Brian was of the arts of magic, he did know one thing. Something was very wrong with the queen. She'd grown even more cruel and deadly since her sister's exodus.

He passed into the grand entranceway. The carvings were ancient and beautiful beyond words. Here was one of a dragon standing at the gate of the castle. Another of two dragons in battle. This one was of the horned creature that had assaulted the kingdom a thousand years ago which was turned away by the king. He examined them all as he moved through the area. It was as though he were a man doomed to never look upon them again. He entered the grand throne room where the black eyed Sealla sat dressed in red and blue. The grand dress she wore was far more eloquent than she needed. It was all about appearances though.

"My queen," he said dropping to one knee. His voice carried none of the respect he pretended to show.

"What is the news?" she asked staring at her bloody colored fingernails.

Brian licked his lips. "The Seers report the princess Keiara is no more."

Sealla sat up on the throne. "This is good news; I hoped when she left that her life would be short indeed. What have they said else?" she said, her features blurred by some sort of screen surrounding her face.

"They say she may not be alive, but she still exists."

Sealla stood up with a confused look on her face. "This is not possible. What is it, tell me, boy," she spat stepping towards him.

"The Seers say Princess Keiara has died. She has died by your hands but has risen as someone new yet old."

Sealla's eyes grew wide. "Priestess!!!" she yelled turning away from Brian.

A woman with pitch black hair entered the room. She wore robes as red as blood. Brian shivered. She was the high priestess of Rhen. Rhen was the goddess of many horrible things, and Brian hated to see her enter. Normally they operated under a veil, since like all other groups of Faith, they too were a dwindling lot. The gods had abandoned them, too, though they took a longer time to come to terms with it. No one could deny their power over nightmares though. She lifted her head and her eyes burned deep red.

"You called, my queen?"

Sealla walked to her and dropped her hands to her hips. "You said Keiara would be destroyed. Now, the Seers say the... You know what this means. Tell me."

The High Priestess nodded. "The Prophecy has become true."

Sealla's face twisted. "You can't be serious, how is that possible?"

The priestess shook her head. "I must consult the Great One."

Sealla nodded and stepped backward.

The Priestess made a motion and around her five robed figures appeared. She stood in the middle and chanted. Brian watched, and his knees shook. Above them appeared a large black bird suddenly. It spread its great wings and landed beside the circle. It was partially real and partially not though. Parts of it were transparent.

The high priestess approached it.

"Oh, great Timal. Your advice is needed, oh greatest of the Itemlnoga."

The bird stared at them for a moment. Then it began to speak in a female voice which sounded almost like Keiara's voice.

"On the night of the hidden moon, dark fire shall consume her, and from the flames the Dark Phoenix will once more rise."

The creature paused and stared at each of those present in the room. It was almost as though it were thinking.

"The night has come and gone, fools. The Dark Phoenix has risen, and you have created her. She gathers the followers as you settle your petty ways. The Darkness has come to Chaos. The Light has come to Order. All are being drawn. The rest will find her soon, and then you will not be able to fight her."

The bird stood taller and transformed into a woman. She was still transparent, and thus was not there in the slightest. She was tall and beautiful. She had hair of midnight and eyes of eternity. Around her left swam the eternal chaos. She locked eyes with Sealla who stood transfixed. There was look of pain and fear for once on the queen's face.

Sealla screamed. "You cannot be this! I only wanted the kingdom. This is not what I intended!" Yet in the back of her mind the whisper came, Oh, I want so much more than a kingdom.

The figure smiled. "Ah but you caused this. You started this by killing me. You, dear sister, released the Dark Phoenix within me. Now, it is out of our hands. Your kingdom, or rather my kingdom, is inconsequential. The prophecy is what it is."

She held a rusted sword. Sealla knew the sword, the rusty sword she'd killed her sister with. She smiled. "Good bye, sister..."

The image faded away into nothingness.

Brian watched. He thought his life was forfeit walking into here, as did everyone he had passed along the way. And now he was certain. Sealla stared at the place her cursed sister had been and then turned to Brian. She pointed her finger at him and he felt invisible hands ripping his heart from his body. Then he saw the blood and fell to the floor. But his spirit did not leave. He stood up once more. He was not alive though. Sealla's eyes were hard and did not waver. He had no will of his own, yet still inside, he remained.

Raise the armies. Embrace the corrupt. Shelter the deceitful. Arm the heretics. Call them to you. They will come to you. I will accept them all, the voice whispered in Sealla's mind. Sealla was coming to believe the voice was her own.

"Raise an army that can defeat anything. Make them stronger and better and make them mine," the Queen of Lineria said with a curse in her voice and with her back to the High Priestess. "Send out a call to all the dungeons and prisons. Send me the scum and villainy. Tell them I will grant them full pardon if they come join me. Send it out into all the lands. Bring them to me. Bring me the corrupt, the vile, the heartless. I want them all. Bring them to borders where the solid fog rests, they will be allowed through."

"Yes, my lady," she whispered and left, with the newly undead Brian in tow.

She paused outside the door. Rhen was many things, but these were not the words of Rhen. Ashelane, the last high priestess of Rhen was beginning to doubt the queen's claim that the Nightmare Walker spoke to her in her sleep, and whispered words of instruction. The Black Star had never used undead abominations before that she knew of. Then Ashelane thought. No one had heard from Rhen or any of the gods in a thousand years. Who knew, perhaps she did use undead... She shook her head and walked on. But what about when they started to decay? Wouldn't they stink? She walked on, contemplating the ways to avoid the event.

Sealla sat down on her throne. She stared into space. No prophecy would stop her from having what she desired. Even though her desires appeared to not be her own any more, she had to have them. You will get what you desire. I know how to take care of the Dark Phoenix; I've already prepared for her arrival. Sealla closed her eyes. She muttered under her breath, "You mean you've known all this time?" The voice laughed. Oh yes, I've been waiting for her to appear, we will take care of matters soon enough.

Sealla sighed as she sat in her room. Suddenly she heard the humming that meant she was calling her. She swallowed. She hated allowing her in, because she couldn't control her actions like she normally could, but in the name of power she would do it.

She reached inside the drawer at the dresser as she stared into the mirror. The woman who looked back at her wasn't the same as she had been before. Once, her gray eyes had sparkled with the vibrancy of youth and life, now they were so dull and lifeless. She knew making a deal with the Mistress of Death would leave her empty eventually, but she was surprised at how fast the coldness was creeping into her heart and soul. Such was the path to power. She gave her strength where she had none. She slowly watched her reflection lifting a black crystal from the drawer which was making the soft, almost pleasant-sounding hum.

"My Mistress," she whispered. "I am here."

Suddenly, Sealla's head was thrown back, her blonde hair blowing away from the crystal in her hands, and as usual her body was wracked with intense agony, and then she felt the soothing cold slip over her as the presence came to be. She righted her head and stared into the black eyes that were not her own.

Have you a plan for dealing with the Dark Phoenix, yet, my dear? The cold and icy voice said like thunder in her head.

"Not yet, I am unsure how to proceed..." she said softly.

There was a shock of pain left her gasping and the voice continued, Worthless. Why have I invested my time in such a worthless human like you?

Sealla caught her breath and swallowed before speaking. She was used to her using pain, but this was more intense than other times. She was really upset by this Dark Phoenix.

"My Mistress, I am sorry, I...I..."

Speak no more, wretch. You will be receiving a party soon of my own creation. You will extend them the same courtesy you would show me. They will hunt her out and destroy her.

Just as quickly, her presence was gone and Sealla was left sore and shaking from the encounter. She swallowed again and sighed. She reminded herself, if not for her, she would have never murdered her father or her sister. She would have never conducted the experiments she had. She wouldn't be nearly where she was already.

The crystal in front of the dark woman spun. It was a sphere of black oblivion. It was but a piece of her power, though. Power she was taking from the very gods everyone believed had Abandoned them. Imprisoned in the Prison of Eternity, none of them could get out and none of them could use their power. And she'd taken care of those pesky Keepers too, though they couldn't be placed in the Prison of Eternity. The gods had enough power to fuel her desires. Instead she channeled their power into herself, and she grew more powerful by the day. She encased the sphere in her hands and it disappeared to return only when she called it. She would leave her puppet alone for now. She had thought Sealla would be worthless when it came to destroying the Dark Phoenix, which is why she'd created the squad to send after them. Dark Phoenix. She'd expected the Maker and Unmaker to do something but to go to this extreme? It meant she was a threat. She stood slowly, a pale figure with taunt skin over bone and eyes like pits of emptiness.

She walked past skeletal guardians, and past half fleshed zombies. She walked down corridors of stone, her black robes swishing against the ground as she went. The black stone walls and floors echoed the clicking sounds of her shoes as she came upon a gate built into the walls.

The gates stood twelve feet high and were equal in width. They were constructed of a black obsidian-like material that reflected all light, and likewise reflected all magic. Great silver bands crossed the gates in five places, each a foot in height, and running the width of the gates. Unseen, strong, magically laced banding supported the interior of the gates as well. A single hand sized silver plate sat four foot from the ground. The magical enchantments were palatable they were so strong. They should have been strong; it had taken the blood of fifty sorcerers to enspell it, and the talents of twenty more to maintain it.

She placed her hand on the plate and the gates swung open into a place void of all light. This was the antechamber to the holding room. The gates shut behind her and she spoke a single word. The room was lit with a floating light above her head. Ten figures were chained to the wall on the right side, and ten to the left side. Technically, they were not alive. They were the shells of the sorcerers who had once been alive. Now all that remained were their bodies, which produced the magic which continued to ward the doors. Some still resembled the race they had once been, but most had decayed far too much to be recognized. The preservation of their entire bodies was unnecessary, only their hearts and minds needed to remain intact, and they were all that she cared about.

A large set of black double doors sat on the other side of the antechamber. Likewise, these were set with a silver hand plate. She reached out and touched it. The door swung inward and the sound came first, followed by the wash of cold air.

She stepped forward and smiled. The screen which surrounded the prison was clear except for the thick red substance running around it. Inside sat a crystal with sixteen faces that was about the size of a large boulder. Upon each face of the crystal was a horrified vision of an entity. Each entity looked tortured and replete with pain.

"Hello there," she whispered to the crystal. "How are my prisoners holding up?" There was a sound like screaming but muffled. "Good..." she whispered. "Still in Eternal Suffering I see."

She looked around the rest of the room. The metallic smell of blood filled the place, and she breathed it in. It was one of her favorite smells. The walls were black and reflective like all the walls and lined with steel and enchantment. The sound of trickling blood was strangely loud in the small world. She touched the screen and her finger came away red and wet. She suckled her finger for a second relishing the taste of Prophet's blood. It was that, and only that, which kept the Prison beyond anyone's Sight. But it would not matter now. The Veil had begun to fall. She had no need of the Prophets or Seers anymore, well the few which were left. The Forge had served her well over the last thousand years to provide her with every person born with a Mark of Sorcery. Even if they didn't have activated powers, their blood still contained the power and served her purposes.

She turned to the two tortured looking humans standing at the right of the room. Both were thin and their dark skin was nearly drained of color. They were nearly identical save the difference in gender. They were t'Kalima, rare indeed, twins and seers, born of the fire kin elves. Their eyes were wide and glassy. No pupil or iris showed because they were in a constant state of Sight. The two censors beside each of the continually burned enhanced seer's incense.

Seers were good to check on current state of affairs, being able to see past enchantments and webs of spells as well as being somewhat clairvoyant about people and places they were focused on. She had the Prophet's chamber upstairs where the few remaining Prophets under her command lay, their eyes open and dead. There was a pair of skeletal recorders up there to write down anything they said, in case some new prophecy was written. The Forge had been ideal to make sure she had access to all those who were born with the innate powers. Wizards were a copper a dozen, but those born with the ability were so very rare. Of course, over the last thousand years, she'd pulled the strings of the Forge from behind the scenes quite successfully.

She turned toward the emaciated figures.

"Are all the pieces in place correctly?" she asked them.

The female spoke for the two always. "Yes, my Queen. It was the last I saw before the falling of the Veil. As long as the pawn Sealla plays her part, you will succeed."

She smiled. "Good..." she whispered and turned and left.

The mood at the Linerian castle had gotten progressively darker since the King's death. A funeral had been held, and then Queen Sealla made a long, rambling speech about the treachery of those closest and a reminder of her edicts. Most in attendance didn't remember what she said, they were too stricken with grief at the loss of their king followed by the loss of their favorite of the two princesses.

Sealla returned to the throne room and sat down in the deeply cushioned chair of red velvet. She smiled. Such a wonderful place to sit. She reached up and adjusted the crown. It was a bit annoying because it was made to fit a man, and not made for a queenly head. But she'd worked a little magic and managed to shrink it a little, but because of the age of the crown she didn't dare try to make it too much smaller.

"Captain Dunbar to see you, your royal highness," announced the steward in front of her.

A man dressed in the garb of the palace guards walked up the red carpet to stand before his queen. He then kneeled down to one knee, placing his hat over his heart. He deeply bowed his head and spoke in a soft voice.

"Your royal highness, the scouting parties have lost the servant who escaped the barrier."

Sealla sat up, the crown almost falling at the violence of her motion. "What? Where are they! Bring them before me!"

The captain remained kneeling. "Most gracious one, I cannot do so."

Sealla's eyes flashed dangerously as she stood, her voluminous layers of red satin rustling as she stood. "Why not?"

"Please, my Lady, they are dead. They were attacked just outside the border by a group of vampires, all of the squad were drained of blood. We traced the trail to an abandoned cottage where we found dust and bones, as though the vampires had been destroyed somehow."

"Indeed..." she muttered as she sat down slowly. "And Lena?"

"My most gracious queen, we found no sign of her other than this," he said, reaching under his cloak to hold up a blood-stained shirt Sealla recognized as Lena's. "We also found discarded holy symbol bearing the mark of the order of Paladins."

Sealla smiled and began to laugh. The captain looked up cautiously.

"So, she's either a vampire, or she's a dead vampire, then," she said, smiling. "Thank you, dismissed," she said, waving him away.

If there had been a paladin, he had to have been the one who destroyed the vampires whose remains were there. His armor being there meant they must have captured him first, then he got away, but the question was, did he get turned too, or did he destroy Lena and any others who were left behind? Sealla smiled at either prospect, but she would rather know for sure.

The steward returned. "Most royal highness..." he began, only to be pushed out of the way by a woman in a leather skirt and a bustier top that barely covered her large chest. A cloak of deep red and black flowed behind her and her thickly heeled boots clicked as she walked. Her skin was pale, and her eyes burned a fiery orange. She was followed by three others, two men and a woman.

"You know why we're here," she announced.

The steward escaped from Sealla's sight as quickly as he could. "The Black Queen sent you," Sealla said without surprise. She certainly had no trouble identifying them.

"Yes."

"Fine then, you know what needs to be done. Find Keiara, and while you're at it find this brat Lena who ran away, she might be turned by now," she said staring at the pale woman.

"I heard. We'll take care of her," she said.

"Is there anything you need?" Sealla asked, becoming especially uncomfortable with the dark-haired man who kept his hood up, hiding everything of his face but the streaming black hair the flowed out of it and over his shoulders.

"Food. Drink. Baths," the other woman answered. She was slight, very thin, and much shorter than her vampiric counterpart. She wore exceedingly bright colors in a dress which looked like petals of a flower rather than a dress. Her eyes were a strange aqua color and her hair a nearly matching shade of blue-green.

"Sleep," chimed in the second man. He was a thick, heavy man who wore leathers and had a huge sword strapped to his back. His brown beard was sparse, and his hair was a long and tangled brown mop.

Sealla clapped and the Steward returned, nearly shaking. "See to them. Whatever they desire, make sure they have it. Make sure they are provisioned however they need," she said staring at the pale woman. "Make their accommodations for their mission when, and only when, they decide they are ready. Understood?"

"Yes, my mistress," the steward said, bowing deeply and leading the group of four away.

Good, good... the voice in her head whispered, but Sealla couldn't get the chill to leave the man with the hood left her with. There was something about him that was more than disconcerting to her.

The Black Queen sat in the great hall in her throne of bone and black obsidian. Her taloned fingers struck a rhythm on the twin skulls which served as hand rests. The noise was loud in the otherwise silent room. The only other sound came from a constant dripping of water down the roughhewn cavern walls to puddle at the skeletal feet of the guardians who lined those walls. She was waiting. She had been waiting for a very long time. In some respects, she had been waiting over five thousand years for this moment.

"My lady," a soft voice from the only entrance to the great hall called.

She turned, her pale face reflecting no emotion. "Is it time? Has the veil fallen?"

"They say the Sight is beginning to blur. The time has come," the young, blonde woman said with eyes cast downward.

She stood, and walked out, the servant girl scampering out of her way. She walked down a short, dank hallway to a small door. She pressed a hand to the plate beside the door and felt the magical currents ripple as the door slid open. A smell like sweet incense wafted out in billowing cloud. Inside, a ring of people sat facing each other, all their eyes clouded white. She walked to the center.

"You've seen the veil drop?" she asked one, a human female with very dark skin.

She nodded. "I've seen the dark one come to your hands, but no more beyond."

"What of the Seer in the Darkness? You mentioned long ago, has it come up again?" she asked, turning to a pale skinned elven man.

He shook his head slowly, "No, my Lady. It may be that the seer is no more. I did not see the seer's death, but in all my seeking I cannot find this Seer in Darkness. They must no longer be alive."

She nodded and stepped outside the circle. The room was square, and in each corner sat a pedestal. On each pedestal sat a censor. A curlew of white smoke flowed from each of them, filling the room with the slight sweet smell. It was commonly called seer's incense. It was used by seers to initiate a state of sight at will, rather than wait for a vision to come to them. Here it was used to keep them in a constant state of sight, with no release. Of course, she'd added a little of her own magic to help it along... The Black Queen put out the first censor, and then moved to the next, glancing at the circle of half-starved Seers. She gave them enough food and water, so they didn't die, but the sight made them lose so much energy. There were eight in this room. Four females, four males, two of each were human, and two elves. She put out the last two censors and watched as their white eyes slowly returned to normal. They blinked several times and looked at each other, for the first time in years seeing the real world.

The Black Queen stepped outside and shut the door. She beaconed a large stalwart man to her side.

"Kill them all, they are of no use to me now. The twins in the prison chamber too. Drain their blood and put it in the summoner's pool. Then kill the last of the Sorcerers who are in the cells. Drain their blood as well and mix it with the Seer's blood. Be quick. It must be still warm," she said and turned and left him so she could gather the rest of the tools she needed.

The room spread out large and round. Perfectly round and smooth walls made up the perimeter of the dark room. The walls were slightly shiny, and unlike the other walls of this underground stronghold, no water dripped down. The large domed ceiling was also slightly shiny and made of the same black material as the walls. The only thing not round was the floor, which was flat and colored black as well. The floor though was perfectly matte and smooth. Nothing reflected from it. In fact, it almost appeared like light was absorbed by it.

In the very center of the room sat a large round pool of sorts. The sides were made of the same matte black material as the floor. It actually appeared to be a part of the floor, rising up. It was in equal proportion to the room, in the perfect center. There were carved symbols all the way around the walls of this pool, five or ten inches each. The walls themselves stood two feet in height, and the diameter of the pool was five feet. Inside the pool some liquid caught the magical light the Black Queen carried with her. It appeared the servants had already brought much of the blood to the pool.

The man who had been charged with the killing of the seers and sorcerers came in the small doorway quickly, carrying a brace across his back, two large buckets on each side of it dangling heavily. He approached the pool and carefully sat them down. He then poured the contents into the pool. It was a little over halfway full.

"That is the last of it my lady, they all are dead now," he said bowing in reverence and leaving the room as quickly as he could.

With a single motion of her hand, the door closed, sealing her inside. There was no trace of the door afterward. She motioned and high above her at the top of the ceiling, a pale red light began to glow. She reached a pale hand down and dipped a finger into the pool. It came out red and glistening. More than that, though, she felt the power in the pool.

"Seers and Sorcerers, Kalimourne, you've granted me more power than you can imagine," she whispered. "By your ilk alone, I could have done what I have, but things were made easier by the others."

She pulled a flask of water from her robe. Seawater from the Sea of Salwine, created with the firstborn's own tears. She then in turned poured various other substances into the pool. Each one was special and rare. Each one was directly related to the Dark Phoenix's own children. And each one would aid in the capture and binding of the Dark Phoenix.

She pulled a final vial from her robe. She stared into the red substance and smiled. The most difficult component to get was here. The most precious component sat in this vial. Kalimourne's own blood. The final component. The other nineteen were important, but this...

"Mother of the gods, bringer of the flames, I call you to me, and I bind you to me," she began to chant as she poured the god's blood into the pool

The blood turned bright blue as it poured from the vial and began to swirl into the pool of other substances. She continued to chant, and all around the chamber, the sound reverberated.

Keiara was sitting when she felt the spell take hold. She smiled.

"It is time for me to see who we are up against," she said.

Myrstand looked at her with a questioning look. "What do you mean?"

"Whoever this is, she's woven a very complex spell to try and summon and bind me. I'll let her summon me, but once there

I'll reverse the spell and return," she said as a large dark circle began to form around her.

Sanna and Lena exchanged worried looks. "But is it safe?" Sanna asked.

Keiara smiled. "No, but it is necessary. The Veil must fall, and this powerful spell she's trying to use will provide the components which I myself could not gather. It is a simple manner to change the spell once I'm there."

Jovan had been sleeping, or so it appeared. "What, that's mad!" he announced, sitting up quickly.

Keiara smiled. "She has no idea what she is truly dealing with. What you all need to do is stand in a ring around me, linking hands with each other. You'll feel a humming and there may be some visual effects, but nothing too severe."

With that she stood up and faded to nearly transparent. When she said "some visual effects", they weren't sure what to expect. But the sparks, stars and shooting beams of light which began to circle them where they were standing was certainly "some visual effects". They held tight and felt some sort of powerful barrier forming between them and something else.

Keiara's first realization was her feet were wet. In fact, her knees were also wet. Next, she realized she was bathed in a red light and that light was reflecting off black walls all around her. Finally, she realized she was face to face with the one she wanted to finally meet.

"Ackana," she said flatly.

The pale woman smirked, her tight drawn skin making her look skeletal especially when she did so.

"I much prefer the Black Queen," she said in a haughty voice. "I mean, it sounds so much more eloquent, don't you think?"

"You aren't my child, Ackana, so I have to say, I have no attachment to you."

"Why should it matter to me?" she asked, shaking her head, the stringy black hair bouncing off her shoulders.

"Because if you were my child, I might pity you right now," she said, running her fingers in the blood at her knees. Tears filled her eyes and poured over into the water. When her tears hit the pool of blood, a thin ribbon of steam rose into the air.

"Well, it doesn't matter to me. I've trapped your children. I've tapped their power. I've used the Seers and Prophets of the world to ensure it. What will you do about it?" Ackana's face was sickening, even to Keiara who was looking on one of her children's progeny. If only she knew all the details of her origin...

Keiara smiled. "You've given me what I need to defeat you. You've gathered pieces of my children, all twenty of them, and the blood of my favored mortals, the Seers, Druids, and Prophets. You, in your attempt to harness a power you can't even fathom, you've gathered everything I need. I'm sorry, Ackana, but the Veil...falls...now."

Standing knee deep in warm blood, Keiara raised both hands in front of her and muttered ancient words even one of the gods did not understand. The goddess opposite her stepped back in confusion. Suddenly, there was a blue light flowing out of Keiara's hands and into the pool of blood. The blood began to swirl faster and faster until to Ackana's surprise, it became clear as pure water. Keiara smiled and lowered her hands.

"What did you do?" Ackana asked with utter hatred in her voice.

Keiara smiled sweetly. "I used the power you had gathered here to bring the Veil over the Sight. You've used Seers, Druids, and Prophets to your whim and will for near a thousand years. Now, I've taken their blood, their power, and used it to darken your strongest ally. You've used them for so long. It stops now. What will you do without someone to tell you the future and lend you magic?"

The goddess fumed. "You're still mine! You cannot escape."

Keiara smiled and shook her head. "That's where you are wrong. I'm not really here to begin with."

Ackana blinked and then pulled a long thin blade from her hip and swung it violently at the woman in front of her. The blade when through her and Keiara's form started to fade. Ackana screamed in anger as the one person in all of Avern who she needed to power her desires slipped from her grasp.

CHAPTER NINE

MEETING IN THE DARK

*It is often lamented
and often said,
damned are those that dare
to walk among the dead.
Even more damned are we.*
—Seer Viscore, Vampire Hunter

T he mountains were annoying to traverse. She was glad she'd worn her heavy boots in this muddy, snowy mess. The others straggled behind her, their mortal bodies bothered by the chill where her undead one was not. She reached a crest and spotted what she was looking for.

"Camp in the valley, smells like them," she called behind her.

"Mistress," called the brightly colored woman. "I'm not sure if..."

"Kel, I don't ask you to think. I ask you to blast things out of existence with magic," she said with a hiss.

Kel chewed her lip for a moment and then scrambled up the space between her and the more imposing vampiress. She would have told her the position was bad, but she also knew she wouldn't listen to her. She watched as the two male members of the group made it up the slope.

"Graster," she said to the lumbering hulk carrying the large sword. "When do you want to attack them?"

The bearded barbarian snorted. "Doesn't matter. They're dead where they stand."

The hooded one came up last, brushing sand from his hands. "We couldn't find a more hospitable location? The mediocre castle we came from looks better now." The vampire turned her gaze on him, one which could melt metal. "Sorry, Mistress Vestra," he muttered.

Kel sighed. "Kendal, must you?"

The hooded man pushed his hair from his face, his black eyes reflecting nothing as he dropped the hood. Thick stringy black hair hung well past his shoulders to his midback. Vestra shook her head and hissed at him, then tied her own black hair up on the back of her head for the coming fight. She licked her lips in anticipation. Surly this would grant her some fine dining this night. She unwrapped the cloak from around her as the sun began to dip behind the horizon and she felt her power swelling.

"Kel, you go around behind their camp, get some higher ground, and start blasting. Graster, once she starts raining fire, you wade in and take on the stronger fighters. Kendal, do whatever you do, and I'll come in during the chaos Graster causes. Let's make the Black Queen proud, this day, leave no one breathing," Vestra said, smiling, her vampire teeth bared fully.

Kendal giggled and faded into the darkness and Kel took off scampering down the slop until she could find a good position. Below, a fire in the camp was being kindled, and the attackers hoped to keep surprise on their side as dusk started setting in fully.

Keiara paced around the campfire as Jovan and the two dwarves sat in earnest conversation. Jovan was quite a history buff and connecting the pieces of the past of his people with the dwarven past was completely engaging his attention. It was fascinating to him to find out things he had always wondered about over the years. Myrstand stood watch near the opening of the cavern that led deeper into the mountain as the dwarves had warned the area they were in was heavily patrolled by the Noran t'Kalima. Lena and Sanna quietly cooked some snow hares they'd caught nearby. There was tension on the air that Keiara could feel all around her.

"Be alert," she said walking to the fire and sitting.

Jovan and the dwarves looked up from their conversation. "What is it?" he asked glancing around.

"We're being watched, soon attacked I'm sure. Eat what you can quickly, all of you, and prepare yourself. Four of them, I think, but only one poses any real danger," she said sipping from her waterskin.

All the group wolfed what food they could, all the time alert to any movement around them. Myrstand looked up just in time to see a tiny light above them start growing larger as it came closer.

"Fireball!" he yelled and grabbed Keiara and pulled her away from the center of the camp.

Everyone scrambled back as it fell and exploded on the campfire, which had obviously been the target. Just then, they all heard an incredible roar and saw a huge figure of a man running at them. Myrstand had his sword out in a second and the steel clashed sending sparks into the dusk evening air. Myrstand

165

struggled against the man's power but held his own. Another fireball exploded to his right and he heard Lena scream.

Lena stood frozen, her hands over her mouth, looking at the spot where another fireball had dropped. Sanna had been there, just seconds before. Sanna, though Lena hadn't seen it, had dodged the ball at the last second, her superior reflexes and speed allowing her to remain a target until the last second. Lena sighed.

Sanna stood up and began pulling the fire around her toward her hands. "You like fire, little bitch?" she screamed and hurled the fire back at the direction it had come from. "Have it back!"

Above them there was a crash and explosion as Sanna's return fireball hit the rock ledge above them. There was a second before three more lights appeared and smaller fireballs began to rain down on them. Sanna began dodging the balls as they exploded at the ground around her. She couldn't form fireballs like this wizard was doing, but she could control fire to some degree after the training she'd had with the monks.

Jovan, just as the first fireball hit felt like someone had sapped all the strength from his body. It was like something had pulled away every bit of energy. Miira stood over him as Moryn was looking around for the source of this mysterious attacker.

"Over there," Miira said, pointing. "He's in the shadows, entropy, if I don't miss my guess brother. Tend to him, I'll go, you don't have any equipment."

Miira stood, shouldering the great axe and swung it with grace and speed the large weapon would not have had in any other hands. It smashed the tree it hit to pieces and a shocked, cloaked man jumped out of the way. She wouldn't have been able to see through his magic, but her dwarven abilities allowed her to see past it.

Lena felt a presence near her and then felt hands grip her shoulders. "My child, I smell the undead on you, why do you play with mortals?"

Lena turned and was staring at what had to be a full-fledged dark vampire, much like the ones who had tried to kill her and Myrstand. Lena smiled, revealing her own vampire teeth.

"One problem, I'm not really a vampire, I just have the power of one," Lena said in nearly a whisper.

Vestra's eyes glowed brilliantly orange and she swiped at Lena's face with clawed hands, but Lena caught her hand easily despite her being nearly a foot taller than the smaller Lena. For a second Vestra looked confused, not expecting a newly turned vampire to rival her in strength. Lena then set her feet in the ground and twisted to the side, pulling the bigger woman off balance and sending her flying.

Myrstand's fight with the brute was not going well; his much larger sword was taking a toll on the smaller sword he wielded. Keiara stood solemnly in the middle of the battleground, her friends and companions losing ground quickly to the more experienced fighters. They were not yet a cohesive group, each one fighting independently, and she knew they were all unaware and not in touch with their innate abilities. She moved to where Miira squared off with the strange dark cloaked man, stopping any spells with deft swings of her hammer. Jovan was stirring now, but still out for the most part. Moryn stood over him.

"Pull Jovan into the cavern opening, Moryn, then we'll pull back in there too. Can you seal us in?"

"What?" Moryn asked, looking a bit shocked by the idea. "Why are we retreating now, we're not losing yet?"

"We're not ready for this yet, by a long shot, we're safer inside before they show their true power by working together, something they are not yet doing."

Just then another rain of fire fell throwing both Myrstand and Miira to the ground, leaving them open to new attacks from their opponents. The barbarian then took advantage and Myrstand barely dodged a mortal blow but fell unconscious as the blow landed on the side of his head instead of his neck. The hooded man had enough time to cast a quick and energy sapping spell at Miira causing her to drop like a stone. Keiara stepped forward and swirled around, throwing her arms up and building a pillar of black fire around them. Moryn had already pulled Jovan in, and now he grabbed Miira and pulled her into the opening. Sanna ran toward them and grabbed Lena by the arm and pulled her behind, leaving a confused Vestra frozen in place from the power generated by the psychic energy swirling around her. Keiara grasped Myrstand's ankle where he'd fallen.

Once they'd all gotten safely inside, the black pillar dropped and Moryn touched each side of the opening to the cave, and slowly, painfully slowly, the stone strained from each side, trying to join each other. Before the opening finished sealing, they had a horrific glimpse of the vampire woman's snarling face as she lunged at the rock. They all sighed, and Keiara lit a torch and tended to those who had taken a fall.

"You escaped into the wrong place," a voice just beyond the torchlight said as Keiara checked on Myrstand.

A tall, thin Noran t'Kalima stepped into the light. His skin was almost translucent white in the darkness, and his eyes were a pale blue in color, bright even with the slightest light. His light orange white hair was tied up in a topknot on top of his head. He held a crossbow in front of him, and slowly, around him, several more figures stepped into the light. Keiara stood slowly and stared at her children, and she knew for sure they had forgotten her.

"Will you come without fighting, or shall we decimate you here?" he continued, and Keiara noticed the others didn't understand him. Of course not, he wasn't speaking common, he was speaking Elven.

"We offer no resistance," she responded in Elven, bowing her head to him respectfully.

He nodded. "Bind them," he said to the closest elf to him, a young boy with pure white hair and eyes like pale jade stones.

"Let them bind you, we're in no condition to fight them now," Keiara said to the others, who all relaxed.

Soon enough they were all bound and those that were walking were escorted, and those that were still unconscious were carried on makeshift litters. There was little light, as the Noran did not require it. They were escorted past dark alcoves and now and then they saw the pale skin of a Noran in the corner of their eyes. They entered some sort of building and were escorted into a cell. Myrstand had woken up along the way and was shoved harshly into the cell, and Jovan was unceremoniously dumped from the litter he'd been on to the floor with a thump.

"Be quiet. The Chief will be here soon to talk to you," the Noran said gruffly and turned on his heels and left.

"What did they say?" asked Lena, holding her hands folded on her chest.

"Well, we're going to be interrogated, I'm sure. I don't know much about the Noran today, they are nothing like they used to be," Keiara said with a sigh.

"I can tell ye, we're dead," Moryn said from beside his sister who sat with a dazed look against the wall. "They offer no quarter to mine."

Jovan moaned and sat up slowly, holding his head. "Enervating bastard," he muttered. "What, where are we now?" he asked looking around.

Sanna snorted. "We've been captured by the Noran t'Kalima, and probably won't live to leave this cell."

169

Jovan sighed. "I know I won't survive, there's nothing but bad blood between the Whispara and the Noran, that's for certain."

Keiara looked sad in the pale light offered by the two meager balls of light which glowed near the doorway. Vaguely, she thought she saw movement in the darkness, but she wasn't sure at this time.

"How far my children have fallen," she whispered.

Myrstand, still slightly addled from the blow to the head he'd taken wasn't sure she had said what he thought. "Your children?"

She smiled and looked at them all. "Long ago, at the creation of the world, after we had been split apart and after the Keepers and Gods were birthed to the world, the races of peoples that live on Avern were created. Life does not begin without a spark of life which is contained in one piece or another of the phoenix, and so Kalimourne created the elves, each elven race created with a different piece of the phoenix. The elements and the light and the dark. The Lumen were the children of the Light Phoenix, and the Noran were my creation with Kalimourne."

Sanna frowned. "So, you created them? This hateful race?"

"They weren't always like this. I fear that as time passed, the writings where I was revered were changed, as also happened with the Lumen. Today, the Lumen are known as the Maker's children, and the Noran are known as the Unmaker's children. The Maker and Unmaker had no part in their creation; it was I and my consort that breathed life into them. Mortals, unlike gods, are vastly imperfect and susceptible to the swaying of their emotions and desires," she said softly.

Lena, who had sat down beside Jovan and Miira, sighed. "How sad that they have forgotten you."

"Darkness is evil, is it not?" asked Miira slowly. "So, anything made of darkness will be evil."

Keiara smiled. "No, there is no evil inside darkness."

Everyone turned to look at her with wide eyes. "But Aren teaches to stay in the light and never step into the darkness," Myrstand said, standing now.

"My child Aren's words have been misinterpreted, along with a great many other things that have been said since the Beginning," Keiara said softly and put an arm around Myrstand as he stared at her with a look of surprise.

"Is fire evil or good? Is the earth around us? The water we drink? Or the air that we breathe? So why does an element of light or dark have to be either? I have seen many mortals who stand in the light with hearts as black and evil as the worst demon, and I have seen those enshrouded in darkness shine with the greatest good. The three spheres of magic, the three types of energy, they are not 'good' or 'evil', they just are. The energy of nature is the force of the physical elements. The energy of the mind is the force of psychic elements and is called negative because of the way it interacts with the others. The energy of the spirit is the force of spiritual elements and is considered positive. It is untrue that positive equals good and negative equals evil. They must be balanced against each other like everything else in our world.

"Things are not quite what people have come to believe them to be. But no, darkness is not evil, it is what mortals do within the darkness which is evil. Like fire can be used for destruction and evil, so too can darkness," Keiara said, and looked around to all of them.

No one said anything for a long time. The idea that good and evil were not what they had always thought them to be was something that took some getting used to. But their thoughts were a mixture when a voice came from outside the cell.

"Is i' true? We are not t'children uven Unmaker?" the female voice said in halting common speech.

From the shadows, a figure stepped. She was a Noran, but she was different. Half of her body looked to be made out of silver metal instead of flesh, though it was similar in nature to the other side. Only the dim light glinting off the metal flesh told the tale. She wore a corset top, open at the center of the front, where they could see where the flesh met the metal at the midline of her body. The metal then moved along her collarbone, leaving her neck and head flesh. Her eyes were light blue and her hair a strange shade of silvery pink. Her white flesh on the left was nearly translucent.

"We a'not evil born?" she continued, moving smoothly through the shadows, making no sound.

Keiara nodded slowly as she approached, wrapping her flesh hand and her metal hand around the bars. "You were born of the dark phoenix, neither good nor evil, simply born."

She looked around. "They will come soon, t'take away t'dwarves and elf, t' their deaths I am sure, after they a' tortured for information. I can stall there, will y'take me w'you? Away?"

Keiara looked to the others. "Of course, we need..."

The elf turned quickly toward the back and slipped away into the shadows as they heard marching boots nearby entering the room.

"Get the dwarves and the elf, take them to the questioning room. Mistress will see them, and get any information from them that they have, or she will kill them trying to get it," one of them said in elven.

Keiara and Jovan exchanged glances as the doors opened, and the two dwarves and he were removed from the cell. Sanna and Lena looked at each other, not understanding what was being said.

"What's happening?" Lena said, frantically.

Keiara shook her head at her and she quieted down while the others were escorted away.

Jovan was chained hands over his head to the wall, his toes barely touching the floor once the chains were cinched tightly. Moryn and Miira were treated the same, though their height was lesser. And then they were left alone.

"Well, now isn't this cozy?" Jovan quipped with a grin.

Moryn snorted. "It won't a'be cozy for long."

"Of course, it won't be cozy," said a voice from the shadows, her elven smooth and silky sounding.

All three of them turned to stare at a female in the back of the room. She wore a black outfit, form fitting and slick looking. Her hair was a bright white in color and tied up on top of her head in a streaming ponytail which cascaded down her back in complete opposition to the black outfit. Only her head was free of the black colored suit she wore. It appeared to be one full piece with no seaming or closures.

"Because, you see, the pain I inflict won't be cozy at all, I'm Mistress T'ran. Now, please prepare yourself."

Moryn and Miira exchanged glances. This, they had heard of, and were prepared for, but Jovan, had never been prepared for such a thing. Both the dwarves, since childhood, had been trained to handle torture by way of a pouch of potion sewn into the inside of their cheek. As they aged, the pouch was covered by skin, and to release the potion, one had to bite through it. The potion was a powerful sedative that rendered them completely unconscious, making them useless as a victim of torture. It was easy to reverse with the right antidote, which both the dwarves also had sewn into their skin, only just under the flesh of their right wrist. All young dwarves had the sedatives, while older and more important dwarves carried a fast-acting poison.

Moryn turned his head to Jovan and said gruffly, "Sorry, friend. Really I am." Blood flowed from the corner of his mouth.

The black clad woman screamed in rage as she saw the blood dripping down from the corners of the dwarves' mouths. "Blast those dwarves, already done themselves in?"

Mistress T'ran lifted Miira's head with the handle of the whip in her hand gently. Jovan glanced over at his dwarven counterparts, both with their heads drooping. Suicide? He thought and was horrified.

"Ah, nah, pretty ones are asleep. Too young for poison," she said, then turned her attention on Jovan. "You see they do this so we can't torture them. In hopes that we'll dump them before they're useful. If they have a sedative in them, they're useless to us. But you, on the other hand."

Jovan swallowed as she pushed his head to the side with the handle of the whip. She then pulled a knife from her belt and sliced down the front of his shirt, revealing his bare chest. Jovan gasped as the knife sliced through a thin layer of his skin along with the shirt. His shirt hung open and she leaned forward and slowly licked the trickling blood from his chest.

"My, you taste as good as we do," T'ran whispered as she pulled herself up even with his face and Jovan realized how beautiful her face was with its pale almost translucent skin and glittering light blue eyes. "Amazing, isn't it, both elves, but so different."

She walked slowly backward and pulled the whip around and cracked it across his chest. Jovan sucked in a breath. It felt like a small fire had been lit in his chest. Not really like pain, but like a fire.

"A little concoction I coat my whips with. Nice little burn, sweet?" she said smiling at him, and there was an edge to her.

"What exactly do you want from me?" Jovan breathed, gritting his teeth against the rising burn in the wound.

"Oh, everything," she whispered, leaning in and licking his ear. He pulled away, and then couldn't help but yelp as she bit down on the lobe. He felt the blood drip down his neck and shoulder.

Jovan gasped as she petted his other ear with her free hand, her head still nuzzled into the hollow of his neck. "But...I don't know anything you'd want," he whispered.

Slowly, she stood back up. "Oh, but that's not true. I already know who your father is, little prince."

Jovan started, but his surprise was temporary as she suddenly went at him with the whip again, striking him at least seven times in quick succession. She paused, and Jovan caught his breath and waited for the next set of blows.

"How do I know that?" she asked and placed the whip on a rack beyond his vision. "You see, you're actually the second one I've seen. The first one, another little prince, squealed like a stuck little pig."

Jovan's head shot up. "What?"

"Oh yes, he looked a lot like you, I knew as soon as I saw you. I remember all my visitors. I have a feeling you are the lost little prince he was looking for," she said, coming back with a tool that looked something like a riding crop for use on horses. "Now, what I want to know, just like him, why'd you leave?"

"Is he alive? Did you kill him? What...?" Jovan began but his words were interrupted by a stiff slap to his jaw by the crop. It was like ice burning through his jaw.

"See this one is coated with another potion, I call it cold fire potion. Like the fire potion, only this one feels cold instead," she said as she petted the right side of his jaw with the crop. "And as far as your brother, he was bright and shiny when we turned him out. You haven't answered me yet."

Jovan wasn't sure what to say. "I left because...I wanted...to wander."

"Are you sure?" she whispered and pulled back with the crop.

After another round of icy slaps from the crop, he was left almost unable to breathe. She pressed her body against him, her breasts and legs caressing him and despite himself he felt attraction to her. She was incredibly beautiful and smelled like fresh lilacs under the full moon. She moved away and placed this whip on the wall, and he heard the click-snap of another one being removed from the wall.

"You see, I can do this all day, sweet elf prince," she said, her voice low and full of pure malice. "I have so many lovely toys in here, some specially made."

He raised his head as she held up another implement, this one a multi tailed whip with barbs on the ends of the tips. "It's coated in another potion, this one so much more fun, it intensifies the pain when it enters a wound..."

She spun him easily around until his face was buried in the gritty stone behind him. She ripped the remains of his shirt off and leaned into his back. Jovan's breath caught from her presence this close, and he felt his mind fogging and filling with images of the moon lilacs blooming that he could smell from her. But how could he smell a flower which only bloomed in the full moon north of the Anaset forest? She stepped back, and the smell left, but still his mind felt full of sand. Then she went to work on his back, and despite himself, that's when he started to scream. It felt like a million bugs working their way through every vein in his entire body, pushing through into his muscles, his organs, even his brain. It was like being wrapped in wire covered with barbs and then rolled down a steep embankment that never ended...

"Only the answers will stop the pain," she whispered between strikes. "Only the right answers, the ones I want to hear, because your screams are luscious."

"Mother..." came a voice from the front of the room.

T'ran stopped and turned leaving Jovan gasping against the wall. He felt the blood dripping down his back and the throbbing pain still rang through his body. He didn't care who it was at the door he was only glad to get a reprieve.

"What is it, Syera?" she said, her voice tight.

"Father said he wanted to see you about the redhaired one. Something he doesn't understand about her. Something's not right," she said slowly, her eyes drifting to the three shackled to the wall.

"Okay, okay, I'll go. Stay here. Don't let anyone play with my pretties without me around," she said, snapping the scourge into the wall holder and walking past Syera. The door slammed shut.

Syera stared out the small window for a moment then rushed over to the unconscious dwarves. She started feeling their arms and necks.

"What...are you...doing..." Jovan whispered, craning his neck around.

"Looking for the antidote so they'll wake up," she whispered.

"What good is that going to do?" he said, confused.

She looked up and grinned at him. "We're getting out of here."

After a few minutes she smiled, her flesh hand brushing against a slight bulge at the wrist on the male. She picked up the hand and pulled out a knife from her boot. Gently, she slit the pouch open on Moryn's wrist and put it to his lips, letting the liquid drip into his mouth. Then she did the same for Miira. After a few minutes, there was a cough and sputter from each of them.

"What?" Moryn muttered.

"Shhh, I found your pouch, we're getting out of here, and I need you two awake," Syera muttered.

"How are we going to do this?" Miira said hoarsely.

"Mother will be back soon, so stay quiet and feign unconsciousness, your red haired friend is presenting a conundrum for them," Syera said as she checked the door again.

"What do you mean?" Jovan asked.

"I mean, I don't know, something is different about her that they can't understand. She's been taken to another cell, and I'm sure she'll be brought here next, and when she is, we take the chance to go. Mother can be overzealous with her torture, so she'll have a stock of healing potions on her because she wants the information out of your redhaired friend," Syera said.

"Here she comes," Syera whispered and the dwarves dropped their heads. Jovan swallowed.

The door banged open and Sanna stumbled into the room. The first thing to catch her attention was the sight of Jovan's bloodied back, and the two slack bodies of the dwarves. Despite her attempts to keep distance from any of the males in the group, she sucked in a breath. Mistress T'ran stood in the doorway.

"What is the enchantment?" she asked, sternly, and forgetting Syera was still in the room. She slipped out the door and headed toward the cell the others were locked in.

Sanna shook her head. "There is none," she answered and shook her head. "I don't understand it any more than you do!"

T'ran approached her and placed a black gloved hand on her shoulder gently. "You see your little elf boy over there?"

Sanna swallowed and nodded. She could hear Jovan's heavy breathing. She always found him in this state.

"You will look much worse when I'm done with you. And this," she said, taking a bandolier of potion bottles and hanging it on the hook beside the weapon rack. "This is so when, not if, when, I bring you to the point of dying, I can bring you back, just so I can take you there again."

Sanna wanted to laugh, but she was afraid that Jovan would suffer for it. "I'm a monk. Pain is inconsequential."

T'ran stopped. "What?"

"I'm a monk of the sacred flame, the order of the Asumbar Acolytes. Pain is a sense that I can deaden at will," she said simply.

T'ran smiled a wicked smile. She took out a knife coated with the pain enhancing potion.

"We'll see," she said, drawing the dagger across her forearm.

Sanna simply watched as the blood began pouring from the wound. She was mildly glad that she'd chosen her left arm without the Flame of Asumbar tattooed on it. T'ran looked at the complete lack of reaction and frowned.

"How? You should be screaming in agony?" she said, walking a circle around her.

"I told you, pain is inconsequential." She held up her right arm, which had been tattooed from fingertip to collar bone. "These are done with reeds, and each flame represents a level of awareness in the Way of Fire. I surpassed my own master. Pain does not matter," she said, looking at her bleeding arm.

T'ran grabbed her by the wrists and slapped her into the manacles beside Jovan. They clanked and she fell back against the hard, stone wall. She turned on her heels and left the room.

"You made her angry," Jovan croaked beside her, turning his face toward her.

She turned and looked at him and swallowed again. His face was swollen badly, and blood trickled from his mouth and his ear on the side facing her. His eyes were clouded, and he didn't look entirely awake.

"Yeah, I did, but at least she's gone," Sanna said, sighing and settling her back against the wall.

Syera heard her mother leave the room behind her. She smiled, it was even better than she had hoped. She quickly ran down into the open cavern where the others were locked.

"Please, hurry," she whispered, now in halting common. "We have na much time."

Keiara came forward, leading Lena and Myrstand. "Are the others okay?"

"Yes, come," she whispered. "Here, I've hidden your things."

She handed a couple large bags to Keiara and Myrstand. "No time, just come," she whispered.

They hurried down the corridor. Syera stopped them. She heard her mother and father just past the torture room.

"What do you mean?" her father said.

"I mean, she's a monk, of the Flame," mother answered.

Syera knew this conversation would take a while. Monks of the Sacred Flame were legendary, even among the Noran, and father did not believe they even existed. Syera waved them on and she ran into the room with the other four, and ushered the remaining three in.

"Be quiet," she said softly. "They are alive, must go."

She reached up to the shackles holding Miira on the far end and with her silver hand, snapped the lock in two, freeing her. She moved to Moryn, and then Sanna, doing the same. She waved Myrstand and Moryn over.

"He'll need help," she whispered as she snapped the shackles holding Jovan and he slid down the wall to his knees. Myrstand quickly hefted him to his feet.

"Follow me, and don't speak, not a word," she whispered, and they headed back out past the cells they had been in.

She stopped and grabbed some cloaks and spread one on each of them. They were black and had a bright red colored x in the middle of the back. She motioned them forward, and for a while, they saw no one, but then they saw a pair of guards. Keiara stiffened beside Myrstand, and Sanna readied herself for a battle. The guards stood at attention and let them pass unmolested. The group was confused but said nothing. They came to a large room with a pedestal made of stone, and beside it a large axe. Bones of bipedal creatures littered the ground, and they saw at least two headless corpses of dwarves that were just beginning to decay.

Syera led them by this and past several closed doors, and finally into a small room barely large enough to hold them all. She used some nearly invisible hand holds to scurry up the wall and muttered something under her breath. An opening shimmered into existence above them. She motioned to them to go up, and pulled Lena up first, followed by Moryn. Then they helped Jovan get up, though it was tedious at best, even with both Myrstand and Moryn helping him. Keiara went up next, followed by Miira and finally Myrstand. Syera muttered something again and the image of stone appeared again. They were in a tunnel above the room, barely large enough to fit through on hands and knees for Myrstand and Keiara. Syera lead the way and the others followed close behind.

Finally, they came to an opening in the floor of the tunnel and they all squeezed down in turn and dropped into a larger open space. Syera motioned for them to remain quiet and they moved for what felt like a very long time. Jovan was stumbling worse as they moved along, and Myrstand who was helping him walk knew they had to stop soon, but he remained quiet. Finally, Syera led them into a large open cavern beside an underground lake. She stopped.

"Out of range," she said. "I know where t'hide t'mselves. We have to get up and out..."

Jovan leaned against the wall and sighed. From behind him though, they heard the distinct clashing sound of weapons. Syera's eyes were wide.

"Follow me, run," she whispered hoarsely, and they all ran after her.

Syera watched as Jovan shook his head and ran after her as best he could. He would slow them down if he wasn't careful. She just hoped it didn't come to the point where they would have to abandon him.

CHAPTER TEN

ESCAPING THROUGH THE DARK

Be wary children of magic.
The Mind, font of the psychic energy,
The Body, font of the physical energy,
And the Spirit, font of the spiritual energy,
Are all traps to those unwary,
And weapons to those learned in magic.
-Archwizard Crazmore Tebbon, last of the Tri Wizards

❧

Sealla waited for word about the squad she had sent, the Black Queen's own. But when the messenger entered, she already knew the answer. Before he even spoke, she had killed him, and his body left without his spirit within it any longer.

Her head snapped back as the crushing presence entered her body, completely unbidden, and forcefully. Her nose shot blood down her satin dress and the guards on either side of her were startled, but when she rose, no one said anything.

Yes, they've failed. It does not mean the end. It is inevitable. They will fall to us; this merely delays it. Now, give me freedom with your body now, the voice said, and there was no asking to it. Sealla gave control fully to her for the first time and it was like her soul was being crushed into a space much too small.

"Bring me the scribe," she said, and it was but was not her own voice. It was like watching from within a dream as she paced the room, and the look of abject terror on the human guards was enough for Sealla to know it was apparent she was not herself.

The short, fat scribe entered, his hands permanently stained black with ink, and his robes covered in dust and pieces of parchment.

"Take this decree," Sealla's voice said. "The kingdom of the mighty Queen Sealla the illustrious invites the diplomats from Lord Dar Meterc to the castle."

There was a collective intake of breath from every breathing soul in the room. Lord Dar Meterc was a necromancer who commanded vast numbers of undead that controlled his small empire in one of the nearby layers of the underworld. In the days since the Keeper of Death had disappeared, many masters of undeath had taken residence there, but none as successful as the powerful Meterc.

"Tell him I wish to invite him to our cause, to rule all of Avern under the iron thumb of the Black Queen of the Underworld," she continued. "And I will sign it."

Sealla watched her hands take the parchment and the pen and sign a mark she had never seen. The scribed then rolled the parchment and headed to the door.

"One more thing, scribe," she said. "Life is lost on the living, undeath suits you better," and with a wave of her hand, a cascade of black smoke flowed out around her and every living thing in the room breathed its last. She drew the tiny points of light that were emitted from the bodies toward her and smiled as she held them in her hand.

"Souls are so pretty, don't you think Sealla?" she said, and then just as suddenly as she had come, she was gone and Sealla was standing, her gown coated in blood, her entire throne room covered in a chill.

She looked around, and the guards all stared vacant and empty eyed back at her. Her own blue eyes blurred with tears. What had she done?

Keiara found a passageway that looked like a likely spot to hide and ushered the group into the cavern. She then muttered a few words and an illusion spell fizzled into existence over the opening to the cavern. From the outside, the passageway was nothing but a wall. Of course, it was merely an illusion, should anyone poke around, they would find it quite intangible, but at the moment, it was all Keiara could do. They were not in a position to do much else except hide and heal themselves.

The whole event had been trying. All of them, especially Jovan, Moryn, and Miira, were exhausted. Syera helped Miira and Moryn, who were still groggy after coming out of the sedating potions they had taken. Jovan was hanging onto Myrstand for dear life, and then let go and simply slid down the wall to the floor slowly. He breathed a long sigh of relief.

"How are we doing?" asked Myrstand as he moved away from Jovan and looked at the dwarves.

"I'll be fine," Moryn said stonily, crossing his arms and sitting down cross legged on the floor, his eyes slightly bleary, but he was mostly awake. He glanced at Miira, still looking lethargic. Syera smiled at him.

"She'll be fine, th' potion works on dwarves really well, which is only made b' dwarfs, but wit th' ant'dote, they'll be fine," the Noran t'Kalima said slowly, her common greatly improving as she spoke more.

Myrstand kneeled by Jovan who he had helped walk half the time. "And you?"

Jovan looked up, his green eyes bright and smiled. "She was beautiful, though, but she packed a demon's punch in that whip!"

Myrstand clapped him on the shoulder. He was still shirtless, the crisscrossing red lines from the Mistress T'ran's whip still fresh on his chest and his back. His ear had finally quit bleeding, but it looked like she'd tried to take a chunk from his earlobe. At least the swelling in his face from her strikes had started to recede. He still had his humor, which meant he would be fine. Being bound and whipped like that wasn't a prospect many could come through with a smile, but Jovan was a singular individual.

Keiara was frowning when he returned to her, however. She was staring into the wall and concentrating very hard on something. He glanced at Sanna who stood cross armed against a nearby wall, eyeing the newcomer to the group with a suspicious eye. She couldn't very well feel a threat from a lone Noran t'Kalima who had been the one to help them escape. But then he knew the Sanna was suspicious by nature. He turned back to Keiara.

"Is something wrong?" he asked slowly, and very quietly.

"Yes," she answered, which was not the answer Myrstand was expecting.

He looked around, and they were all there, Lena now sitting beside Jovan and talking about the things they had heard from Syera. Jovan was explaining what had been said in Elven that she had not understood and what had been said in the chamber.

He turned to Keiara again. "What is it? Are the Noran following us? Should we be on the move?"

She shook her head slowly. "He's coming for Jovan again," she muttered. "I have to stop him."

Myrstand frowned and started to ask her what she was talking about when Jovan leapt to his feet, his face frantic. There were a thousand snakes slithering around him, coiling around his legs, drawing him down into the floor...

"Keiara!" he cried out, his hands flying to his head as he felt like there were snakes inside his head as well. "Help me!"

Keiara was already moving to him as he fell to his knees, shaking his head back and forth violently. She kneeled in front of him.

"Jovan, fight him, he can only hurt you if you let him do so, push him out of your mind!" she said franticly, grabbing his hands from his head.

Jovan lifted his head and locked eyes with her, but she knew he wasn't there anymore. His bright green eyes had faded to a dull and lifeless color. Sanna faltered for a moment, and started to come over to him, then resumed her position on the wall. She wouldn't help a man like him anyway. But her mind kept slipping back to the bound and gagged man she'd found frightened and alone behind Maelstrom's hooves...

Jovan's eyes flickered, and he muttered, "I can't...can't...fight this...help me..."

The world around him had faded to pure blackness and for a time he thought this was his punishment, to be alone here, but he saw eyes, those cruel red rimmed and black eyes that had haunted his dreaming state ever since he'd found his way to Keiara's side. The eyes materialized and the face around them, and he knew his tormentor to be Cage.

"Oh, sssssweet elf, I have you now. What shall I do with you..." his voice boomed in Jovan's head.

There was a moment when the blackness shimmered and resolved itself into a bright day. Jovan started to run but fell flat, his feet tightly bound together, and his hands bound in the fashion Cage had bound them before. He tasted the bitter taste of the potion on the gag that was cruelly forced into his mouth. He rolled to the side and found his face buried in the fragrant grass of a forest of some sort. He heard a shrill scream and he looked up, unable to do much else, and he saw his sister running past him, but it was like he was moving with her. She was running away but he was staying with her though he was laying on the grass.

"Let me alone!" she screamed in elven tongue, her bluish white hair streaming behind her.

"I don't think so!" shouted a man's voice not too far away from her. Jovan watched as a brutish man with a large sword trundled past after her. A few moments later a man Jovan recognized as the old elf hunter limped slowly past him.

"Catch her, Verstan. She's a noble 'un. I don't have any noble 'uns from the air yet," the old elf hunter grunted and Jovan felt his stomach lurch. He was going to watch her die.

He buried his head in the grass in front of him, refusing to watch it. He wouldn't do it, he couldn't watch her die like this. Suddenly a heaviness crushed the air from his lungs and he felt hands on either side of his head forcing him to look ahead.

"No, no, little elf boy, you get to watch this," Cage's hot breath whispered into his left ear.

For some reason, Jovan's eyes wouldn't close. It was as if they didn't work at all. Then he heard her screaming again and he saw the brutish man holding her with her arms behind her back. She was struggling violently against him, and the elf hunter put a large knife to her throat, calming her struggles.

"Hello, pretty," he said in rough elven. "What brings you out o' the forest?"

She pulled at the man who held her. "I'm looking for my brother, you brute. Release me!"

They both began to laugh. "I don't think so, pretty thing," the elf hunter said and with his knife began cutting away her leather armor.

"See, I'm a head hunter, elf head hunter, and I'm going to take your pretty little head with me today," he said as the chest piece of her armor fell to the ground. "But before that...I like to play with my prey..."

Jovan tried to look away, but Cage's hands held his head in a vice grip.

"Watch what they did to her," he whispered into his left ear. "All because she was looking for you, little elf prince. Why would she leave to find you, I wonder, sweet boy?"

Jovan's breath was heavy, and he started to scream against the gag in his mouth. He struggled violently against the bindings feeling them biting into his wrists and ankles. The weight on his back was great, his chest not getting enough air, and his sister's screams filling his ears.

"Oh yes, and this isn't made up, like you may be trying to tell yourself," Cage continued. "This is what was in that old elf hunter's head after I severed it from his body. You see, he cost me you, so he had to die for it, him and the wife of his. You caused their deaths too, because you ran from me, and if you hadn't run, they would have lived."

Jovan's heart felt like it would explode. Cage had killed them? The elf hunter sickened him but to murder him? There was no justice in it, but still, a flicker of happiness at knowing the man who killed his sister was dead bloomed.

"Oh watch, this is the good part!" Cage whispered urgently.

He didn't want to see. Not at all. His sister was whimpering, begging for her life, and the old man had his brutish companion hold her by the hair over a stump and with one fell stroke, severed her head from her body. The head rolled, and rolled and stopped right in front of Jovan, and he was staring into her lifeless eyes, and then they blinked.

"Why, Jovan?" the severed head asked. "How could you leave the forest, leave me? Look what happened to me, look what they did to me…"

Keiara knew something had to be done and fast. Jovan's whole body was shaking, and a low keening sound was escaping his tightly clamped lips. Whatever was happening in his mind was terrible.

"Jovan!" Keiara yelled. The others had gathered around them. Sanna, from her position on the wall looked uninterested, but kept one eye on them.

"Jovan! Fight him, it isn't real, whatever he's showing you isn't real, Jovan!" Keiara said.

"Is that true?" asked Myrstand.

Keiara looked up at him. She shook her head and felt the heaviness growing on her. That was the worst part; she knew that he was seeing truth in whatever Cage was doing. But she didn't know what.

"I…can't…help…her…" Jovan muttered through tight lips—every word forced.

Sanna felt something tug at her heart. Again, talking about her. She found herself stepping forward and standing beside Myrstand now. Jovan jerked violently, seeing the world in his mind shift.

The world spun sickeningly, and Jovan found himself sitting against the stone wall of the Mistress T'ran's chamber again, his arms painfully chained above his head. Physical torment, he thought to himself, he could handle that. He could be whipped all day long and be okay. He steeled himself as the dark form raised the whip and struck him across his bare chest, but to Jovan's horror, the pain was like someone slicing through his body, and in his mind, in a few seconds his mind was filled with the terror and horror his sister had gone through. He screamed again, this time without a gag, between the pain and the horror he felt.

The figure with the whip stepped forward, and it was not the Mistress of the Noran, it was Cage.

"Do you like it?" he asked, holding up the whip. "Want to feel it again?"

Jovan shook his head violently and tried to escape as the whip lashed out again, sending him into a writhing world of pain and torment. It faded again and Cage was kneeling beside him. He recoiled to the right, away from him.

"Jovan, I can be cruel, but so kind," he whispered into his ear though Jovan struggled to get away from him.

Cage reached out and traced a finger down his face and Jovan thought his entire brain was going to explode from his head. He saw his sister's death again, he saw Cage killing the old elf hunter and wife, he saw the passes where Cage had found him, it was littered with dead bodies, and Jovan knew Cage had killed them to keep Jovan from joining up with anyone else.

"All dead because of you, sweet Jovan, how do you feel about that?" he whispered, then as Jovan lay there his mind wracked with pain, crawled onto his lap and lay his head against Jovan's chest.

Jovan couldn't move anymore. He couldn't even fight him, his weight on his body was too much for him. "Stop it, please," he whispered hoarsely.

Cage reached up and gently stroked Jovan's cheek. Suddenly, Jovan was filled with peace and calm, all the horror was gone from his mind, as if it had never happened. Jovan sighed with relief and then just as suddenly, it all came crashing back as Cage removed his hand. He still sat on him, and stroked his cheek once more, allowing the peace to enter then taking it away.

"I can help you; I can make it all stop, just say one thing," Cage whispered into his ear, and Jovan wanted to know what that was.

"Tell me you submit," Cage whispered and for a moment Jovan nearly spoke the words.

Keiara couldn't control what was happening. "I don't understand this, the dark is my power, which includes the power over the mind, but I've never seen anything like this. Whatever is being done to him is something I've never even dreamed of. But he's almost gone."

Sanna frowned. "Gone?"

"This Cage is trying to break him, get Jovan to willingly come to him, so to do that, he's breaking his mind apart, and he's taken him to the breaking point, and I can't stop it. Unless Jovan finds the will to say no, to fight, he's lost to me, to us," Keiara said, dropping her hands. She'd laid him down on the floor, and his keening had stopped, in fact a nearly peaceful look was on his face at the moment.

Sanna dropped to her knees on his other side. She slowly picked up his left hand and squeezed it in her own.

"Jovan," she whispered into his ear. "Please, fight him, come back. I don't know...I don't think I want to lose you..."

"I..." Jovan started then stopped. "I..."

Cage squeezed his hands above his head in the shackles. "Yes, you just have to say it, and I'll take all of it away and you'll never feel it again...just say you submit..."

But there was another whisper, something warm and comforting in his ear, something that was overcoming the pain he was feeling, stronger than the desire to get rid of Cage's torture.

"No...no...no..." he started to mutter. "I won't, I won't say it, I'm not going to submit to anyone..."

Cage's eyes flashed red and he put both hands around Jovan's neck. "Defy me? You are MINE, my toy, mine, do you understand? You will be mine and you will submit to me and to my master's hands. Why? Because I desire you to do it!"

Jovan shook his head, his lungs starving for breath. It didn't matter, he would die here, in this nightmarish world of Cage's making. In his mind, he was assaulted by so many terrible things, the deaths he caused, all he caused... He screamed silently, completely blind to everything but the unbearable pain that was crushing him. From out of the ground around him, tendrils of smoky fire began to come up and wrap around him and it felt warm, oh so warm...

I won't. I can't. I...

His eyes fluttered open and he found himself staring up into Keiara's black sparkling eyes. His breath came in panting gulps of air, and he tried to rise up. He felt hands on him gently pushing him down.

"Stay there, Jovan," Keiara said softly, pressing a hand on his forehead. "You mustn't move yet."

He glanced around and saw Sanna on his left, and he locked eyes with her, and he knew it was her voice in his ear that he had heard. "It...was...you..." he rasped at her. "You..."

Keiara put a finger to his lips. "Shhh, Jovan. You need to rest."

Jovan couldn't rest, not now, but there was a creeping blackness he couldn't avoid, but this time, it was only sweet, dreamless unconsciousness that found him.

As they watched him, his eyes rolled up into his head and his head flopped to the side. "Keiara, what..."

Keiara smiled at her. "He's fine, he just passed out. Stay here with him. I don't want him left alone. Watch for any changes. Sleeping is fine, but if he looks to be dreaming or something, tell me immediately."

Keiara stood, nearly stumbling herself. Myrstand caught her as she did so. He stared at her as she walked away, supporting herself against the wall for a moment. Myrstand followed her after a moment.

"Something is bothering you greatly," he commented.

She nodded. "I don't know what he is."

Myrstand looked at her. "What do you mean, this Cage? He's a human, right? Sanna knocked him out easily enough."

"He was unprepared for her, and angry at losing his prize, that of Jovan. As far as human or not, Myrstand, I don't know. He was human at least at one time. But now, something else is in him that I don't recognize, and that's saying something. I should recognize everything that has been or ever will be on the world of Avern. I created much of it. And the magic that he is using, or power, or whatever it is, it is not of the Stars. No sphere of magic influences what he is doing. I tried everything. Only Jovan's will brought him through, and I'm not sure what will happen next time, I managed to get into his mind and help him pull himself out of the nightmare, and a nightmare it was, but I don't know if I can do it again, it nearly knocked me out along with him. I only hope this Cage is as exhausted as Jovan after this," Keiara spoke staring at the ceiling.

She turned to Myrstand. "There's more to this than I or even the Maker and Unmaker imagined. I have to find someone who knows what happened directly. And I think I know who."

Myrstand glanced back. Sanna had laid down beside Jovan's sleeping form, using her backpack as a pillow, her eyes intent on him. Lena sat at Jovan's head, gently petting his black hair. Syera and the two dwarves had sat down and drowsed against the wall.

"We won't be moving for a while, Keiara," Myrstand said slowly.

Keiara patted him on the back. "I know; we must rest. I think the danger from the Noran has passed, now that we have Syera, we can avoid their traps until we make it back to the surface. But I need to know where to go from there."

Myrstand was confused. "You said we had to find the True Litany?"

"I know. I did, and we do, but I am afraid it may only be one of the tasks for us to complete before we can free my children, and free Avern. So, I need to find one of my young ones, and I sense one nearby. We will set out once everyone is rested. I only hope Cage lets Jovan be, we cannot afford to lose him," Keiara said, heading back to sit beside Jovan's feet.

Myrstand thought for a moment. Why could they not afford to lose Jovan? Who were these young ones? Things were very curious right now. But then, the paladin had gotten used to that lately...

Syera sat quietly beside the sleeping form of Jovan. Sanna sat beside her and watched Jovan's chest rise and fall. She couldn't believe she was afraid to lose him. Something about his desire to save someone he could not save had stuck with her, from the beginning.

"He's a prince, y'know," Syera said softly, reaching down and brushing his hair from his face.

Sanna looked up at her. "A prince?"

Syera nodded. "They don call themselfs princes, they have a tribe system, but yea. His father ruled the Airkins. I can na tell him, but hi' brother was here, with us, looking for him. Their father is dead, and his brother was ruler, but someting happen, and he is gone. Jovan is their ruler now if he go home."

Sanna stared down at his face, now clear of the blood that had stained it. Sanna pushed his dark hair from his face again as he slept in peace. She glanced back at Syera.

"Why did you leave? She was your mother, she was in a high position among your people..." Sanna said slowly, looking up at the strange pink haired elf seated on the other side of Jovan's sleeping form.

"Yes, indeed, dark child, why did you leave?" Keiara's voice spoke from the shadows to their right.

Keiara sat slowly beside the two, pulling her dark skirts up around her legs. Lena sat up and yawned beside them, feeling Keiara's presence even in her sleep. She rubbed her eyes slowly and glanced at the other girls beside her. Miira and Moryn were resting not far away and Myrstand paced the small room they were in. The sound reverberated easily, Syera's voice carrying despite her quiet speech, and even Myrstand, his attention on the room around him, listened as the new addition to the group spoke in her halting common.

Syera nodded. "I am sure th' explanation i' needed. My mother, T'ran, was indeed powered. She was head of interra-in-terrog... questions. I am sorry, common language is hard. Father is head of medical researching."

Syera held up her silver hand. "I had accident when I was young girl. A rockslide, ruined arm and leg. I could not walk, and once I stop growing, father make new arm and leg, think it be for soldiers too, but not good, heavy for older men. I was a girl, so I grew with it. Experiment was a failure for him, and I was not good for much in my world. I helped them, carry messages, carry things. The arm is strong as metal it is made from, but my other arm is only flesh."

"You were an experiment?" Lena said, a look of amazement on her face. "A failed experiment?"

Syera looked down at her body where the lines of metal met her flesh, hard yet softly curving along her body. She touched the metal with her flesh hand and nodded.

"I was his greatest failure, because I was useless once I was hurt, and then the experiment gave no results," Syera said, sighing as she looked around to the faces staring at her.

"It was as I read through books in our archives that I found entries about a dark one, and it did not match what we are taught about the Unmaker in our schoolings as children. This dark one was talked about with reverence, not fear, with passion, not venom. I keep looking and looking and in the oldest items I see this picture of a black phoenix. I asked Mother what it was and she said to speak not of it, that it was heresy to talk about it, an affront to the unholy Unmaker. So when I heard they had captured upworlders, I came to see, and then I heard you talk, and I knew who you were. I knew you were someone I needed to trust," Syera said, her eyes coming to rest on Keiara's form in the darkness.

"Yes, child, it is well you did," Keiara said. "If you hand not interceded, we would no doubt be dead."

Syera nodded, glancing down at Jovan. "She would have killed him at least once and brought him back before she was done, and then she would have killed him, and both the dwarves. Elves and dwarves are given no quarter, though the wars ended long ago. They are vicious, and they work together. I knew it was not right, and I wanted to leave."

"What wars?" asked Sanna, leaning forward now and listening intently.

Syera smiled, "I do not..."

"The Elven Ascension wars," Keiara broke in. "When Kalimourne's children stopped being one people and became six different groups with nearly no communication."

Syera nodded. "Yes, when my people separated, and the wars began."

"It is a very long tale, I'm afraid, a tale too long for tonight, but one I'm sure either I, or Syera when her common improves, can tell you, or perhaps even Jovan. But most likely each of us will have a different version. No, please, sleep, we set out tomorrow to find someone, hopefully an ally, which lies in these caverns nearby. But we need to be rested and wary for the trip," Keiara said with a soft smile and patted Syera on the back.

"Child, do not fret, your people will yet be brought out of the dark of their own making. Maybe it will be you that brings them out of it," Keiara said as she passed Syera. "I do hope that, my child."

CHAPTER ELEVEN

UNLOCKING ELMLOCK

All that are born into the world, do not live.
There are some in which the spark of life, was never lit.
And there are some in which the spark of life fades too fast.
And then there are some whose bodies cannot contain their spark.
It is those that we should fear the most.
—Master Wizard Alchert on the Nature of Life

M yrstand woke suddenly to a sound like scratching on the stone wall next to him. He started and sat up and saw nothing in the blackness. He turned his head toward the middle of the room where a light shown from a torch Keiara had just lit. She placed her finger to her lips and nodded to him. He did hear something.

He crawled quickly over to where the two dwarves were sleeping, and shook first Moryn then Miira awake. Both stared at him and said nothing, the severe look on his face enough to set them on edge. He gently pushed at Lena who started with a yelp, which he quickly shushed her. He pointed to Sanna and Jovan who lay side by side. Lena crawled over and gently shook Sanna awake. She gasped but looked around as the torches they'd lit began to lighten the room. She nodded and then shook Jovan awake, or at least tried to shake him awake.

"Jovan," she whispered, and then looked down at his eyes which were rapidly rolling underneath his closed eyelids. His face had gone pale and his jaw muscles were tight.

"Keiara!" she whispered harshly and Keiara came back to where he laid down.

"Oh no," Keiara whispered as the others gathered.

Sunshine was the first thing he saw when he opened his eyes, and for a moment he thought it was kind of strange, since he had gone to sleep underground. But his mind discounted it quickly as the world filled with the smell of full moon lilacs. He smiled, glancing down at his bare feet as he walked through the green grass. He looked up into the clearing. His brothers and sisters were there, they had a picnic today, the morning after the full moon lilacs bloomed. Jovel, his eldest brother stood looking into the distance, while his other brothers, Jomel, Joser, and Jomack each laid around the field. Jokara and Jokeiva picked the flowers around the edge of the clearing. It was a beautiful day.

Jovan smiled as he walked into the field and expected to be noticed.

"Why, Jovan?" asked Jovel as he turned to dust before his eyes. Jovan felt rooted to the ground as he looked to the others.

Joser and Jomack turned at the same time. "Why?" they said in unison and their bodies turned to dust and blew away in the wind.

Jovan wanted to scream, but nothing would come from his mouth. Now Jokeiva, his eldest sister who had always treated him so very well began to cry as she turned to dust. Around them, the sky was darkening like night falling. Jomel, his last brother shook his head and looked at Jokara.

"We looked for you, we looked for you because we needed you," he said and burst into flames, burning away and the ashes spreading themselves on the wind.

Now only poor Jokara stared at him. Her eyes teared up and to his horror, her head fell from his shoulders like he had seen so many times.

He felt hands on his shoulders. "I can be so kind to you, Jovan, just submit to me. You see, I know more now. I know they're all dead. You know they're all dead, and I wonder why?"

Jovan tried to pull away but the familiar hands had him again. It wasn't even like hands, it was like five twisting snakes came from each hand and wrapped around him. He felt Cage again against his back, holding onto him.

"What are you doing this for?" Jovan asked through tight lips.

Cage moved around to stand in front of him, looking every bit like the man Jovan met in the forest the first time he saw him. "I told you, submit."

"Why?" Jovan said, struggling against the snakes that enveloped his arms and legs now.

Cage smiled. "Oh you have no idea my reasons. Now just be a good little boy and submit? There's so much fun you and I can have for a while..."

Cage touched his face gently and Jovan sighed deeply with relief as the touch once more brought and overwhelming feeling of peace and tranquility into him. He didn't want it to stop. He wanted to feel like that forever. Then he released his face and Jovan's knees buckled.

"Are we going to do all this again?" Cage asked, taking out a whip like weapon and striking Jovan across the chest.

Jovan's mind filled with the assault and murder of his sister, then Cage's murder of the Elf head hunter, and the murders of all the others Cage had killed to get to him.

"Why me?" Jovan screamed. "Why am I so damned special to you?"

Cage put the whip away and kneeled in front of him. He leaned over and whispered into Jovan's ear, "Because you are special to him."

"Him?" Jovan said, then yelped as Cage bit down on his earlobe.

"Oh yes, him. I'll give you time to think, but for now, something to remember me by," Cage said and walked away.

From the ground around him, snakes began to boil up like some sort of bubbling liquid and all at once, they struck, and it felt as though a poison ten times stronger than T'ran's pain potion had been released into his veins and he screamed with all he was worth.

Keiara looked up to Myrstand when he started to scream. For a second everyone was shocked into silence, then they all acted, knowing someone was on the other side of the wall. They didn't know if it was a Noran patrol, or some underground beast, but whatever it was they all knew it was far better for them to not be found than for them to be found. Sanna put both hands over his mouth to squelch his screaming as best as she could.

"Hush, Jovan!" she said.

His eyes were open wide and he was fighting them all as Lena and Moryn both held down his arms. Then he suddenly stopped as though he realized he was now awake and he stared up at Sanna who was covering his mouth rather painfully. He saw Keiara staring down at him from above his head. He panted and made eye contact with Sanna and nodded, and she slowly released her grip and he took a great gulp of air. The others let go and he sat up, running his hands through his hair and panting.

"We have to go, now," Myrstand whispered hoarsely from the piece of wall they had enchanted to hide themselves the night before.

"I'm sorry," Jovan panted as he scrambled to his feet. "I..."

"Shush," Sanna said, helping him to his feet. "Just move!"

They were out the doorway in seconds, and seconds after that an explosion rocked the small cavern they had been in, and a very angry looking Mistress T'ran stood staring into the ruins of the empty cavern.

They quickly ran through the mazes of tunnels, following Keiara, not even Syera knowing where they were going now. Jovan had gained most his faculties back but was still not back to normal after the last two days affairs. Sanna stayed behind him, and Syera kept a watch on their rear.

Keiara was not worried about the pursuing Noran at the least, her main concern was finding the presence she was seeking. She had to find out what was happening. What had begun as simply locating and releasing her lost children was turning into something much bigger than she had ever imagined. Even with all the power and knowledge of the Dark Phoenix, she had no way of telling what exactly was happening. The Veil had fallen, blocking prophecy and blocking the ability of using Sight because they were two things which Ackana depended on. But now, they were hindered without someone who could see future events. Now, Keiara wondered as she stopped at an intersection of four tunnels, now she had to wonder if Ackana was even the one who had orchestrated this.

The tunnel she picked dead ended after about an hour of walking, but she was certain this was the right place.

"A dead end?" Myrstand asked as he came up beside her.

"It would appear so, but I know there is something beyond it. Lena!" she called over the others, and the small girl made her way up to her.

"What do you see?" she asked her.

Lena stared at the blank wall, and for a moment, there appeared to be nothing but a wall of stone, but as she watched it, discreet lines of a door began to take shape and a large inscription appeared at the arc of the top.

"It's a door," she said and reached out to grasp a handle no one else could see. "You have to see into the spirit world to touch it."

She grasped the handle and turned it. There was a feeling like lightning striking in the air as a light resolved itself in the form of an arched doorway. The doorway swung open and settled against the stone to the right. They all entered the room and after the last, the door swung shut behind them.

"I doubt anyone but you could have opened the door," Keiara said softly. "What did the inscription read?"

"It said 'Reach into Spirit', so that's what I did," she said looking up at Keiara with a smile.

They were now in a large open room with a set of double banded stone doors in front of them. There was a plaque in a language few among them recognized. Keiara moved forward and touched it.

"Ancient elven," she whispered. "I haven't seen this in thousands of years."

Lena stared at it. "It says Those who enter Seeking the Sun shall die by its fire."

Myrstand reached forward and to his surprise, the door opened easily.

The group followed him in and found themselves staring at a large statue. Past the warning on the doors, inside the room starting at a statue of pure marble, they now found themselves. It looked like an old man, the lines in the face chiseled and it looked like it was as pristine as the day it was carved, if it had been carved at all. There was a banging boom as the large doors slammed shut behind them. All of them stared at the statue because now, with the lights gone, the statue glowed in the darkness. They were tired of running, and somewhat out of breath, and tired of being wary. Jovan and Sanna slid to their knees in front of the door, Syera and Moryn stood silent, breathing heavily near where Lena stood staring at the statue. Myrstand stood against the closed doorway with Miira beside him. Keiara walked up to the statue.

"It is alive," Lena whispered. If she had a living heart, it would have been beating very hard at the moment.

Keiara stood up straight and stared. "What do you mean, Lena? It is alive? The statue?"

Lena walked closer. "But it isn't, a statue, I mean…"

The others came around, still out of breath from their desperate run, and stared. The statue was at least six foot in height, on top of three-foot diameter platform that stood two feet high at least and was inscribed with runes and symbols. Lena walked around it slowly.

"Those who touch the effigy of a god, should expect that which they wish, whether they know what it is or not…" she read slowly. "Touching the stars will blind the weak, touching the moon will deafen the unworthy, touching the sun will kill the impure…"

Around the statue, as a testament to those words, there were bones, ancient bones, some crushed to dust. Many, many had died here. Lena turned to Keiara.

"This is for you," she said. "Look," she said pointing at the statue's outstretched and open hand.

"That hand," Myrstand breathed. "It wasn't like that when we came in. It is reaching for you..."

Keiara nodded and walked toward it and then shifted her wings out, which unfortunately shocked Syera into screaming. She reached the out stretched hand with one good motion of her wings and stared into the open hand. In the hand was a medallion. A brilliant, multicolored phoenix shown in the darkness on the disk of gold on a fine gold chain lay there. Keiara reached out and gently took it by the chain, careful not to touch the stone.

Then Myrstand looked at his other hand, which was against his side. In it as a wand, topped with a brilliant star. There was a clasp at the throat with a crescent moon, and on his hip a sword with a sun on the pommel sat.

"His treasures. That's the sun, moon and stars. Anyone who tries to take them suffers the fate described on the base," he said slowly.

He turned to Keiara who was opening the medallion which was a locket. Keiara smiled slowly.

"Sly old son of a goddess," she muttered.

Myrstand and the others turned to her. "What, you know what's happening?" asked Jovan, slowly getting to his feet again with Sanna's help.

She gently flapped her wings, sending her upward a few more feet. She then moved closer to the statue and then gently placed a kiss on his forehead. There was a loud crack and a sound like thunder that sent everyone to their knees. As they looked up the marble began to turn into flesh starting at the point Keiara's lips touched his forehead. Keiara landed, folding her wings behind her and watched as the light began to emanate from where the stone returned to flesh.

The others watched astounded as he rolled his old, white haired head on his shoulders and eyes of brilliant purple glinted from the shriveled face. Slowly, the robes of deep midnight blue began to take shape and the clasp with the moon on it was carved of pure diamond. Slowly, his arms came free and he lifted the ruby tipped wand, the star ruby at the top shimmering. He stretched and they could see the brilliant gold hilt of a massive sword strapped to his back. Keiara waited with her arms crossed, staring amused at him as he transformed. Finally, he stood there completely human looking on top of a marble base. Keiara stood in front of the pedestal. He leaped down with a spryness not be possible for a man of his apparent age.

"Grandmother!" he said, his wrinkled face smiling.

Keiara arched an eyebrow. "I was sure you were killed when you mother was captured."

He tilted his head to the side. "Well, of course you were. Only way the bastards wouldn't bother me until I could help free her was to pretend to be dead."

She held up the locket. "Grandmother's Kiss?"

"What else was I supposed to say? 'Only the touch of the Mother of All Gods will free me from my self-created stony prison, anyone else is going to die if they touch it'?"

Keiara looked around at the bones. "Might have not been a bad idea..."

He looked at the bones. "Humans, all, they can't resist the treasures of the hidden god."

Keiara rolled her eyes. "And who started the rumors about the 'treasures of the hidden god'?"

The old man looked sheepishly away. "Well, now, I thought you'd be pleased to see me, Grandmother."

"Okay, this is too weird!" announced Sanna.

Keiara and the old man turned to her. "What is?" they said in unison.

"He calls y' grandmother, and looks like y' great grandfather," Syera answered from beside her. The others stared too.

Keiara snickered. "I supposed it is a bit odd. What's with the old man look anyway?" she asked.

"I was hiding at the end, masked my powers and went underground, played the part of the crazy old hermit for a few years, but I realized pretty fast it wasn't going to work as long as Ackana was looking for me, so I decided to use the stone prison on myself," he answered, removing a black cap from his white head.

Keiara nodded. "Why don't you resume your normal visage now, the Veil has fallen already."

He looked at her surprised, and then smiled. "Of course, it was you all the time who made the Veil fall. I don't know why I never realized it."

He stared at the others and locked eyes with Myrstand and grinned ear to ear. He started to say something and Keiara put a hand on his arm. "No," she hissed. He looked crestfallen and nodded.

"Okay, back to normal, it's kind of rough looking like an old grumpy man..."

The man closed his eyes and a soft purple glow began to surround him. Slowly his face shifted into the same face, only much, much younger, his hair turned blonde, his ears lengthened to almost elf-like, and his beard disappeared. The wrinkled pale skin firmed and became tanned and the only thing remaining the same was the shining violet eyes. He had been stooped and standing six foot, now he straightened and shrunk in the shoulders a bit and became a long, lean and gangly figure.

"So, is that better?" he said turned to the group.

Just as he said it, the robes slipped off his no longer stooped shoulders and he stood before them in all his glory. Keiara sighed.

"You size altered yourself but not you clothes, Elmlock," she said.

He looked down, standing in front of them with a pile of clothes at his feet and smiled. "Well, that won't do."

He picked up the robe and held the wand to it and it transformed into a different set of clothes entirely. He dressed quickly, slipping on a white cloth shirt and a pair of heavy blue pants. He wiggled his bare toes from under the pants. He looked at Keiara.

"Shoes, Elmlock. Shoes," she muttered.

He smiled at her again, his roguish face almost comical as he pointed at his feet and materialized a pair of shoes. "Better?"

Keiara nodded slowly then slid down the wall and passed out cold.

"Keiara!" Myrstand shouted and went to her.

Elmlock smiled. "Don't worry; she'll be fine in a bit. To release the spell, it sucked a lot of power out of her, no other way. Without her, the stone prison is permanent with no hope of release." He rubbed his head slowly and shrugged.

"Actually, that was probably the first time anyone's ever used it on themselves, since only the person who casts Stone Prison Lock can release it. And when you cast it on yourself, you can't really release yourself. I'm glad I wasn't wrong!"

Miira looked up from beside Keiara. "Wrong?"

The roguish man smiled. "I honestly didn't know for sure that Grammama would even be able to release it."

No one said a word, but everyone exchanged glances with each other. Who would put themselves into living death without being sure someone could ever get them out?

"So how long were you in stone?" Sanna asked as Elmlock shoveled half of her week's worth of rations into his mouth.

Elmlock tilted his head to the side and shrugged. "I have no idea."

"Elmlock, if you can stop eating, this is serious, I need information about who is behind this, and where your mother and the rest of my children are," Keiara sad standing with her back to the wall beside him.

Myrstand sat beside Jovan along the wall. They had decided to stay and rest in this cavern for the day, since the enchantments on it were so heavy. The Noran hadn't found it before they did, so the chances of them finding them now were slim. Myrstand had applied the healing energy he could muster to Jovan's wounds, which looked much better. However, even Myrstand could see the ghostly look in his eyes. What was happening to him in his mind was taking a sure toll on him.

"I wish I could tell you something, but I really can't tell you more than you already know. They started disappearing, one by one, the lesser powerful gods first, then the more powerful ones, and finally the Keepers. The three of us knew Ackana was involved, and we scattered to the four winds trying to keep ourselves safe. We were the only children the gods had ever borne, so we figured we would be pretty easy to kill, since you weren't involved," he said, drinking deeply out of the waterskin.

Keiara snorted. "Since I wasn't involved. The hubris of my children."

Lena looked up quizzically. "You weren't involved in Elmlock's creation? You said a part of the phoenix was required for the creation of life."

Keiara's face changed drastically to one of disgust. "Even my most cherished children decided they wanted to make life. They wanted to create their own children, without our help. So they tried and tried and tried. And mostly failed. Only Ackana, Elmlock and two others ever came from the hundreds of attempts to create gods by them."

Elmlock shrugged. "You always bore ill against them for it, didn't you?"

Keiara turned quickly toward him and for the first time, they saw real anger rising in the normally composed woman. "Of course. I will always harbor ill against them for trying to create what was impossible. Without the spark of life, they were destined to fail, and I told them so."

Elmlock, slightly worried by her anger, smiled, "But four made it out of their attempts! At least they quit trying after we didn't live up to their hopes."

Keiara stared at him for a moment. "Nothing came of their attempts."

Elmlock stopped, turning his purple eyes upon Keiara in the dim light. "But we're here, you didn't..."

He put down his food and stared for a moment. "You did."

Keiara snorted and stared the other way. "Of course, I did. If I hadn't stepped in without them knowing, the four of you wouldn't exist."

"Wait, so you gave them the spark of life after all?" Sanna asked quietly. "Why?"

Elmlock sat shocked into silence.

"Because I was tired of hearing them die, not that they were ever truly alive." Keiara didn't look at him when she said it.

"Hearing who die?" Elmlock asked slowly.

Keiara felt tears in her eyes and she didn't stop them. "I heard every life they attempted to bring into existence. Some lasted seconds before they faded from existence, some lasted torturous minutes and hours or more before they finally faded away, and they screamed in pain the entire time because there was no spark of life to bring fire to their souls. And yes, they had souls, and they simply vanished and were gone from the world. At first, I thought they would just stop when their attempts met with no success, so I waited for them to stop, but they didn't. They were convinced it could be done, and then Kalimourne began to try, and it was then I couldn't take it any longer. Elmlock, you were the first I whispered life quietly into before you could fade away. There were others but some faded too fast. And that was how it went," Keiara finished with a deep sigh and turned away.

Elmlock nodded slowly. "Somehow I always knew. I think all four of us knew at some base level. But I think the worst is that we all remember the time before you whispered life into us as you put it. This aching darkness and struggling as if to breathe under water."

Keiara nodded. "I was glad after Ackana was created when they decided the results were not worth the effort."

"So, what happened to them?" Lena asked quietly after a few moments of silence.

Keiara turned to here and shook her head. "What do you mean? They vanished, ceased to exist."

Lena nodded, "Yes, I understand that, but if something is brought into existence, even for the shortest amount of time, it has to go somewhere, doesn't it?"

Elmlock and Keiara glanced at each other and back at Lena. "I...I suppose that is true," Keiara said slowly.

"Does it even matter?" Myrstand asked standing from where he had been kneeling beside the others. "What became of those lost ones doesn't mean anything to us now, does it?"

Keiara shook her head. "I suppose not, we know that Ackana has them imprisoned, and we must release them."

"But she doesn't have the Keepers," Elmlock said, thoughtfully biting into a piece of jerky.

Keiara looked at him sharply. "What?"

"She caught them, of course, at the end, but they aren't in the same place as the rest, I know that much. They were too powerful to be contained in whatever prison she built," he said, sipping from the waterskin again. "No, she imprisoned each of them, locking them away, with some sort of artifact as the key."

Keiara nodded. "I had wondered about how she had contained them, they have control over the base elements of Life, Death, Magic, and Nature. They cannot be put within the same prison as the others without needing vast amounts of power to contain them. Power it would be impossible for her to draw."

Keiara stood up and folded her hands behind her back. "What did she do to get them in containment?"

Elmlock, shook his head. "That I couldn't find out before I had to escape into hiding. All I know is all of the Keepers disappeared around the same time, and seemingly without a whisper."

Keiara sighed deeply. "So, the question is, if we are to release my children, can we even do it without the Keepers being released first?"

Elmlock stood against the wall and crossed his arms. "You have no idea what you're doing, do you?"

Keiara looked up sharply. "I had planned to find the Litany."

Elmlock arched a brow. "Thinking the words of the old days would release the enchantments binding them?"

"Of course, the power behind the True Litany is insurmountable," Keiara said, staring at him with a sharp look.

Elmlock snorted. "If you can get to it."

Keiara growled under her breath and turned her back on him, her shoulders tight. Behind her, Myrstand and Sanna locked eyes. They'd never seen her like this before. Her omnipotence had limits. Severe limits. Elmlock smiled.

"She didn't tell you, did she?" and Keiara turned and stared at him with a look that could have melted stone.

Myrstand shook his head. "Tell us what?"

Elmlock grinned a sideways grin. "Oh, you're sly, old gram."

"How could I tell them?" she said with an incredulous tone.

The entire group looked at her with a mixture of confusion and fear.

"I'm sure she had the best intentions," Elmlock continued. "She always does. But the truth is, she's as mortal as you are, and all her vast knowledge comes from before she entered the mortal world, how long ago?"

Keiara sighed. "I entered the cycle shortly after my children disappeared."

Myrstand narrowed his eyes and moved toward her. "You mean, you've got no knowledge of the world and what's happened since then?"

"Of course not. How could I? My soul has been bound into mortal bodies for centuries until Keiara carried it and it woke, and merged with her soul," Keiara said, and sighed again. "There was no other way. I could remain outside the physical world, in the astral and outer planes, and remain powerful and see everything, or I could choose to come to the world and try to save them. Only Lena's help has made things possible this far."

Everyone's eyes turned to the small girl. "What? Why Lena?" Sanna asked, placing a hand on her back.

Lena smiled. "I'm different. The Seer in the Darkness, I still can See even though the Veil has fallen."

Keiara nodded. "I didn't know how long it would be, but I knew I would have to Veil visions and sight to succeed against whoever I was fighting against. But doing so would cripple me as well, so I imbued two mortals, one with Prophecy and the other with Sight. Lena is the descendant of the Seer."

"I'll give you one thing, gram, you have foresight," Elmlock said nodding.

"But that still leaves us with the question of what we are supposed to do now?" Sanna said softly from her place beside the wall. "Do we go after the Litany? Do we try to release the Keepers? Or do we just go after Ackana?"

Keiara sighed. "I don't know."

"Ah!" Elmlock exclaimed suddenly. "I do!"

Everyone turned to him and he smiled broadly. "The House of Oracles! I may have been in stone for a few hundred years, and you, Gram, may have been floating around in mortals for a few more, but if one thing will have stayed the same, it is the House of Oracles!"

Keiara nodded slowly. "Yes, the House of Oracles. We aren't far, and it may hold the answers we seek."

Jovan spoke up from where he sat beside the snoozing Moryn. "I can lead us there, at least as far as the end of the mountains where they let out into the Wildlands. But beyond that, it is up to you lot to figure out where to go."

Elmlock nodded. "I can find it once we are above ground again. I've got more than a little magic left in this old wand," he said holding up the ruby tipped wand.

"So, it is settled then, we head out to the House of Oracles, and we hopefully find a direction from there," Myrstand said with a sound of confidence.

CHAPTER TWELVE

SHADOWS ON THE SUN

Shadows will grow on the sun, in the year of the Veil,
Shadows will grow on the sun, in the beginning of the Tale,
The Shadows on the sun will take flight and fly away,
And in the end, tears will stop, the very world will sway.
—Prophetess Truesa of the Lost Tribe

∞

Avari shivered in the tiny room. Well, it wasn't so much of a room as the space above the ceiling. One could not even call it a proper attic. The winter wind whistled through the rafters into the tiny space chilling her to the bone. This was something she was used to. She wasn't allowed down in the house during the day except in the windowless kitchen to cook for her "father". She'd shivered in the cold here for nearly sixteen winters now, since she had been four years old. She could take the cold. She would rather take the cold and be forgotten.

She swallowed hard the fear that rose in her throat when the door slammed below her.

Please let him forget me, please let him forget me.... she thought over and over again as she sat pulling the thin remnants of the old, gray cloak around her.

She didn't want to be remembered right now. He'd promised her punishment when he returned. It had been her fault, of course. The dinner had burned, because she'd been foolish, as he'd told her before he left. But the knock at the door had meant he couldn't punish her right then, so instead he forced her up the rickety ladder into the attic space. Maybe he'd bring someone with him, someone he didn't want to see her...maybe...

Her hopes were dashed with the loud bang slap of the trap door opening and the ladder sliding down.

"Down." That single word was enough to set her heart beating faster and her eyes to well with tears.

She slowly climbed down the ladder, and as her feet touched the midpoint she felt the world spin as she was yanked down from it onto the floor. She moaned despite herself as she felt, once again, the cracking pain as something in her hand snapped. Before she'd even had a chance to draw second breath, a thick, heavy hand connected with her jaw, sending her reeling once more, but this time, no noise issued forth from her tightly clasped lips. Blood filled her mouth and leaked from the corners, but no sound came from her.

She stared at his feet. The dark brown boots were well worn, especially on the toes. There was snow caked around the edges of them, and up to the hem of the brown wool pants above them. She tried very hard to find a point on the left shoe to focus on. There was a small white scratch there, crossed several times by others, and she tried to focus on it while her head rung from the blow.

"D' ya know who tha' was?" The heavy, thick voice of Dobius Fletcher was not raised, no he wouldn't raise his voice for fear of being found out. She didn't dare answer; she was not expected to answer.

"No, a course ya dn't, ya whelp uvva girl. It was th' Bloufs, next door. Says he hears strange sounds comin' from th' house in th' wee hours of th' mornin'. Worryin', he was. Now, what do ya thin' makes him say tha'?"

She swallowed hard. She shook her head, knowing voicing any answer would mean the boot she was staring so intently at would be meeting her ribs. She knew exactly what the sound was. It was her, in the night, calling out in her dreams. Or, nightmares, as she more accurately described them. She had tried to do everything she could to keep the noise down, to chase them away, but nothing had worked.

"If'n I hear thi' agn' then thar will be hell to pay," he said in a dangerous whisper.

"Ah, Pa, yer home!" came the shrill voice of her "brother". He was a year older than she was, and just as horrible as her caregiver. She refused to even think of him as her father. She had known for as long as she could remember he was not her father. He was not really related to her at all but had been entrusted with him. She hurt inside to think her mother would leave her here with this terrible man, did it mean she'd been as bad as he was?

"Ah, Val, m'boy, how was th'..." his voice trailed off as he placed a thick, hairy hand onto Val's broad shoulders and steered him into the kitchen.

She lay there for a moment, swallowing the blood in her mouth, knowing better than to spit it on the floor. She gasped and felt the pain radiating from the side of her hand. Another break, no doubt. She reached up and rubbed her eyes, oh how they ached, her strange purple eyes. They called it a Mark of Sorcery before the Regulations had begun. But then, anyone caught with the Mark was shipped away and never heard from again. Sent to the Forge. She couldn't remember her mother very well, but she knew her mother had the mark as well. She could see her face sometimes behind her eyelids if she tried. She had been four when she watched them come and drag her away while she trembled inside the broom closet, her dad swearing to the Regulator that his daughter had died last winter as his wife was dragged from the small cottage beside the wood.

After they had gone, he'd grabbed her and bundled her up tightly, and took off on their old horse to his friend, Dobius Fletcher's, home in the next town. Dobius, even then, had been a gaunt, heavy handed man, but he had been fair. His wife, Anagelica, also bore the Mark, but so did many people then, and even though the Mark did not mean that they were gifted with sorcery, the possibility was there, even though a Prophet hadn't been heard of in over a hundred years or more. Their son, Valentor, was a year older than she was, and she felt safe in Ana's arms.

"I'll come back, with your mom, I promise," he whispered to her and kissed her lightly on the forehead. She remembered his head of thick, black hair as he disappeared out the deep mahogany door. Thick, black hair much like her own. But she remembered the only semblance to her mother had been in the eyes.

Two days later, they came back. She ran and hid again as the Regulators' burst in and dragged Ana from her son and husband's arms. She remembered so clearly, Dobius yelling as they did so, "Please, please, don't take her from me! Take the brat, she's got the mark, just don't take my Ana!!"

The Regulator walked into the house and lifted the small four-year-old up by the front of her night gown. She squeaked with horror as the man had pushed her hair from her face and stared at the Mark burning there. He touched a finger lightly to her eyes. And then he dropped her. She fell with a thump, the strength suddenly drained from her body.

"She's a non-possible. No residual power. You wife carries residual power. No reason to take the child," he said, pushing the then strapping Dobius out of the way.

"But...but Ana's never had a..."

The Regulator turned on him and lowered his eyes. "The potential is there, so she comes to the Forge with us. She may not always stay so. That one...no potential. Her Mark is merely an annoying reminder that there are those who bear it who are just as worthless as you are, Dobius."

With that the Regulator left, dragging the screaming woman behind her. Dobius sat at the door for hours. When he turned around to see the child standing there he rounded on her.

"Your pa drew em here. You drew em here."

And that was the first time she had ever tasted blood.

She climbed slowly into the space. Tomorrow was Val's eighteenth birthday, and the day he would become a "man" according to the traditions of Darna. At eighteen, he would be considered able to court a girl he would marry, and he would be able to go alone into the towns. So, tomorrow was a big day. She clutched fervently to the thin blanket she covered herself with.

The next morning, the sun awoke her, as usual, and she waited for the distinct slap bang of the door opening. It did not open from above, only below. Then she would make breakfast for her "brother". Soon enough the door was opened, but it was not Dobius, but Val who stood below as she climbed down. Val, like his father, had a shock of dark brown hair, and dark, almost black, glittering eyes. He stood about a foot over Avari's small frame. She stared up at him, her brilliant purple eyes full of fear because Val had never let her down before. He was pressing up against her so she was nearly pinned to the ladder behind her.

"Pa's up in th' village getting my birthday trials arrange fer t'day. Said ta make me breakfast."

Avari swallowed hard, inching away from him. She scampered to the kitchen and began to make his eggs and toast as quickly as she could. The quicker she was done, the quicker she could return to her small safe room. But after he finished, he sat there, watching her clear the dishes, watching her wash them, put them away. Never before had he lingered after his food was gone. She put the towel back on the rack to dry and went to leave the room.

"Where do ya thin' yer goin'?" Val asked, leaning back in the chair and crossing his arms.

"B-b-back up to m-my r-r-room..." she stammered, standing stock still inches from the doorway. She wanted to run. She didn't know why but she wanted to run. But inside a voice told her it wouldn't matter, because when Dobius got home, she'd be whipped for not staying when Val, now a man of the house, told her to do so.

"Nah, yer not. See Pa, he says there's only one way t' make a man. The trials, ya, they're good and all tha', prove I can take care of myself, and Pa. But no. Tha' not wat make's a man of me."

Avari felt her heart trip-hammer in her chest. She swallowed hard and flinched as he got up and approached her. He stood in front of her, towering over her, his dark eyes glittering with malice like his father's did before he hit her his hardest. There was something wrong, something diseased in them, and at that very moment she was elated there was no blood between them. The elation didn't last long as he moved on her. Without thinking, she ran, her instincts kicking in suddenly, knowing without knowing standing there in front of him was only going to lead to more pain.

But the only place she could go was up. Irrationally, she thought if she could just get to her attic room, he'd leave her be, he'd just give it up. She couldn't have been more wrong.

"You dare run," he said as his thick, hard hands closed around her waist as she clung halfway up the small ladder.

"No...please," she cried, gulping air, knowing he was going to hurt her. It is just pain, some part of her brain whispered. But something was different, something was very different about Val right now. She kicked hard with her left foot and connected with his nose. He let out a startled, strangled cry and let her go. She scrambled the rest of the way up and crouched in the corner. She looked down to her bare foot and saw blood, Val's blood, there.

Suddenly the weight of what she had done hit her. She bit her lip and looked from the busted rafters and wondered if she got out on the roof, could she survive the nearly twenty-foot drop to the ground below? It was snow covered, there would be...

She suddenly lurched violently away from the rafters and fell, her face smashing into the floor, blood from her mouth blooming out. She realized then he'd grabbed her foot. She scrambled, trying to gain a hold of something, not even realizing she was sobbing

"No...no...please...stop..."

She felt the fingernails on her right index finger dig into the wood, but then she watched in horror as the whole nail began to splinter as he pulled her with his full weight. Blood spurted from her ripped fingers and she tried desperately to hold on. But why? The though passed through her head quietly. It wasn't like she could go anywhere....

There was a half second between the time her hands let go and she hit the floor sprawled out, her fingers on fire, her mouth bleeding profusely, and she wasn't sure, but she felt something crack in her chest. Then she felt him grab the back of her head, his fingers twining into her long, thick black hair. He easily lifted her off the ground by her hair and held her as she grasped at his hand.

"You. Dare." It was all he said, and all he needed to say.

His nose was still bleeding, and she could tell her kick had broken it, swelling up across the bridge. Her own bright violet eyes were welling with tears as she tried to speak words of apology, but instead he dropped her to her feet and dragged her by her hair into his bedroom. Her heart began to beat even faster as he held tightly to her hair. She struggled still. How could she not. He let go of her but as soon as her head raised, he raised his hand and backhanded her as hard as he could. She could barely think, let alone breathe as she flew over his bed into the wall beside it.

Her head ringing, she tried to get up, still struggling to get away from him, but was met with a swift kick into her ribs, sending her sprawling once again, her breathe gone now entirely. Again, the searing pain of something breaking made her whimper. He wasn't done, of course. He grabbed her by the wrists and lifted her up easily, her small body easy for his powerful arms. He reached down with his free hand and pulled the belt from his waist.

"Manners." He whispered the word like a threat. "You will learn manners."

She couldn't fight the sobbing and started to wail. He struck her across the face violently with the folded belt. He smiled at her, blood freely running from several cuts on her face.

"Now, remove yer clothes," he whispered into her ear. He dropped her to the floor once more.

She started to back away, trembling with fear and pain. "No...please...I... I..." she stammered her eyes darting beside him to see if she could possibly run from him.

His face turned to something far worse than it had been. His eyes widened, and he grabbed her by the throat this time, lifting her off the floor the turning and slamming her into the wall. Her hands grasped feebly at his thick hand. He leaned over and smelled her neck, stroking the belt over her face with his free hand. She choked back a sob, already turning red from lack of air.

His grip didn't loosen, and stars were twinkling in her vision. "Yer scrawny. But yer gud enough for the fir' one."

She was beginning to see the black patches forming in her vision as he lifted her up and threw her to the bed. She took great gulps of air, still scrambling to be away from him, almost making it off the bed, but he was there so fast, his hand coming at her again, sending her reeling, her eyes crossing and her ears ringing. She felt him take her hands and wrap the belt around them tight. She muttered protests through swollen lips, but he didn't care as she lay there, limp and helpless. She couldn't have moved any more than a newborn kitten at that moment. She stared up at the ceiling, a dark dot on the ceiling, and felt the hot tears streaming down her face, wetting the bed beside her. Then his weight was on her and she cried out loudly and couldn't move, he was so heavy, his hands pressing her into the bed, his body hot against her. He was trying to get her clothes out of the way, but she pushed back, making it difficult for him.

Suddenly, there was a great slamming crash as the door burst open to the room. He was off her already, standing at the side of his bed, staring at whoever had interrupted him. The bed to either side of her face was sopping wet, her hair matted against her head. Her whole body ached. Even the crashing of the door opening violently only gave rise to her head turning slowly toward it and seeing a man and woman standing there. It didn't register as odd at all to her mind the man and woman said something, and Val responded back, trying to say something about his sick sister he was tending to. Val was standing in front of her so all she could see was just the shapes of them in the door frame.

There was a deep roaring in her ears, though and she couldn't hear anymore. Suddenly Val's shape was pushed violently aside, and she heard the woman give a mild gasp, and just as the world began fading finally to black, felt a blanket being thrown on her, and felt herself lifted by someone. It was so warm, so warm, she thought as she slipped into the comfortable darkness.

Lena's scream woke everyone in the cavern. It was one of those piercing sounds that once it has gotten into the mind it reverberates forever. Something about it made every single one of them sit bolt upright and gasp for breath, but not one of them uttered a sound. Only the heavy breathing in silent darkness of the cavern they had slept in during the night.

In the darkness, Lena's voice had incredible power, and as everyone turned their heads toward her, her eyes glowed intensely white.

"The Shadow on the sun has awoken, but without knowledge of destiny. Rescue them and they will lead us. Destroy them and they will save us."

Lena closed her eyes and there was a soft thump sound as she fell back into her bedroll. A cracking sound in the darkness signaled the lighting of a torch with flint. The brilliance blazed into existence showing them all spread around the enclosed cavern, all except Keiara and Elmlock, who were gone.

Myrstand slowly stood and looked around. They were sealed in, Moryn and Miira had made sure of it, so how had they left?

"Yes, I felt it. The Shadow on the Sun," Keiara said, staring up at the moon.

Elmlock stood beside her on the peak of the mountain in which below her the rest of the rested.

"They've awoken, Gram, you know of course," Elmlock said, his face severe as he stared at the stars with her.

"No doubt they know we've gone," she replied.

"No doubt at all," Elmlock said. "Have you decided the course?"

Keiara leaned back, appearing to sit on a chair made of dark clouds. "Yes, I have. You won't like it."

"You mean to split up the group, don't you?"

She nodded. "After the House. We don't have time to scamper across the world together, cozy as that might be. I'm not sure what we'll find there, but of the Keepers have been bound, they must be released first before we can do anything about the rest. And whoever is at fault no doubt has made it difficult."

Elmlock looked confused. "What do you mean, whoever is at fault? I thought my cousin, Ackana, did this?"

Keiara smiled. "And before, I thought it was dear sister Sealla. All is not what it seems all the time, godling boy. No, Ackana did not do this on her own. What I saw of her was not possible. Even a Keeper could not have done what she did. Alone, it would be nearly impossible for me to do what she has done. No, there is a puppet master behind these puppet queens, and that is in the end who we must defeat."

Sometime later Avari opened her eyes and found herself staring at a clean, white ceiling. She was still warm and comfortable, a feeling she was quite unfamiliar with. Even the pain that was radiating through her ribs couldn't take away the comfort.

"Oh, you are awake," a quiet woman's voice said from beside her. She turned her head to see a tall, stick thin woman with a shock of bright blond hair standing beside her in a blue smock. She blinked her eyes wearily and wondered where she was.

"What's your name, dear?" she asked leaning over and peering into her face.

"A-A-Avari," she whispered.

The woman smiled, her face warm and kind. "Avari," she said, picking up a parchment on the rolling tray beside her. She dipped her quill into the ink and Avari could hear the scratching as she wrote the name quickly onto it. "And how old are you?"

Avari swallowed. Why was her throat so sore? "Twenty, my birthday's just past, on the Solstice."

Even as dazed as she was she saw the woman jerk her head up sharply and suck in a breath. "Twenty?" she repeated stiffly as though there were something stuck in her throat. "Twenty. Birthday, winter Solstice." The scratching continued as she wrote the information, she assumed. "Parents?"

Avari shook her head. "Don't know. My mom and dad have been gone since they left me with Dobius when I was four. Mom was taken to the Forge, and Dad went after her. They never came back."

Avari had never spoken these words to anyone. It felt odd to do so. The woman was staring at her now, not writing anymore. "And you, have the Mark. I assume with parents who were taken you are considered non-potential?"

Avari shrugged, desperately wanting to go to sleep. "I suppose. That's what they said when they took mom away, and when they took Ana."

The woman made a note on her parchment. "Who is Ana?"

"She had a mark, was Dobius's wife. After that, he wasn't the same," Avari whispered.

The woman scratched again. It was beginning to annoy Avari, she wanted to sleep. "Is that when it began?" she said, not looking up.

Avari was confused. "When what began?"

The woman looked up, one eyebrow cocked. "The neglect and abuse."

Avari didn't understand. "What do you mean?"

The woman set her parchment down and stared. "You are emaciated, skin and bones, you've been beaten many times, and now..." her voice trailed off.

Avari stared upward. "But I did bad things, I should have been better, grateful that Dobius gave me a home, all he wanted was me to stay quiet, to keep food on the table and a clean house. I couldn't do it properly, so he had to punish me."

The woman cleared her throat. "And today, when the boy attacked you like he did?" she asked, her voice terse and taking on a strange tone.

Avari started to cry again. "I should have listened. He's a man now, I shouldn't have run from him like I did. I shouldn't have kicked him, it was very bad to do so, after all him and his father do for me, I shouldn't have tried to get away. I...I don't deserve to be in this warm bed, I should be in my room," she whispered and tried to push away the covers from her badly broken body.

The tall woman carefully pushed her down onto the bed, and as Avari looked up at her face, there were tears glittering there.

"Stay here, please. Stay here. I'll be back in a moment."

Avari lay back down. She supposed she was going to get Dobius or Val. She had to apologize, she had done something so terrible. Weak, she was, to try to escape Val's desires. He was a man now, to do as wished. She turned her head to the side and saw the tall, thin woman speaking with a shorter, plumper woman in a set of purple robes. They were pretty she thought as a pain struck through her ribs causing her to sharply intake her breath. The thin woman looked upset, very upset, she thought. She supposed they were angry at her actions. But the warmth of the bed was too much, and sleep soon stole over her.

"So, you're saying we have to go to this House of Oracles?" Sanna said slowly once Elmlock and Keiara returned to the cavern with the massive pedestal.

Keiara nodded. "Yes, it's in the Wildlands. But I can't ask you to go all the way with us, because it will be incredibly dangerous going there. I have no guarantees we'll make it at all. After Miira leads us out of the underground, you are all free to go your separate ways. Elmlock and I will take the trek on our own."

"But how in the world are we going to get there?" Myrstand asked. "We only had one horse and wagon, and they're long gone after the attack forced us underground."

Keiara smiled slowly. "He's not lost, Maelstrom is nearby, outside the mountain range. But we will need help."

Sanna picked up her pack and tightened the straps and looked at Keiara. "Well, let's pack up, crew, we're wasting time. Let's get to this place as soon as we can."

The others all stood and did the same. "Agreed," they all said together.

Keiara smiled softly and glanced at Elmlock.

"I told you, Elmlock, they would insist on going with us," Keiara said.

"She's only twenty," the tall thin woman said to the shorter, plumper woman in the purple robes. Agna was the tall thin woman.

"What?" answered the other, Thress. "She's twenty? He told Horace she was seventeen and his sickly sister."

Agna snorted. "The only thing wrong with her is that she's been beaten, starved...and very nearly violated."

Thress looked at the bed, the girl was sleeping now. "What? Are you sure?"

"Thress, yes, I am very sure. Her legs were bruised and there were cuts on her thighs. She didn't say it, bt I'm sure the boy meant to violate her."

The plump purple clad Thress nodded. She swallowed hard. "Why? Why would a young man do something like that?"

Agna cocked her eyebrow. "She's been abused for a long time. She has more bones healed from untended fractures than I care to think of. I don't even think she can walk without a limp. As it is, she's had at least five ribs broken, her right hip was dislocated, and her arm was broken in two places. There's another injury, her hand, that looks to have healed a little, but wasn't from today."

Thress was silent for a long time. "Should I call the Regulators? She has the Mark..."

Agna didn't let her finish. "After what the girl's been through? No. She can't go to the forge in this condition and she's a Noppa anyway. We detected no trace when she came in. You know how careful they are, getting anyone with the Mark secreted away if they've got powers. Might as well send her to die if you send her there with no trace of magic. You know what they do there to the ones without powers."

The plump lady nodded. "Let's just heal her up first, then we'll decide where she should go..."

"She says it is her fault, too," Agna said with obvious disgust.

"What is?" Thress said, confused.

"Everything. Her being beaten, confined, and she thinks since this boy turned eighteen today, he had every right to take her, and she shouldn't have fought him. She thinks she should be punished."

"Oh dear," whispered Thress.

Lena stopped Keiara as the others filed out of the cave. "This shadow on the sun, who are they?"

Keiara looked at her closely for a second. "I don't know; they're beyond the Veil for me."

"I get the feeling we have to find them soon, maybe they are the prophet you created long ago," Lena said, looking at nothing in the distance. "I can see that much is possible through the Veil."

Keiara smiled and followed the others. "You are the Seer in Darkness, Lena. You would be the one who knows the best about this at this point."

Lena frowned. "But why?"

"Whatever do you mean?" Keiara said.

"Well, if you are all powerful, mother of gods, why can't you see through the Veil and why can I?" Lena asked, kicking a rock out of the way. "Why could you have not simply imbued yourself to see beyond the veil when you entered the mortal world?"

Keiara smiled again. "The Maker and Unmaker do not want any one being to have total power, because to do so can easily bring ruin on the world we are trying to save. That is why the Phoenix was split in six parts. The Phoenix was an Eternal, and they are a race of beings which brought many worlds to life, but also brought many worlds to ruin as well. Power does not know good nor evil, and without balance it can run rampant. Corruption and power go hand in hand, so thus the Phoenix was split as the progenitor on this world."

"I don't understand," Lena said slowly. "Why didn't the Phoenix just leave?"

Keiara smiled. "You are very astute. That would seem to be the obvious, wouldn't it? But the Phoenix brought the flame of life to the world, what came to be known as the Flame of Asumbar, the Phoenix had brought life, but not death. The cycle was incomplete. So, the Phoenix had to return with the flame of death, and this was also the Flame of Asumbar. Because of bringing both, the Phoenix became one with Avern itself, and being an Eternal, would be reborn even after being consumed by the Flame of Asumbar. So, the Maker and Unmaker split the Phoenix as it rose, sowing six seeds in Avern."

Lena nodded. Ahead of them, Jovan's attention had come to rest on their words as well. "I thought you said it was split into seven?" Jovan piped in.

"My, these students are quite good!" Keiara said with a grin. "I did, the Legend of the Seven Parts. Six Parts of the Phoenix came to be, Light, Dark, Earth, Air, Fire and Water, all the elements of life, but there is a seventh part. That part leads to the ultimate resurrection of the Phoenix as a whole. It is said that should the Phoenix be united with a seventh mortal host, the once great Phoenix will arise and defend Avern."

"So, is that what you have come back for?" Lena asked.

Keiara shook her head. "I do hope not!"

Jovan nearly stopped walking. "Why not?"

"The soul of the phoenix rests in a mortal when in this, the physical world, as I and Keiara have become one soul once death came to claim Keiara's soul. For the Phoenix to return, all six parts must be awakened, and a seventh mortal must be used as a vessel for all six souls, and then all the souls will join in the seventh body. Meaning all six would cease to be, because all six souls would become one," Keiara said with a smile.

"They'd all die?" Jovan asked, slightly horrified.

Keiara nodded. "It would take the ultimate sacrifice to bind that much power."

They walked in silence for a while, following Miira's lead along the myriad of tunnels. Lena's mind wandered for a bit, and then she stopped, supporting herself against the wall. To the others, her eyes glowed white in the dimly lit corridors. Her voice was scratchy and eerie sounding, and she appeared to have no knowledge of her surroundings.

"There is a place forgotten beyond reality where the godlings have gone."

Lena blinked to see both Jovan and Keiara kneeling beside her. She glanced from one to the other.

"I have no idea what that is supposed to mean," Lena said slowly.

Keiara shook her head. "Neither do I, but it was a message. I have no idea from whom, but it is something we must listen to."

CHAPTER THIRTEEN

THE WILDLANDS

So, it came to be, lo, the Wildlands were abandoned by those civil,
As the orcs, goblins, and wild beast ran rampant
Beside the creatures that changed between beasts and men.
Wildlands became fearsome and wild, no more a haven to us.
—*History of Avern by Tobus Fletcher, Chapter 8: The Wildlands*

❧

"Here we are," Miira said as they moved upward toward a light ahead of them in the tunnel.

Syera covered her eyes as they all emerged from the rocky underground world into the light of a midday sun shining off the white snows around them. Some of the snow was melting, and the temperature was not quite as cold as it had been when they had gone underground, but they had traveled much further south in that time.

"How do you come by knowing this?" Syera asked, wincing as she tried to uncover her eyes.

"We study escape routes to the surface from early on, in case we need 'em," Moryn answered for his sister. "There are many more than this, and of course the Noran do not know of them.

If they do, they are removed from our maps. Noran usually don't come above ground, though."

Syera stretched out and stared open eyed into the light for a long time before she finally allowed herself to close her eyes. "It is painful at first."

Moryn and Miira both clapped her on the back at the same time, nearly knocking her from her feet. She looked at them and found them both smiling at her. She knew how strange it was, for her to be here with dwarves of all people, but she had to change things in her homeland, for the better.

"It is good," she said, looking up again. "My eyes grow less painful."

Moryn smiled up at the sun. "Yeah, it does that. Give it a while, and it won't be painful at all. The surface is different, though, remember. There are dangers here you do not know of, and things look different."

Syera nodded. The others had come out behind them and now looked around. The exit had brought them out of the Burning Furies close to the border of the Wildlands and Phomean. They could see in the distance the guards at the border to keep the creatures of Wildlands out of the country of Phomean. Every mile or so there was a guard tower, staffed by at least two guards who took turns patrolling between their tower and the next one to the west of them.

Myrstand looked at them in the distance. "We'd best avoid the guards from Phomean. I'd rather avoid political questions at this point, especially with these four with us."

Syera, Miira and Moryn all stood together with Jovan who was explaining surface world details to them with gusto. Apparently, his horrific mental trials had not broken him, because he frequently laughed and made jokes at them as he instructed them. Lena and Sanna headed over to where they were to see what was so amusing.

"Too right," said Elmlock softly. "Phomean was already becoming xenophobic when I went underground, I can only imagine it has gotten worse. I do not think showing up with two dwarves, a Noran t'Kalima and a Whispara t'Kalima who looks like Jovan does now would bear good will towards the humans there. And if things have continued in the direction they were heading when I was last there, I'll be lynched as soon as looked at."

Keiara looked up at him. "Why would that be?"

He pointed to his eyes, shining and brilliant purple in the sunlight. "I'm sure you've heard of the Forge, as the Princess Keiara knew of it."

Keiara nodded. "Yes, that's information which came from the human experience. The dark phoenix had no knowledge of it, but Keiara was quite knowledgeable. Some sort of place to heighten the abilities of those with magical marks and training of wizards. They came once to see Sealla, but because she was the princess, they came to the castle to train her instead of sending her there. Father refused to allow her to leave."

"He was a smart man," Elmlock said, nodding. "That would be the public and political face of the Forge. I had my eye on the place for quite some time, and no person who entered ever came back out. In the years before I went underground, they started raiding towns and taking anyone who had the Marks, whether they had ever shown any power or not. It was not a pretty sight."

Keiara nodded. "I sensed as much, I knew something was not right, even as a child, when they came to talk to Father about Sealla's magical training. I can remember him arguing with the stuffy old wizard who came to the castle. They wanted to take her to the Forge to train her for five years, but Father would have nothing of it. They instead sent a tutor for about half the year. It was never the same guy, though, always a different wizard."

Jovan had found some strange appearing flowers that he was showing to the others. They were so happy, as though there was nothing strange going on, as if the military just to the north of them wouldn't kill them as soon as they saw them. Keiara smiled and looked to Elmlock.

"I've been away too long. I never expected to have to wait nearly a thousand years in mortal limbo before I was awakened. However, I suppose this awakening happened now for a reason," Keiara said and held up the rusty old sword. She looked at it as though it were the first time she'd seen it.

"Where in the wide world of Avern did you get that old thing? And why are you even carrying it?" Elmlock asked, staring at the old weapon.

Keiara shook her head. "Sealla killed me with it, so I figured it might have significance, and despite everything else, I've managed to keep it with me. Strange, but I feel like it is something I have to keep with me."

Myrstand nodded. "Strange, yes, but I think so too…"

Elmlock crossed his arms. "It is just after mid-morning. If I don't miss my mark, we should be at the House of Oracles after about a day's march. We might make it before midnight is high if we hurry, or we could head there and sleep for the night, then finish the trip by morning."

Keiara glanced at the rest of the group. Jovan was being sat on by Lena at the moment and they could hear him laughing. Lena giggled and slapped his head playfully. Beside them the dwarves shook their heads. Syera sat nearby laughing at their antics. Sanna watched leaning against a tree, but even from this distance, Keiara caught the smile on her face. Keiara herself smiled. Jovan was warming her heart that had grown so cold over the last few years. This was certainly good. But still, under that strong sheen of power, Sanna's heart was in pain and in desperate need of healing.

"Keiara?" Myrstand asked, dropping his hand on her shoulder startling her out of her reverie.

"Oh, let's not push everyone too hard. We'll move forward until dusk, then make camp when we find a good spot safe from the wilds around us," she said.

She smiled and stepped out and whistled shrilly through her thumb and index finger. Everyone startled at the sound. A group of birds went flying into the air nearby and everyone stood and stared. In a few moments, a large grey stallion with packs came meandering towards them. Jovan and Sanna exchanged glances.

"Maelstrom!" Sanna exclaimed and headed over to the horse.

Jovan approached and nuzzled with the horse, very glad to see him. Jovan looked over to Keiara. "But how? He bolted when we were attacked..."

"Maelstrom is a good horse, Jovan, and I gave him a little enchantment so he could follow us. He took the gentle paths while we were underground, and made it here," she said, patting the huge horse.

Introductions were made all around, and both the dwarves and Syera eyed the horse very suspiciously. Myrstand managed to find a shirt for Jovan and found a few healing salves to heal up the rest of his open wounds. Once they were all suitably equipped from what had remained on Maelstrom, they headed out, south towards the House of Oracles. Or at least, everyone hoped Elmlock was leading them to the right place.

"Sedate him, quickly!" Avari heard nearby, waking her from her fitful sleep.

Avari turned her head to see a boy thrashing wildly in the bed next to her. She couldn't see much, other than his rough and wild gray hair. The sounds coming from the bed sounded more like growling and animal sounds. She watched as the nurses sedated him with something in a needle and his thrashing calmed slowly.

The nurses murmured in their subtle way. Avari only caught whispers of voices from them as they passed by. She tried to stretch and then remembered they had bound her to the bed because she'd tried to leave several times. She was tired of being here. They'd counseled her again and she understood she could not go back to where she had lived. Both her adopted father and brother had been jailed. She vaguely understood she was not at fault, but she could not help but pine for someone to take care of like she had done for so long.

She turned her head to look at the young man beside her. She blinked wondering if she was seeing things. He had dog ears. Silvery gray triangular ears sitting on top of his head, his gray mess of hair puffed up around them slightly giving him a slightly comical look. His face was smooth and a brown shade with a button nose in the center. His eyes were closed, but they were graced with thick lashes. Underneath his button nose, a boyish mouth hung half open, his tongue lolling half out, and she could see his teeth were sharp and pointed, and slightly feral. He wore a healing house robe and his feet stuck awkwardly out from under the white sheet, his toes bearing nails that looked more like claws. He wasn't quite human, but his visage was not fearful at all.

Moments later, the nurse, Agna was her name, came back and strapped him to the bed in much the same way as Avari herself was bound. She feigned sleep so she could listen.

"Is he a demon?" a younger nurse asked Agna.

"No, of course not, he's one of those from the Wildlands, just part beast, is all," she answered, yanking the straps tight to his wrists and his ankles.

"Well what do we do with him?" she asked softly.

Agna snorted. "Treat him, of course. He's been run through by a sword in the belly."

"But..."

"No buts, Nellis, treat the boy," Agna said.

"And then? Aren't we supposed to report outsiders?"

Agna sighed. "We aren't doing anything until he's well."

Avari turned her eyes and watched the nurses leave. She then turned her head back to watching the boy again. His eyes fluttered and opened, and she found herself even more enamored of him. His eyes were beautiful and vertically slit, like a cat, and one, the right, was vivid blue, and the left was bright green. He blinked several times, and surely should not have woken up after a few moments with the shot they'd given him.

He murmured slowly. "Hey, who are you?"

"Avari," she said quietly.

"Wilder is my name," he said smiling, baring what on anyone else would have been fearsome fangs. "I know why I'm locked down, what about you?"

"I just want to leave," she said sadly. "But I'm Marked so they'll take me to the Forge soon anyway."

Wilder snorted, "Yeah, well, if I'm lucky that's where I'll go. They don't take to Wildlanders here in south Phomean. That's how I got skewered by some idiot guard while I was out hunting in the north of our lands."

"So, I guess we're both doomed," Avari said softy, turning her gaze back to the ceiling.

Wilder sighed deeply looking upward as well. "So it would seem."

The trip was thankfully uneventful under the sun. Jovan managed to hunt using an old bow they'd brought with them from underground and managed to kill a couple rabbit like creatures they boiled and made stew with some root vegetables they found. They paused for a lunch for a little while then moved on again. They saw a few wild animals, but luckily, with the winter, most the wildest and fiercest beasts were hibernating. Jovan was interested in every tree and brush he found, trying to identify it as best he could, but trying not to hold them up with his interests in local flora and fauna.

As the night started to fall, they built a camp fire and Jovan looked around to see if he could find some more small snow hares for dinner, and was not disappointed. They sat around and hoped the night would also pass uneventfully, because they really did not want any run ins with anything else. Jovan stood outside the ring with the others and stared at the moon.

"What's on your mind?" Sanna said, walking up behind him.

He smiled and spoke, still staring at the waning moon. "Oh, just thinking about the nights like this when my sister and I would sneak out and sit under the moonlight until my father came to find us."

Sanna was quiet for a moment. "When you were in the Anaset?"

Jovan nodded. "Yeah, I'm the seventh born of my family, the youngest. Jokara was my closest sister. My father was very old when I was born, so I was young when he died. I miss Jokara the most because I know she won't be there if I ever return."

"Is she the one you couldn't save?" she asked softly.

"What, how do you?" Jovan stammered, turning to her.

"You've said it a couple times, about not being able to help 'her'. I'm sorry if you don't want to talk..." she said and turned to go back to the fire.

Jovan put a hand on her shoulder. "No, no, it's fine. No, that's her. When Cage had captured me, he took me to this Elf head hunter's house, and he had her head mounted to the wall. Cage has delighted in using her death to sway me to give up to him."

"How so?" she asked, as Jovan's eyes went back to the moon.

"He has this ability to get into someone's memories, and he did that to the elf hunter when I escaped him because he killed him and his wife, so he's replayed the scene from the hunter's memory. And now since I know one of my brothers was here, he's using that. I still don't know why they were looking for me. There were six others who should have been given the... well. It doesn't matter," Jovan said, sighing.

Sanna nodded but said nothing more, merely put her arm around his shoulders as he stared at the moon. She felt his sadness and knew he would talk more if she asked, but she knew that pain. It was a pain you could only release when it as ready to be released. Sanna herself had not come to the point when she could release the pain herself. For a long while, the fire flickering at their backs, they stood in silence and watched the moon. Such a tranquil winter night it was that they could have been alone for the entire world. They of course were not.

There was a flurry of excitement that woke both Wilder and Avari early in the morning. Wilder tried to jump to his feet but found himself tied down still.

"Dammit, what's happening?" he growled. "I hate the fact I can't get up."

Wilder's bonds had been tightened to include a belt restraint, thigh and bicep restraints, and a neck restraint. He was quite strong. Avari glanced slowly over where the commotion was coming from.

"A demon for sure," one of the nurses exclaimed loudly.

Agna shouted. "Be quiet, all of you. Take him to the back behind the curtain and treat him."

In a moment, the curtain which separated Wilder and Avari from the other patients moved, and a man was brought in on a litter. He was lifted onto the bed next to Avari. She turned her face slowly as a tall, thin man was laid there. Her eyes were fixated on his left eye though, open for some reason though he was unconscious. His other eye was closed. It was like nothing she had ever seen. Where it should have been white it was bright yellow, and where it should have been colored it was bright red. Like Wilder, his eye was vertically slit. His hair was long and a deep blue in color, and pooled around his head, but she could see it was bloody on the other side. He was wearing the shredded remains of an officer's uniform from the Phomean army.

"But Nurse Agna, he's obviously..." the young blonde nurse started to say.

Agna turned and slapped her squarely, causing both Wilder and Avari to jump in their bonds.

"We treat the sick, no matter who they are. Treat him. Just like these other two, when they are well, we turn the over to their fates, but while they are in my care, they will be treated," she hissed. "Do not even begin to argue with me. I know he's been impersonating an officer. I know he's probably a murderer. I know he's probably going to be shot once they come get him. But for now, he's in MY care, and he's going to be treated, and I don't care if they're going to execute him later! They're all in my care for now, no matter what ill fate awaits them when they leave here!"

Every nurse in the place was staring at the enclosed section of the room. They all knew who they were talking about. And they all knew how Agna felt about her patients, no matter who they were. They all knew it was breaking her heart to know that all those in the enclosed area of the house would probably be dead once they left Agna's healing house.

The young blonde nurse gasped and backed out of the curtained area. Agna slowly sighed and sat down on a short chair, and found herself being stared at by six eyes, including the newest one, his other eye, a brilliant deep blue color, fixed on her. She stared at each set of eyes in turn. The poor girl, her violet eyes shining with tears. The boy, his one eye blue, other green, showing for the first-time real fear since he'd come here. And the demonic man looked at him too, awake now it appeared, his one blue eye, his other demon eye, fixing her with a look that could only be described as pained.

"I'm so sorry..." she whispered and left.

Avari turned toward the new arrival and watched as his head slumped back down to the bed, his white bandages around his head already staining red from his wounded head. She turned her head and stared at Wilder. He shrugged as best as he could as restrained as he was. He'd known his life would end once the sword had run him through; being treated here only delayed the inevitable.

Jovan woke with a start. He swore he heard something nearby. He grabbed his bow and stood up, moving quietly as he could away from the fire. Why was no one else awake, he wondered to himself. He heard the sound again, it sounded like a large creature whatever it was. He looked back at the fire and saw no one was moving at all. There was a strange feeling on the air though, and as he pushed back the foliage, he felt it rebound on him suddenly. He blinked, and he was sitting in the tavern where he'd seen Sanna for the first time. Only he was watching from across the room.

He saw himself and Cage enter the room, talking and laughing. His wrist was bound, and he knew they had just come from the healing house where a small amount of a healing draught was given to him. Of course, then he had no idea it was only a mild pain reducer and wasn't a healing medicine at all. He watched, feeling strange as he viewed himself. He wanted to stand up and tell himself to leave, get away from him, but he was rooted to the chair he was in.

"Funny, huh, watching yourself?" a familiar voice whispered in his ear.

"Why am I seeing this?" Jovan whispered back, feeling his breath on his neck now.

Cage moved and sat beside him. "Just keep watching, my lovely elf boy."

Jovan watched as the familiar scene played out before him. But this time, he noticed something he had not seen when he sat beside Cage. Cage got their drinks, but paused, and dropped something into the mug of ale. Jovan frowned and turned to the Cage beside him.

"Oh yes, I was drugging you. I bought it before we left the healing house, a little sedative, told them you'd be in so much pain you wouldn't be able to rest, so the obliged and gave me enough for a week's use. I just dropped two does into your drink there," Cage whispered into his ear.

Jovan watched as Cage sat the drink down and they toasted mugs and told various stories of adventures they'd seen in their lifetimes. Jovan watched with a keen eye this time, not clouded by the thought Cage was his friend. He noticed the sideways glances he passed at him.

"Jovan, you getting sleepy yet, my friend? I booked us each a room, you know," the past Cage said.

Jovan watched himself smile and shake his head, "No, friend, let me buy a round this time!"

Jovan caught Cage's confused look as Jovan got up and returned with another round of ale. Sanna had just walked in, catching Jovan's attention, and Cage took the chance to drop some more of the drug into his drink.

"Two doses this time. I was wondering why you were still conscious about then. Then your little red head girlfriend came in, and I too was distracted," Cage whispered in his ear.

Jovan watched again, still feeling strange about watching himself, and this time, he saw his eyes starting to droop slowly. He caught himself and after the damage Sanna left in her wake watched the owner clean up the mess. After things were back to normal once more, Cage turned to Jovan again.

"Are you certain sleep does not come yet, you've been through a lot these last few days, you should really rest," Cage said softly.

"No, shall I get us another round?" Jovan said, feeling the effects of the ale as his head grew fuzzy.

Cage's look, though back then Jovan could not see it, could have shot flames. "No, my friend, I will get it, you stay here."

Cage went to the barkeeper and got another pair of ales and he watched as he dumped what had to be the last two doses of the powder into the ale.

"By this time, I wasn't sure why you weren't unconscious or dead, and quite frustrated, as I'm sure you can imagine," Cage whispered into his ear.

Jovan didn't like being frozen in place like this as he sat in a chair watching himself, but Cage gripped his shoulders tightly. "Ah, the good part, watch close and we'll follow!"

Jovan saw he was more than tipsy. His head drooped and bobbed. Only a few ales would not have set drunkenness on him like this.

Cage helped him to his feet, whispering encouragements and helping him walk. Jovan's feet stumbled, and he nearly fell several times. Had it not been for Cage holding him up he would have fallen flat on his face and stayed there passed out. As it was, Cage practically dragged him up the stairs and dropped him onto a raggedy looking bed. Jovan and Cage had somehow followed them and was now hovering over the head of the bed watching.

"I love this part," Cage whispered harshly into Jovan's ear.

Jovan watched as Cage pulled his boots off his feet as he murmured softly in his sleep. Jovan barely moved as Cage then crawled on top of him, straddling his stomach, and turning his head from one side to the other. He then yanked off the cap he was wearing and leaned back and started to laugh.

"You see it all made sense now, why I couldn't knock you out with the medicine, you were an elf, and that meant without a special medicine, I couldn't put you out easily. So, with the drug and the alcohol, it finally took effect, and you dropped out, but there's more!" Cage explained.

"What the hells did you do to me?" Jovan asked, disgusted.

"Oh, don't worry, nothing bad, I enjoy screaming too much to do anything while my lovelies are unconscious..." Cage whispered harshly in his ear again.

Cage leaned over him and brushed his hair from his face and stared at him in the dimly lit room. He then opened Jovan's mouth and leaned over as though to kiss him, but Jovan's point of view shifted, and he could see clearly from his mouth a smoke began to roil. Then, a pale ghostly snake emerged from his mouth and slithered into Jovan's open one. Once the snake was gone a second puff of smoke issued forth, this time from Jovan's mouth. His unconscious body began to recoil at the intrusion, and as Cage slipped off his body to the floor, he began to convulse violently. Cage sat down in a nearby chair and calmly waited.

"I was waiting, you see," Cage said, the point of view now from above the bed again. "Very few survive what I did to you. I was a little worried after I saw you were an elf, thinking you might not be able to handle it. Most humans die within the first moments."

"What is it?" he asked as he watched his own body continue to convulse wildly on the bed, and he wondered when it would finally stop, because it would obviously since he was still alive.

A smoky puff issued from his mouth every few moments, along with a black liquid substance that was running down his chin and face. Finally, the convulsing started to ease off and then to his horror, he vomited a huge amount of bright red blood onto the floor beside the bed. Jovan was horrified, but in the scene, he was watching he couldn't do anything. There was a knock at the door.

"Sir, is everything alright, the man on your left heard something..."

Cage went to the door and opened it. He smiled his gregarious smile and shook his head. "Oh, I'm sorry we disturbed him, it's been a while since we've had our own bed, if you know what I mean!"

The innkeeper looked at him for a moment. "Keep it down or you'll be out on the street."

"Of course, of course!"

Cage returned and took care to clean up the blood on the floor, and then took rags and wiped off Jovan's face. He took his shoes and dropped them from the second story window of the Inn, and then began to wrap rope around Jovan's ankles and wrists, the way it had been when he woke up in the wagon. He gagged him tightly and then lifted him from the bed and dropped him onto the floor. He tossed the extra blanket over him, then put himself into the bed for the night.

Things became fuzzy and the sun was streaming in through the window as morning dawned. Cage stood up slowly and stretched and glanced over at Jovan where he laid on the floor. He kicked him squarely in the ribs, and Jovan didn't move at all. Cage smiled, and the world spun to show outside as Cage murmured over the cart for a moment. There was a poof of black smoke and a small cracking sound. Cage emerged and headed up to the room. A short while later he came back with a bundle wrapped in the blanket from the room, and Jovan knew he was moving him. He disappeared into the wagon, then began tossing the hay into the back, over the top of where Jovan then slept.

Jovan now stood in the middle of the road, watching the wagon pulling away to begin what had become one of the most horrific trials in his lifetime. He reached out, tried to scream out to anyone, but his voice was gone, and he was rooted to the road where he stood. The world spun out of control and for a while, he was sure he would be sick. There was a thunking sound and he blinked to find himself once again chained to the wall of a stone.

"I like you like this," Cage said, sitting on his heels in front of him. "Now, submit, and this will be over."

"I'm not submitting to you or anyone else!" Jovan said with a growl in his voice. "I don't care what you do to me in my head, I'm not coming to you of my own will. If you want me, come and get me. Just come and kill me and stop all this. Why all these games?"

Cage smiled. "I like these games, but also you have to come to me, that's just the way he wants it."

"Who? And what did you do to me in the Inn anyway? What was that thing?" Jovan asked, struggling against the bonds that held him.

"I can't tell, and it's a little trick I call the Zyphius. Yes, it is a living thing, something I called from outside this realm, and it's right here," he said poking him on the forehead. "As long as it is there, you are bound to me and won't be able to escape my grasp, so there really is no use in trying. I won't kill you, I'll just continue to do this and make you miserable until you come to me."

Jovan shook his head. "Never."

"Have it your way, our time tonight ends, but I'll leave you with this," Cage said.

From the ground, black, green and yellow striped snakes began to rise and wrap around Jovan's legs. He squirmed and struggled against them and held back his fear as they crawled over him one after another. He wouldn't give in to fear. But then, once again, they all rose up and sunk their fangs into his flesh, injecting poison into his body. He gritted his teeth against the unbearable pain. When Cage saw he wasn't giving in, he struck him with the whip which sent the horrific images spiraling through his mind. With both of them warping his mind and body he couldn't bear it much longer and finally released the scream pent up inside.

"Jovan!" came a familiar voice, piercing through the haze of pain in his mind and body. "Jovan, wake up! Please!"

He was sucking in a gasping breath and his vision cleared and he was staring into Sanna's emerald eyes and Keiara's black ones. He took gasping gulps of air and looked around to see the rest of their group all standing around staring at him with concern faces. The dawn was just now breaking, and he was laying where he had laid down to sleep last night, having never moved from the spot.

"I...oh. Again," he said, grinning sheepishly at them.

Just then there was a howling from nearby. The noise had drawn predators, and he knew it.

"Quick, to your feet, we're surrounded by now, they're Bracken Wolves, double the size of normal ones, and three times as vicious," Myrstand said with a glance around them.

Jovan started to stand, his legs, shaking still. "Jovan, no, stay here," Keiara said. "We can handle this, you aren't in any shape to fight right now."

She turned to Sanna and Lena, "You two stay here with him, we don't know if he'll be attacked again, with these wolves around."

With that her great black wings unfurled, and she set off into the direction of the nearest howls. The others all engaged them as well. From Jovan's left there was a grunt and he looked up just in time to see a enormous wolf jump directly for him. Of course, he was the injured one of the group, making him their target as the weakest member of the pack; it was basic animal instinct.

With one swift blow, Sanna knocked it away, cracking a bone or two in its ribcage in the process. Lena likewise took one on, only she did so hand to hand, the wolf screaming in pain as the claws she could bear when she took a mind to it sliced deeply into the animal. Jovan scrambled to his feet but fell swiftly to his knees, completely unable to stand up on his own. Sanna and Lena were both busy with wolves, and he saw another one stalking them that they couldn't see. He crawled to his belongings and managed to grab a bow and an arrow from the weapons they'd gotten from Syera. He quickly knocked one just as the wolf pounced at him. He managed to get it off, straight through the beast's forehead, but its momentum carried it forward where it landed on top of him with a thudding sound.

"Jovan!" Sanna exclaimed after braining the one she was fighting with the staff.

She looked around and suddenly they all began leaving, retreating, and Sanna saw the broad white stripe running down the back of the wolf which had landed on Jovan. She gasped. The packleader. Both her and Lena ran toward Jovan and started heaving the huge beast off of him with all their might, and finally it fell backward. Jovan lay very quietly on the ground, covered in blood from head to toe, but it was not clear if it was his own blood or the beast's.

"Jovan," Sanna said softly, kneeling beside him as the others began returning from their positions. "Are you alive?"

There was a long pause and then he gasped air, nearly arching his back completely off the ground. There was a collective sigh because he was a sight to see. He began breathing heavily and looked around at the others who stared down at him with concerned faces. He reached up and wiped his face and made a very disgusted face at the blood that came away coating his hands.

"Hey, look at that, it's not mine this time!" he said and grinned a very grim looking smile. "I really need a bath now..."

Sanna smirked and shook her head and looked up at Keiara. "I think there's a small stream over to the east a little way which runs out of a mountain spring," Miira said, almost smiling herself.

In short order, they packed up camp and headed that way, and by then, Jovan's body had started to cooperate again. They found the small stream easily enough, but the pool it created was only about waist deep and barely big enough for one person to fit into. Jovan had to get the blood smell off of him, or he really would be attracting predators at an astonishing rate.

Myrstand handed him a chunk of soap and promised to bring back a pile of dry clothes since the ones he had were practically ruined. Jovan sighed and peeled the shirt off of him, wincing as he got to his ribs. Where the wolf had landed on him, he was sure he had a broken rib or two. Now as he stood beside the water and looked down, the huge black bruise on his right side confirmed it. He sighed. Just what he needed, already a burden on them, and now this too. He wouldn't let them know, because he wouldn't slow them down any more.

He gingerly peeled away the pants he'd been wearing, both legs were pretty much shredded, and stuck to him with prickles of his own blood where they had taken a raking from the wolf's giant back legs when he fell. He glanced down, seeing there were indeed a pair of matching rake marks down his legs, one beginning on his thigh, the other starting around his calf. He carefully stepped into the freezing water and started shivering.

"I hate w-w-wint-ter here..." he muttered as he began soaping his hair and his upper body up.

"Oh, you do?" a voice said from behind him. He turned to see Sanna standing there with a pile of clothing for him.

"H-how long have you b-been th-th-there?" he said, scrubbing furiously as his face turned red. He couldn't stop, he had to clean himself and the only option was this freezing pond.

Sanna smiled and sat down. "Not long, just enough to hear you hate winter."

He nodded and quickly finished his upper body and turned to the side, only to hear Sanna gasp slightly. He looked at her and realized she could see and was staring at the huge bruise on his right side.

"It's just a bruise, its fine," he said, trying to be strong about the whole thing.

"It's broken ribs, is what it is, why didn't you say something?" she asked, standing up.

Jovan snorted and stepped upward on the slope to clean his lower half, forcing Sanna to turn quickly about, hiding a blush in her own face. He scrubbed his legs and lower body rapidly and then eased back into the water to rinse the soap off of him and his hair. He dunked himself under and rubbed the soap from his hair and then came back up to see Sanna watching him as though she was waiting for him to not come up.

"I'm fine," he said. "Do you have a blanket or something to dry with?"

She smiled. "I'm all you need to dry off."

She turned her back again, and he climbed his way out of the water and stood behind her. "How's that?" he said in her ear.

She almost started, then held out a hand and a flame blossomed in it. She breathed into it and a warm wind began swirling in her hand instead, and washing over Jovan's ice cold body.

"I've got to turn around, but I'll close my eyes," she said, with a cheeky grin.

He stood for a moment and waited as she turned, as promised, with her eyes closed, and continued holding the funnel of heated air in her hand. In a few moments he was dry and incredibly warm all except his hair. He reached out and took the clothes and she put down her hand. As he pulled on the

255

white shirt, she opened one eye, unable to resist, then closed it quickly before he noticed. He pulled on the fresh brown pants and the leather boots and then grabbed the thick cloak he'd been wearing.

"Okay, I no longer smell like a dead animal," he said smiling, as Sanna opened her eyes.

"That's a good thing, are you ready to head out?"

"Of course," he said raising his arms and wincing.

Sana didn't say anything, but she noticed it as they headed away back toward the others.

Keiara and Elmlock stood together nearby watching quietly. As the two headed back they exchanged glances with each other.

"What has him, Elmlock?" Keiara asked. "There is something maintaining the connection between him and this Cage. Something physical because all the mental barriers I put up don't make a difference at all."

Elmlock nodded. "You have the means to find out."

"Lena."

"Yes, she's the only one with functional Sight right now, and I have a dread feeling I know what has been used against him. Had the Veil not fallen, it would be apparent to both you and me, but as it is we are blind."

"You know it was essential to bring down the Veil, Elmlock, do not pester me on the issue."

"I'm sorry, I don't like being blinded, that's all. Without Sight and Prophecy, I feel as though I am powerless," he said, breathing a deep sigh.

"I understand, but remember how powerless our enemies are," Keiara said watching as Sanna and Jovan sat down with the others.

"I know, Gram, believe me, but right now, I'd give anything to have those powers to figure out who has a hold on your friend there."

Keiara nodded and sighed. So would she.

CHAPTER FOURTEEN

FREEDOM FROM CAGES

We strive to reach for freedom from our cages.
Cages wherever we look, in our minds, hearts and souls,
We can be caged beasts without bars or chains to bind us,
We can be caged in our own minds just as easily,
And it is we who hold the keys.
-Mantarose Vertrue, Last Prophet of Darna

W ilder woke with a start. He smelled someone close by him, and he recognized her scent immediately. He opened his eyes, preparing to strain against his bonds, only to find his arms slipped free from the strap on his right wrist. He didn't see anyone and whipped his head either direction. The room was dark, the dead of night, and he heard Avari and the new man sleeping soundly beside him. He held up his clawed left hand and found he could just reach the bonds at his upper arm on the right and began digging at them furiously. Soon enough, the leather strap on his right snapped through, and he quickly cut through the rest of his bonds, though not carefully. He felt the blood running from various cuts from his own tearing. He grabbed the sheet and wrapped it around him, the thin robe not much to cover him.

He dropped to his knees beside the girl next to him, so sad and lonely, and ripped through the wrist straps and the ankle straps.

"Wilder?" she whispered, sitting up, rubbing her wrists.

"Shh, don't talk, just get up, we have to get out of here, they're coming for us tomorrow morning, remember?" he said in a rushed whisper and he crawled from her bed to the blue haired man.

He sliced through his bonds quickly and shook him to groggy wakefulness. Wilder wrapped his sheet around him and looked over to see Avari doing the same.

"Wake up, friend, we're getting out of here," Wilder said pulling him to a sitting position.

Aside from the eye and the oddly shaded hair, this fellow looked normal, though his ears were more pointed than most humans. Wilder pulled him to his feet, though he stood a good foot taller than him, and grabbed Avari's wrist. He pulled back the curtain and saw the night nurses seated around the table near the door, but they were all sleeping. Wilder arched a brown and shrugged at his two sheet clad companions.

The moon gazed through the window as the trio headed through the maze of sleeping patients. They paused to stare at the nurses who were indeed out cold, snoring quite loudly. They slipped in a line, hand in hand from the doorway into the frozen world outside. Without clothes or shoes, though, Wilder knew they wouldn't last long out here. He motioned them toward the nearby trees.

"Okay, so why she let me go, I don't know," Wilder said quietly.

"Who?" Avari asked.

Wilder smiled at them. "Nurse Agna, I didn't see her, but I smelled her, she loosened one of my wrist straps enough that I cut the rest myself."

The blue haired man leaned heavily on the tree behind him. "What's your name?" Wilder asked. "You've been out since you got to the healing house."

He nodded, touching his still bandaged head gingerly. "Hinto," he said softly. "I'm still not clear, and I don't really remember what happened..."

Avari smiled. "That's okay, Hinto, I'm Avari, and this is Wilder. I think we were all due to be shipped out come morning to meet our unlucky fates."

Suddenly Hinto realized they could see his strange eye. "Oh, you must think I'm a monster," he said, covering his eye with his hand.

Wilder snorted. "No more than me, friend." He pointed to the doggish ears on his head.

Hinto smiled and dropped his hand. "I guess you're right, we're all pursued by those who hate us for being different, aren't we?"

Avari shivered. "What now? We're close to the Wildlands, aren't we Wilder? Can we hide somewhere there?"

Wilder smiled. "I know a place, not far from the border that my people call cursed, and the humans don't dare go near it."

Hinto looked a bit worried. "Is it really cursed?"

Wilder smirked. "I don't know, but nothing's ever bothered me there, so I am pretty sure it's safe. It is maybe a day's trip from here. First, we steal some clothes though, and you guys need shoes before your toes freeze off."

It didn't take long to find an army barracks. Wilder shushed them and snuck in through a window. His small frame moved easily and quickly through the cold snow-covered ground leaving nearly no trace. He returned in a few moments with clothes for them. They each pulled on a pair of pants and shirt, and a long woolen cloak. He had found boots for both of them.

"Don't you need shoes?" Avari asked as she laced the boots.

Wilder smiled. "Nah, I rather have my feet free. I have furry feet when I need them."

To Avari's amazement, a thick coat of gray fur began to grow on his feet and the backs of his hands. Hinto just stared, keeping his strange yellow and red eye shut.

"Here, Hinto," Wilder said, handing him an eye patch he'd found. "I noticed you close your eye when you're awake, so I got this for you."

Hinto held it for a minute and looked up with tears in his eyes. Avari and Wilder exchanged glances as he knuckled the tears from his eyes. He sniffed loudly and smiled at them, slipping the eye patch over his demonic looking eye and pushing his long bluish hair behind his ears.

"Sorry, I'm just used to people running from me. Half breeds like me aren't accepted anywhere, you know."

Wilder smiled. "Oh, well, we're all unique here so you're in good company."

He glanced at them. "You're some kind of half beast, but you look fine, dear, just a human girl..."

Avari nodded shyly. "My eyes are the Mark of a sorcerous ability. No one is born with this color who is allowed to walk free, even though I've never had any powers."

Hinto, who stood at least a foot and a half over Avari's slight frame, clapped her gently on the back. "At least your mother wasn't a succubus that abandoned you after you were born with a father convinced you were unclean..."

Wilder and Avari exchanged a very apprehension filled glance as the taller Hinto walked past them looking around. Neither one knew how to react to the statement.

"Oh, don't worry, I don't expect your pity, I just mean, there are worse scenarios for all of us. Being different in this world isn't easy, especially right now. I have my mother's blood, but I also have my father's as well, and I spend every day trying to prove I am more than the demon which lives inside me, unfortunately, it has been met with varying success over the years," Hinto said and turned his near six and a half foot tall frame back to look at the two young people before him.

"You two can't be more than sixteen turns," he said, as if suddenly realizing they weren't very old.

"I'm twenty-two turns," Wilder said and stood to his full five-foot eight inches height. "And I'm more than capable of taking care of myself, thanks."

Avari shrank. "I am twenty turns as of the Solstice, and I've never been alone in the world. It is so big to me, and I just want to find a small corner to hide in until I find some way to live."

Hinto kneeled before the young woman and cupped her face gently. She started and began to pull away but his hand was warm against her face.

"Avari, I see the pain life has brought you, but that's over. You're with us now, and Wilder is strong, and I am strong, but most of all, even though you don't know it yet, you are strong," Hinto said and his voice was intoxicating, and she nearly felt herself drawn into his arms even though he didn't pull her toward him.

He stood up quickly. "I'm sorry, sometimes it happens when I am impassioned, I'm sorry."

He stood back, and patted his pockets looking for something frantically. Avari stared at him strangely, the moment his contact with her face was broken, the strange feeling of wanting to be in his arms left completely.

"It's my demonic blood. A succubus uses seduction to bring males and females to her. When I touch anyone flesh to flesh it happens. It isn't really something I can control, but I usually wear gloves because of it. I just forgot, it won't happen again," he said, turning his head in shame.

Avari grasped his hand of her own will suddenly. His eye widened, and he gasped, beginning to pull away from her.

"I know," she said quietly, and dropped his hand once more, unfazed by the demonic ability he had. He frowned, his smooth brow furrowing.

"Well, that explains why you're so perfect, there, blue hair," Wilder said, leaning against a tree.

"What?" Hinto asked, confused, finally finding gloves in the coat's pockets.

Wilder walked up to him. "All this," he said, motioning around him. "Your skin is perfectly smooth and cream colored, your hair falls nicely no matter what condition you're in, and you are tall, with an ideal body type, broad shoulders, thin hips. Your ma was a succubus, aren't they supposed to be 'perfect' women when men see them and fall for them?"

Hinto nodded. "Yes, they are the ideal of whoever looks upon them, whatever that ideal may be. But that is only the surface, underneath, they are twisted, ugly creatures, and not something you ever want to see."

Wilder nodded. "We better get going, the sun is rising, and they're going to send out army patrols. If we hurry, we can make it by the time night falls again. We're so close to the border here with the Wildlands that we'll cross over before the sun is high in the sky. Come, let's go."

With that, the trio of forgotten and forlorn souls headed out away from the large healing house of Agna Starbrightner. Far above, though none of them knew it, she watched them. She knew questions would be asked today when the Regulators arrived for the girl, and when the general arrived for the demon and the beast. She looked down to her arm, where deep furrows were cut into it from the beastly boy's claws. Of course, he had been unconscious when she used his claws to cut herself with them. She headed downstairs and into the curtained area. She took a knife from her belt and reopened the claw wounds so the blood flowed and rammed her head into the shelf behind and blood flowed over her face and clothes.

A moment later after she felt enough blood was let she screamed. Two nurses, looking groggy still from the sleeping draught they'd had came running in.

"Sister Agna!" one screamed. "What happened?"

"They've escaped!" she cried, slowly standing. "I don't know how long I was out..."

Keiara and Elmlock finally came back to the others and Keiara whispered something to Lena.

"Jovan, come here," Keiara said when she stood.

He looked up from his morning meal of winter berries and tact bread and nodded. He went over to Keiara, followed closely by Sanna. Keiara read the look on Sanna's face behind him, one of worry at what she was about to say. Jovan ran a hand through his hair.

"Look I understand if you don't want me with you anymore, I mean, it's okay," he began.

Keiara placed a gentle hand on his shoulder and pushed his downward gaze up into her face. "No one is leaving anyone behind, Jovan."

He looked at her with pain in his eyes and she knew that part of him had wished it were so that they would leave him behind, so he would not be responsible for them. So, they would not have to care for him. Elmlock came up beside him and sat down. Keiara, Elmlock and Lena sat, motioning the others to do the same, as the rest of the group had quickly congregated on the spot.

"I should not have tried to make this anywhere near private, I see, so it is, we are of course worried about you, Jovan," Keiara said, smiling. "So, we are going to see what is going on. Well, Lena will See, that is, since Elmlock and I don't have the capability currently."

Jovan sat down sheepishly. "Um, I hope it's not too painful, I've had enough of that lately..."

Lena stood up beside him. "Of course not, just sit there so I can take a look at you and see if there is anything out of the ordinary which is beyond normal vision. I'm not so good at this yet, this making it happen on purpose..."

Elmlock patted her on the arm from beside her. "Just concentrate on him and will yourself to see past reality into what is just out of the range of normal vision."

Lena closed her eyes for a while and as the rest watched, a soft glow began to emanate from around her eyes. She opened them slowly, and her eyes were white with the power of vision she had brought into existence, but as soon as she opened her eyes, she wanted to close them. She let out a yelp and stepped backward, falling over and landing on the ground open mouthed.

"What do you see Lena?" Keiara asked, glancing at Elmlock.

"It...I can't believe how you can't see this, it..." Lena sat and stared, unable to really comprehend what she was seeing. During episodes of sight, she could see the world around her, though it was hazy. What wasn't hazy was the things that couldn't been seen by normal sight. Jovan's form was grayed and blurry, but the bright yellow, black and green snake twining its way around his body was brilliant and visible. From the crown of head, the head of the snake emerged, almost the same size as

Jovan's head, and fanged with gigantic fangs dripping a thick, viscous yellow liquid.

"What is it, Lena?" Keiara asked. "Turn off the sight, relax and see only the real world."

Lena breathed deeply and closed her eyes. Slowly the whitish glow dissipated, and she was staring only at the normal Jovan, sitting looking at her confused, without a huge grotesque snake emerging from his head. She walked up to him and touched his head and his arms where she had seen the snake.

"Amazing, how can I not even feel the presence now?" she breathed. Jovan looked at her with utter confusion.

"I'm sorry, Jovan, I'm sorry," she said and sat down beside Jovan, still staring at him intently.

"What is there something growing out of my head or something?" he said and touched his head.

Lena swallowed. "I'm sorry, but yes, a snake."

There was a set of collective murmurs from around the group. "A snake?" he asked, his eyes wide.

"I saw this huge snake's head growing out of the top of your head, with huge fangs dripping yellow venom, and then it was wrapped around your body, the tail coming from your back and coiling around you, and it was truly horrible, because it looked like it had burst out through your skull..." she said and looked at Keiara and Elmlock.

"What color was it?" Elmlock asked quietly.

"Yellow, green and black," Lena said. "What does it matter?"

"Because now I know what is happening," he said standing up slowly.

Keiara looked at him and nodded. "It is as I feared, isn't it, Elmlock?"

"What?" Jovan exclaimed, looking between them, his eyes fearful for the first time that they had ever seen.

Elmlock sat down beside him. "It was long ago, before things changed and the gods were captured. Ackana and I were young, and she had yet to become thoroughly evil hearted. We met a man in the Wildlands, not far from here in fact, a man who said he was a Beast Lord."

Syera looked up. "We hear of Beast Lords, dangerous to those who are against them, even Noran know to leave them be."

"Yes, there are stories among the dwarves of the Beast Lords, great and powerful animal spirits which inhabit the bodies of mortals," Miira nodded from beside her.

"Yes, they are what some consider to be 'gods of nature'. They epitomize the ultimate in a species of animal kind, the kings of the animal kingdom if you will. And there are seven of them. Madtraline the Lion, Uventap the Bear, Chrones the Spider, Selc the Python, Anga the Eagle, Vertas the Shark and Gerack the Wolf. Ackana and I ran afoul of Selc in these woods. Ackana had always been proud of her powers and was quick to use them on anyone she deemed deserving, though with me she tended to focus on the unruly and lawless. There was a young bald man and a small gang of what we thought were average hooligans robbing a caravan. We intervened, made short work of the men and were left facing the young bald man. He was very unusual, and we knew something was amiss.

"Ackana attacked him despite my warnings, and from the ground sprung dozens of black and green snakes. When Ackana tried to dismiss them, they remained and attacked, piercing even her bone hardened skin. She retreated to me out of shock more than anything and we wondered who we were facing. He proclaimed he was Selc, the mighty Python, and one of the Beast Lords, and we would pay for attacking his vassals and him. Ackana and I decided it was in our best interest to let him be and transported ourselves back to my realm. Never before had we faced a foe who feared not even a god.

"It took some research, and I wanted to know more, so eventually I tracked down Gerack, the Wolf Lord, who would eventually become my friend. I found over the next few years that these group of mortals were empowered by pure nature energy which permeates the world, and they are set on it as protectors, however, they act in the nature of the beast. Chances are, Selc was provoked and thus attacked, like any snake will. We simply did not understand what we saw. I would come to find out Selc was the most unfriendly and animalistic of his Beast Lord fellows, and one of the few who did not spawn half breeds, or lycanthropes, which would eventually spawn the shifter races."

Jovan shook his head. "What does this have to do with a giant snake in my head?"

"Patience," Elmlock said, clapping him on the back. "I'm getting there."

Keiara nodded. "I've heard of the Beast Lords. A unique group in that their power is passed from generation to generation not by blood but by ownership of the sacred talisman. The only thing is, no one knows what the talisman for each of them is except for the ones they choose as their successor."

"Wouldn't that make it easy to be stolen?" asked Jovan, interested in the story at this point.

"One would think," Elmlock said. "But it isn't so because of the power of the talisman. Not only is it heavily enchanted, to the point of being blocked from Sight, but it is a seemingly innocuous item, and it is different with each generation that takes procession. When I knew the Wolf Lord, it was a piece of stone he wore woven into his braids that remained in place no matter the form or shape his body took."

"Interesting, and what form can these Beast Lords take?" Jovan asked, still interested in whole idea.

Elmlock shrugged. "I am not entirely sure. I know the Wolf Lord could be a wolf, half wolf/half man, and man, but I believe he was able to shift into any canine breed."

"I'm sure this has some relation to what Lena saw in her vision, is there any way to get there?" asked Sanna, standing behind Jovan now with her arms crossed, obvious irritation showing on her face.

"Oh, yes, forgive me, after hundreds of years, sometimes I forget the short nature of those alive today. Well, after I left my friend, I wanted to meet the other Beast Lords. I traveled for over thirty years, and managed to locate all of them except for Sect, who I had already encountered. I had heard he was in the swamps near the border with the San T'shi desert, and it was there I encountered his favorite monster, Zyphirus."

"The Zyphirus?" asked Keiara, her face concerned.

"The Zyphirus," Elmlock confirmed.

"Excuse me what is the Zyphirus?" asked Sanna with one eyebrow cocked.

"I think the Zodiac is rarely used today, but Zyphirus is the Snake of Franel, god of lies. The two headed snake was banded black, yellow, and green, and the legend was after Franel sent him to the stars, he could be summoned by the Lord of Snakes, or Sect at the time. The other celestial creatures can also be summoned by those who hold power over their beasts. Those who don't align to the Beast Lords have other ways to be summoned, but that is no concern. Our concern is Zyphirus," Elmlock said shaking his head. "Zyphirus has two heads, and a massive body, but what is most dangerous about Zyphirus is his attachment to the psychic plane, where he exists. He only manifests partially in this plane, and that part can only be viewed with the Sight. Because of my mother, Kalimourne, I am able to see into the spiritual realm and the psychic plane, and I saw the great Zyphirus curled at the feet of Sect. He greeted me coldly, but said he knew I had been to see the others and would allow me to speak before he tried to kill me. In the interest of diplomacy, I apologized for Ackana's attack and our interference. It was apparently enough, as Zyphirus did not attack me. I was fascinated, and I asked Sect about the great serpent.

"It was from him I found out the greatest and most terrifying power of the serpent, and that power is what you see here. Because he exists in two places at once, he can separate the psychic half, the right head, from the spiritual half, the left head. The right can then burrow into the victim, literally embedding himself into the mind and psyche of the victim. The spiritual snake remains inside the body of the summoner, because once separated, the snake cannot survive in the physical plane and has to be inside a host."

"So, you're telling me there is physically a link between them?" Keiara asked, concerned as she looked to Jovan, who'd dropped his head into his hands and looked ill.

"Every time he uses it, you get weaker, don't you Jovan?" Elmlock asked.

Jovan was pale when he picked his head up. "It's true. He showed me what he did, that night, I was in that pub when Sanna destroyed the table, I saw her then, and Cage drugged me."

Sanna's face drained of color. "You were there? That night? And I...I could have stopped this...?"

Elmlock reached up and put a hand on her arm. "Don't do that, Sanna. You didn't know."

"She left, and I guess that's when you found her, but it was that night, he got on top of me and this snake like thing, he showed me, passed from his mouth into mine, then I just watched as my whole body rejected it and convulsed, and he said he was surprised I lived because most don't..." Jovan said, staring blankly into the distance, the scene replaying in his mind as he spoke.

"It is amazing you didn't die," Elmlock said softly, placing a comforting hand on his shoulder. "Let's move onward for now, I think best when I'm moving, are you well enough to do so?"

Jovan nodded and stood up and began to gather things together. They loaded Maelstrom quickly and then headed toward the House of Oracles. They were relatively confident they would find their way there before the sunset, or at least be able to come within sight of the place.

Suddenly, Lena screeched. "Stop! Jovan, sit down, now, you're going to want to..."

Jovan turned and just as he did his head felt like it was going to explode, dropping him to his knees. He gritted his teeth together as the world began to waver around him and he tried to hold onto reality. The biting cold of the snow began to work its way into his knees and calves, keeping him conscious, but even it was fading. He felt hands on him as the cold faded and he was warm again. So very warm, and everything was so peaceful. His sister was standing in front of him smiling warmly and reaching out her hand. He took it and they embraced. Such peace...

They laid him back down on a bedroll and looked at Lena. "What did you see?"

"I just saw in a flash, the snake it reared up and sunk its teeth into his head suddenly, and as soon as it did, the yellow venom began to course through his body, and it...it was almost everywhere, everywhere but his heart, but it is so close..." she said, touching Jovan's chest gently.

Elmlock nodded. "When it takes his heart, it is too late."

Everyone was quiet as they bundled his unconscious form and put him on Maelstrom's back with Sanna behind him to hold him up. Lena checked now and then to make sure the poison hadn't consumed him yet. But it got closer and closer the more they walked.

"Shhh!" Avari said. "I hear someone coming!"

Wilder and Hinto both hit the dirt beside her in the scrub brush and watched as a large group began to pass by them. Two dwarves, a strange looking elf like thing with a silver arm, a human with fiery red hair and a limp boy in front of her, a shiny knight of some sort, and the leader was a woman in black walking with purpose beside a boyish looking blond human man. Avari glanced at her fellows. She could read their faces easily. They were as much of a rag tag group as they themselves were.

After they had passed they crawled out of their hiding place and watched them as they disappeared over the crest.

"They going to the same place we are, you think?" Wilder asked.

She shrugged. "Does it matter?"

"Not really," he responded.

"What if they see us?" Hinto said worried and wringing his hands.

"What are they going to do, kill us?" she asked. "I doubt it by the look of them. And they aren't from the military, you don't see dwarves outside the mountain. No, I sense something about them, almost a comfort with them."

They moved on, staying behind the group enough so they were unseen, but close enough they could watch them. Avari was wary, though not as much as Hinto who kept glancing ahead and behind them. She figured if they could see them, they would know what was going on with them. Soon, the sun was setting, and just over the next rise, they could see a great stone building rising from the ground. The group in front of them began making camp.

"Smart," Wilder said.

"Why? Wouldn't it be safer inside the building?" Avari asked.

Wilder shook his head. "No, because if there was anything in there with them, there would be nowhere to go if they got trapped. This way they can set out at dawn and investigate the ruins instead of taking chances of dark roaming creatures."

They watched from afar as they set up camp, and Avari noticed the young man who had been limply riding the horse. Something was wrong with him, very wrong, and it made her head hurt to look at him. The red-haired woman was apparently strong as an ox because she lifted him easily and laid him on a sleeping roll as the others set the campfire.

The blonde boyish looking one stared directly at them for a long time, so long, they wondered if they had been seen, but he diverted his gaze and continued preparing for the night's watches. Avari kept her eyes on the dark haired one who was sleeping deeply. After a while, when the moon was high, and both Hinto and Wilder had faded to sleep, she checked again on him. The red-haired woman was sleeping beside the sickly one, and the shiny knight was sitting watch across the way, looking away from him. There was a sudden shooting pain in her head, and to her surprise the sickly one slowly stood up and began walking toward the ruins. And to her horror, he began to take off his shoes and walk barefoot in the snow. A light snowfall had begun again. She shook Wilder awake and took off toward the wayward traveler. Soon, she heard both Hinto and Wilder's footfalls behind her. As the dark-haired man walked, he dropped his fur lined cloak, then his coat, and his white thin shirt. He looked unaffected by the biting cold. Avari couldn't understand what had possessed him, but she knew something had because her head was fit to split from watching him.

Sanna woke with a start. She didn't know what had done it but she was glad she woke because Jovan was gone. She scrambled to her feet and found his tracks easily enough in the fresh snow.

"Myrstand, Jovan's gone! I'm going after him!" she said as she ran past him, leaving him speechless.

She found his boots and wondered why he would have removed them, then his cloak and coat, and his shirt. She gathered them all as she walked, and she followed his footsteps. She felt her heart rise to her throat. Why would he take off his clothes? It was freezing.

She stopped when she heard laughter ahead of her. She ducked down and moved quietly through the underbrush until she came to the edge of the ruins that must have been the House of Oracles. There was a small alcove with a broken pillar, and Sanna saw Jovan bound with rope to it. Beside him sat a man in a bright red cloak with a mop of brownish blonde hair. She did recognize the Linerian crest on the cloak, and knew it must have belonged to Jovan. She watched as he stoked the fire to his right while Jovan shivered and muttered, his eyes closed.

She stepped out of the shadows and pointed her staff at him. "Cage."

He looked up, his eyes red rimmed and black. "Ah, the red haired Sanna. Come to rescue your little boyfriend? Well you can't have him, he's mine."

"What have you done to him?" she asked, dropping his clothes in front of him. "Why'd he do this?"

Cage smiled. "Isssn't it wonderful? He was with his sister, swimming, you see, so he had to discard his clothes ss-so they couldn't get ruined, after all they were his good clothess. He's ssss-so happy right now. Don't you want him to be happy? He'sss happy with me."

"It's a lie, what you show him," she said, her fury rising. "And using Zyphirus on him, why?"

Cage's smug look faded, just for a moment, before it returned. "Even if you know about him, what doesss it matter?"

"How'd you do it anyway? Take the Beast Lord Sect's power?" she asked, stepping closer.

He smiled. "Oh, that was easssy. Can you believe his talisman was his tooth?" he said, pointing to his front left canine. "How obviouss. After I killed him and yanked it out, I made it mine, then called the powerful Zyphirusss to my aid."

"Let him go," she said. "I will fight you, again. You didn't fare so well last time."

"Oh, well, I wasn't really prepared for a full-fledged master of the Sacred Flame, I am now," he said, and held up his hands.

A funnel of blackness emerged from them and struck Sanna from her feet, knocking her staff flying. She couldn't dodge it, which was a rare thing for her. She stood up, blood dripping from her mouth and nose.

"He's my toy, and he will submit to me," he said in a near growl. "An unwilling sacrifice is no use to my master."

Just then, Sanna looked up to see her staff come flying through the air back at her. She saw no one, but there was a flurry of movement and a man that stood taller than she did stood between her and the man in front of her. She blinked, and realized his hair was...blue?

The tall man uncovered his demonic eye and moved forward. Cage stood and tried to move, but his eyes had entrapped him. He stood immobilized and staring at him. Sanna stood somewhat dumbly as a short, furry boy came running and sliced through the ropes holding Jovan to the pillar and came running back past Cage and the strange blue haired one. She felt someone take her hand and looked down to see a young woman with purple eyes staring up at her, tugging her away, and she didn't need more of a hint. The blue-haired man told Cage before him to sleep and he slumped down into a deep slumber, and they headed away as quickly as they could back to their camp.

Keiara met Sanna as they ran up and looked at the three newcomers then the nearly naked Jovan. "What happened? Cage?"

Sanna nodded. "Get him warm, he was controlling him, said he was 'swimming with his sister', so he's got him locked into a pleasant dream, I suppose."

They quickly wrapped him up and he finally stopped shivering, though the blue color around his mouth had yet to fade.

"I have these three to thank, I don't know how they did it, but he knocked Cage out flat without doing a thing," Sanna said staring at Hinto.

"Hinto," he said and bowed to him. "I wasn't exactly doing nothing," he said, and sheepishly uncovered his demonic eye. The effect was immediate, everyone who saw it was drawn toward him and then he dropped the patch back and the feeling stop.

"Succubus?" Keiara asked. Hinto turned with a wide eye. "Mother, if I don't miss my guess," she said looking him up and down. "You are a very lucky half breed to be so human in appearance."

Hinto said nothing, only glanced at his two companions. Keiara next looked at the boy. "Shifter...no...you're a child of the Beast Lord clan, wolf."

Wilder nodded. "Wilder is my name, and this is Avari and she..."

Keiara's eyes settled on the young woman and she lifted her face up. "Sweet child, you're a prophet, no, a seer? Or a druid?"

"None, I don't have power," Avari stammered.

Keiara winked at her, "Yet."

They all then turned their attention to Jovan, who had opened his eyes finally, but their vivid green color was significantly dulled. "What, where...why do my feet hurt so much..."

Sanna kneeled beside him. "You went off in a dazed dream and thought you were swimming and walked to the ruins without your boots, you daft fool."

He looked around. "You should have left me with him. It would have been better for you all."

Syera kneeled on the other side. "Jovan, no. Listen. I know about this, I watched many years mother work her torture on all kinds, and in the end, they gave up to her, either to stop their pain or another person's pain. What he is doing to you, it is working because you think it would be better if you left us, do not think so, it is not true. Fight this though, or you will give it all to him."

Jovan's eyes filled with tears and he gripped her hand hard. "But I put you in danger, all of you, I'm getting weaker and I am losing my mind, I think, what if one of you died because of me? I just submit and let it go. It has been too much, since that night it began when you found me."

"The night it began?" asked Sanna. "I thought this started after the Norans?"

Jovan shook his head. "No, he's been in my head since I came to you all. He came into my dreams that night, the night you found me and Myrstand healed my wrist, and he sent me on being chased, and being hunted, and other things, but I could handle it. That day after the Noran, he must have killed the elf head hunter and gotten the memories, because then he started using them against me, and that's when I couldn't hide it from you anymore. He was more aggressive and came at me while I was awake where before it had just been as I slept."

Elmlock kneeled beside Sanna. "Then Jovan, you are so much stronger than I ever knew, to be fighting him this long. There is only one way to defeat him, and that is to use Zyphirius against him the way he is using it against you. You have to control it."

Jovan shook his head. "How can I control it? You said it lives in him and me at the same time, it answers to him because he's got the power or whatever..."

Keiara stood behind Elmlock. She smiled. "No, he's right. If you take control, he cannot control you, and you will be free of him. Removing Zyphirius is dangerous, and you may yet die, but I know of no other way..."

Jovan was so tired though. So tired of fighting it. Giving in appeared so sweet sometimes and he didn't know how to fight any more. Sanna gripped his hand tightly, and then her face began to waver. He vaguely heard Lena's voice saying something about his heart being taken, but he couldn't hear that anymore. There was a dull roaring sound in his mind. He was free, though, and he stood up and walked toward the sound. There was a snake. Not just any snake, a huge great snake with stripes of yellow, black and green. Its yellow eyes focused on him, and the fangs dripped yellow venom which pooled on the floor. As he watched, the venom ran towards him as though alive and disappeared under his feet.

The will to fight was fading, but he felt pressure, comforting pressure, so he kept staring at the snake. It stood easily three times as tall as he did, and he wondered what it would do if it struck him right then. Vaguely he heard Cage's voice, and he stared to his left and saw an opening in the blackness, and through it he saw a large pond where his sister swam, calling him to her. He looked to his right and he saw a grave scene of himself surrounded by the people he knew, but he still felt the comforting pressure on his hand. He looked at his sister, so happy and free, and alive, and not dead because of him. He walked toward the opening and watched. She called to him again, and he reached his shaking hand toward her.

Cage's voice reverberated in his head, "I can be cruel, but I can be so very kind. This life is for you, forever, just give yourself to my will, Jovan."

He stared at the snake and for the first time, he could see it was indeed half a snake, the other side was missing, and it looked like it had been forcibly ripped away. And for the first time, Jovan saw something in the snake's eyes. It was sad, so very sad because it was not meant to be two separate beings, it was meant to be one whole creature. Jovan felt the keen sadness now that he understood, and he slowly walked toward the snake instead of his sister. It simply stared, the venom dripping and flowing in to him. But now he understood. The venom was hatred, but it wasn't toward Jovan, no it was hate and anger at the one who had summoned, bound and hurt it.

Jovan touched the snake's torn flesh. This was not the half that was inside him, no this was the half that Cage had inside himself.

"Zyphirus," Jovan whispered. "Be whole again and return home."

It was then he heard the shriek, but this time it was not from himself. The snake in front of him lurched forward, and dimly, where the snake had been, he saw Cage's outline, as the snake severed himself from Cage's body, and the screams sounded wet and bloody as he watched the shadowy outline of Cage's body fall and dissipate. The image of the lake and his sister also faded. The great snake reared up and shot forward like a lightning strike and he felt the snake enter him. And then, this time, it was his own voice he heard screaming.

Sanna jumped back as Jovan's body lurched violently, almost sitting up completely and then fell back onto the ground into violent convulsions. She looked at Lena. "What's happening?"

Lena was staring, her eyes shining white in the darkness and she couldn't really comprehend what she was seeing. "I think he's fighting it, no, there's another snake and its twining into Jovan's body…"

In the distance they heard a blood curdling scream that made them all stare off in that direction, all but Sanna who stared at the still convulsing Jovan. She gasped as blood began to bubble up out of his mouth. She turned to Elmlock.

"Wait, this is his fight, we cannot help him."

Then he screamed and there was a great gush of blood from his mouth and along with it the semi-transparent form of a snake forced its way out of him. Jovan fell back with a thump into Sanna's lap, and they could just see the shadowy outline of a huge two headed snake. Sanna couldn't believe her eyes, and she couldn't believe she could still feel Jovan breathing beneath her hands as she clutched him against her.

An eerie voice could be heard by them all in their minds. "Two become one again, and I return home. He will live, the other will not."

Then, the image faded into sparkling lights which faded an instant later. Everyone stared at the spot for a moment and were completely silent, not really sure how to react to any of it.

"Well, how's that for a night out, I end up tossing up a snake and covered in blood again, some evening, huh?" Jovan's voice croaked from Sanna's lap.

Sanna looked down, tears in her eyes still, and saw him smile, covered in blood, but still the same Jovan he had always been.

CHAPTER FIFTEEN

PATH OF ORACLES

When the Sight left me,
I was alone.
Until on the steps of
The Oracle's Path I fell.
—*Talas Treath, Servant to Oracle Teavari*

"So, who are you?" Avari asked as she sat down beside the strange dark-haired woman.

Keiara smiled at her and stared into the brightening sky. Dawn was breaking, and the ruins of the ancient Citadel were lighting up. In the open field below her, the rest of them slept, even Jovan, after their recent trials. For this moment, there was peace to be had by all of them.

"I used to be the crown princess of Lineria. But that has changed now. Keiara, the princess was born with the essence of the Dark Phoenix, one of the six parts of the Eternal Phoenix that brought life to Avern. When the conditions were right, and I died by this sword," she said, holding up the old rusted hunk of metal she still carried sheathed at her side. "The separate soul that had lay sleeping awoke, and now, the soul of the Dark Phoenix and the soul of the princess have become one soul."

Avari nodded, swinging her boot clad feet. Keiara could tell the purple eyed one was wearing stolen clothing from the Phomean army, all of her group was. "And you are a special young person."

"I'm not so special. I'm just me," she answered, watching as the sun rose over the mountains to their east. "I don't even know a lot about me yet. I can't even say for sure if I'm a boy or a girl some days."

"All mortals are special because mortals are able to die. It is the ability to face an end to the life led that makes mortality a gift," Keiara answered and looked on as the sun rose as well.

"What are you doing here?" Avari asked, watching her carefully.

"Searching for answers. I became a part of the mortal world to find out how to release my children, the gods, but things like this Cage individual, are unexpected, and troubling. I must find out how to release my children before this world topples down," Keiara said and sighed deeply.

"But if you are a phoenix, aren't you powerful enough to do it by yourself?" she asked.

"I'm hoping the rest of my brethren awaken. I am afraid this is going to require the ultimate sacrifice in the end," she said.

Avari nodded. "How will they awaken?"

"Different ways. It depends on the part of the phoenix which rests inside, but I don't know for sure. This sword released the barrier between the Dark Phoenix's sleeping soul and Keiara's human one."

"But where are they?" Avari continued, staring up into the sky.

"They are drawn to me, we are always drawn together, because we are pieces of the same being. I have my suspicions of who carries the slivers of the Phoenix soul, because I can sense it sleeping inside a mortal's body."

"Can't you tell them you think they're a part of it?" Avari asked.

"I cannot. The vessel that contains a piece of the soul of the Eternal Phoenix must awaken on its own, and it may not ever awaken. For nearly a thousand years we traveled from mortal to mortal, never to awaken. No, I may be the only one to awaken," Keiara said sadly, and her glance fell on the sleepers below her.

"They're among your group, aren't they?" Avari asked.

She nodded. "Yes. Because of the sleeping soul, they all carry more powerful abilities than normal mortals, making them formidable, even unawakened. So, they are my friends now, and we go forth and find the answers."

Avari nodded. "And me and my friends?"

Keiara smiled. "You are all welcome to come as well as they are. It is always the choice of my companions if you wish to travel with me. I offer you the same choice they had. Do you wish to help me?"

Avari stared into her strange eyes swimming with stars, and the black patch on her face and nodded. "Yes."

Jovan woke slowly, and was for the first time in a while, rested and his head was not whirling with the horrific images Cage put there. But then he went to sit up.

"Holy gods of above and below!" he exclaimed and wrapped his hands around himself, tears immediately welling in his eyes.

"What's wrong?" came Sanna's voice from beside him, as she rolled over and placed a hand on his shoulder.

"I feel like a dragon sat on me," he responded, lowering himself back down to his position on the ground.

Sanna couldn't help but smile. "I'm sure, your ribs are still broken from the wolf attack, and then you did just have some sort of weird out of phase with reality giant snack come vomiting out of you."

"Oof, I think I'll stay here while longer," he said staring up into the morning sky. "In fact, maybe I'll stay here all day. Why don't you go with Keiara and the rest to explore the ruins, I'll be fine here."

Sanna shook her head. "Don't think so. I'll stay here, and a couple others I'm sure will as well. Everyone doesn't need to be trampling around the ruins anyway."

"We'll stay as well," Moryn said with a gruff nod. "Just to watch our backs and make sure you don't get made a meal of."

Jovan snorted. "Well, in this state, I can't do much to stop you now can I."

Sanna smiled and leaned over him. "No, there isn't. Now keep still, your body heals incredibly fast, but it has a lot of work to do."

Keiara and Avari walked back into the camp area. The others all perked up to see what they would end up doing about the ruins.

"It is pointless for all of us to go, so if you would like to go, Avari, Myrstand, Elmlock and I will be going soon. Jovan...you look...better..." Keiara said slowly, realizing better did not equal well.

"The dwarves and I have decided to stay here with Jovan," Sanna said promptly.

"I think I shall stay as well," Syera said. "I have questions for t'dwarven folk."

Hinto and Wilder glanced at Avari. "We'll go with you guys, I think," Wilder said, obviously still suspicious of the new people.

"Lena, I would ask you come as well, but it is your choice," Keiara said, looking at the smaller woman.

"Of course, my Sight would be useful," Lena said, standing.

"Very well, I am hopeful we will find some answers," Elmlock said with a smile.

Together, the group headed to the ruins, leaving the other group behind to mend and discuss the options for the future. The ruins were very large; spreading easily over two miles of ground, but the main building appeared somewhat intact in the middle. They headed that direction and found themselves staring at a massive stone carved door. Keiara stepped forward and found it pushed easily open.

The inside was nearly completely ruined by whoever had ransacked the place most recently. Elmlock began looking over the floor.

Hinto glanced around. "It's been many years, but I came here once, as a child."

Elmlock turned to him. "This place has been deserted for at least a hundred years."

Hinto smiled sheepishly, pulling at the too short sleeves of the stolen uniform. "I'm the son of a succubus, so I've been around for a while."

"Longevity was one of your gifts," Lena said, putting a hand gently on his arm.

"My father brought me here. We'd been to every temple, and church in the world it seemed. He thought after my mother brought me to him as an infant that I needed to be cleansed. My mother couldn't keep me with her. She said as half human, I'd be killed by the others, so it was up to my father, and finally, we came to the Temple of the Oracle at last," Hinto said, walking and running his hand along the ruined walls.

"I remember going down the long stairs," he continued, staring up into the sky through the broken rafters. "When we came into the room with the marble chair I couldn't breathe. She was so pretty, a little girl, no more than ten years old. She wore this little circlet around her head with a purple stone resting between her eyes, the same color as her eyes. Her silver robes were so pretty in the lamplight. She had black hair with this shock of white which ran right down the front that she had pushed behind her left ear."

The others had stopped moving, all enraptured in the story Hinto had to tell. Even Elmlock had stopped searching for access to the inner sanctum. And it wasn't the impossible lure of the succubus blood that enraptured them. The story itself had them held. The fabled Oracle s.

"I remember father pulling me by the hand to the marble seat upon the dais in the middle of the room. As we got closer, on her right cheek was a birthmark that looked like a green leaf. And I knew she had the three Marks. Which made her the Oracle . My father walked up and said he'd been everywhere, and every priest had said I was unclean. I'd been bled until I was faint. I'd been beaten with purified canes. I'd been dunked in consecrated water. So many things. I was scared of what she would say. Then she stood up and stood in front of me, possibly a year older than I was at the time. She was tall though, almost as tall as I was. I remember the look in her eyes, utmost mercy as she placed her hands on my shoulders, then embraced me in the first real hug I'd ever had in my life. My father was silent, and no one there spoke.

"She then pushed me back and smiled. She told me I'd been through too much already then looked at my father. She said I was purer than anyone in the room and my fate in life would be to do more good than all of them put together. She told him to take me home, and raise me as his son, and think no more of the state of my soul."

They could all see Hinto's raw emotion. And they all gave him a moment. But it was about then that the slapping bang sound of the hidden trap door broke the silence. Everyone turned and stared at Lena who looked up from an opening in the floor with a shocked expression.

"Sorry…"

"That's it, those are the stairs…" Hinto said, almost excitedly. It was like he expected the girl he knew to be found in the sanctum below.

The others quietly followed him down the stairs in the darkness. In the dim light, they could make out a winding set of marble stairs, heading into the base of the building they had entered. The stairs were tight, but soon opened up into the inner sanctum approach. There was a set of banded wood and steel doors. The doors nearly hummed with a magical power which bound them and kept them locked tightly.

Hinto walked toward them almost mechanically. Keiara started to reach for him, then stopped, remembering what the Oracle had spoken to him. She stared up at the script written above the doors, proclaiming "Only the pure of heart withstand the Oracle s judgment". The warning, of course, was for anyone who tried to enter the room without permission of the Oracle within or sanctified by the Oracle would die. Hinto gently pushed open the doors, which gave at his touch easily. There was a moment when the air was electric around him and then the doors stood wide. The others quietly followed, with Elmlock lighting a torch as they entered the room.

The cavernous room was larger than they expected, untouched by marauders it appeared, the spell on the door successfully blocking them for these hundred or so years. Keiara lit another touch, and then touched it to the sconce on the wall. Another ancient spell enacted, lighting all the sconces in the circular room. Elmlock slowly doused his own flame and they were staring at what was perhaps one of the most impressive looking rooms any of them had encountered.

Elmlock sighed. "Dusty and missing the items of value, but otherwise, it is pristine."

The air was musty and choking, but none noticed the fact as they walked around the room. In the center, a marble dais rose, with two steps on each of the cardinal directions. Upon the dais sat a marble carved seat. It was far too plain to be called a throne, a simple seat. But there was something magical about it, something just past the normal range of vision.

"So, how exactly do we find answers here?" Avari asked.

"Even with my Sight, I see nothing. The seat is magical, some sort of aura surrounds it, but nothing else..." Lena said, running her hands over the seat.

But Keiara had stopped and was staring intently at Avari. "Avari, what is that?"

Avari turned and shook her head. "What is what?"

Keiara moved up and pulled her long hair around in front of her, and pulled from the underneath a thin row of shock white hair. It couldn't be seen from most angles but ran from the back of her head behind her ear.

Avari shook her head and shrugged. "It's always been there, just some white hair, no big deal."

Keiara shook her own head. "It is a mark of the Seer. Lena carries it, tucked behind her left ear. Barely noticeable in some, obvious in others, this does not occur often. And you have the Mark of the prophet. Are you also carrying Druid's Mark?"

Avari was amazed at this thought. "I don't, I mean, I've never seen anything..."

"Let me see your back," Keiara said slowly. "Hinto, Wilder, turn your heads, you too Elmlock."

The males turned their backs as Keiara lifted the uniform shirt Avari wore and was not disappointed. Between her shoulder blades sat a birthmark, shaped like a four petaled flower. It was small, and unlikely anyone had seen it since she was a baby.

"Three Marks," Keiara whispered, dropping her shirt back down. The others all turned around.

"I'm not an Oracle ," Avari said, frowning.

"Only Oracle s have all three."

"I've never had any power!" she complained.

"It doesn't matter if you've never shown power before, sometimes Oracle s have pronounced their only prophecy on their deathbeds," Elmlock said quietly. "That's why the Forge comes from anyone with the Mark, whether or not they've ever shown a sign of power. The ability exists with the presence of the Mark."

Avari shook her head. "I'm not an Oracle."

The others glanced back and forth between each other. It was surprisingly Hinto who broke the silence. "Prove it, then."

Keiara smiled. "You're right, Hinto...she can."

Avari shook her head again. "What do you mean? How?"

Hinto, who stood by the seat of the Oracle, smiled and patted the arm. "Here. Sit here. If nothing happens, no one will say anything again about you being an Oracle."

"Will it work?" Avari asked.

Keiara shrugged. "This was built after I went into the Cycle. Maybe, maybe not. But perhaps it will do something."

Avari slowly walked up to the chair and stared at it. Would she do it?

Jovan sighed and winced at the piercing pain in his ribs still.

Syera and the dwarves had gone foraging for some fresh winter berries and roots. Sanna had opted to stay just in case something came along. The others had been gone for a short while, Jovan wasn't sure exactly how long, as he was dosing in and out of sleep. He heard Sanna sit down beside his head, and he rolled over towards her.

"How are you feeling?" she asked.

"I'm doing better, I think," he said. "I feel like I've healed some of the superficial damage, but my ribs...ugh."

Sanna looked up, her bright red hair shimmering in the sun that was streaming down around them. "How long have you had the fast healing thing?"

Jovan thought for a minute. "I guess as long as I can remember. As a little kid, I'd scrape my knees, my elbows, and I'd heal up within a day while it took others a week or more sometimes. And I just never got sick either. Never got scars from when I got hurt either. And I found if I was really hurt, I could concentrate on the pain and make it go away."

Sanna nodded and looked thoughtfully into the morning sky. "It is interesting. I've always had to ability to use fire, almost like it was a part of me."

Sanna brought a small flame to life in her hands and showed him. Jovan wasn't surprised, and as Sanna extinguished the flame Jovan smiled. Sanna looked down at him, looking a bit confused.

"I'm not surprised because I've never met a woman with as much fire in her soul as you before," Jovan responded, smiling up at the sky. "The flames, tattooed on your arm, do they mean something special?"

Sanna nodded. "Yes, they are each skill I've mastered as a Monk of the Sacred Flame. There are ninety-nine flames on my arm. I am missing only one flame that would make me a master in my order."

Jovan turned his head, curious, "Which flame is it?"

"The Flame of the Past. The final flame, that shows I have left the past behind completely and have only forward to go toward. I have not yet come to the ability to move past things which lie in my own past," Sanna said, her hands reflexively clenching into fists as she spoke.

Jovan was silent for a while and thoughtful. "I know the feeling."

They were both quiet and then Sanna turned to Jovan, a new look on her face. "So, you're some sort of prince, huh?"

Jovan snorted and laid flat on his back again. "I'm the seventh child of the chief of the Whispara, so maybe a prince, but never a king."

"So why would your brother and sister be away from the forest looking for you? I assumed you were next in line or something..." Sanna asked, a little confused.

Jovan frowned. "I would like to know the same. My older sister and my older brother would have no reason to come looking for me. If my eldest brother had died, they would have been in rule well before me. I can think of no reason for them to seek me out."

Sanna nodded. They were quiet for a while again, until Jovan decided to sit up. He let out a long, low whistle. Sanna looked over as he did so. She arched a brow at him. He slowly got to his feet and stood up, taking a moment to stretch to his full height. He felt a wracking pain shoot through his body, to which he gasped and breathed heavily for a moment.

"You shouldn't get up yet," Sanna said matter-of-factly.

"Yeah, I know, but if I don't move around, I'm going to go crazy," Jovan said, wincing at the striking pain across the ribs where they had yet to mend.

Jovan looked across at the ruins, wondering what was happening within them, and wishing he could be there to see the results of their trials. He sincerely hoped it would be worth everything they had gone through.

Avari stared at the seat and wondered what she would do if something did happen. What if she was more than an orphaned child? What if she was more than some purple eyed freak? But then, what if she was not?

Finally, under the eyes of those around her, she stepped onto the dais and turned to sit upon the seat of the Oracle. Those present took a collective breath, waiting to see if something did indeed happen. For a long time, nothing did happen, and Avari smiled and started to speak of this fact when a sound like silent thunder could be felt in the room. A great pressure was felt by all. Avari's eyes began to glow silvery violet and all the air blew outward from the seat and the entirety of the scones were extinguished. The glow from Avari's body left plentiful light for all to view her easily.

Avari's voice rose and reverberated throughout the room, "Find the Crown in the Northlands among the people of the sea and open the way for the Keeper of Life to return to thee. Find the Cloak in the human heart among those who flee and open the way for the Keeper of Death to return to thee. Find the Staff in the jungle's breath within the one tree and open the way for the Keeper of Nature to return to thee. Find the Ring in the sands of time before the holder of the key and open the way for the Keeper of Magic to return to thee. Break the seals and open the gates for the truth to now flow, and then you can seek the truth that you must eventually know. The True Litany will break away the torturous crystal that binds, only once the

Keepers have fled and it is the phoenix that finds the true evil that has been released into this world one true. So, it is spoken thus that there is so much more to do."

Just as suddenly, Avari's head dropped and the brilliant light faded, the scones relighting once more. Avari was silent, and so were the rest. No one knew how to respond. They had received the instructions they had come to this place looking for, but not in the way any of them had intended.

Avari slowly lifted her head, and they all noticed now, the slight shock of white hair Keiara had earlier noticed in the back of her hair had expanded, becoming more noticeable, extending from her right temple, down to the underside of her hair.

After a short discussion about what had transpired, and Keiara taking the time to write down the prophecy Avari had delivered on two pieces of parchment, they all sat and stared for a moment.

It was Jovan who broke the silence. "So, now what?"

Keiara looked at them and sighed. "We have only one course open. We have four points in the world, essentially the four corners of the world, what I am assuming are the San T'shi desert, the realm of the water kin elves to the north, the jungles to the south, and one of the northern human kingdoms most likely Darna since it is currently being taken over by neighboring kingdom. In the case we are right, there is no way to get to all these places and retrieve the Litany in time."

Myrstand, who had remained silent all this time looked up. "In time for what?"

Elmlock placed a hand on Keiara's shoulder. "We have a time limit. This is the nine hundred and ninety ninth year since the gods were trapped, essentially, having their power cut off. The gods of our world can be destroyed, or rather sent to the Void much like my failed brethren. After one thousand years of having been bound as they are, with no access to the planes they live in or even in the physical plane, they will simply cease to exist."

Lena frowned. "Why would they cease to exist after a thousand years?"

Keiara nodded. "It isn't something anyone of this world would know, but the Maker and Unmaker knew, as did those of the phoenix blood. After a thousand years, their divine spark would die, starved of the nourishment of the cosmos. Unlike mortals on the world of Avern, the divine are created from and live on the cosmic energy of the universe. That is why they cannot exist in the physical realm like mortals without taking an avatar, or a mortal shell. Without access to the cosmic energy of our universe, they will cease to exist...or rather, cease having ever had an existence. Anything that is sucked into the Void in this manner becomes as if it never was. That is why only I can remember the dying godlings, and no one else can. They only know they failed, they do not know how many times they failed."

"Wait," Sanna said, looking up. "But the eternal phoenix and the Keepers created the mortal and sentient races..."

"Then, that means they'll never have existed," Keiara finished.

Moryn spoke up this time. "But how can we be sure they are cut off? Starving if you want to put it that way?"

There was murmured assent among those present. "Because I can't find them," Keiara said softly. "If they were anywhere receiving the energy, I could trace it. I can see the lines of energy which flow into divine beings, even Elmlock feeds on the cosmic energy of life. And that is what it is, pure life energy generated by the Eternals at the heart of the universe which powers the worlds and the planes around us. But before I entered the mortal cycle, I could find none. That was how I knew something was terribly wrong. It was as though the streaming energy that flowed into the world around me was nearly gone, with only a few small trickles flowing down here in the physical world of Avern. And that was why I came down to the world in this form."

They sat in silence and contemplated this, the end of their existence. "But why would Ackana do this?" Lena asked softly.

"She doesn't know what she is doing; the undoing of the gods would also undo her. She could not have done this alone, she has had help, and something tells me the one pulling the strings on her may understand these things and desires them. I do know one thing, if we don't free them before the year's end, it may be too late," Keiara said, standing and beginning to pace.

Jovan, who sat slightly hunched over still nodded. "But what about the law of balance you spoke of? I thought you said things couldn't just cease to be?"

"No, they can't, but they can go into the Void, where they become something else, something we know nothing about. We can't enter the Void, and the Void cannot enter our world, so there is no way to tell what happens when they enter the Void, we only know they disappear from our reality," Elmlock said, standing slowly. "I studied the Void for several years, wondering if it could be used as a magical power source to find the gods, and all I found was those who dabble in the Void usually end up dead or missing, and missing from the memories of those that knew them."

Syera had been silent and listened carefully. "So...we split t'group."

All eyes turned to her. Keiara nodded. "It is the only way. Two groups, one to the east, one to the west. I will take Myrstand and head to Darna. Avari, and her companions Wilder and Hinto, have agreed to come with us. Sanna, I would like you and Jovan to head to the Water-kin Elves to the north. I know the Whispara have been out of contact, but the relations between your tribe and the water-kin elves were better than many of the other elves, Jovan. Lena, I would like you to go with us, so we have a person with the Sight to help Avari with her newfound ability. Miira and Moryn, you both know the mountain ranges well enough to navigate easily, so if possible, I would ask you to split up. Syera, I will leave it to you who you wish to go with. Elmlock will travel with Sanna as far as the north of the Wildlands, but he has another errand to attend to while we seek these artifacts of the keepers."

Sanna frowned again, her forehead deeply furrowed. "But what are we looking for and how do we release a Keeper once we find it?"

"Another reason to split our group, there will be less to keep track of. The artifacts are items the Keepers were never without. The Crown of Life is a living wreathe of leaves he wore all his days. The Ring of Magic is a piece of crystalized magic formed into the shape of a band. The Staff of Nature is a living staff that will take root if sat on the ground. And the Cloak of Death is a black cloak which was formed of the silk spun by the death's head worms in the Realm of the dead," Keiara responded.

Jovan frowned this time. "So we have to find a headband of leaves in the realm of the water-kin elves, a ring in a desert, a growing staff in a jungle, and a cloak in a warring country of humans....and say we do find them, how do we find the Keepers?"

"The items themselves will lead you to them, and no, I don't know how exactly, but it should do so," Keiara answered.

The others thought for a moment about what that would mean. Moryn spoke up.

"It must be done. We will do it."

Wilder stood. "There is a frontier town that still survives south of here. We can go there for provisions, but only a few of us should enter the town. They've had...issues with outsiders over the last few years and I don't recommend agitating our only source of provisions."

Keiara nodded. "It is settled then."

A day's easy walk took them to the outside of a walled village. Wilder took Myrstand and the horse in with him. The rest waited in silence outside, somehow feeling the next morning would mean the end of their time together. Strangely, though the dwarves had agreed to split up, they were nonplussed about it, simply going about the preparations. By the time Myrstand and Wilder returned with a provisioned Maelstrom and another strong horse, the others had set camp for the night, leaving only what was required unpacked.

They ate a meager meal of bread and roast rabbit around their fire. The snow had stopped for the time being, and around them they could see bits of earth and rock jutting out of the broken cover of snowfall. Even those who were normally chatty were quiet. They heard a sound and looked up to see an older man walk towards them from the town. They silently moved hands to weapons but waited to see what he would do.

"Ho, there travelers, why do you not sleep within the safety of the walls of our city?" the man asked. As he drew closer, they could see he was a broad man, dressed in furred leathers and bearing a bow and quiver upon his back. He had scraggly brown hair sprinkled liberally with white, and a scraggly beard to match it.

Myrstand stood up and moved forward. "I'm afraid our guide suggested staying out of the city might be better, considering the size and composition of our group."

The man sat down among them and glanced around. "I see. Quite a group you have here, isn't it?"

Keiara nodded as Myrstand sat down beside her once more. "Yes, we're seeking some artifacts," she said slowly.

The scraggly man locked eyes with her for a moment, then looked away toward the others. "Ah, well, that's a noble effort."

There was a silence that no one knew how to break until the scraggly man continued. "I've heard that there is a strange tree down there in the jungle, seems it never stops growing and changing, and no one can seem to cut it down, seems its surrounded by an aura of some sort." The group was still silent. "And I've heard telling of this cloak that the princess of Darna had when they pulled her of her throne and she disappeared into exile. They said it protected her somehow when they tried to cut her throat."

Myrstand had heard that the princess had been sent to exile, but to have her be the one to hold the Cloak of Death?

"And this here ring of leaves they tell about up north, seems that wearing it gives them the ability to cure just about anything that ails a person," the old man continued. "But my favorite artifact story has to be the desert dwellers out to the west. There's a ring lost in the desert which they say finding would make the wearer the most powerful magician of all time. I'm not sure I believe that one. And then of course, the crown jewel of all ancient artifacts has to be the original copy of the Litany. That's been debated hotly for years, you know. If it is real, what would happen if a mortal read the words?"

Who was this man that knew already what they were seeking?

"And who are you, anyway?" asked Jovan from his position lying beside the fire.

"Ah, I'm Jacos, the Truthseeker. In my younger days I used to be a hunter of the artifacts that would reveal the truth of cosmos. But that was long ago. Now I'm just mayor of this little village. I heard we had visitors, and I was hoping to see you before you left. Reminds me of my days tramping around the woodlands," he said, smiling and staring up at the stars.

The group, though somewhat suspicious of the newcomer, spent the rest of the evening hearing his tales of adventure, and found he asked very little of them. He wanted company on this cold night and sitting under the pale moon reminiscing of days past was enough for him. When the moon was high, and most of them had gone to sleep, only Myrstand, Sanna and Keiara remained awake.

"You intend to find them, don't you?" he asked slowly.

"Find who?" Keiara asked innocently.

The scraggly Jacos smiled. "I know the signs too well. The time of the Veil has come, and the Blood Moon rose, and then the Night of the Hidden Moon passed. All of the old prophecies have come into play. You can't fool an old adventurer. You've come to find the gods and bring them back."

Keiara and Myrstand exchanged looks. "It would seem you are more astute than I originally thought," Keiara said. "The answer is yes."

Jacos smiled again. "I hope you do find them, because if the thousandth year comes, the old ones who spouted the end of the world when the gods disappeared may be proven right."

With that he stood, wrapped his dark cloak about him and headed back to the town. He stopped and turned back. He handed Keiara a small locket on a chain. "This might help you, someday."

As Keiara opened the locket, she gasped. The pictures in there were rough sketches, but both Keiara and Myrstand could tell the profiles looked somewhat like Avari, but one had short hair, and the other had longer hair. The back of the locket was inscribed with a name, Talmavari the Oracle.

"Is that the Oracle? Or is this something she saw in a vision?" Myrstand asked.

"I do not know," Keiara said, and looked up, seeing no sign of their Truthseeker. "I haven't heard of a Truthseeker walking the world of Avern in a long time, they were the clergy of Samastain, the one who wrote the True Litany."

Morning came far too early. Everyone was quiet and spoke very little. Most of the discussion was non-committal and had to do with packing the campsite away. Keiara stood and watched from a short distance with Sanna beside her.

"Why me?" Sanna asked. "Why do you want me leading them? You could have sent Myrstand."

Keiara smiled. "I know there is something waiting for you and it is without us. The flame you are missing, it will come on this journey. I believe in you. And Myrstand has some issues to wrestle with soon enough."

They stood in silence for a moment watching. "I've never led anyone before."

"Doesn't mean you can't lead them. I haven't made a mistake, just trust yourself," Keiara said and walked away back to the group.

Sanna stood and watched and wondered. Could she do this? Could she lead this group and find what was needed? She would have to try. She sighed and headed back down, and her thoughts were on the one flame she was missing. The flame of the past. It appeared the one she had been unable to receive was going to be coming to her in the future, if she believed Keiara. She didn't have any reason not to believe her, but she didn't know how she could resolve herself with a past she couldn't remember. A past she was afraid to remember.

There was not much more to be said as they finished preparations. Miira and Moryn said a farewell, but in the knowing fashion of twins. Hinto joyfully hugged both Miira and Syera, both of which looked a little uncomfortable at the spontaneous affection. Elmlock left Keiara with a hug as well, though she reciprocated the gesture. They were headed out in separate directions, one toward the northeast and Zerri T'Ves, and the other to the northwest toward Darna. They stopped at the crossroads, one leading to the northwest, the other to the north east. Sanna nodded and smiled at Keiara.

"I guess this is good luck and farewell," Keiara said.

"Yeah, I hope to hear from you soon," Sanna said with a nervous laugh.

"You will be fine. In fact, I'm sure you will have your own adventures to tell when we meet again. After you are done in Zerri T'Ves, you'll have to make your way south to San T'Shi, and we'll head to the southern jungle, the Seran. I'm not sure how much I will be able to communicate, but I'll find a way," Keiara said as the others headed down the two paths.

Sanna nodded and slowly followed Maelstrom and Jovan, and Keiara followed their pony, Charlie, and their group. Sanna kept looking toward them until she could no longer see them. She looked ahead now. Ahead was the only way she could look now.

EPILOGUE

SETTING OUT

Within the echoes of the night
A voice will spin a tale,
And you will listen to it.
Red eyes shall give you a fright.
—*Red Eyes and Echoes, poetry by Treve Mandera*

◦∞◦

Tyla sat on the stone fence that surrounded the tower and looked into the distance. She ran a hand through her thick black hair and heard someone approach.

"Pin," she said, turning her gold eyes to glance back at the other woman.

"Tyla," Pin responded.

Pin, unlike Tyla, who wore short breeches and a shirt with no sleeves, wore a set of rugged leather pants made of a patchwork of different-colored leather and a heavy cloak that obscured the tight bustier underneath. Her hair was cut short, its blonde strands falling just around her face and the back of her neck. Eyes dark as night stared back at her.

"What brings you out here?" Tyla said, knowing Pin rarely left the confines of her tower.

"Our prey is next," she said, sighing a bit. "It is troublesome and will be a lot of work for me, and you as well. We cannot work together as they have split into two groups, one heading northeast and the other northwest."

"Already? Cage hasn't returned," Tyla commented, looking over the mountains.

"Cage won't be returning. He has failed."

Tyla turned and looked at her sharply. "Failed? Even with the Zyphirius?"

"Even with that, though, I think he may have depended too much on otherworldly help as it was. He should have depended solely on his own capabilities," Pin pointed out.

Tyla sighed. "He was so confident when he left. I was sure he could do it."

"Well, that's what happens when one is too confident in their abilities and depends on something other than themselves," Pin stated, crossing her arms over her chest and glaring into the distance.

"I don't know why he just doesn't let us all go at once instead of just one or two," Tyla grumbled. "At least I'll get to leave soon, but I guess you'll be leaving first since he hasn't talked to me yet."

"You know as well as I do why he doesn't want us all pursuing our prey at once time. He can only dedicate his power to one or two of us while we're away from the tower. Besides, if one of us is successful, his power will increase vastly and then he is more likely to get to the others he desires," Pin told her.

Tyla nodded, settling her elbow on her knee and her chin in her hand. "I know, I know. I'm just bored with the waiting. I'll feel better when I can leave. Torturing wizards can only entertain me so much, y'know."

Pin did smile a bit. "Ace and Chase were complaining about that as well."

"Hmm, yeah, maybe we'll have to get together and make a game out of playing with a wizard or two that the Master doesn't want. I mean, he has so many, surely he won't miss one or two," Tyla frowned as she spoke.

Pin glanced at her. "Do not take any of the wizards without the Master's permission. He might kill you if you do," Pin reminded her.

Tyla gave a dismissive wave of her hand. "I know, I know. I won't do anything without permission. Last thing I want to do is end up on the Master's bad side. People don't last long when they are on it."

"You know, there's something I have been wondering about," Tyla said after being quiet for a moment. "Is the master a man or a woman? I mean, I know we call him Master and all, but really, which is he?"

Pin was silent a moment as she thought. "I think he is neither. Or perhaps both. It is not something I wish to ask of him. It does not matter, though. He is simply the Master and will lead us to glory."

"True," Tyla admitted as she thought about it. "Do you really think his whole plan will work?"

"You question the Master?" Pin admonished.

"Well, not really, I mean, I know why I'm here and why I follow him, but the whole plan, this trying to gather them to his side, will it work?" Tyla asked as she thought it over.

"The Master knows the outcome already," Pin said, huffing a sigh through her nose. "We simply have to trust in him."

"But Cage failed. What if more of us fail?" Tyla continued. "What if we aren't able to get them to his side? What will happen then?"

Pin didn't speak for a long while. "Trust in the Master. Things will work out just the way he has planned. He doesn't inform us of all of his plans, remember?"

"True. So, maybe Cage failing was part of the plan," Tyla said slowly as she thought about it. "Does that mean the Master knew and sent Cage to his death anyway?"

"Would you die for the Master if he willed it?" Pin asked, looking at her seriously.

"Well, yeah, that's why I'm here. I gave my life to him."

"Then don't worry about it. Your life belongs to the Master now, not to you. If he sends you to die, that is up to him. You gave him your life to use as he will." Pin turned back toward the mountains again.

This time, Tyla was quiet as she thought over Pin's words. Then she nodded and spoke. "As long as my life is used to help the Master, I don't mind dying."

"I'm going in; this cold is annoying," Pin told her, turning on her heel and heading back to the tower, leaving Tyla on the stone fence.

Tyla thought about a great many things. In particular, she thought of how she had come to the Master and given her life to him. She had been nothing before the master. Now, she could do so much with the power he had given her. She looked down to see a large spider crawling up her leg. She smiled, reaching down to pet its back. It stopped, thinking about whether to bite or not, most likely.

"Shh, pretty one. Don't be ill-tempered," Tyla told it, and it appeared to relax.

Tyla brushed her fingers over the small creature's body and smiled. Soon enough, it would be her turn, and she would be wrapping up her prey in her own webs.

Pin pushed open the door and went into the tower. She almost didn't hear Chase come into the room. He came up beside her and nodded. "You look like you're thinking about something."

Chase stood somewhat taller than Pin, but not much, as Pin was a tall woman. His hair was an orangey red color and lay about his face like the mane of a lion. He was clean-shaven, though, and had golden brown eyes that glittered under the fringe of his bangs. He wore simple breeches and a buttoned shirt made of linen. Overall, Chase was a rather simple man. His intellect, though, was sharp and cunning.

"I was just speaking with Tyla about some things. She didn't know of Cage's failure," she said, turning to him fully now. "The Master told me my chance is next. Then Tyla will be allowed to leave with his blessing."

"Ooh, that true? That's exciting. Even though Cage failed, it should still be fun to try and get to these...people. I look forward to the time when I am released and hope it will come soon. Do you know where you're heading?" Chase said as he crossed his arms across his broad chest and smiled at her.

"The northeast. They're headed up, possibly to the water-kin elven kingdom. I wonder, though, what they are doing by going there," she said with a frown.

"Does the Master know?" Chase asked her.

"He has not said if he does know why they are going that direction, only where they are now and possibly heading. Most of the job of finding out their purpose will be up to me and Tyla. If we succeed and bring them willingly to the Master's side, then we will know more, I am sure," Pin told him with surety.

They were quiet momentarily; then Chase brought up something that Pin had been thinking. "What of the one Cage was supposed to go after? Will the Master send someone after him again, or is he done trying to get to him?"

Pin sighed, shaking her head. "I don't know. It would be in his best interest if he tried to persuade him again, but I don't know if he can. I think he will try to get to the others in hopes that they will increase his power, making it easier to get to the one Cage failed to get."

Chase nodded. "That would make sense," he said and let out a sigh himself. "Well, good luck to you in your pursuit. I do hope you can succeed where Cage has failed."

"Cage depended on the Zyphirius too much. I only depend on myself and my own power," she said, reaching up and pushing a stray hair out of her face.

"As I would expect from the Master of Bears," Chase told her and bowed slightly before he left her alone.

Pin watched him go and wondered if she could indeed do it. She had every confidence in herself, but knowing that Cage had already failed in his mission made doubts creep in.

"Mistress Pin," came a voice behind her. She turned and looked at the stooped servant who was standing behind her. She cursed the fact they were so stealthy when they moved around.

"Yes?" she asked.

"The Master will see you now," he said, gesturing toward the door.

She swallowed hard and wondered why the Master wanted to see her. She'd already been handed her orders by way of the missive he had sent via a servant. What he wanted to see her in person for, she had no idea. She steeled her resolve, though, and followed the servant up the stairs to the uppermost tower. He opened the door, and once more, she felt a shiver as she entered the room, which was too cold. He was once again sitting on the window ledge, looking out the window at the mountains below. She could not see his eyes, which glowed with a constant red hue.

"You are setting out soon," he said.

"Yes, Master. I received your communication that I would set out immediately to the northeast. I believe Tyla has not yet received her instructions, though I told her she would be going as well soon," Pin said, trying not to show her nervousness at speaking to the Master.

He was quiet for a time, not speaking, and Pin wasn't even sure if he was breathing. She had no idea if the Master even required breath anymore. Not that it mattered to her. She would follow the Master anywhere he told her to go. He had been the one to give her the power of the Beast Lord that she now carried. That gift alone would have beholden her to him for life, but she also believed in his aims.

"Do better than Cage. He was ill-equipped for the power of those he was faced with. Do not make the same mistake he did. Those you face are not weaklings, even if they appear on the surface. The abilities of those you seek are not to be underestimated," he said finally.

"Yes, Master, I will do as you say."

He was quiet again for a time before he spoke again. "You will not encounter the most dangerous member of their group, I sense. They will be in the group Tyla follows. The group you pursue has no Seer, so use this to your advantage. However, be wary of the redheaded monk. She is more than she appears."

Pin nodded. "Yes, Master. I will take all your advice to heart."

He turned toward her now. His red eyes again unsettled her. She swallowed thickly again. He nodded and then looked away. She was glad to no longer be under his gaze.

"You may proceed," he said.

Pin bowed deeply and went back out the door as quickly as she could. The chill did not leave her as she reached the bottom of the stairs. She shivered and went to provision herself and take one of the horses. As she mounted the horse, she looked back on the Forge and swore at the top of the tower; she saw the Master's burning red eyes.

Appendix A

Countries and Capitals

This is a handy reference for some of the locations on Avern. If you are so inclined to check them out, you can very easily match them to the map below. I've provided another map just for you to reference alongside this list.

Countries and Capitals

Country	Capital	Government	Leaders	People
Phomean	Childers	Democratic Republic	President Samus Harmett	Human
Lineria	Meitan's Rest	Hereditary Monarchy	Queen Sealla	Human
Darna	Kingshome	Hereditary Monarchy	King Jaxon Brevace	Human
Vestern	Seterest	Parliamentary republic	Maxim Trustblooded	Human
Republic of Namas	Vera	Constitutional Republic	Eriana Secretkeeper	Human
Dwomer	Kalapamoor	Constitutional monarchy	Fastem Dulope	Human
Luxen	Avonic	Aristocracy	Cannvek Newhope	Human
Perta	Celestistic	Liberal democracy	Serama Intenica	Human
Ruark	Chavnerise	Social democracy	Vrayne Mistwalker	Human
Kranos	None	Anarchy/ Tribalism	There is no central leader.	Human
Sern T'sal	V'minist	Elective Monarchy	Queen Estel'ner	Sprit-kin Elves
Zeri T'ves	V'aquane	Tribalism	Multiple	Water-kin Elves
Grumach	Rustume	Hereditary Monarchy	King Boden Stormwatch	Dwarves
Holiess T'me	V'shera	Theocracy	High Priestess Mala Swiftriver	Dark-kin Elves
Lerestis T'mis	V'isterna	Tribalism	Multiple	Air-kin Elves
Grua T'gara	V'gama	Elective Monarchy	Queen Eldana	Earth-kin Elves
Mix T'nexus	V'resta	Tribalism	Multiple	Fire-kin Elves

APPENDIX B

KEEPERS OF AVERN

There are four keepers, each one representing one of the four forces of the world of Avern: Magic, Nature, Life, and Death. Each of these is among the firstborn of the gods and is more worshipped than any others among the pantheons. Even after the Abandonment, the four Keepers are often whispered about, and some old ones remember what they were. Common sayings related to them exist, even if the origin has been forgotten. During the harvest, Charin is invoked, and her symbol is often etched on farming equipment, even if it has been forgotten why it is done that way. Four holidays are named after the Keepers. Each of the Keepers is the sovereign of their own realm beyond the physical plane. The Keeper of Stars resides in the Astral plane, the Keeper of Nature resides in the Physical plane, the Keeper of Life resides in the Upper planes in the Halls of the Souls, and the Keeper of Death resides in the Lower planes, in the Halls of the Dead. The Keepers are all neutral in their outlook on life, the four aspects being neither good nor evil nor aspects of lawfulness or chaos.

Worshippers of the Keepers feel that those who worship the other deities are incredibly small-minded and do not understand the broadness of the universe. Of all the Keepers, the

Mother of Elves is perhaps the best known. After all, her children all take from her name.

There are those who worship the four keepers together. When these are found, they use a holy symbol that combines all four of the keepers' symbols. Usually, it is an hour glass laid over a spiral background with a leaf to the right and a seven-pointed star to the right. There is debate among people as to whether the Maker and Unmaker are really two of the Keepers, but it isn't so in reality, of course.

Keepers of Avern

eeper	Domains	Known as	Symbol	Weapon: Iconic Weapon	Followers
alimourne	Magic, elves, non-natural elements	Keeper of the Stars, Mother of Elves		Shuriken: Whirling Stars	Star-keepers
harin	Elements, nature, druids	Keeper of the Earth, Mother of Elements		Staff: Tree of Life	Earth-keepers
varin	Life, Birth, Fertility, Cycle's Beginning	Keeper of Life, First Guide		Chakram: Circle of Life	Life-keepers
umar	Death, Dying, Cycle's End	Keeper of Death, Final Guide, Pale One		Scythe: Soulpassage	Death-keepers

APPENDIX C

MAJOR DEITIES OF AVERN

The Primary deities were the second born at the dawn of creation. These deities were born with a balancing opposite. The order of their birth is presented in the chart, born in pairs with their equal and opposite. The neutral and evil nature of the deities determines their place of residence, either the upper or lower planes. Those that are neutral in nature take up their residence in the planes of law and chaos, to either side of the physical, but neither upper nor lower.

The people who follow each of the primary deities tend to align with each other. They group in fellowship, and in the worst case, it leads to fanatic tendencies among them. Some groups have subgroups and occasionally, some groups worship groups of more than one god/dess as a group. These groups are looked upon several different ways. Single god/dess worshippers sometimes call these blasphemers, feeling that worshipping more than one god/dess is tantamount to being a traitor to all the gods. Those who worship multiple gods feel that the single god/dess worshippers are missing out on a world they cannot even understand. They often refer to them as single or closed minded and much too narrow in focus. There are pantheists, those who worship the entire pantheon, and are often disliked by the multitheists and monotheists alike because they are not choosing a path at all. They also feel that those that worship the secondary or auxiliary deities are too narrow in focus because of the specificity of the foci of the secondary deities.

Major Deities

jor Deity	Foci	Know As	Symbol	Weapon: Iconic Weapon	Followers
en (Male)	Paladins, Cities, Codes, Crusades	Paladin father, The Patron		Longsword: Virtue's Kiss	Paladins
akas (Male)	Barbarians, Destruction	The Destroyer		Greataxe: Destruction's Hand	Destroyers
erome (Male)	The Wilds, Hunters	Great Hunter		Spear: Heartseeker	Hunters
ema emale)	War, Slavery	The Slaver, The Matron		Chainwhip: Slave's Embrace	Slavers
asha emale)	Mercy, Healing, Angels	Great Angel, Lady of Hope, Healer		Light mace: Mercy's Touch	Healers
ean (Female)	Disease, pestilence, Demons	Great Demon, Lady of Despair		Scourge: Despairfires	Plaguebearers
lmn (Neutral)	Government, cities, judgment	Lawgiver, Lawmaker		Heavy mace: Lawmaker	Justice-bringers
kreas eutral)	Chaos, chance, gambling	The Gambler, Chaos Bringer, Smiling Lady		Morning star: Chaoswhisper	Freedom-makers

APPENDIX D

MINOR DEITIES OF AVERN

The secondary deities were the third grouping of gods born to the Phoenix of Light and Phoenix of Dark. Once again, they were born in pairs, with their equals and opposites. They are somewhat lesser in scope than the primary gods, their focus tends to be on some specific area, but even that specific area can be extensive. They are born in opposition, but some of the pairs are Neutral in their outlook, such as Joryn and Soryn. These two don't necessarily engage in fighting with each other, they are simply opposite aspects of the world. Others, such as Luan and Ravera, are in constant contention with each other. They all have a specific purpose that could be in another god's domain, but rather than others, they have been born to assume the powers over that area. There is a still a lot of debate among their worshippers as to whether they are as powerful as the primary deities. The truth is that they are just as powerful, they are just created for an even more specific purpose as the primary deities. Like the primary deities there are monotheists and polytheists. There are those that choose to worship the secondary deities as a whole pantheon, and those that choose to worship all the deities together. The secondary deities seem to not prefer chaos or order at all, unlike the primary deities.

Minor Deities

Minor Deity	Foci	Known As	Symbol	Weapon: Iconic Weapon	Followers
Joryn (Neutral)	Dawn, sun, daylight, sunrise	The Rising Sun, Sunchild		Longbow: Shaft of Daylight	Dawnbringers
Soryn (Neutral)	Night, moon, dusk, twilight, sunset	The Rising Moon, Moonchild		Short bow: Shaft of Moonlight	Twilightbringers
Samastain (Female)	Records, Scribes, Truth	Truthsayer		Rapier: Ageless Pen	Truthspeakers
Franel (Male)	Lies, Espionage, Subterfuge	The Liar, Great Spy		Dagger: Lifestinger	Venomspeaker
Luan (Male)	Undying, Spirits, Guardians	The Undying		Club: Deathsheart	Spiritwarders
Ravera (Female)	Undead, Ghosts, Restless Spirits	The Undead		Flail: Deathshead	Wraithwardens
Whesta (Female)	Dreams	White Star, Queen of Mistalan		Scimitar: Dreamerlight	Dreamwalkers
Rhen (M)	Nightmares	Dark Star, King of Pranithan		Whip: Nightmaredark	Nightmarewalke

Appendix E

Avern's Calendar

There are four hundred days to one Avernese year. The calendar is divided into sixteen months, each consisting of twenty-five days. There are four six-day weeks per month, with the last day coinciding with the new moon and the first day with the full moon. Avern has one moon and one sun.

The days of the week are Lumasday, Ruanaday, Marisday, Ravasday, Whispasday, and Shadasday. The extra day at the end of the month is Nereday. Each month is named after one of the major and minor gods and goddesses, though these names are rarely used except by Elves and Truthspeakers.

The names of the four holidays, those of the equinoxes and the solstices, come from the names of the Keepers. These are generally known, however, the origin of the names has been lost to most. Each day of the week, which is still often used, is named after one of the pieces of the Phoenix, though that is not remembered by any; even the elves do not remember the ancient names of the predecessors of the gods.

The zodiac is commonly used, though the stories behind the constellations are generally ignored or forgotten. Each month is associated with one of the gods (where their names come from), and each of the zodiacs is associated with that god.

The calendar must be adjusted slightly every few years to account for changes in the celestial bodies, but no more than a day or so every couple hundred years. The beginning of the year is celebrated on the first day of fall, coinciding with the beginning of harvest times.

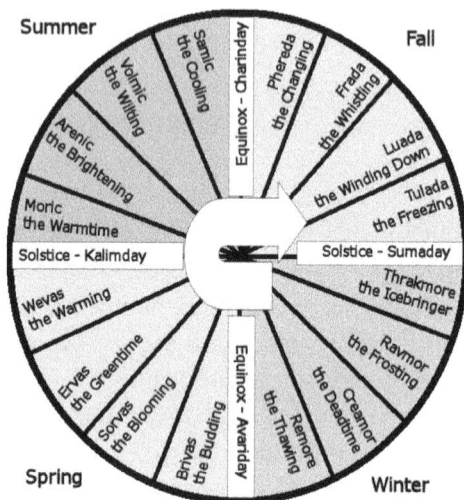

Calendar of Avern

Month	God	Common Name	Zodiac	Holiday
Fall				
Pherada	Pherome	the Changing	Lupene, the Wolf	Autumnal Equinox (Charinday)
Frada	Franel	the Whistling	Zyphirius, the Snake	
Luada	Luan	the Winding Down	Edre, the Turtle	
Fulada	Telema	the Freezing	Kran, the Chain	
Winter				
Thrakmor	Thrakas	the Icebringer	Ales, the Axe	Winter Solstice (Sumaday)
Ravmor	Ravera	the Frosting	Skel, the Raven	
Creamor	Crean	the Deadtime	Vad, the Vulture	
Remor	Rhen	the Thawing	Essex, the Spider	
Spring				
Brivas	Briasha	the Budding	Ana, the Dove	Spring Equinox (Avariday)
Sorvas	Soryn	the Blooming	Shov, the Owl	
Ervas	Erikreas	the Greentime	Pendulum, the Coin	
Whevas	Whesta	the Warming	Luen, the Dreamer	
Summer				
Joric	Joryn	the Warmtime	Loasta, the Lizard	Summer Solstice (Kalimday)
Arenic	Aren	the Brightening	Tamar, the Horse	
Volmic	Volmn	the Wilting	Brita, the Torch	
Samic	Samastain	the Cooling	Shamis, the Tome	

APPENDIX F
ZODIAC OF AVERN

The Zodiac of Avern is based around the deities and the stars. Each one has a mythos of how it came to be. On the following pages, find the charts for the various zodiac signs along with the generally agreed upon traits associated with them.

Zodiac of Avern

Name	Symbol	Attributes	Mythos
Lupene	Wolf	**Positive**: Persevere where others might not, great leaders, strong, great stamina. **Negative**: Can succumb to the pack mentality, sometimes too dogged.	Lupene was once the greates companion of Pherome. After dying t protect his friend, Lupene was cast int the skies to create the constellation.
Zyphirius	Snake	**Positive**: Wary individuals, may be able to wriggle their way out of tough situations, make good politicians and diplomats. **Negative**: Often tends to hide the truth and can become vicious when attacked.	No doubt, Franel speaks with a forke tongue, so it was no surprise tha Zyphirius became his favorite follower When Zyphirius pleased him greatly, h promised to make him immortal whe his time came. Ever the liar, Fran instead changed Zyphirius into a tw headed snake and sent him to the stars
Edre	Turtle	**Positive**: Perhaps best known as survivors, those born under Edre are often hardy and can be happy even if alone. **Negative**: Sometimes become isolated; find it hard to trust others in their lives.	One day, Luan found Edre upon th shores of the Sea of Tears nearly dea The Father of the Undying knew tha she would not last long and asked he preference: undeath or death. Edr chose undeath as long as she coul stay with Luan.
Kran	Chain	**Positive**: Make lasting attachments to others, loyal, and often trustworthy. **Negative**: They tend to dominate those around them, can become too wrapped up in their own lives, sometimes insensitive.	Telema's weapon, Kran, gaine sentience during repeated battles ove the years. After serving his master fo many years, Kran was grante immortality in the stars.
Ales	Axe	**Positive**: Strong as a stone, they are often creative thinkers and can sometimes buck established rules that lack fairness and don't like to be tied to one place. **Negative**: Often, a wild streak defines those born under Ales, and there is a tendency to let anger get the best of them.	Thrakas carried Ales into many blood battles. Somewhere along the way, Ale gained sentience and became an eve faithful companion to the grea Destroyer. After many long years o service, he heaved the axe to the skie where it landed among the stars, eve able to show the way to glory for hi followers.
Skel	Raven	**Positive**: Observant, risk-taking, and willing to go the extra mile, loves to find new places and things. **Negative**: They are often perceived as cold, can have a hard time understanding others, and can be highly distractible.	Ravera walks the line between deat and life, and Skel the raven stalks thos dying from the shadows. For many lon years, Skel was the eyes on th battlefields for Ravera, and was know to herald the appearance of man undead creatures in a battle.
Vad	Vulture	**Positive**: Opportunists, find opportunities for success and advancement where others cannot, can be very successful in business. **Negative**: Often misunderstood by others because their demeanor does not often match their intentions, sometimes seen as materialistic and selfish.	Crean is known for her cruelty i spreading pestilence, and Vad, th vulture, watches and waits for he victims to pass from the world. Afte many years of doing his duty to Crean the Plaguebearer allowed him to ascen to the stars. Vultures are still a sign tha Crean is near the field of battle.

Zodiac of Avern

Name	Symbol	Attributes	Mythos
Essex	Spider	**Positive**: Known for their fearlessness, those born under the sign of the spider rarely shy away from anything. They are known to be some of the best adventurers in the land. **Negative**: With their fearlessness comes a degree of recklessness. Sometimes, they take things too far and put themselves and others in danger more than necessary.	The master of the Nightmarwalkers, Rhen often could be found with creatures that frequented the nightmares of mortals. One such creature, a spider named Essex, became well known to him and often walked into the world of nightmares with him. After being his companion for a long time, Rhen decided that Essex should be elevated to the stars.
Ana	Dove	**Positive**: At their best, those born under the sign of Ana the dove are positive and upbeat at the worst times. They are known to wear a smile and spread joy where they go. **Negative**: The positive nature wears on those under this sign. They can easily burn out and succumb to despair if they are not careful.	Briasha, to compete with her sister Crean, also chose a bird to be her herald. Ana was once a regular dove until Briasha put her hand to her and elevated her to get intelligence and wisdom. For many years, she heralded the coming of the merciful one, until she wore down and was placed among the stars forever to be viewed from the world.
Shov	Owl	**Positive**: Wise beyond their years, those born under the owl, Shov are often sought out to be wizards and healers. They seek knowledge and are often night people. **Negative**: Wisdom comes with a price, and some of those born under the owl lack common sense while retaining that wisdom.	Soryn became lonely following the moon and being separated from their twin, Joryn. Along the way, they acquired the company of many nocturnal creatures. The wisest among those creatures was Shov who was able to keep Soryn's spirts up despite being without their twin.
Pendulum	Coin	**Positive**: Those born under Pendulum are excellent gamblers and often take chances. They can be great persuaders and speakers, often having good charism. **Negative**: The winds of chance are fickle, and those born under the Coin can just as easily be plagued with bad luck as they are able to turn luck in their favor.	Erikreas carried Pendulum for many years, a coin minted from an Ancient Avernese country. For no other reason than it suited them at the time, they tossed the coin to the skies to create the constellation of the coin.
Luen	Dreamer	**Positive**: Those born under the Dreamer often are dreamers. They reach for the stars, and sometimes they have very lofty goals. They are often positive and hopeful. **Negative**: They can often be flighty and live with their head in the clouds. Sometimes, they spend more time daydreaming than living life to it's fullest.	Whesta spent a lot of time in the dream city of Mistlan, and there, the dream wraith named Luen became her constant companion. For many years, they were inseparable, and eventually, to reward Luen for their service over the years, Whesta elevated them to the stars.

Zodiac of Avern

Name	Symbol	Attributes	Mythos
Loasta	Lizard	**Positive**: Bright personalities are the hallmark of Loasta, and an ability to fit into new circumstances easily. They often are people who try to do good in the world, bringing light to it. **Negative**: They can be prone to despair if they aren't careful. They are often light bringers, but sometimes they need to have the light brought to them.	Joryn, like their twin, became lonely and made companions out of animals that would often follow them as they walked the world. One of those, perhaps the most interesting among them, was Loasta. For years, Loasta kept Joryn company and eventually was elevated to the stars by them.
Tamar	Horse	**Positive**: Exceedingly Loyal to friends, seek to mediate, often listen well to others. **Negative**: They can get too wrapped up in others' lives to the detriment of their own, sometimes considered naïve because they take people at their word.	Said to have borne Aren himself in battle, the great warhorse Tamar was blessed near the end of his long life with a place among the stars by Aren. Though he was sad to see his trust steed leave his side, he knew it was Tamar's time to go.
Brita	Torch	**Positive**: Those under Brita make excellent judges, able to remain neutral in many situations. **Negative**: Often unable to understand motivations of others, tend to be rather literal.	Volmn was known for carrying a torch to light his way to the truth. Eventually, the torch became very old and worn. Volmn sent the now sentient torch Brita to the sky to forever be a guide to those who traveled Avern. The Star of North is the peak of Brita's formation.
Shamis	Tome	**Positive**: Shamis means that those born under her sign will be born with a thirst for knowledge and seek it out voraciously. **Negative**: While a thirst for knowledge can be good, they are often dogged and will pursue something until they are satisfied. This can sometimes lead to ruin.	Shamis was the book that Samastain wrote the original Litany in when time began. Given life on her own, Samastain sent her to the heavens once she no longer needed to bear the burden of the Litany.

Appendix G

History of Avern

Avern's history is rich and varied. This is exclusively for those of you out there who love a little peek into how the world got the way it is currently. Please be mindful, there may be some spoilers to the stories, so read at your own risk.

History of Avern

Year	Events
1 OR	Banded Court established; all elves are in residence on the islands of Sern T'sal (Spirit Isles). There is peace among them. They have not yet ventured to the large continent to their East which they call only the "Eastlands". All events previous to 1 OR are considered BR (Before Reckoning) but there is no role of years to organize them save the oral history of the t'Kalima.
75 OR	The elves begin to separate into their distinct tribes, choosing to be somewhat separate, but still connected through the Banded Court.
256 OR	The Spirana t'Kalima decide to launch an exploration boat to the Eastlands to see who and what they encounter.
306 OR	After several years without contact, the expedition, called the Iveson, is deemed lost at sea and considering lack of magical contact, it is unsure where they went down.
407 OR	The Noran t'Kalima come to the Banded Court with an exploration plan, once again, wanting to take a crew of each of the Elven tribes. After much debate, the plan is approved by the Banded Court.
410 OR	The next expedition, named the Kranos, leaves Sern T'sal.
411 OR	Kranos makes landfall in what will become Darna, on the northern lands of the Eastlands. The elves make contact almost immediately with primitive human tribes. The humans at this point have little power, and the elves offer protection from the ravaging wilds.
413 OR	The elven explorers continue to come to the Eastlands, bringing with them settlers who settle alongside the humans within their tribes. They bring with them technology, writing, and mathematics.
456 OR	Humans begin to build the kingdoms of Darna and Luxen.
539 OR	Vestern established, a kingdom headed by humans but mostly populated by a people called the Halifast, a race very similar to humans, but about half the size. The Halifast are peaceful and enjoy working with the Humans. While the king is human, his advisor is a Halifast.
701 OC	The Marin t'Kalima establish a large outpost on the island to the north of the Eastlands, which they name Zerri T'ves.
731 OC	Humans establish the kingdom of Namas and Phomean. Slowly the humans are being brought the advances of the elvenkind.
789 OC	Humans establish the kingdom of Lineria. Kranos sends word of the success of their mission. Other Elven tribes send expeditions to the East lands.
801 OC	The Isle of Night is discovered, an island ringed with cliffs and mountains, and seemingly impenetrable.
905 OC	Whispara t'Kalima claim a large forest in the center of the continent for their outpost, named the Anaset forest.
1125 OC	The Tryst Dynasty begins. King Tryst of Lineria starts forging alliances with other smaller nations nearby. Last year of Old Reckoning.
1 NR	The Banded Court forges the first Broad Alliance with King Tryst and other members of the human nations.
5 NR	A joint mission between humans and elves is sent to the Jungles to the southern peninsula for the purpose of exploration.
25 NR	Discovery of the Shifters in the center of the continent around the edges of the Anaset forest. A fast alliance between the Shifter tribes and the Whispara.
88 NR	Discovery of the Zamos on the peninsula.

3 NR	Strife between the elven tribes begins over petty matters; the Banded Court takes little notice. They are more concerned with the growing power of the humans.
9 NR	The Ruana t'Kalima send an expedition into the desert to the south east and end up establishing an outpost before the end of the year. They make contact with the native Wraiths of the forest and establish a trade relationship with them.
03 NR	Restel t'Blanisa is found dead by her advisor during a meeting with the Lumen t'Kalima. Noran t'Kalima leave th Banded Court over the incident. They form a colony in the mountains west of Lineria.
04 NR	Lumen investigators fine evidence that the representative of the Marin t'Kalima. Furious with the Lumen, the Marin as well as Whispara leave the Banded Court. The Marin take up residence on the northern island they had established an outpost on, and the Whispara took up residence in the Anaset Forest, feeling a great connection with the ancient wood.
05 NR	Ruana t'Kalima lose a number of high ranking members of their court. Ravsa t'Kalima representatives feed them information that the Lumen are involved. Both tribes leave the Banded Court, the Ruana taking up permanent residence in the great desert, naming it the San t'Shi and the Ravsa taking underground in the Windsong mountains close to the Noran stronghold.
AW	The Ascension war begins with attacks on the Noran t'Kalima by the Ravsa.
-45 AW	Several skirmishes between various tribes occur over the next several years, each one violent and leading to loss of life and nothing productive.
8 AW	Finally tiring of the battles, the Lumen retreat to the homeland of their island and leave the rest of the elves to their own devices.
9 AW	Ruana t'Kalima soon also leave the battles and close their borders, threatening death to any who dare come into their lands.
0 AW	The generally peaceful humans begin establishing empires. Lineria's current king begins taking over surrounding areas with an iron will.
3 AW	Ackana is visited by a prophetic vision in which she rules all of Avern and is inspired to begin creation of the Crystal of the Gods.
8 AW	The Ravsa and Dwarves form an alliance and decide to establish themselves and fend off the increasingly violent Noran t'Kalima.
9 AW	Marin t'Kalima seal their borders an establish their own society with threat of death to trespassers.
2 AW	Whispara officially cut off relations with all other races and insulate themselves in their forest.
5 AW	Human kingdoms begin to flourish, and with the success, various wars spring up across the lands.
8 AW	The Orc Wars begin. Orcs decide to spread out from the Wildlands into the civilized nations nearby.
9 AW	Human kingdoms begin allying with each other to fight the Orc menace.
2 AW	The Orcs, their numbers greatly reduced, are left to their own tribes in the wilds of the Wildlands. Meanwhile, humans begin forming lasting alliances with the Shifters of the same land.

92 AW-265 AW	Reasonable alliances were formed during this time, and there were few all out wars, but the peace was very tense, leading to much espionage and infiltration exercises. During this time Ackana, is gathering her forces and has completed theortress that will house the Crystal of the Gods. She begins gathering Prophets, Seers and Druids before the Forge can find them.
266-498 AW	Ackana's forces incite rebellion and advancement of the war forces during this time. The attempt to continue the constant wars is successful and it seems Avern's people are on the brink of implosion. She provides weapons to any who ask, as well as undead soldiers when they are needed.
499 AW	Continued fighting and lack of compromise brings the priests to gather and ask for help from their deities. This, the Convening of the Faithful, lasted one month. At the end of that time, each priest/priestess received a vision confirming that the Divine had heard their pleas for salvation.
499 AW – Eve of the Autumnal Equinox	In an attempt to stem the self-destruction of the people of Avern, the twenty gods, and four lesser gods including Ackana gather in mortal avatars on the Isle of Night. At the stroke of Midnight, all of Avern witnessed an explosion of light emanating from the sacred island. Many priests, priestesses, prophets and seers die immediately. The current Oracle, Aresena, also succumbs after delivering a final prophecy.
1 AY	The Abandoned Years begin.
10 AY	After the apparent complete loss of divine powers, skirmishes between kingdoms begin to increase at an alarming rate.
39 AY	Leaders of all the largest human kingdoms and some of the smaller ones come together in what became known as the Conference of Nine.
52 AY	Skirmishes between the human kingdoms and non-humans begin to rise and fear begins to increase among the people.
78 AY	It is decided that everyone has lost significant power, both those who worship the light and the dark.
97 AY	Most Prophets report the Veil.
236 AY	Out of fear, the current Oracle, Trimertam goes into hiding, keeping the line of Oracles secret from that point forward. The House of Oracles is constructed in the Wildlands.
380 AY	Age of Destruction begins. Overall this time was marked with strange and extreme weather and many rivers and lakes were reshaped.
509 AY	The landscape of the north is reshaped as a third mountain range rises from the land and merges with the already existing two, effectively isolating the kingdom of Lineria.
560 AY	Several small islands south of the Seran jungle sink into the ocean taking their indigenous populations with them.
598 AY	The Conference of Nine reconvenes when it seems that the weather patterns are beginning to stabilize.
600 AY	Age of Law begins.
623 AY	The Conference of Nine approves the building of the Forge, the creation of the Regulations on Magic and deployment of the magical enforcers known as the regulators.
990 AY	Age of Chaos begins with the resurgence of Orc warlords in the Wildlands attacking nearby areas.
999 AY	Current year

Appendix H

Magic of Avern

Magic of Avern

Magic, like the universe, is based on the three spheres. Like the planes, there are three spheres of magic, from which all magic is drawn depending on where the spheres intersect. The spheres are Light, Dark, and Elemental. Much like the planes, which consist of the light planes (upper planes), the dark planes (lower planes), and the world of Avern (elemental planes), there are places where the spheres cross each other, giving rise to different types of magic. The three energies of Avern are present in the planes: positive, negative, and wild.

To learn magic, one must have the Talent. Talent is the capability to channel the raw energies of magic into something else. Identifying one with the Talent is relatively easy for a Master and somewhat more difficult for a Teacher. Using an ability that all who can use the Spheres of Magic can use, the Master or Teacher examines the potential Sphere User. If a certain color is found in his or her aura, then that person may channel magic. The color is a complex color of violet and black, with a sprinkling of sparkles that look like stars. For Masters, it is easy to separate the different Auras, but Teachers may have a more difficult time. For this reason, most Teachers do not attempt to identify those with the Talent; they instead take them to a Master.

One with the Talent can use any Sphere; they only have to be taught. Many people with Talent never know that they have it, and they go through life just as happy as they do not know. But sometimes, Teachers seek new students and go forth to find those with the will and without the fear of Magic.

Spheres of Magic

Star Sphere – The other three spheres rest inside the Star Sphere. Star is another word for Magic, describing that Kalimourne gathered the Stars for her to give to the mortals at the beginning of Time. Also, magic tends to take on visual effects similar to stars. Masters of the Star Sphere are called Sorcerers or Sorceresses. Their magic flows very naturally as the Keeper of Stars, Kalimourne, has shown them the Path of Stars before they are even born. The Path of Stars shows itself when the person is both mature and mentally ready. Sometimes, it may be fifty years before the ability shows itself, and sometimes, it only shows itself when another Sorcerer appears to train the younger one. Since the Abandonment, no one has been born with the ability to use the Sphere of Stars. It is assumed that without Kalimourne to show someone the Path of Stars, there is no way to learn the ways. Even before this Forgotten Sphere was practiced, those born with the ability to channel Star magic were rare; perhaps one in ten thousand who was born with the Talent would be those of the Star Sphere. Those who carry the Path of Stars are obvious to even the newest Sphere users because their Aura is a deep royal purple with stars all around. No other color exists in their Aura. The Star Sphere cannot be learned; it is entirely innate. Practiced by: Sorcerers

Light (Spirit/Spiritual/Positive) Sphere—The Light sphere encompasses the beginning of life, the start of a cycle, or anything related to that type of area. It draws from positive energy. Since this sphere draws on pure positive energy, those who practice it must ward against overdrawing themselves. They must often recharge themselves. Overusing the light sphere can lead to the separation of the soul from the physical and send them into a period of spiritual flux.

Spirit – Pure light sphere magic focuses on the spirit of everything. The power of the Spirit is deceptive. It appears nonexistent in so many ways because the power is subtle. At the core of every being, there is a Spirit. Spirit Magics can alter the very Spirit of beings and things. Using Spirit magic brings help or harm to something far deeper than any other magic, and those who Master the Spirits, called Spirit Walkers, can more than defend themselves. Pure Spirit magic is often a feminine trait, as spirit walkers, or can be combined with other paths to practice it differently, such as paladins. Practiced by: Spirit Walkers, Paladins

Spatial: Intersection of Light and Elemental – Those that use this type of magic can move from place to place within a moment's notice or may transport people or things just as quickly. Those who deal in place magic and learn all aspects of it can be very useful for their ability to go anywhere and send things anywhere. However, those that have the place magics are rare because it takes an extremely long time to learn how to bend space. Practiced by: Guides

Elemental (Nature/Physical/Wild) Sphere—The Elemental sphere comprises all magic that draws from wild energy. This can be practiced in a couple of ways. It is often called four-point magic or wild magic, and each type of magic often looks different.

Four Point Magic: Pure elemental magic: fire, water, earth, and air. The four "Points" may be combined in various ways to different effects. Masters of Four Points can ruin entire regions if they desire, or they can help just the same. Generally, students at Four Points are trained for at least ten years at each point. Then they must spend anywhere from 10 to 30 years learning how to combine them. Other practitioners of Four Points choose to practice only one, two, or three of the Points. This type of magic, referred to as either single-point, double-point, or triple-point magic, is the faster route, taking much less time to master. However, to be considered a Master of this Sphere, one must master all Points, and the ability to combine the Points. The practice of Four Points is an ancient discipline and is thought to have been the first type of magic discovered. Practiced by: Elementalists (All), Firamancers (Fire), Aeromancers (Air), Aquamancers (Water), Terramancers (Earth), Stone Brothers (Earth and Water), Storm Children (Water and Air), Bloodfires (Earth and Fire), and many others.

Nature/Wild: Wild magic is sometimes called natural or green magic. It takes perhaps fifty or more years to become a Master, but Wild Masters can re-grow entire forests within days, and repair almost any living, natural thing. Their magic is unable to harm the Natural World. They cannot harm natural creatures unless they threaten the Natural World or other natural creatures. These practitioners appear almost to be pacifistic until someone does something to damage their lands. Usually, one Wild Master will live in a fifty to hundred-mile area of the wilds and train other Wild Masters there. Any who entered his or her area called their Wild Tract, had better beware and not disorder the natural world around them. Among Those who practice the wild, there are those who specialize in using animals and beasts; these, called summoners, summon creatures to aid them. Practiced by: Druids, Wild Women, Summoners

Temporal: Intersection of Elemental and Dark: This magic deals with time. The time sphere is rarely, if ever, used. A large amount of time must be spent on this area, and many races need to possess the longevity to even begin to learn mastery of time. Those that do, however, can appear to live forever by manipulating various things. However, wanton use of this can upset the Balance and cause unknown misery upon the wielder of this magic. Those who become Temporal Masters are rare indeed and usually ancient by the time they come to power. If any Masters currently exist, they are unknown. Practiced by: Chronomancers

Dark (Psychic/Mental/Negative) Sphere – The Dark sphere draws from negative energy. This does not necessarily mean that the magic is evil. There is a natural ending to all things and that is present in the Dark sphere. Thus, the magic associated with the Dark Sphere is that of Psychic magic. Psychic energy draws on negative energy because it manipulates the energies of the mind and removes energy as it is working. Workers of the Dark Sphere must frequently recharge in various ways and must protect themselves from overdrawing their own energies.

Psychic – This magic does everything possible to use the target's mind against them. There are different ways to practice psychic magic. Enchantments make the target more willing and take over a target's mind, while Illusions make someone see and possibly feel things that are not there. Those who Master both sides can do many things without others remembering that they were even there. Practiced by: Enchanters (Enchantment) and Illusionists (Illusions)

Cycle: Intersection of Dark and Light – Cycle magic is simply Life and Death magic, also called Entropy magic. The magic of the Cycle provides life to everything and death to everything. One may take the path of life alone or the path of death alone, but to become a Master, one must learn both aspects. The Cycle

Sphere is one of the more difficult Spheres of magic, taking at least 20 years in each aspect and more to learn the intricacies of putting two opposites into effect. A true Master of Cycle Magic can turn entire cities to ravaging undead or bring an army of twenty thousand men back to life. These types of magic are integrated and cannot be separated. A healer must deal with both positive and negative energy, and so must a necromancer. Practiced by: Cyclists (Both), Healers (Life), or Necromancers or Entrophists (Death)

The intersection of all three spheres gives rise to Shadow magic. No one except Sorcerers accesses this particular magic. Sorcerers do not have a label for this type of magic, but it can be magic that balances other magics.

Magic of The Void – There are places between the spheres where there is simply nothing. There is only blankness. There is neither life nor death nor law or chaos. Such is the place of the Void. Those who tamper into the Void are doomed to succumb to it, but many try. The power of the Void is quick and self-destructive, but there are many who will trade everything for power. There are others who simply believe that the Void is a living creature like the Maker and Unmaker, and thus should be worshiped and abided by. Those following the Void are loosely aligned under the calling of the Master of the Void and refer to themselves as the Prophets of the Void, though none have any sorcerous abilities. The majority believe what they do is what is meant to be done. Practiced by: Prophets of the Void

Oracles and True Sorcerers

For a true Oracle to be, they must exist of three parts.

Seer: A seer can see through enchantment and illusions and often has flashes of insight from the minds of others. They essentially are immune to psychic powers, much like the natural power of the dwarves, making them impervious to magic from the others that practice in the psychic sphere, especially wizards. Often, they cannot be lied to or fooled by others. They can sometimes glimpse coming events, but usually not in detail, nor very far in the future. Mark of the Seer is a star pattern that appears in silver over their eyes when using the powers of a seer, and they often have shocks of white in their hair. Some are born blind except for during episodes of seeing past that which is not real. Seers access the magic sphere of the dark, that of the psychic.

Prophet: A prophet is one who views the future and is often put into a deep trance in which they can receive extended visions of the future, past, or present. Prophets always see the truth, but sometimes it is possible to change the truth. They are also often exorcists, able to see deep into the world of spirits and otherworldly creatures. Wizards trained in the psychic sphere can never quite see extra planar creatures as effectively as Prophets, though they do make the attempt. They can sometimes, like Seers, see past enchantments, but they do so by viewing the real spirit of a creature, not seeing past the enchantment or illusion itself. The Mark of the Prophet is a child born with a brilliant violet eye color. Prophets access the magic sphere of Spirit, that of the light.

Druid: A Druid wields all the power of nature. They naturally can use the magic of any of the four elements. Druids also have a natural affinity for animals and plants, and they can communicate with either one if they so choose. There are varying degrees of druidic powers, and it is thought that many who live close to nature have some degree of green powers. They go by many names throughout the world of Avern and, in some of the more primitive areas, are considered blessed by the gods or nature. They are generally marked by having some connection to the natural world (green hair/skin, bark-like skin, etc). Druids access the elemental sphere, or that of nature.

All of these are referred to as sorcerous abilities or natural practitioners of magic. A True Sorcerer, one who can practice all the spheres of magic naturally without being marked, is very rare. A True Sorcerer only practices magic of the spheres without the other abilities associated with the three sorcerer abilities. For example, they aren't able to see past illusions, read minds, see the future, or speak to animals unless they use their magic to do so. An Oracle is all three of the sorcerers combined with all their powers.

The last and final type of magic, shadow, is only accessible by True Sorcerers and Oracles. Shadow is powerful and also a balancing magic. It combines the three parts of the world (physical, mental, and spiritual).

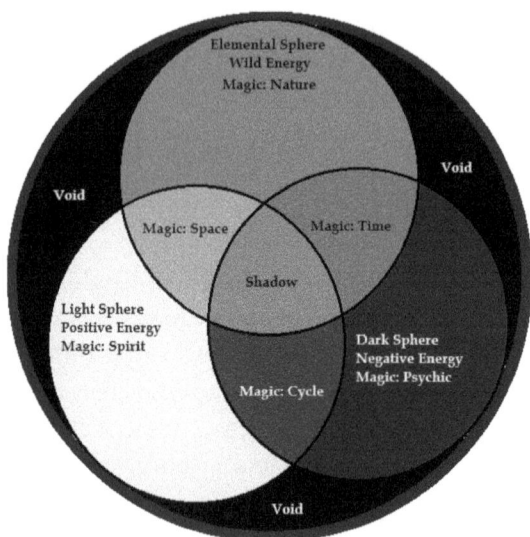

ABOUT THE AUTHOR

BEVERLY L. ANDERSON

Transgender. Bigender. Asexual. Panromantic.
Kinkster. Pagan. Autistic. Polyamorous. Queer.
Poet. Writer. More.

She/Her or They/Them

Beverly L. Anderson started writing at eleven, and when they did, it was apparent they would stick to something other than the every day. Her first story, written in spiral notebooks, was about a kidnapping. There were endless story ideas featuring fantastic places, monstrous creatures, and forbidden love in her mind even then. There's no surprise that these days, they favor the dark corners of the psyche over the happy and fluffy parts. Enamored with the mind, she studied extensively in psychology and related fields. She spends most of her days dreaming about stories and deciding how to make the unruly characters do as they tell them. As everyone knows, sometimes the characters take off and do what they want, no matter what the author has planned.

Beverly's other hobbies include gaming of all types, including a great love of tabletop, transgender and autism advocacy, and writing fanfiction when she can. Their interest in the BDSM community began as a simple curiosity but has led her to the road to finding a place for herself there as a Domme. She has gone on the journey of self-discovery in the last few years, finally pinning down their identity after nearly thirty years of searching. Coming out as bigender, asexual, panromantic, and polyamorous was one of the hardest things they've ever done, but it gave them the confidence to become themselves even more. An autistic person and an eclectic pagan, Beverly finds themself at odds with a lot of what society calls "normal." They don't mind, though, because they find that they are uniquely queer in every aspect of her life, and she's just fine with that.

Beverly started their writing journey seriously in 2013 when she found their way to fanfiction. She spent several years writing over three million words in various fandoms. In the last few years, they have been drawn to making those stories into original pieces and publishing them for a wider audience. Finding her publishing home helped make that dream a reality, one that they try to help others find.

Visit online: https://www.phoenixreal.net/

phoenixreal.net
Queer Love

ALSO BY BEVERLY L. ANDERSON

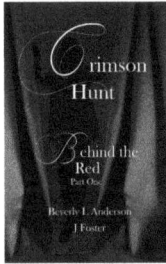

Crimson Hunt - Behind the Red Part One

Kerry Graham surprises his father by coming out as gay and cross-dresser and possibly non-binary. Then again, when he starts performing in drag at a local Cabaret named The Red, where his cousin works as a tailor. He finds himself free and able to be himself in a world that has always treated him as an outcast. He's among people that understand him, and he can finally relax. At least, that's what he believes. Then, a dress arrives, seemingly an apology for a bit of bigotry from a shop clerk. No one thinks a dress can cause any harm, so he wears it under the stage lights. Things go awry, though, and Kerry wonders what could possibly be happening. A bounty hunter named Martin swoops in, convinced that he can be of aid in the situation. Along with Martin, there's an intrepid FBI agent named Zak on the trail of a pair of sadistic serial killers who target and manipulate young, attractive, feminine men like Kerry.

Kerry doesn't believe it at first. Can he be targeted by these people? Then, things start happening, and his phone and email is full of messages with horrible images of what these people plan to do to him. He's frightened but staunch in living his life. He is adamant that he won't let them win, no matter what they do to him. Still, as the manipulation and gaslighting continue from afar, he starts to doubt everything he's ever known. He begins to lose purchase on reality but finds that Martin and Zak ground him. He refuses to give in to their sadistic games, but in the end, he begins to wonder if his willpower is enough to keep these people away from him.

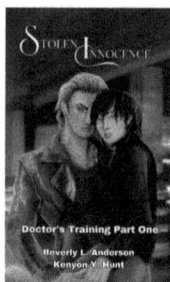

Stolen Innocence - Doctor's Training Part One

When desperate criminals find an easy target in the autistic neu-rosurgeon Kieran Sung, the young doctor is soon at the mercy of a local Irish mob boss with perverse desires. Despite suffering at his hands, rescue finds him with relative quickness. Pulled unwillingly into circumstances that bring his world crashing down around him and destroying the carefully laid routines and structure he desires; Kieran must find a new way to live. He discovers comfort in ways he never imagined, within sensations of pressure and binding. Taking the hand of a childhood friend who desires nothing else but to help him, Kieran realizes his heart aches for more in his life. Circumstances bind him to a tattoo artist named Varick Jaeger, an actor named Carmine DeAngelo, and a bartender named Devan Sullivan. With this unlikely trio, Kieran must learn how to handle the upheaval in a life he sees desperately needs change.

Stolen Innocence, part one of the Doctor's Training Trilogy, is a story of healing that examines D/s culture, the complexi-ties of polyamory, and how people often deal with mental and physical trauma. Follow Kieran, Devan, Varick, Carmine, and the rest of their pack; they navigate a world that rarely accepts people who do not fit in with expectations.

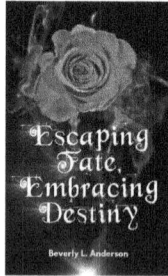

Escaping Fate, Embracing Destiny

CJ Kim is a normal college student. He is doing what most college students do, figuring himself out, sometimes the hard way. He has some strange dreams now and then, but he just thinks they are just dreams. They're certainly nothing to worry about when reality is pressing down so hard on him. Between the demands of school and family, he has enough on his mind.

He ends up with a huge crush on a senior that is on the baseball team. He doesn't even like baseball, but he goes to games just to see him. Of course, he'll never notice a gay and nerdy English major like CJ. Things are good, though. He even has a good relationship with his parents and his twin sisters.

He never expects his family's past to come back to haunt him. It rears its head in the worst way possible and CJ finds himself the prisoner of a vengeful man. Thrust into something that goes beyond what can be considered normal, CJ finds out that there's a fate out there trying to destroy him. He doesn't know how, but he has to reach for a destiny that he can just barely see.

Dark and the Sword – Legacy of the Phoenix Book One

The world of Avern has moved on. It has been almost a thousand years since the day the entire pantheon disappeared. Since the Abandonment, the mortals have learned to live without gods and goddesses. The world became mundane, with little magic and even less hope. Tyrants have risen, and those able to wield what is left of magic are powerful. Forces surge in the darkness that threaten to topple the already fragile world. However, the plight of the world of Avern is not unknown, and those who watch from a distance have decided to intervene. The mortals are sleeping, however, unknowing that two great powers will soon be vying for control.

Then something happens that changes things. A young princess makes a bid for power by murdering her father. She then attempts to murder her sister, the crown princess of Lineria, Keiara. Despite a true strike aided by dark powers, Keiara doesn't die. Instead, the strike pierces the barrier between her human soul and the soul sleeping within her, the soul of the Dark Phoenix. More than a goddess, the Dark Phoenix is the legendary mother of the gods. She is a part of the Eternal

Phoenix that brought life to their world eons ago, one of the primal forces of the cosmos.

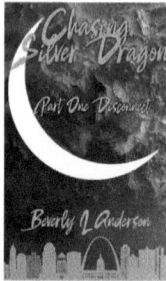

Chasing the Silver Dragon – Part One Disconnect, Book One of the Dragon Trinity Cycle

Silver Dragon has become a bane to the werewolf community in recent years. Designer heroin, one that actually affects were creatures where normal drugs are simply a passing fancy, has infiltrated the St. Louis werewolves. One of these, a young woman named Anna Maddox, wants her brother back somehow from the brink he's standing at. To do this, she reaches out to the ancient order, the Children of Asclepius. Duncan Powell hears her plea and pledges to help her rescue her brother from the streets of St Louis.

He goes to Detective Sebastian Pearce, a member of Unit Zero, the law enforcement agency that deals with supernatural creatures that pose a threat to the peace in the world. Sebastian implores him to leave things to Unit Zero, but Duncan is stubborn and goes down to the Red District to find the young Were. Sebastian and his partner follow and then begin the mission that will either save Kacey Maddox or doom all of them.

Let Sparks Fly – Short Story Compilation

Romance can come from the most unexpected places. Sometimes, two people meet, and the sparks just fly between them. Then, sometimes, two people see each other every day, and don't realize the spark that exists between them.

In this volume, you will find stories of many kinds. You'll meet a pair of fellows just looking for a sub to share when they ask out two people, and a secret is revealed. A young man is pining for his very best (straight) friend when a strange entity shows him pleasures beyond imagining, along with some truth. Join a guy who secretly harbors a taboo wish he thinks will never come true. Watch the sparks as a pair of swimming rivals find themselves in a compromising position. A demon on a mountain demands a sacrifice and receives something he isn't expecting. And finally, a man finds his bliss in a woman who can completely own him.

Journey through these pages and enjoy short erotic stories of love found in some quite unusual ways.

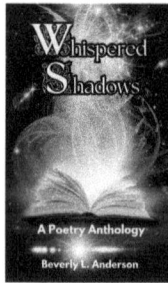

Whispered Shadows – A Poetry Anthology

The twisting paths of a poet's mind lead to intriguing places, there can be little doubt of this. These places contain whispers of the writer's soul. Some paths show desired sights; others uncover unforeseen knowledge and, at times, unwanted things. The shadows conceal unknown discoveries on well-lit paths through the poet's mind. Travelers, beware: uncertain destinations await along these paths. Tread carefully. Becoming lost in the pages of the poet's thoughts may be a very real danger to these travelers.

So, come along and visit this place of shadows. Here, there be dragons, monsters, truth, and more to enjoy. Fantasy, Reality, and Truths form one hundred and fifty poems by Beverly L. Anderson. The first path is one of fantasy with mythic beasts of yore and darkness that creeps into the very bone. Fairies may fly, and dragons may soar. The second path is one of reality and perhaps questions of what is and is not within that reality. Questions of existence and what the world shows us daily are spoken here. And the final path is one of truths. These truths may be surprisingly uncomfortable or may not be the truth expected. In any case, travel the paths at your own risk.

Open these pages and see if something draws you into the whispered shadows of the very soul.

Reflections of the Shadow Dancer

In an abandoned dance studio, there's music and dancing un-heard and unseen by anyone. The whispers in the shadows laud praises upon the figure who spins around the room, her body translucent and flickering in the night. Nothing is in motion, and yet everything moves around the room. Darkness and light intertwine and dance to cast the shadows of the world. The Shadow Dancer performs a dance that crosses the borders between the world and other surprising places within flickering shadows.

The Shadow Dancer knows the truth. Without the darkness, there can be no light. Without the light, there can be no darkness. Between them lies the shadow in which the Shadow Dancer twirls.

Enter the world of the Shadow Dancer and immerse yourself in 150 poems, living in the light, the dark, and the shadow.

COMING SOON - CHAINS OF BLOOD

FROM BEVERLY L. ANDERSON AND J. FOSTER

The Chains of Blood Trilogy

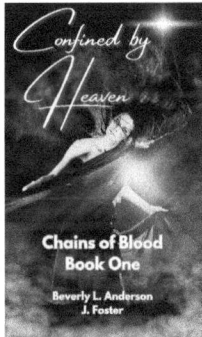

Confined by Heaven – Chains of Blood Book One

The day started as any other day would. Bellamy Delacroix was shopping with his brother, and then he headed home to the inevitable discussion about his future with his mother. A woman who still cooks despite technology that doesn't require her to, his mother is an old-fashioned type in a future world.

Then, his world explodes quite literally, and he's swept up into a world beyond his imagination. A war between extraplanar creatures who call themselves angels and demons draws him in because of what he is. And what he is, no one has ever seen before—a Nephilim. He is the child of an angelic mother and a demonic father and is thus capable of channeling both the positive and negative energies of the planes. This makes him dangerous and a target for both the minions of heaven and hell.

An angel named Saniel takes him under her wing and helps him adjust as he is brought to the underground city of heaven, Elysium. He learns about what he is, who they are, and their enemies in Zion, the demons. A warning from an ally of his mother, though, rings in his head, and he wonders who he should really be trusting. Things begin to spiral in ways he doesn't understand, and the world is changing before his very eyes.

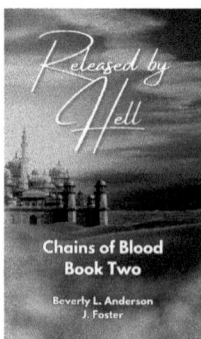

Released by Hell

**Chains of Blood
Book Two**

Beverly L. Anderson
J. Foster

Released by Hell – Chains of Blood Book Two

Driven insane by the very people he trusted, Bellamy is caught between worlds in a way like never before. He's in the hands of Addariel, the angel both at fault for his fall from grace and the current King of Hell. His mind is only clear when he is inside his own head and his world is spinning out of control. A terrible experiment that went wrong has left him on the verge of death, and it is up to the Codex of Hell and Addariel to save him.

Then, the strangest things happen among the demons. They devote themselves to his salvation, claiming him as their mate and, more than that, dedicating the hearts they didn't know they had to him. In his madness, he captures their very souls and changes the nature of the beasts around him. Even Addariel, once only interested in power, shifts his focus to taking care of the mentally fragile Bellamy. For the first time in Zion's history, the King of Hell cares more for something other than power and conquest.

Elysium, though, is not letting go of him easily. In a misguided attempt to help him, they make a move that could destroy the fragile peace between Zion and Elysium.

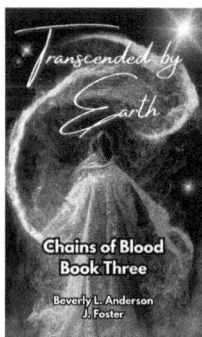

Transcended by Earth – Chains of Blood Book Three

Rescuing Bellamy has become a priority for both Elysium and Zion. Adding to the mix are the Arcadians, who will stand to fight for Bellamy. Held by the angel Usiel in a location no one knows, Bellamy fights for his survival and the survival of his unborn child. Usiel wants to breed an army of angels capable of fighting demons without fearing their use of negative energy, and by doing that, he needs to rid Bellamy of the demon's child within him.

A human woman senses something off with a strange neighbor and investigates the situation. What she finds shocks her, and she knows what she must do. Taking Bellamy, unstable as he is, she flees, unsure what to do with what she thinks is a young girl pregnant with her a child her captor wishes to kill.

Meanwhile, in Arcadia, angels from Elysium and demons from Zion work together with a pirate radio station to try and find the missing Nephilim. The world is unsure, but they know they must find him before Usiel captures him again.

Milton Keynes UK
Ingram Content Group UK Ltd.
UKHW031908201124
451474UK00001B/29